FACE OF THE EARTH

*Behold, thou hast driven me out this day from the
face of the earth; and from thy face shall I be hid;
and I shall be a fugitive and a vagabond in the
earth; and it shall come to pass, that every one that
findeth me shall slay me.*

—*Genesis 4:14*[*]

*White House officials said the new strategy would
include the option of reconsidering the use of
nuclear retaliation against a biological attack, if the
development of such weapons reached a level that
made the United States vulnerable to a devastating
strike.*[†]

—*New York Times, April 6, 2010*

---

[*] Genesis 4:14, The Bible: Authorized King James Version.

[†] "Obama Limits When U.S. Would Use Nuclear Arms," David E. Sanger
and Peter Baker, *The New York Times*, April 6, 2010, p. A1.

PROLOGUE

Galen's Ghost

As a further example of the diagnostic value of the microscopical demonstration of virus, mention might be made of its use in smallpox. This virus is of a size readily visible under the microscope.

—S. P. Bedson, *Journal of Clinical Pathology, 1947*[*]

New York City, 2001

Galen Fischer saw things that other people couldn't see. She was a virtuoso with a microscope, earning her reputation during the 1947 smallpox outbreak in New York City.

She knew immediately. *It's smallpox. There's no question about it.*

Using her microscope to examine skin scrapings from those suspected of contracting the virus, Dr. Fischer could diagnose smallpox faster than any other doctor in the city.

In contrast to the horrible outbreak of 1902-03, very few people died in 1947. Medical authorities quickly identified the single person who had come to New York already infected with the disease. The city initiated a massive vaccination program and isolated those who became ill.

Galen became legendary in medical circles in New York City. Like her father, also a doctor, she would always maintain a private

---

[*] S. P. Bedson, "The Laboratory Diagnosis of Virus Infections of Man: A Review," *Clinical Pathology*, Vol. 1, 1947, p. 2.

practice. She lived and worked in the Manhattan brownstone on the edge of the financial district that had been her childhood home. Unwilling to retire, the 84-year-old physician continued to see patients in the brownstone's first-floor office.

On a beautiful September day, with all the indications that summer was nearly over, Galen stepped outside to retrieve her copy of the *Times*. The sky was crystal blue, and the view of lower Manhattan's skyline was breathtaking in the sunshine. A flash of reflected sunlight caused her to look up.

After the first collision, she stood on the sidewalk with her neighbors. Everyone was confused. *It must have been an accident, but how could that happen?*

She was already walking toward the Towers, her medical bag in hand, when the second plane hit. Slowly and deliberately, desperately trying not to think about what she would surely find, she walked against the tide of people streaming from the exits. Those who needed her help most were still inside.

Galen went into the building. She was never seen again.

The killers, like those in 1947, were indifferent.

* * *

New York City, 2013

Samantha and Bob Winters were delighted with their new home. A New York City brownstone was considered a real prize, and the old Fischer house was in good condition. It had been rented out for nearly a decade, but the previous owners had been there a long time, they were told. Almost 100 years ...

For several years, they focused on redecorating the living areas, but in the summer of 2013, they finally tackled the basement. Behind the furnace, in what was once the coal bin, they discovered a number of boxes that must have been there for years. Most of the stuff went directly into the trash. But there was a collection of old medical journals dating back to the early 1900s. Samantha recalled that several generations of doctors had lived there. In one of the boxes, they found a microscope and some medical specimens. "I'm going to list these things on eBay."

But there wasn't much profit to be made. Nobody wanted the medical journals, and the microscope was snatched up by someone in Connecticut for only fifteen dollars. The microscope specimens brought even less. Samantha enjoyed telling the story that described her lack of business acumen. "The top bid for the box of slides was only two dollars, and it cost me five to send them to her. I should never have offered free shipping."

* * *

1

National Security Council

... the existence of a single case of smallpox within
the entire Western Hemisphere would signify a
terrorist attack.

—*Center for Defense Information, Terrorism*
Project, 2002[*]

Day 24: Washington, D.C.

"**N**ext slide please."
Those seated around the table were silent as
they listened to the man speaking from the front of
the semi-darkened room.

"Gentlemen ... and Ladies ..." The speaker caught himself as he
glanced briefly at the Attorney General, sitting to his left. "As you
can see from the data, we have every reason to believe that the
United States of America is under attack.

"Smallpox was erased from the face of the earth in the late
1970s, and suddenly we have an outbreak in New Mexico. There's
no question that this is the work of a hostile force, and we have
strong suspicions regarding several possible perpetrators of this

---

[*] "CDI Primer: Smallpox," A. Keats, Center for Defense Information,
Terrorism Project, Jan. 6, 2002.
http://www.cdi.org/terrorism/smallpox.cfm.

monstrous attack. Unfortunately, we cannot be certain at this time just which one of them had primary responsibility."

"We know exactly who the fuck did it," came a low growl from the far end of the highly polished mahogany table.

"Our nerves are sufficiently frayed, Trevor. We don't need profanity." President Alexander's voice was gentle, but it commanded the Vice President's attention.

Trevor Richards stiffened, glanced at the Secretary of Defense, and cleared his throat. His face had turned to stone. "Excuse me, please, Mr. President."

"Mr. President," the Secretary of Defense interrupted on cue, "We can provide more information on origin of the attacks ..."

"When your turn comes, Quentin, we'll be happy to listen to you. Right now, I'd like Mr. Hayes to continue, so we can get some clarification."

Hayes swallowed his irritation at the Vice President and the Secretary of Defense. Those bastards were up to something—he was sure of it. If the interruptions were intended to rattle him, it wouldn't work.

The President continued, "Mr. Hayes, it's not at all clear to me why we're calling this a foreign attack. Smallpox outbreaks have occurred naturally over millennia. How can we be so sure that the same thing hasn't happened here, however unlikely that may be?"

Arthur S. Hayes was the National Security Council's bioterrorism expert. A former CIA analyst, he had served on the White House staff through five administrations.

"The real point here, Mr. President, is that we—and by that I mean our people, both at Centers for Disease Control and in the intelligence community, as well as our allies in the international community, through the United Nations and the World Health Organization—have been monitoring illnesses in every country around the globe. The last case of smallpox was in 1977 in Somalia, and that was *Variola minor*, a mild form of smallpox with a relatively low death rate. The last known case of *Variola major*, the more lethal form, was two years earlier. It was in 1975, in Bangladesh. By 1980, the World Health Organization officially declared that the disease had been eradicated completely.

"If it's been eradicated, how has an outbreak occurred? I want to make sure I understand, Mr. Hayes."

"Certainly, Mr. President. Unfortunately, scientists in several countries studied smallpox for many years, not only for medical purposes but also for use in biological weapons programs or for research into defense against such weapons.

"As we know, bioweapons were outlawed by the Geneva Protocol of 1925. Eventually, we had the Biological Weapons Convention, which we signed in 1972, but even that allows countries to have small amounts of smallpox virus for research. The United States maintained a small stockpile, and so did the Soviet Union. And ever since the Soviet bloc fell apart in the 1990s, we've never been entirely sure just who else might have samples."

"That doesn't answer my question, Mr. Hayes," the President said. "How do we know this outbreak isn't a natural occurrence?"

"Because, frankly, that's impossible, Mr. President. Our planet has gone 35 years without a single case of smallpox. There's no virus left for a natural outbreak. The only way for infection to happen now is by growing the virus from samples kept by the United States or Russia—samples that may have fallen into the hands of a terrorist group or rogue state. I must emphasize, Mr. President, there are no natural reservoirs of smallpox on Earth. There are no other possibilities. May I?"

President Alexander nodded, "Go ahead, Mr. Hayes. Please proceed. For now."

The Vice President's eyes narrowed to slits: *What the fuck is Alexander thinking? This was no accident.*

"Next slide please."

His thoughts interrupted, Richards' attention snapped back to the man at the front of the room.

Hayes continued with his presentation. "As you can see, there are a number of possibilities. So what do we really know? It's difficult to pin down, but several countries are clear possibilities: Besides the United States, three countries had known smallpox biowarfare programs during the 20th century: the U.K., Japan, and the Soviet Union. We can pretty well rule out Japan and the U.K. because they are our close allies.

"Even Russia has to be considered an ally in most instances, despite a variety of ongoing policy differences. But some of the former Soviet states are worrisome, specifically those listed at the bottom of the slide: Azerbaijan, Kazakhstan, Kyrgyzstan, Tajikistan, Turkmenistan, and Uzbekistan. All of them are known to harbor a variety of known terrorist organizations. Al Qaeda is just one of them. State has had varying levels of success in forging links to these regimes, but even those countries with whom we've had good working relationships must be on our list of suspects.

"Our colleagues at the Defense Intelligence Agency have advised us that they have narrowed down the list pretty well." Hayes nodded slightly to Robinson Edwards. "I believe Under Secretary Edwards will be taking over the briefing at this point, if that meets with your approval, Mr. President."

"Please proceed, Mr. Edwards."

Edwards knew the President well, having briefed the Security Council when he was a senior defense liaison to the White House—when he still carried three stars on his shoulders. Ever since being named Under Secretary for Intelligence at the Defense Department, he'd been making trips across the Potomac from the Pentagon less frequently. His position was, by law, a civilian position, so he had to retire from the Army, but his allegiance was to the military. He also served a second role as Director of Defense Intelligence under Bert Morrison, the Director of National Intelligence. Both of his bosses were seated at the table—Morrison and Quentin S. Walker, Jr., the Secretary of Defense.

Edwards thought that the President and the Director of National Intelligence seemed to be straight shooters, and he believed they would listen carefully to his arguments. He couldn't say the same about everyone in the National Security Council. The Secretary of State, in particular, made him a little nervous, and the President's Chief of Staff and the National Security Advisor seemed quick to agree with each other, almost as though they'd been doing some behind-the-scenes planning.

Edwards stood up, his years of military background leading him to prefer a ramrod-straight posture when making a formal presentation. "Mr. President, Ladies and Gentlemen, please allow me to summarize the intelligence data and present you with the evidence—what we believe is incontrovertible evidence—demonstrating the precise origins of this cowardly attack on our great nation."

• • • • •

Ten minutes later, the meeting was over. President Alexander, recognizing both the gravity of the situation and the emerging conflicts among the members of his Security Council, ended the meeting clearly and firmly.

"Ladies and Gentlemen, our discussion is going in circles. We all share the same concerns and the same desire for action. But we cannot, and we will not act precipitously—not in my administration. We will gather the facts first. I need not remind you of the responsibilities of your own departments and agencies. We will meet again on Monday. I expect each of you to come with information. Fact, not opinion. Information that is accurate, documented, and reliable. We are adjourned."

The President stood and walked briskly out of the room with his chief of staff.

The others drifted slowly from the room. Vice President Richards caught Walker's attention, and they walked together toward the Vice President's office. Only when they were beyond the earshot of others did Richards begin to speak.

"That weaseling coward Alexander is just hiding his fucking ass behind the political cover of what he's calling 'information.' It's a smokescreen, and he's just stalling. We know what happened. And I know who did it. And most of all, I know what we're going to do to those bastards."

* * *

2

Redhouse

The disease most commonly confused with smallpox is chickenpox, and during the first 2 to 3 days of rash, it may be all but impossible to distinguish between the two.

—*Emerging Infectious Diseases, 1999*[*]

Day 11: Farmington, New Mexico

It was the day before Jackson Redhouse's second birthday, and he was miserable.

"Mama ... hurts."

"I know, Jackson. We're going to see Dr. Parker. He'll help you feel better." Evelyn Redhouse tried to sound cheerful, but she was dead tired and worried. She'd been up much of the night with her son. Dr. Parker had office hours on Saturday, and his receptionist told her to come right over. Her husband, Jack, already had left for the job site, but she could take care of this herself. One of the neighbors gave her a ride.

• • • • •

"You look a little under the weather, Jackson. Are you itchy? C'mon—let's have you sit up here on the table while your mom tells me what's been happening."

---

[*] "Smallpox: Clinical and Epidemiologic Features," D. A. Henderson, *Emerging Infectious Diseases,* Special Issue, Vol. 5, No. 4, 1999, p. 537.

"He's been cranky for a couple of days, Dr. Parker. And he has a temperature. And last night he started saying that he hurt, so that's when I decided I'd bring him in to see you this morning. But now he's got some sores on his face, and some in his mouth, too. It's really got me kind of worried."

"Well, let me take a look. It's okay, Jackson, I'm not going to stick you or anything. How old are you now?"

"Toooo—I two."

"Well, then ... you are getting big. Now, let's see just what's going on here. Hmmm ... I can definitely tell that you're running a bit of a fever. What was it when you checked Evie?"

"It was 102 this morning. Last night, when he woke me, it was 103."

"All right, we'll check it again in a couple of minutes. Have you been having headaches, Jackson? Has your head been hurting? Up here ... has it been hurting you?"

"Uh huh."

"Let's get your shirt off. There, that's good. You're a very good patient, Jackson. I wish all the children that came in here were as cooperative and nice as you are. You know what? I've seen this before, and I don't think you have too much to worry about."

"What is it Dr. Parker?"

"You don't remember, do you Evie? You had it when you were a kid. Chickenpox. The headache and fever, then the rash and the lesions? It used to be that almost all kids would get it. But the vaccinations have really cut down on chickenpox. I'm a little surprised that Jackson has it now, because he got his MMRV shot last year. Some children who are vaccinated still get it but it's usually a mild case."

"Do we need to keep him at home? I mean, to protect the other children?"

"Oh, I don't think so. In fact, it might be a good thing if they caught it now. It's a lot better to have the virus for the first time as a child than as an adult. Before the vaccine, it was pretty common to have what people called a 'pox party.' That way, all the children would contract chickenpox, and they would have protection against the more serious adult illness."

"What about medicine? Can you do anything to make him feel better?"

"There are some things we can do that will make you feel a lot better, Jackson. First of all, some acetaminophen to help with the aches and fever. And then some lotion to help with the itching. You're probably going to be itchy a lot for a couple of days, Jackson, and it's really important that you try not to scratch. That will be hard, but I know you're a strong young boy and you can do it. And your mom and dad will help, too. Baths are also good to help the itching, and in case it gets really bad, I'm going to give your mom some sample packets of antihistamines. We'll have you as good as new in no time at all."

"You be a good boy for your mom, Jackson. And Evie, please say hello to Jack for me. And don't worry, little Jackson is going to be all better in just a few days."

* * *

3

Sarah

In the past seven years, the federal government has spent more than $57 billion to shore up the nation's bioterrorism defenses, stockpiling drugs, ringing more than 30 American cities in a network of detectors and boosting preparedness at hospitals. The result: modest gains, at best ...

—*Washington Post, 2008*[*]

Day 22: A Call from the West

"Sarah Lockford." The newsroom of the *Washington Post* was so loud she had a hard time hearing who was on the phone.

"Sarah, it's Jillian." The connection was bad. "Can you talk?"

Sarah scanned the ring of offices and small conference rooms that surrounded the bullpen. She saw one that was empty. "Jillian, it's too noisy here, and you're breaking up. I'm heading over to a conference room. Call back there, okay? Extension 7307." It was the day before Thanksgiving, and Sarah was excited to chat with her old college friend.

The phone in 307 was ringing as she entered. "What's up, Jillian? Happy Thanksgiving!"

Silence

---

[*] "Modest Gains Against Ever-Present Bioterrorism Threat, An Attack Could Be Hard to Predict With Current Tools," Spencer S. Hsu, *Washington Post*, Aug. 3, 2008, p. A10.

"Jillian, how are you?"

"Something's wrong. I don't know what to do. One of the kids at school—his mother is a teacher's aide—the kid had a really bad case of chickenpox, and he died. Now some other kids are getting it too."

"God, Jillian, that's horrible. I knew that normal childhood diseases can be awful. One of the kids in my neighborhood almost died from the measles when we were little. I'm really sorry about the child in your school."

"You don't understand. It's not just one child. There are others, and they seem to be the worst cases of chickenpox that any of us have ever seen. But that's not all. A bunch of people who look like cops just showed up. They're armed, Sarah. And they're telling us that we can't leave. We're being quarantined."

Sarah felt her calm begin to dissolve. "Let me do some checking on this. Can I call you back tomorrow? Even better, why don't you call me again tomorrow? Here in the conference room. This same number. Could you manage that?"

"Sarah, I'm scared."

"I know. I'll find out what I can and let you know what's going on. Tomorrow. You call me. Okay? Jillian? Are you crying?"

"I'm really, really scared. I'll call tomorrow."

As soon as Jillian hung up, Sarah dialed Jake Overman's number at the Centers for Disease Control and Prevention in Atlanta. If anyone could tell her about chickenpox or medical quarantines, it was Jake.

She waited impatiently while Jake's phone rang a half dozen times. It was 4:30. *Why the hell doesn't he pick up? He told me two weeks ago that he wasn't going anywhere for Thanksgiving.* The last few times they spoke, it sounded like Jake was almost living at his office, working such long days that he hardly seemed to need his condo anymore.

Finally, after the seventh ring the line clicked, and a female voice said "BPR. May I help you?"

Sarah hesitated. "I'm trying to reach Dr. Overman." Sarah was confused, because Jake always answered his own phone or used voicemail. And she didn't recognize 'BPR.' Jake worked in the Division of Emerging Infections and Surveillance Services, devising strategies for identifying and controlling disease, and he hadn't said anything about changing jobs.

"I'm sorry. He's not available. Your name please?"

"He and I worked together before he joined the CDC. I need his input on a snag I just hit in my research. Can you tell me when he'll be back?"

"I can't give out that information." The reply was as chilly as it was officious. "Give me your name and number, and I'll ask him to return your call."

"I'll just try calling him later," she said and hung up.

Sarah headed back to her desk in the bullpen and typed her password into her computer. Her Web browser was already launched, and a moment later she was on the CDC website. There was the new set of letters: Division of Bioterrorism Preparedness and Response (DBPR). "Weird," she said aloud. Then silently, *He's never said anything about bioterrorism.*

Deciding that she'd been taken sufficiently off task, Sarah logged off her computer, threw a few papers into her bag, and headed out of the building. On the short walk down 15th Street to the McPherson Square Metro Station, she pulled out her cell phone and called Jake's cell. After a moment, a tinny voice announced, "The number you are trying to reach is not available at this time."

Now Sarah was irritated. She'd never had trouble getting Jake on the phone. Everything that had happened that afternoon was weird, and she didn't like it. She dropped the phone back into her bag.

Damn! I promised Jillian I'd call her back tomorrow, and Jake would know what to tell her. Maybe this won't be on the front page in Washington, but it sure as hell is a big deal in New Mexico. What the hell is going on?

* * *

Day 22: Sarah and Jillian

Jillian and Sarah became fast friends when they met as freshmen at William & Mary. They roomed together for the next three years, and their friendship remained strong despite their different career paths.

Sarah went on to graduate school in the molecular biology program at the University of Virginia, where Jake Overman was in the fourth year of his Ph.D. in the same department. Despite their attempts to be discreet, it wasn't long before their romantic involvement was the best known secret on campus.

After getting her degree in biology, Jillian was accepted into the Teach for America program and was sent to New Mexico to teach on the Navajo Reservation. When she finished her stint with "The Corps," she decided to stay in Farmington, in the northwest corner of New Mexico. It was just a few miles from the only place in America where four states converge at a single point. This intersection of Arizona, Colorado, New Mexico, and Utah gives the entire area its nickname. Jillian found it a strange and wonderful place.

She signed on to teach at Apache Elementary School, and she arrived with a sunny outlook. There were many challenges and many obstacles, but she always tried to see them as opportunities.

Not until the past few days had Jillian ever been unhappy with life there. The child's death had devastated the community, and the entire staff at Apache were scared to death that their kids might be next. At least four other children had come down with bad cases of chickenpox, and she'd heard that a couple of adults had caught it as well. She desperately hoped that Sarah would have some information for her the next day.

* * *

Day 22: Where's Jake?

Sarah lived in Arlington, Virginia, just across the Potomac River from D.C. She had a gorgeous view of the nation's capital from her 12th floor apartment. From her balcony, she could see the Lincoln Memorial, the Reflecting Pool, the Washington Monument, and finally, in the distance, the Capitol.

As soon as she got home, she dropped her bag in a chair and called Jake's CDC number again. After five rings, he hadn't answered, so she tried his cell phone, expecting that he'd pick up after regular working hours. Instead she immediately got the same recorded message. *Damn! Where has he gone?*

She made a grilled cheese sandwich and heated a cup of tomato soup. Halfway through the sandwich, she suddenly realized that she'd missed an obvious answer—call his housemate.

For the past two years, Jake had been sharing his condo with Charles Evans, an assistant professor of public health at Emory University. The two met through a mutual friend when Charles had interviewed for his faculty position. They'd hit it off, and when Charles was hired, Jake took him on as a renter.

The condo had two large bedrooms, a guest room, and an office area that they shared. Both men spent long days at work, and their modest social schedules didn't lead to conflicts. If either of them were having friends over, the other was always welcome. Financially, it was a great deal for both of them.

Sarah had first met Charles at a meeting of the American Epidemiological Society, and the trio had hung out when she had been in Atlanta for long weekends with Jake.

She looked up Charles's number in her contacts file, recalling that he had a separate phone line at the condo. He answered on the third ring and sounded delighted to hear from Sarah. "God, I haven't seen you in nearly a year. What's up? Are you coming in for a visit? Jake's not here, but I guess you probably know that or you would have called him rather than me."

"That's exactly why I'm calling. I've been trying to reach him all day, but I couldn't get him at his office or on his cell. He picks up his cell unless he's in the middle of a meeting."

"Hmmm." It was more of a grunt than a word. "I know he's off on a trip, but he didn't say where. Did you try leaving a message on his voicemail at the office?"

"I tried, but after the phone rang a few times, a woman picked up and just said he was unavailable. She wouldn't tell me anything else, and she wasn't particularly friendly. I don't know, maybe 'snotty' is the right word. It kind of bugged me."

"That's odd. He always takes such pride in answering his own phone and leaving a personalized voicemail message when he's on travel. But he was in one hell of a hurry when he left yesterday. We were supposed to meet up for dinner last night, but he showed up at about 5:30 and fired right into his room to pack. He said he needed go out of town on business for a few days."

"Where?"

"Don't know. When I asked him where he was going, he just said it wasn't anyplace glamorous. He was back out the door with a suitcase in 10 minutes."

"I wish he had stayed in contact. I had a question that I was hoping he could answer."

"Maybe I could help."

"You probably could. I guess I wasn't thinking. Okay, here's the deal. I got a call from an old friend out in New Mexico who teaches in a school on the edge of the Navajo Reservation. She was totally freaked out that one of the kids—the child of one of the other teachers—came down with chickenpox and died. And she said that other kids are really sick, some of the adults too. Then she said that a military unit had swooped in, and they were cordoning off the whole area."

"Wow! Military? Anyway, an outbreak of chickenpox isn't that unusual Sarah. Especially since some parents haven't vaccinated their children in the past few years. And some of the chickenpox strains can be bad. I don't have the statistics at my fingertips, but there are still a number of deaths every year. I'd have to check into this to get better answers, though. Childhood diseases are outside my research area, and I haven't looked at those stats since grad school."

"What about the idea that they're being quarantined? I haven't heard of anything like that happening during my lifetime—and certainly not since I've been reporting on this kind of stuff."

"That is weird. I'll put in a few queries in the morning. Some of my colleagues will be in the lab for a couple of hours, even on Thanksgiving. If your friend is right, this might make a good story for you. Give me a call after ten, and we'll see if there's anything to it. Realistically, it's probably nothing. Usually these common diseases don't lead to serious epidemics."

"Thanks, Charles. I'll talk to you tomorrow. Give me your office number again."

Sarah wrote it down on her notepad. She never went anywhere without a small spiral notebook in her pocket, and the stash of old notebooks in her desk drawer contained a wealth of old phone numbers, many of which never made it into her computer files.

* * *

4

Redhouse

*A growing number of New York parents are
scheduling chicken pox playdates where kids share
lollipops and trade germy pajamas to spread the
disease and avoid vaccinations.*

—*New York Post, 2009*[*]

Day 12: Pox Party

When Evelyn and Jackson got home, Jack was already
there.
    "We closed the job site down early. There was
some snow, and it was icing up. Colder than usual for this time of
year. I don't think the guys were real happy, losing a day's wages
and all. But I had to make that decision. It wasn't safe out there. Too
bad, though. We kinda need the money too."
    Evelyn hugged him. "It's okay, Jack. We'll manage. And
Jackson will be okay, too. Dr. Parker said he has chickenpox, but he
should be over it in a few more days. He'll be uncomfortable, but I
got some medicine. And Dr. Parker said that baths would help, too."
    "They would, huh? How about it big fella? Would you like to get
into the bathtub? And maybe start to feel better?"
    "Uh huh. You too, Daddy?"
    "Well, I'll give you a bath, but I'm not gonna take one. This'll be
special, just for you. C'mon let's get you undressed."

---

[*] Kate Torgovnick, "Inside New York Chicken Pox Parties," *Page Six
Magazine, New York Post*, Jan. 11, 2009.

In a few minutes, Evelyn joined them in the bathroom, where Jackson was playing with one of his bath toys. "You're looking a whole lot better now, Jackson."

"Yes. Better." It sounded more like "butter."

"Evie, what should we do about Jackson's birthday party? The other kids are supposed to come over tomorrow. Maybe put it off until next week? It would only be a few days after his actual birthday on Tuesday."

"Bffday?"

"Oh, gosh. I forgot all about it. We already ordered the cake, Jack. It's got writing and everything, so they'll charge us even if we don't have the party."

"Yeah, but we can't just expose the other kids to this."

"Dr. Parker said Jackson only has a mild case, because he was vaccinated. And he told me it's not a problem for the other kids. He said that before the vaccines, people would have special parties to expose all the other children on purpose. That it's much better to get it when you're a kid."

"Well, maybe. But you have to talk to the other moms, Evie. If they agree, we could go ahead. What about it, son? Do you still want to have a birthday party tomorrow?"

"Uh huh. Bffday potty."

They tried not to laugh, but they weren't very successful. Evelyn just leaned over the tub and gave Jackson a big kiss.

The other parents thought the party was a good idea, especially when Evelyn explained what Dr. Parker had said.

The birthday chickenpox party was a big success. There were four other children, ranging in age from one to five, from two other families. Jimmy and Stacey Shepherd brought Ethan and Emily, and Shannon Apachito brought Ryan, Rebecca, and Sienna. The children all had great fun playing and eating cake. Jackson seemed to think that the two candles on the cake were just the greatest thing ever, and he really knew he was special when everybody sang to him.

* * *

5

Sarah

'The vaccine has reduced infections in every age group, including among babies under 1 year old, who are too young to be vaccinated,' says study author Jane Seward of the CDC's National Center for Immunizations and Respiratory Diseases.

—*USA TODAY, 2008*[*]

Day 23: Varicella Numbers

Sarah woke early the next morning and went for a run. The exercise was a great stress buster, and there wasn't a better place for running and biking than where she lived. A network of bicycle paths went across the Potomac into the District, and there were even longer trails on the Virginia side of the river.

The 20-mile trail down to Mount Vernon was only a few blocks from her apartment. National Airport was only a couple of miles downriver, with views that Sarah thought were unmatched anywhere in the world. She was fond of telling people, "The river is beautiful, and there's nowhere else that you can look around while you're running and see the Lincoln Memorial, the Washington Monument, the whole city of Washington, D.C."

On this morning, Sarah decided instead to run on the Martha Custis trail. After going north several blocks from her apartment, she entered the trail and headed west. The hills and overall uphill climb

---

[*] "Chickenpox vaccine does a number on the number of cases," Liz Szabo, *USA Today*, Sept. 1, 2008.

for 20 minutes were a good workout. The return trip was a little easier, and she didn't need to push as hard to finish a total of five miles in just under 40 minutes.

During her run, Sarah thought about the prior day's strange events. She had some work to do before she talked to Charles. Several publicly accessible databases might prepare her to ask the right questions when she talked to Charles. Without even noticing, she had switched from being Jillian's friend who was asking Charles for help to being a reporter who was using Charles as a source.

Thinking about databases, she remembered a lecture she had attended while she was a graduate student. The speaker had been from CDC, and he had seemed old, maybe already retired at the time. He was an epidemiologist, and his lecture was on the importance of maintaining accurate and up-to-date statistics on diseases. She knew she could find his name on the Web. After a quick shower, some cereal, and a cup of coffee, she turned on the desktop computer on the kitchen table that doubled as her home office.

A quick Google search did the trick. Michael B. Gregg had been a pioneer in providing information on disease outbreaks, and there was the stuff she wanted near the top of the column:

> *Under his editorship from 1967 to 1988, the Centers for Disease Control and Prevention's Morbidity and Mortality Weekly Report not only was a scientifically reliable compendium of disease outbreaks and death statistics, but it also put the sometimes-dense data into perspective with the addition of a then-innovative editorial note.†*

Morbidity and Mortality Weekly Report was exactly what Sarah was looking for. MMWR was a treasure trove of official information regarding disease outbreaks, but she didn't see anything about chickenpox. On the other hand, some of the other entries used Latin names, so she quickly double-checked and confirmed her memory that the name of the virus responsible for chickenpox was varicella. But there were no entries for that term either. *Dead end.*

Next she began searching the whole CDC site for "chickenpox." One page said that before vaccines were available, more than 10,000

---

† "Michael B. Gregg, 78; Journal Editor Led Coverage of Disease Outbreaks, Patricia Sullivan," Patricia Sullivan, Obituaries: *Washington Post*, July 23, 2008; p. B08.

people were hospitalized and about 150 died from chickenpox every year. Another page said that the death rate had gone down by 80 percent since the early 1990s, again because children were being vaccinated. There was a heading labeled "Diseases Under Surveillance" on that Web page. Sarah was surprised to find that there was no entry for a New Mexico outbreak. *I guess they haven't had time to update it yet.*

Before logging off, Sarah signed into her home e-mail account and composed a quick message. "Jake, where the hell are you? I need to ask you a question. –S." She sent the message and shut down the computer.

After another cup of coffee, Sarah dressed and headed to work. She reached her desk at about 9:30. Thanksgiving was always a slow day. She answered a few e-mails and organized some files for a story she was working on. At 10:05, she called Charles at his office. He picked up on the first ring.

"Hi Charles. It's Sarah. Happy Thanksgiving."

"Good morning, Sarah. I've got some information, but I'm not sure it will be of much help. I asked a couple of colleagues about quarantines. They said that a few people had been quarantined in 2007 after being infected with a particularly bad strain of tuberculosis, but nobody remembered any examples where a whole town was quarantined in the past 50 years. On the other hand, they reminded me that quarantines have been discussed as part of an emergency response since September 11, 2001."

"It's possible my friend was just overreacting, but that's not like her. Maybe the people she thought were military were just from the Public Health Department, and they were only asking people to stay home if they were sick. Maybe my friend just misunderstood. I'll call her later and ask about it."

"I also checked into the mortality rates."

Sarah interrupted. "Yeah, me, too. I should have done that before I called you the first time. It looks like about 40 or so people die from chickenpox every year in the U.S."

"That agrees with what I've seen."

"So you don't think it's likely that there's some really bad strain of chickenpox in Farmington?"

"Probably not. And besides, almost all children are being vaccinated in the U.S. these days, so even if kids in an isolated area aren't all vaccinated, there should still be enough resistance in the population that the outbreak will settle down pretty quickly. Adults shouldn't be much of a problem, because almost all of them had chickenpox or were vaccinated when they were children. So they would have relatively good immunity. Overall, I think you should be able to tell your friend that things will be okay."

"That's what I thought, Charles. Get this, though. When I was looking online, I tried to see what I could find out about chickenpox outbreaks. I found some stuff on the CDC website, but it was pretty old and wasn't very helpful. I went to the—let me check my notebook here—the MMWR, and there was nothing about a New Mexico outbreak. And I also checked 'Diseases Under Surveillance,' and there was nothing. Isn't it strange that they don't have the data posted by now?"

He laughed. "That's a good one. We always tease Jake and his crew over at CDC about how slow they are getting useful data up on their site. It isn't really that funny, though. If we had a serious outbreak of something, speed would be really important. But here's another site to check out. Have you got a pen?"

"Always."

"Look at the website called HealthMap—all one word—and it's probably 'dot org' or 'dot com.' You could always Google it to get there. This was set up about five years ago by a guy I know at Harvard. They use Web-crawling technology to search the media around the world for all sorts of disease reports. I bet you can find something there about your New Mexico cases. But don't expect anything too exciting. Like I said, chickenpox isn't really a big deal."

"Okay, Charles. Thanks for helping me out. I was starting to think this was going to be some big story, but I'd rather have things turn out well."

"It should be okay. But there is one other thing before we hang up. I was a little puzzled by what you said yesterday, so I tried calling Jake on his cell. I got that same 'not available' message that you told me about. I also sent him an e-mail, and I haven't heard back."

"Well, he didn't answer my e-mail either, but at least with me, he always has preferred phone to e-mail. I guess he must be someplace where he has bad reception, or maybe his battery died."

"No, that's not it, Sarah. This is a different kind of message—almost like he's been disconnected by the phone company. Maybe he forgot to pay his bill. But what's really got me curious though is the person who answered his office phone. Probably the same person you talked to. She just gave me that same answer, that he 'was unavailable.' And she wouldn't give me any other information about where he was or when he'd be back."

"Did she say 'BPR' when you called? Did Jake move to the Division of Bioterrorism Preparedness and Response?"

"Nothing to worry about there, Sarah. Jake has always worked in that part of CDC. They just haven't emphasized the terrorism stuff. My guess is that they're doing some sort of hush-hush training exercise. Jake's getting a pretty good reputation at CDC, so I wouldn't be surprised if they tagged him as an instructor. He doesn't talk to me about things that are classified, but I know he's up to date on the worst diseases that people are worried about for biological warfare—tularemia, anthrax, even plague."

"Maybe you're right, Charles. I'll try to stop worrying about it. Anyway, you've been a big help on the chickenpox stuff. At least now I can tell my friend Jillian not to worry. If Jake ever answers his phone, I hope I'll be down for a visit sometime soon. Atlanta is nice this time of year, and it would be good to see you again."

"Sounds good, Sarah. I'll look forward to it."

"Okay, Charles. Thanks again. Take care of yourself. Happy Thanksgiving!"

* * *

Day 23: No More Phone Calls

Sarah had several hours before she would hear from Jillian, so she turned again to her regular reporting assignments. She was working on a feature about the Food and Drug Administration. Underfunded and understaffed, the agency had a hard time meeting all of its regulatory and oversight responsibilities. Even the President's promises to safeguard the nation's food supply hadn't stopped the various warnings and recalls: *E. coli* in lettuce, salmonella in peanuts, tainted dog food from China, and drug recalls. Sarah had heard rumors of illegal activities in the drug-approval process.

A potential whistleblower gave Sarah a huge electronic file and told her to look at the numbers. To be on the safe side, she kept the files on her home computer. At the newspaper, she limited her efforts to background research.

Unable to get her mind off Jillian, Sarah decided to check the HealthMap site that Charles had told her about. A few seconds later, she found it.

HealthMap | Global Health, Local Knowledge

www.healthmap.org/

Tracking map of the latest alerts around the world and in the U.S.

She was looking at a world map with several menus on the page. She quickly discovered that she could select a variety of source feeds as well as a variety of different diseases. Once she figured out how to use the map, she activated all the possible feeds, including published information compiled by Google News and official sources such as the World Health Organization. She clicked on "chickenpox," and the screen refreshed to show several "thumbtacks" on the map. Two were in Mexico and one was in South America. And there was the one she was looking for! A single marker in the southwest United States. Clicking her mouse on the marker, she saw a pop-up menu with a result from Google News Español: "20 Nov. Brote de varicela en Farmington."

She felt a surge of adrenalin. *That sure as hell looks like what I'm after.* The active link brought up a new page with the same title and a dateline of "Farmington, NM—20 de novembro." This was followed by two brief paragraphs of text.

Sarah's Spanish was limited, but it was clear that this was what she wanted. It was in Farmington, and it was about varicella. A Spanish online dictionary confirmed that "brote" meant "outbreak", and the second paragraph seemed to be talking about a small number of cases, mostly children. It all fit with the situation that she and Charles had discussed—a mild outbreak that really wasn't much of a problem.

She copied both the file and the URL into an e-mail message to herself using her Gmail account, a habit she had developed for saving personal or confidential information. The account also used an alias, a diversion that she assumed would give her extra protection when she was working on sensitive issues.

At 1 p.m., Sarah decided to get some lunch. She left the *Post* building and walked the street. One of the real advantages of having an office right in the heart of downtown was that some really good restaurants were only a block or two away. Nothing seemed to be open, but then she remembered something. *Hotels don't shut down for a holiday.* A few minutes later, sitting by the front window of a hotel dining room, she ordered a soup-and-sandwich special and read the newspaper.

Shortly after 3 p.m., she was back at the office, walking toward the conference room. It was early for Jillian's call, but the phone was already ringing. Sarah picked up the phone. *"Washington Post,* this is Sa—"

"No names!"

Sarah recognized the voice instantly.

"Look, we may not finish this conversation. We just heard that all the phone lines are being cut. Do you still have that gizmo that your father gave you a few years ago?"

After a moment of confusion, Sarah realized that Jillian was talking about the shortwave set that her dad had given her during her senior year in college. She'd had it in her dorm room, and it became something of a curiosity. Everyone else used cell phones, fax machines, and e-mail, but Sarah still had an occasional conversation with her dad over the radio. He was an old-school techie, and his technologies preceded the digital age. The radio was different enough to be fun, and people from up and down the hall would sometimes stop in and listen for a couple of minutes. "Yeah, I still have it."

"Good, you ought to fire it up this evening. My friend Elmer will call … nine-thirty." Then the line went dead.

* * *

Day 23: A Blast from the Past

Sarah was alarmed by Jillian's call. She still couldn't reach Jake by phone or by e-mail, and now she'd been told that phone contact to Farmington was about to be cut off. *Just for a case of chickenpox that's no big deal?*

She wanted to talk to Jillian immediately, but the instructions had been clear. The radio contact had to wait until evening, when Jillian would contact her. Jillian knew how to use the radio, and it sounded like she had a friend named Elmer.

With more time to kill, she put in another call to Charles. He answered more gruffly than the last time. "Evans."

"Hi Charles, this is—"

"I can't talk now. Things are really busy here. Maybe I can call you at home later." Then the line went dead.

Wow, *paranoia must be contagious.*

Sarah got home around 4 p.m. and spent some time poking around in the FDA files on her external hard drive. She was working on a story about insider trading by a scientist at the Food and Drug Administration, but she found that she couldn't concentrate.

She was startled when the phone rang. "Hello?"

"No names!" It was Charles. "It's been suggested that I stop discussing my research on the phone. It seems to me that this would be a good time for you to just take the weekend off and go visit your erstwhile boyfriend. He's got a nice condo, and I understand his roommate is agreeable to providing you with the space you need." And with that, he hung up.

This is crazy! Somebody told Charles not to talk to me. Because I'm a reporter? Or because the topic was chickenpox?

Sarah turned to her computer and went to the HealthMap site. This time, she let the program search for all the diseases that might be related to food and sanitation. One by one, she added "cholera," the broad category of "foodborne illness," "*E. coli,*" "hepatitis," "diarrhea," "gastroenteritis," "dysentery," "norovirus," "botulism," and "salmonella." Continuously scanning the map, she found a many locations around the globe for these diseases, and a fair number in the United States. But none were anywhere near New Mexico.

She cleared all those diseases from her search and looked at the category of "Not Yet Classified," thinking that maybe the Four Corners outbreak was still preliminary. Once again, there was nothing in the Southwest. The final category was "Undiagnosed," but when she tried that category, there still was nothing in the Southwest—or for that matter, anywhere in the entire United States.

Finally, just to see if there had been any changes since earlier in the day, she cleared all the other diseases and selected "chickenpox." There were three entries for chickenpox worldwide, but none of them was in the American Southwest! *What the hell is going on here? How come the entry I found earlier today has disappeared? If anything, there should be more entries now, if the situation is as bad as Jillian says it is.*

In a near panic, she looked through the list of diseases on HealthMap. *Is it possible that there's some other, similar disease that is causing serious problems and they're trying to prevent a panic by keeping it quiet?* She found a listing for "Monkeypox," but the report was from Africa. Another entry for "Sheep/Goat pox" reported cases in China.

Sarah was sure that something important was happening. *Maybe a training exercise, like Charles said. Maybe just a training exercise, like Charles said. Maybe something for Homeland Security. But if they're manipulating the news feeds—it could be a big story.*

The only concrete step she could take, at least until she'd heard more from Jillian, would be following up on Charles's cryptic suggestion to visit. The reference to the condo and the "agreeable roommate" meant that Charles, not Jake, wanted to meet with her. Whatever information he had, it was something he wouldn't share by phone. And there was nothing in any of her e-mail in-boxes. He really didn't want their communication to be traced.

But he just made a phone call to my number. That certainly seems risky, if he's so concerned. Sarah reached for her telephone and pushed the button for "new calls." The caller ID displayed the Atlanta area code, 404. She was about to look up Charles's number to compare it to this one, when she stopped short. *Jake's number.* Charles was worried that someone might be monitoring his telephone. But the one person they wouldn't be worried about was Jake Overman, who was traveling somewhere on government business—maybe for the same people who might want to find out what Charles was up to. What they didn't realize was that Charles could just walk across to the other side of the condo and use Jake's personal line. In fact, chances were they didn't even know that Jake and Charles shared the same address.

In a strange way, this was starting to make sense. Charles had something to tell her, but it had to be untraceable. Face-to-face, apparently, and he wanted her to come to Atlanta. *Now.*

Turning back to her computer, she stopped, dumbstruck. *Oh shit! Jillian was talking in code too.* Jillian's friend "Elmer" wasn't the name of an actual person. It was a well-known term for someone in the amateur radio community, a ham radio operator who mentored a newcomer. Jillian was going to contact her with the help of a seasoned operator.

When Jillian said "nine-thirty," Sarah had taken the numbers to mean a time that evening. But now Sarah realized that Jillian was only being careful. It wasn't a time at all—it was the frequency that she'd use—9,030 kilohertz—"nine-thirty." When Sarah's dad had called via shortwave back in her college days, he'd use the same frequency every time. For her dad, it was the high end of the 15-meter band, at 19,020 kHz. *We always called it "nineteen-twenty," and Jillian knew that.*

Sarah's set was an Emerson, a really good one, or at least it had been at one time. It wasn't actually the same one that she'd had in college, but there were neither time nor cause to tell Jillian. Her dad had since bought a newer digital system, and he gave Sarah his old set. When he first got it back in 1985, it was the best and most powerful ham radio on the market. Even now, it was still something special. As she turned her dial to 9,030 kHz, she heard a lot of interference and some static. And then, a voice. "This is AFG411 calling N4MEX. Do you read me? Repeat, do you read me?"

That has to be him. Elmer. Jillian remembered my call sign! Sarah grabbed the microphone, pushed the transmit button, responding as calmly as possible. "This is N4MEX. I read you loud and clear."

"Just a second N4MEX." The male voice had an accent that Sarah couldn't quite place.

"Sarah, listen carefully." It was Jillian. "It's getting worse out here. They've stopped all vehicles from entering or leaving the area, and now they've cut all telephone contact. The cell phone towers have been disabled. We can't even make local calls."

"AFG411," said Sarah, looking at her pocket notebook, where she'd jotted down Elmer's call sign. If being secretive was how this needed to be done, she could play that game, too. "I don't understand what's going on out there. Is this just some sort of civil defense exercise? Nobody should be getting upset about chickenpox, even if it is a severe strain. Everything I've read says that it will all be over soon."

"Sarah, listen to me!" It's not getting better, and it's not chickenpox. And more children have died. Her next words were the most chilling Sarah had ever heard. "It's smallpox."

There was complete silence for several seconds.

"That's impossible."

"N4MEX," said the male voice. "It's not impossible. Some of us here on the reservation remember the stories. It's smallpox. And it's not the first time that Indians have been smallpox victims. That's why we're calling. We need help."

Sarah was stunned by the emotion—more accurately, the lack of emotion—in his voice. "I don't know what I can do."

"You're a reporter!" It was Jillian again. "Ever since you decided to become a reporter, you've talked about Vietnam and Nixon and the Pentagon Papers. And the torture memos, and the Iraq war. You said that the free press, the first amendment, those were the keys to the safety of our country. You're a reporter, Sarah. Report."

"Okay." She said it quietly. "I'll start working on it."

"N4MEX," said the man's voice. "If you happen to get out this way, look up an old friend in Cortez, Colorado, by the name of Raymond Morgan. Write down this number …"

"AFG411, I've got the number." She repeated it.

"N4MEX, over and out."

* * *

6

National Security Council

Future generations will know by history only that
this loathsome disease has existed.

—*Thomas Jefferson**

Day 23: Back to Washington

The National Security Council met in emergency session on Friday, the day after Thanksgiving.

For the NSC staff, much of the Thanksgiving holiday had been spent contacting officials who would be needed at the meeting. Many were out of town, celebrating the holiday with family or friends, and someone had to interrupt Thanksgiving dinner.

Telling people about the meeting was only the start. Making travel arrangements was next. Everything was jammed on Thanksgiving night: bumper-to-bumper traffic on the Interstates, trains filled to capacity, and overbooked flights at the airports. Cabinet Secretaries could get a helicopter, and the Defense Department helped with its regularly scheduled military flights, and additional flights were added to for high-ranking civilians. The emergency meeting provided whatever bureaucratic justifications

---

* Quotation from an 1806 letter from President Thomas Jefferson to Edward Jenner, who recently had developed a vaccine against smallpox: D.R. Hopkins, "Princes and Peasants: Smallpox in History," Chicago, Illinois: University of Chicago Press, 1983.

were necessary. But commercial flights were a different story. The overworked staffers found themselves wheedling, cajoling, even begging airline representatives to find a space for their "essential personnel." And all of the arrangements had to be made in a way that would not create a panic.

Arthur Hayes spent Thanksgiving in an office at the White House, using the title "Acting National Security Advisor." At three o'clock on Thursday afternoon, in response to a directive from the President, he found himself placing a call to T. Parker Cunningham, the President's National Security Advisor, the person who effectively ran the National Security Council, even though it was officially chaired by the President.

"Acting" didn't mean that he took over the position. This was a bona fide crisis, and his first order of business was to get the real number one back in the saddle. He could hear the phone ringing at the other end.

Parker's daughter handed him the phone. "This is Cunningham." The hum of conversation and laughter Hayes had heard while he waited for his boss made Hayes feel guilty for interrupting.

"Arthur Hayes here, sir. Sorry to disturb you, but we need you back in Washington. Immediately."

"We're visiting family in Ohio, Hayes. What is this about? It's Thanksgiving!"

"I repeat, sir. You're needed back here in Washington. We've made travel arrangements, and a car from Wright Patterson will be arriving in a few minutes to take you to the airport. We can't talk on the phone—at least not until you get on the aircraft with a secure phone. But sir? I'm not sure that right now we have all that much to be thankful about."

* * *

Day 24: Laying the Groundwork

On the day after Thanksgiving, a few hours before the start of the National Security Council meeting, four men met in a secure conference room in the Eisenhower Executive Office Building. Vice President Richards had quietly summoned Quentin Walker, the Secretary of Defense; Robinson Edwards, the Under Secretary for Intelligence at DOD; and George P. Radisson, the Chairman of the Joint Chiefs of Staff. This was to be a meeting of the minds—military minds—to develop a strategy for the National Security Council meeting—a strategy to assure a decisive and immediate military response to the attack.

Richards suspected that other Council members, in particular the Secretary of State, might be having a similar meeting a meeting that in his mind would be treason. *Any attempt at negotiation with terrorists is treason, by definition.* As he saw it, there was only one choice. *We have to bomb the bastards back into the stone age!*

The Vice President assailed the Secretary of Defense as soon as he arrived for the meeting. "Just what the hell is going on, Walker? We've got a giant clusterfuck here, and you didn't see fit to give me advance notice? That's not why I got you into Defense in the first place, and you'd better remember that."

The two men had a long history. Trevor B. Richards, a graduate of West Point, had cut his teeth in combat as a young officer at the tail end of the Vietnam War, earning commendations for bravery as combat operations were winding down. During the substantial period of peacetime that followed, his military career flourished, aided by advanced degrees in military history and political science. He'd been introduced to the political landscape of Washington, D.C., during an assignment at the Pentagon, when he was detailed to the White House as a military attaché to the National Security Council. He had spent more time than any other NSC member in the conference room where that group soon would soon convene.

Like many of his contemporaries, Richards' views had been shaped at a time when the primary threat to the United States was the Soviet Union. The fall of the USSR had left many in the military without direction while they sought a new enemy. But not Richards. Then a Colonel, he had understood that change was on the horizon, although he didn't quite know what that change would be. From a military viewpoint, it didn't matter that much. What he saw was a change in how wars would be fought. Vietnam was just the first instance in which guerilla tactics were a major part of the enemy's approach. He knew there would be more.

His superior command abilities gained the attention of the top brass during the Bosnia-Serbia campaign, and he was rewarded with promotion to Brigadier General. He earned a second star during the Persian Gulf War. He developed widespread support and respect both at the Pentagon and with the public. Not since Colin Powell had an active military figure been discussed so widely as a possible candidate for national office.

So, when James Fallon Alexander was nominated for President by his party, Richards was seen as an ideal balance for the cerebral Alexander, whose Quaker background was being used by his opponent to label him as reluctant to defend his country. The vice presidential candidate promptly reminded the electorate that Richard Nixon's Quaker background hadn't kept him from continuing to send troops to Vietnam, nor did it dissuade him from initiating the bombing campaigns in Cambodia and Laos. Richards greatly strengthened the ticket, and the pair achieved a narrow victory in the general election.

An integral part of the Alexander Administration, Richards was consulted on all of the President's appointments in the areas of defense and national security. That gave Richards the opportunity to push Quentin S. Walker, Jr. for Defense Secretary. Walker became the administration's most vocal hawk, Richards its most powerful.

After a mediocre undergraduate career at the Louisiana State University, Walker had, through family ties, managed to get an appointment to the Coast Guard Reserve, which allowed him to avoid Vietnam. He did have to put in some time on what his friends always called "weekend cruises" in the Gulf of Mexico. He'd always felt guilty about dodging meaningful military service in Vietnam, where too many of his high school and college friends had died. He also harbored a deep anger over those deaths, which his guilt and narcissism caused him to take as personal rebukes.

Walker had been too old for military service by the time of the Persian Gulf War, but he had decided by then that he would honor those who served the nation by doing whatever was needed to support them and their families. He also understood that war was sometimes necessary, and he would not hesitate to send the country's men and women off to fight—and to die—in the cause of the nation.

Walker worked in his father's shipbuilding and dry-dock operations for a dozen years after college, taking two years off in the middle of that time to earn an MBA. He was no academic star, but for the most part, he did attend the classes and pass the exams. And, more important, he began to make political contacts.

During his last several years at the shipyard, where he and his younger brother worked as managers, his political star began to rise. A decline in the shipbuilding industry hit their part of the Gulf, and Walker bet on the wisdom of working with the unions. He bet right. The result was increased profits for the business, along with modest growth that helped people find jobs. He became a bit of a local hero, and when the political contacts he'd made while working on his MBA came calling, he agreed to run for a vacant seat in the U.S. House of Representatives.

He barely won that election, finishing ahead of his opponent by just a few votes. But he understood the game and how it was played. He worked tirelessly to bring new business and dollars into his district. With this approach—and an uncanny ability to stay on the right side of ethical issues, or at least not get caught while on the wrong side—he had been reelected a dozen times.

Quentin Walker had become one of the most powerful members of the House of Representatives, and he served as a highly influential member, whether in the majority or minority, of the House Armed Services Committee. In that role, he was an unfailing proponent of anything the Pentagon might request.

As Walker's star ascended in Congress, so Richards' did in the military. The two men crossed paths many times, first, during Walker's occasional visits to the White House when Richards was detailed to the Security Council, and later, when Richards would testify before the Armed Services Committee as a representative from the Pentagon. Richards recognized that Walker would always support Pentagon requests, even when the justification for the requests might be flimsy. When the time came for President-Elect Alexander to name his cabinet, Richards had been a strong—and ultimately, successful—advocate for appointing Walker to the position of Secretary of Defense.

While Vice President Richards publicly praised Walker as an unfailing supporter of the military, he also saw the appointment as one that would give him—and him alone—an additional source of power. He knew how to manipulate Walker's guilt about Vietnam to ensure that Walker supported him on each and every question of national security.

Walker wasn't offended when the Vice President greeted him with a stream of profanity. Neither the foul language nor the accusatory tone bothered him. It was just the way Richards spoke under stress. Walker also respected the office that Richards held. "Mr. Vice President, we couldn't give you advance notice about what happened. We didn't know. Nobody knew. This was a terrorist attack—a surprise attack on innocent people."

"Let's hear the details. What do we know?"

"First of all, let me report where we are. Then we'll tell you—actually, Under Secretary Edwards will tell you—how we've learned what we now know. The whole thing started when we received a call from a Dr. Steven D. Rasmussen at CDC, the Centers for Disease Control and Prevention. Actually, he called Col. Jason Bradshaw at Fort Bliss in Texas. You recall that we've started up these rapid-reaction forces to respond to domestic disasters or terrorist attacks? Well, Bradshaw commands the rapid-reaction brigade down at Fort Bliss. He's worked with Rasmussen on simulation exercises. Rasmussen is the—let me see, here—the Director of CDC's Coordinating Office for Terrorism Preparedness and Emergency Response. That's a mouthful. I'm told they just call it COTPER."

"Get to the goddamn point, Quentin. What did they tell you? I don't like being kept in the fucking dark."

"Sorry, Mr. Vice President. Just trying to give you all the background. Well, on Tuesday, three days ago, some small-town doctor called CDC to say they might have a case of smallpox. The guy's not even an American, from the sound of his name—and everybody thought he was just some nut case. But CDC did what they had to do. They sent one of their top guys out to New Mexico to investigate. And then all hell broke loose. On Wednesday they confirmed the illness as smallpox. There were several cases, and one death. A little kid. An Indian kid—this is by the Navajo Reservation out there—but it was still a little kid. So CDC decides to implement their smallpox response plan. That's when Rasmussen called Col. Bradshaw."

"And Bradshaw called you?"

"Actually, he called Under Secretary Edwards here. He realized right away that this needed to be hush-hush to avoid a panic, so he did the right thing. He went right to the top of our Military Intelligence operations. He and Edwards know each other. That's when they called me in. This was on Wednesday. And I approved a full counter-terrorism response."

"And you didn't contact me? Or even the President?"

"Yes sir—I mean actually, no sir. It was just out there on the Indian reservation—out in the middle of nowhere. And even with the CDC call, we weren't really sure at the start that this whole thing was real. That it was actually smallpox, I mean. We needed to be certain first. So we set everything up like a training exercise. Bradshaw said he could get his first troops there by the end of the day—that was the day before Thanksgiving—and start sealing off the area with a full quarantine. That first wave would go in by helicopter, and the real troop strength would begin moving out that same afternoon by motor vehicle from Fort Bliss. Troops would arrive in Farmington—that's where the reservation is. It's in an area that they call the "Four Corners." It's where Utah, Colorado, New Mexico, and Arizona all meet at one place. Bradshaw said it was about 400 miles by road, so the bulk of his troops couldn't get there until after midnight. It was already Thursday, yesterday, when it was Thanksgiving."

"I don't need all this bullshit detail, Quentin. I'm trying to figure out why you didn't call me right off the bat. I've been involved in counterterrorism for a long time. The Defense Department has been brought into the terrorism-response effort, but that's fairly recent. It was always the CDC, the public health people, that had the authority and responsibility."

"Yes sir. That's right. When we—I mean Bradshaw, Edwards, and me. When we talked on Wednesday, I said maybe we should call your office, and the President too, of course. But they said … I mean I decided that action was more important than words in a crisis. We needed to get those troops up there to Farmington without delay, and a bunch of meetings would clearly slow things down. So I just approved the operation. Right then and there. It was the right thing to do. This was a terrorist attack, so we threw the entire response into high gear."

"Quentin, have you actually read the official CDC Smallpox Response Plan?"

"Of course I have. I mean, I looked at it when it first came across my desk. I wouldn't claim I knew every word by heart."

"But maybe you remember the parts about how open communication was one of the cornerstones of the plan? That the public must have complete confidence in the public health system?"

"Well, yes. But this was different. It was a terrorist attack, and that could have caused a panic. So we decided—I decided—that the best way to keep the public confident was to not scare them in the first place. The outbreak—the attack—was in such an isolated area that Bradshaw and Edwards said we could contain it completely. So we imposed a complete blackout on the area. We've completely cut all communications as well as all traffic by air and land. All the roads are closed as of yesterday afternoon. We've got this under control, Mr. Vice President."

"Something like this happens again, you tell me first, Quentin, but I like the way you handled it. The rapid-reaction force out of Fort Bliss is in charge. I like that. It's a lot better than the way they wrote up the CDC plan, which put the medical people in charge. They don't know anything about real emergencies. But the Army? They know how to take care of things. If you get any push-back on this, you let me know. Our country is under attack, and we don't want a bunch of pussies telling us that it's 'Be Kind to Terrorists Week.' We need real men in charge."

"Mr. Vice President? We should probably review the intelligence information. One of the members of the NSC is likely to ask what we have." The Chairman of the Joint Chiefs had remained quiet up to that point.

General George P. Radisson didn't reach his current position by giving his opinion unnecessarily, but when he saw his advice as essential, he wasn't reluctant to offer it. Up to a point. He understood the military chain of command, and he didn't contradict his superiors in public. When a decision had to be made, he contributed fully, and his contributions were invariably intelligent and well-crafted. But once a decision had been made by his superiors—in this case the Secretary of Defense and the Vice President—he considered it his responsibility to support the decision. He would stand at attention and salute, and he would not undermine Quentin Walker.

In theory this could cause an awkward conflict. For example, if the President specifically asked him to state his own view on some particular issue. But in reality, it had never been a problem. By the time the President asked such a question, the matter would invariably have been decided by Walker, and Radisson's opportunity to raise objections had already occurred. The only voice that the President would hear from the Chairman of the Joint Chiefs was the one that supported the Secretary of Defense.

The Secretary of Defense turned to his Under Secretary. "Robinson, would you please brief us on what your people have learned? When we go into this meeting of the Security Council, the four of us need to be on the same page. We need to be the leaders; the others don't have our background. We have to be in full agreement on what the facts are, and we must be able to demonstrate that the actions we've taken and will take are both absolutely necessary and completely defensible. We don't want to leave any openings for others to fuck this up."

* * *

Day 24: Intelligence Sources

Robinson Edwards unlocked his briefcase and removed four
folders marked TOP SECRET. "This information is not to be shared
with anyone else, not even the other members of the National
Security Council. I have a cleaned-up version that I'll be able to
show them later, but this background is only for the three of you."

"Get on with it!" The vice president was edgy and impatient.
"Have you ruled out the damn Russians, Edwards? They've been
acting like our friends, ever since the Soviet Union collapsed,
assuming you ignore some of what that bastard Putin has done. It
seems to me that if the Russians are really the only ones other than
ourselves that have the virus, then this attack must have started there.
And if that's the case, we may be talking about a full-scale nuclear
war. Which makes it absolutely essential that we keep everything
about this smallpox outbreak completely secret. If the Russians
realized we were about to nuke them, God knows what they might
try to do first."

"I agree with the need for absolute secrecy, Mr. Vice President,
and I've been resolute in compartmentalizing everything about the
outbreak. My deputy is the only one in our office who knows there
has been an actual outbreak. Everyone else is operating on the belief
that there has been a threat. Only a threat. Other than my deputy and
the four of us, there are only two people who know what has
happened, both at CDC. That's Steve Rasmussen in their terrorism
unit and Eleanor Torlander, the CDC Director. And Rasmussen
understood from the beginning, from Col. Bradshaw, that this had to
be completely secret."

"Hold up a minute, Edwards. We can't tell the NSC that only a
half-dozen people know about this. Not after we've sent a couple
thousand troops up to Farmington."

"With all respect, Mr. Secretary, we do have this covered. The
only people in Fort Bliss who know what is actually happening have
been moved to Farmington. And that area is sealed. And I don't
mean just restricted, I mean locked down as tight as a ... Well, let's
just say it's secure. All the communications links—land line,
satellite, cell phone, Internet, all of them—have been completely
shut down. The only way anybody in Farmington can talk to the
outside world is through Col. Bradshaw's secure telecommunications
devices. And even Bradshaw doesn't know that everything his

people send out gets routed directly to our offices in the Defense Intelligence Agency."

"You're not bullshitting me, are you? This is fucking brilliant. I've got to hand it to you, Edwards. You've done this right. General Radisson, did you know this kind of communications control was possible?"

"No, Mr. Vice President. I have to admit that I didn't know that it could be done—at least not as effectively as this. Mr. Edwards, do we need to worry that others at DIA could become a source of leaks that could undermine the operation?"

"No sir, that's the beauty of our plans. Other than the small number of people who we've already discussed, everyone else, both at DIA and at CDC, thinks this entire flap is just a large-scale joint planning exercise. They know that they need to provide whatever resources and assistance might be needed, but they think it's just an exercise. Now admittedly, this might not have been so easy to pull off if the outbreak had happened anywhere else. But damn ... out there in the middle of nowhere it just wasn't that hard."

The Secretary of Defense tried to assert control. "Get us up to speed on what we know about who carried out the attack, Robinson."

Before Edwards could respond, Richards lifted his right hand. "We're going to need a game plan when we go into the Security Council meeting, and I think we should base it on what you've already put in place. Do any of you remember *Dark Winter*? It was a simulation exercise for a smallpox attack back in the summer of 2001—before the attacks."

"I don't remember anything about that." Walker looked nervously at Radisson and Edwards. They were both shaking their heads as well.

"That's not surprising. I probably wouldn't know about it either except that I sat in on a briefing after the exercise was finished. Mostly it was kept pretty quiet except for an article in the *Post* about a month later.

"After that we did some work on how to control an outbreak. From the Army's point of view. That was one of the findings of *Dark Winter*. That we just weren't prepared back then. The whole exercise ended in chaos. Nobody knew how to control the spread of the disease. They didn't have any kind of effective quarantine."

"Did they try to use any kind of quarantine at all?" The Secretary of Defense was confused.

"No, not in that exercise, Quentin. Keep in mind, the whole thing was just a bunch of people in a conference room for a couple of days, and they were supposed to follow a script that was written out ahead of time. The point was to illustrate how the government would react and what the consequences would be. Afterwards, the Army brass developed some contingency plans. If it becomes necessary, we can say publicly that this is a new training exercise to test our biodefense capabilities. But this time it's full scale. The National Security Council will accept that approach as a way to keep from creating panic across the whole country."

He looked at the Secretary of Defense. "And if anything does leak out, the public would understand why it had been kept secret. You'll need to draw up an official plan here, Quentin, even though it's after the fact. I'll lean on Torlander so she understands the need for CDC to cooperate on this."

"We'll make sure we have copies of those earlier contingency plans by the time of the next NSC meeting, Mr. Vice President. And we'll have a detailed plan to present. But in the interest of time, may I suggest that we turn to the Under Secretary now for an update on the outbreak in New Mexico?"

The Vice President nodded, and Edwards began.

"First off, this is terrorism. That's policy, but it's also factual. Since smallpox has been eradicated, except for cultures maintained by the United States and by Russia, there's no way to have a naturally occurring outbreak of the disease. Period. And before you ask, we've made some discreet inquiries with one of our agents who has sources in the GRU, the Russian counterpart of our Defense Intelligence Agency. As far as he could learn, there's nothing unusual happening in any of the relevant areas—political, military, or scientific."

"So you trust those weasel-nosed bastards?"

"Yes, I do, Mr. Vice President—at least in this case. There are a couple of their senior people who really seem to understand the realities of working with other countries. But your point is well taken, and we didn't stop there. It's like President Reagan said, 'Trust, but verify.' We have agents over there. Officially, they're military liaisons, but they're first-class intelligence agents as well, and we've asked them to do some checking. They don't have any idea why we asked, but they were able to give us up-to-the-minute reports on Russian activities."

"What did they say?"

"There isn't any unusual activity. No secret meetings, no people suddenly reporting back to Moscow, nothing indicating any sort of heightened alert level. We got the same reports for the military, and perhaps most important, the same with regard to the two laboratories where they maintain their smallpox samples, the old biological weapons labs. So overall, we're confident that the Russians had nothing to do with this. Even when they disagree with us, they're not stupid. They know what would happen if they attacked us, and they sure as hell wouldn't want to risk an almost certain nuclear response—especially for some rinky-dink attack on a second-rate town in the middle of nowhere."

"On that basis, I don't see why *anyone* would want to launch an attack in Farmington, New Mexico," Richards observed. "Why not go after New York or Washington instead of some shithole out in the middle of nowhere?"

"I think it was a test run," Edwards said. "It's not the first time a terrorist group tried this approach. The first bioterrorism attack in the U.S. used a test run. Back in 1984, some wacko religious group in Oregon used salmonella bacteria to contaminate salad bars. They were testing a plan, which they later abandoned, to influence the town's elections, and they caused food poisoning in almost a thousand people."

"You're suggesting that this was done by some fucking religious cult? How would some nutcase hippies get hold of smallpox virus? That just doesn't work for me, Edwards."

"With all due respect, Mr. Vice President, not all religious fanatics lack the resources to carry out this attack. We're not talking about a homegrown group drinking Kool-Aid. I suspect this was done by an offshoot of Al Qaeda, maybe with the assistance of an unfriendly government in the Middle East."

"Let's not fall back into that goddamn trap. Bush and Cheney kept claiming that there were WMDs in Iraq then years ago. They even got Colin Powell to show pictures of those trailers at the United Nations and claim that they were mobile biowarfare labs. But nobody ever found any WMDs over there, and that's because there weren't any. Saddam destroyed the damn things long before we invaded. I can assure you that my administration—the Alexander-Richards administration—is not going to start claiming that Iraq is giving biological weapons to terrorists."

"You are absolutely correct. This attack didn't come from Iraq. Very likely, it came from a different country in the same part of the world. All signs point to Iran."

Richards exhaled slowly. "Sonofabitch. Those bastards! After all this time. Go ahead, Edwards."

"We've been monitoring Iran for a long time—ever since the Islamic Revolution in the late '70s. Quite a few of their senior military officers, good men that we'd trained here, were forced to flee the country. They've always been willing to pass on to us whatever information they could get on the current regime. By 2001, the United Nations reported that Iran was working on biological weapons—including smallpox—even though they were signatories to the Biological Weapons Convention. By 2003, our sources inside Iran had confirmed that they were working on smallpox, and they haven't stopped."

Edwards picked up a piece of paper and began reading.

Iran is often accused in Western circles of secretly developing an offensive biological warfare (BW) program. In a ... report to the U.S. Senate, the Central Intelligence Agency claimed that "Iran has had a biological warfare program since the early 1980s. Currently the program is in its research and development stages, but we believe Iran holds some stocks of BW agents and weapons ..."[*]

"So overall, it looks like we have a couple of smoking guns here. We know that Iran has been antagonistic toward the U.S. for more than three decades. They hate us because we supported the Shah, because we support Israel, and because we don't accept Islam as our religion. It's no wonder that they've decided to provide terrorists with the means to attack the very heart of our homeland. And there can be no question that this is just the first round. They're going to hit us again."

"No they won't," Richards snarled. "Not a fucking chance in hell. We'll make sure those damn religious fanatics can't attack

---

[*] Iran holds some stocks of BW agents and weapons: "Current and Projected National Security Threats to the United States and its Interests Abroad," Central Intelligence Agency, written responses to questions before the Select Committee on Intelligence of the United States Senate, Hearing, Feb. 22, 1996, U.S. Government Printing Office, response # 82.

anybody. When we get through with them, they won't even be able to pray for salvation. America isn't going to sit back and take this any longer. Not if I have anything to say about it. You've put together the right arguments, Edwards. There isn't any question what happened."

Richards paused, almost as if he were trying to catch his breath. "We're going to walk into that NSC meeting in a little while, and some of the candy-assed people in that room will refuse to see a smoking gun. So we need to get more proof—evidence pinning it on the Iranians so that even the dumbest asshole in the State Department will be able to understand."

The Vice President scowled at his subordinates. "Those damn Mullahs in Tehran had better get ready to go into their nuclear bunkers or whatever ratholes they hide in. In another week there won't be enough of them left to get on their knees and beg for mercy. Edwards, you go and get the evidence. And Walker—you make sure that Edwards gets whatever he needs to do his job. I want him to brief me on a daily basis, so just get off your asses and get this done."

* * *

Day 24: Roots of Bitterness

The Vice President had a personal reason for his utter hatred of Iran. During his final tour as a general officer in Afghanistan, he had authorized an operation in the western part of the country near the border with Iran. Intelligence sources had informed the American forces of a major Iranian effort to move military equipment across the border to aid the Afghan insurgents. The Intelligence had come in part from cooperation with the Kazakhstan government, and the plan had been developed with the assistance of a Kazakh military liaison who had an Iranian intelligence source.

The special operations team of 25 men, including two senior officers who had served for almost a decade with Richards, was deployed in what was expected to be a straightforward mission to capture a senior Al Qaeda leader. But the only straightforward part of the operation was the ambush. Of the 25 men who went out that day, only four returned. They were so badly shot up that they would never be the same, and Richards could never even bring himself to visit them in the hospital after they were flown back stateside. What Richards had done instead, was make a solemn vow to himself. *Someday Iran will pay for that.*

Now, as he walked toward the conference room prior to the start of the National Security Council meeting, a grim smile crossed his face. *That day is almost here.*

* * *

7

Sarah

The right of the people to be secure in their persons, houses, papers, and effects, against unreasonable searches and seizures, shall not be violated, and no Warrants shall issue, but upon probable cause, supported by Oath or affirmation, and particularly describing the place to be searched, and the persons or things to be seized.

— Bill of Rights, Amendment IV to the Constitution of the United States*

Day 24: Delta to Atlanta

After talking with Jillian and her friend "Elmer," Sarah didn't have the energy to do more work on her FDA story. She managed to eat a light supper and turned on the television. Flipping through the channels, she found a Wizards game on TV. It was against the Lakers, and it would probably be a pretty good game, but she couldn't pay attention. At halftime she turned it off and went to bed.

Sarah was at her desk at the *Post* by 7:00 the next morning. She turned on her computer and ate a bagel as she scanned the *New York Times*. Then she checked her several e-mail accounts and made quick notes of some things she would need to take care of during the day.

Still trying to make sense of everything that had happened, Sarah knew her next step had to be a trip to Atlanta. She had gotten

---

* Bill of Rights, Amendment IV to the Constitution of the United States sidetracked the day before, but now she logged on to the Delta Air Lines website. It was her preferred airline, and she had a good store of frequent flyer miles. After entering DCA as the code for Reagan National Airport and ATL for Atlanta's Hartsfield-Jackson Airport, she quickly found several flights that would work. Before she ordered the ticket, she decided to be a little more discreet.

She wasn't aware that she was talking to her computer, but the office was almost empty on the day after Thanksgiving, so nobody heard her. "Okay let's make this a little less obvious. We can kill two birds with this stone." Sarah knew how to disguise her travel—nothing illegal, nothing unethical—just a little caution. There was no need yet to tell Sue Parkinson what she was up to. Sarah didn't want people at the paper to know about her visit to Atlanta, just in case someone tried to interfere with her pursuit of this promising story.

Sarah had been doing background work on another story, about a chemistry professor at Florida State University who was developing an environmentally favorable process for making polymers. They had talked about having Sarah visit his laboratory, and the travel had been approved. Tallahassee wasn't that far from Atlanta.

There were no nonstops to Tallahassee, and all the good flights went through Atlanta. Sarah figured that if she conveniently missed her connecting flight, the resulting delay would allow her enough time to spend a couple of hours in Atlanta visiting Charles and still catch a connecting flight to Tallahassee the same day. Nobody would know that she'd been outside the Atlanta airport.

A quick call to Granger's office confirmed her expectation that he would be in the lab on Saturday afternoon. He previously said that weekends were the best time because there were fewer distractions, and now he told her that Thanksgiving weekend was perfect. They agreed to meet at the chemistry building on Saturday afternoon at about 1:30.

With her Florida plans all set, Sarah went back to the Delta site, booked her flights, and printed a copy of her itinerary.

> *Friday (Delta 821) depart Washington 4pm, arrive Atlanta 5pm*
>
> *(Delta 1019) depart Atlanta 7:45pm, arrive Tallahassee 8:49*
>
> *Sunday (Delta 1280) depart Tallahassee 7:20am, arrive Atlanta 8:30*

(Delta 808) depart Atlanta 10:20am, arrive Washington 12:09

She sent a copy of the itinerary to Sue Parkinson with a note explaining that she was going to do her follow-up visit with Professor Granger. If anyone asked Sue where Sarah was over the weekend—something Sarah regarded as highly unlikely—Sue would only be able to say that Sarah was on assignment in Florida.

Sarah managed to put in a good day's work. A bit of preliminary writing on the science feature to get into the right frame of mind for Florida, a list of questions that she would ask Granger, a few phone calls on other topics, and several e-mail exchanges kept her busy until 1:00 p.m. *Time to wrap things up. I've got a plane to catch.*

One of the e-mail messages that Sarah had sent earlier in the day was a request for a loaner laptop to use on the trip. Two floors up, she walked to the reception desk and showed her photo-ID badge. "I'm here to pick up my laptop."

"Sure thing. It's all ready, and I've double-checked that your word processor and Internet browser are working properly. And the wireless modem works okay too. You traveling someplace nice?"

"To Florida. But it's to a chemistry laboratory, so I'm not sure whether or not that meets your definition for nice."

"Hell no! Chemistry wasn't my thing. I switched over to computer science before I was halfway through my first semester in college."

"Okay," said Sarah with a laugh. "Thanks for getting the laptop ready. I've got to run if I'm going to catch my plane." She walked toward the elevator and turned back as she got on. "Have a nice weekend."

Thirty minutes later, she was in her apartment, packing a small duffel bag that was a perfect carry-on.

She checked the apartment to make sure that things were reasonably orderly. She didn't want to come back home to a mess, and she didn't want dirty dishes lying around to attract ants or roaches. She started the dishwasher and double-checked that the stove and coffee pot were off. Her desktop computer was shut down, the external hard drive was powered down and disconnected, and a single compact fluorescent lamp illuminated the small entry hallway. After confirming that she had her wallet with photo ID, cash, and credit cards, Sarah threw her duffel over one shoulder and the laptop case over the other, left the apartment, and locked the deadbolt.

It was only a block to the Metro Station, and a Blue-line train took her directly to Reagan National Airport. She checked in at one of the automated kiosks, and in another 10 minutes she had cleared security and walked to her gate.

After verifying that her flight was on time—the gate agent said that the incoming aircraft was due momentarily—Sarah walked over to the food court. For the time being, at least, she was off the clock, so she ordered a cheeseburger and settled down to relax for a half hour.

The sudden ringing was her cell phone. It was Sue Parkinson. "Hi, Sue. What's up?"

"I'm not sure. I just stopped by the office to pick up some files and got a visit from some guy with a badge. His name is Joseph Silver. He's FBI. The security guard in the lobby said you weren't here and sent him to me."

"I hope they're not checking up on that parking ticket I got last month." A light-hearted response seemed better than admitting how startling this information was.

"Actually, he wouldn't tell me anything. If I had to guess, I'd say there's something going on with your FDA story. If your hunch is right about what's going on, the feds may have found out something as well. And they may have learned that you're looking into it as well. Anyway, I said you were gone for the weekend. And I didn't say where you were going on your assignment. You don't need any more headaches."

"I'll agree with that."

"Maybe when you get back from your Florida trip, you can touch base with your FDA source to find out what's going on. I don't want you to be blindsided by the feds, Sarah. You don't need to tell them who your source is or what you've learned so far. If there's any problem, let me know, and we'll get the legal office involved, pronto."

"Thanks, Sue. I'll let you know if anything develops."

"Sounds good, Sarah. Have a nice trip."

"Okay. Have a good weekend."

Sarah walked back to the gate, wondering why the FBI visited Sue Parkinson. Sarah wasn't convinced that the FBI wanted to ask about the approval process for new drugs. Something in her gut warned her that the feds were much more likely to be looking into people who were interested in chickenpox.

Sarah was struck by a sudden wave of anxiety, and she reviewed her steps to be sure. *Nobody knows I'm spending time in Atlanta. There's nothing on my computer, even if somebody checked and found the plane ticket I ordered. I didn't use my own phone account to talk with either Jillian or Charles, not even at the office. Oh screw it, there's no need to worry about this now. I'll see Charles in a couple of hours, and then I'll know for sure if I should be scared.*

Within five minutes, Sarah was on the plane. The flight attendant advised her that the aircraft wasn't very full, and she would have an empty seat next to her. After stowing her duffel in the overhead compartment, Sarah opened a magazine. It wasn't great reading, but it kept her mind off all the craziness. They took off at the scheduled time, and soon she was sound asleep.

* * *

Day 24: Atlanta

Shortly after 4 p.m., Sarah walked past the airline gate into Hartsfield-Jackson Airport. She continued past the Delta agent who was giving directions to connecting flights and took the underground train to the main terminal. After leaving the secure area, she went into the MARTA station. The Metropolitan Atlanta Rapid Transit Authority runs trains directly to downtown Atlanta and its suburbs.

Sarah still had a Breeze Card with enough value for several trips, but she stopped just before inserting it into the machine. *Shit! I paid for this with a credit card the last time I was in Atlanta. I don't want any electronic traces of this visit. Not outside the airport.* She went over to a fare machine and purchased a new card with a $20 bill. A train headed toward the center of Atlanta took her to the Five Points Station, where she boarded a train to Avondale.

Jake lived a few blocks away. Sarah walked through the enclosed pedestrian overpass above East College Avenue, then along the sidewalk. As she approached Jake's building, a new thought struck. *Shit! Maybe they're watching the condo.* It was getting dark, and it wouldn't be easy for anyone to recognize her at a distance. Still, she turned up the collar on her coat, laughing to herself about her cloak-and-dagger paranoia.

At the corner of the block she walked around to the back of the building, out of sight of anyone who might be keeping an eye on the front door. With a sigh of relief, she saw that there were lights on inside the condo. Charles was already there. *I hope he's expecting me.*

Using the back door, Sarah went into the entrance hallway and knocked softly on the condo door. There was a brief pause and then a rustling. Sarah's heart was pounding. The door opened slightly, and she could see Charles Evans. He quickly put a finger to his lips and motioned her inside. Then he handed her a note. "I think the house may be bugged."

Sarah's knees nearly buckled. She had convinced herself that she was just playing a game by being overly cautious. That there wasn't really much likelihood of surveillance. That her efforts to be secretive like Woodward and Bernstein in "All the President's Men" were just role-playing. But this wasn't a movie. She gave Charles a puzzled look, and shrugged. "What the hell do we do now?" she asked herself.

Charles quickly scribbled an addendum to his note: "Dinner out?"

Sarah nodded, and Charles motioned for her to leave her duffel and laptop in the hall closet. He put on a windbreaker and a baseball hat. Then he reached back into the closet, took another baseball cap, and handed it to Sarah. Charles crossed the room and clicked off the stereo, and just as he turned toward the door, Sarah reached back into the closet and removed the name tags from both her duffel and the laptop case. *If anybody starts nosing around, they wouldn't connect the computer to me right away. The loaner is still registered to Aaron Jacobsen, and he left the Post a year ago.*

Sarah went out the back door and Charles left by the front. They walked around the building from different directions and met at the corner. Charles greeted her with what sounded like genuine surprise. "Hey, how're ya doin'? Haven't seen you around for a while. You headed over toward the park?"

"Yeah, I was." She made a major effort to sound casual because she didn't know who might be within earshot. "Want some company?"

They walked along the sidewalk making small talk about the weather. Then Charles spoke quietly. "Why don't we head up to Avondale? There are a couple of places up there where we can talk without anyone bothering us." The anxiety in his voice was clear.

In a few minutes, they had crossed through the park and were sitting in a booth in an Irish pub—not usually the quietest of places, but the Friday night crowd hadn't arrived yet. It was quiet, but with enough hum that nobody would overhear them.

They each ordered a draft beer. As soon as the beers arrived, Charles leaned toward Sarah. "I'm glad you're here. We've got lots to talk about. What have you figured out so far?"

"I'm not certain. It's all pretty confusing, but I'll run through the facts. To start with, Jake is missing. Well, maybe not missing exactly, but we don't know where he is and nobody will tell us. Then we've got the calls from New Mexico. My friend first described everything as a bad outbreak of chickenpox. God, I can't believe that was only two days ago! Anyway, after we talked yesterday morning, I checked out the HealthMap sight on the Web. There was one report of chickenpox in Farmington—from a Spanish-language newspaper. But here's what's weird: When I went back to the site later in the day, the entry was gone. There were no reports at all of chickenpox in the United States, just a couple in South America and Africa.

"I'm not sure ..."

"Let me finish, Charles. My friend called again, and she told me that they were cutting all the phone communications. Then we talked last night by ham radio. It's something we learned in college. She said a bunch of people from the outside had cut off the whole area. So it wasn't just communications that were blocked. The roads were closed, too. And here's the worst part of all: She said that it wasn't chickenpox at all. It was smallpox!"

Charles was silent for a few seconds. Then he spoke slowly and softly. "Now it's starting to make sense. At least part of it is. If the government thinks there's a smallpox outbreak, it would be logical to try to seal off the area. That's part of the CDC strategy for controlling an outbreak, and it's something we teach in our graduate program—to isolate any kind of disease outbreak. I think I know where Jake has gone and why nobody's talking about it."

"But it doesn't make sense. You and I both know that smallpox has been eliminated."

"Yes and no, Sarah. The last naturally occurring case was in 1977. Subsequently, there were a couple of cases in England in 1978 caused by accidental exposure from a research laboratory accident. After that, international agreement was reached to place all remaining samples either at CDC or in the Soviet Union. Now it's the Russian Federal State Research Center of Virology and Biotechnology. They call it VECTOR. The original plan was to destroy all the samples But then people started worrying about biological warfare or bioterrorism if somebody secretly kept a sample. So the two superpowers maintained their stocks to facilitate development of a vaccine in case of an attack."

"An attack? Do you think that's what has happened?"

"Hard to say. But I think we can be pretty sure that the feds are operating under that assumption. It would explain a lot."

"Yeah, I guess. Why wouldn't you talk to me on the phone?"

"I wish I had a good answer for that. I told you I called Jake's office and talked to the same woman who answered your call. Right after that, I got a phone call from the University's Vice President for Security Affairs."

"Security Affairs? At a university?"

"Yeah, everything changed after September 11, 2001. And then the shootings at Virginia Tech in 2007. It's a different world. Anyway, this guy said he'd been contacted by one of his security liaisons at CDC. They asked him to talk to me and 'suggest' that I shouldn't discuss communicable disease issues on the telephone. The VP repeated some lame excuse about a report that some Internet hackers had been trying to manipulate the stock markets with fears about disease outbreaks. But the point is, chickenpox isn't a big deal. And furthermore, why me?"

"It's must have something to do with Jake."

"Yeah. That's why I think they've tapped my phone. And bugged the condo. At the very least, they were looking at who I was talking to. Maybe it's because I share the house with Jake, or maybe it was after I first called his office."

"Then they would have done the same with me, so why didn't they get on my case right away? Oh shit—I know why! I called from one of the conference rooms at the *Post*. They wouldn't have known who made the call. Not at first. But some guy from the FBI came looking for me today after I left the office."

"I'm really glad you thought to come to the back door tonight. Watching the house wouldn't be too difficult. I took a chance when I called you the last time, but I used Jake's phone because I figured they wouldn't monitor that."

"Even if they did, you never told me to come here. You just mentioned my 'boyfriend,' and they wouldn't know enough to make that connection. But why in hell would they be watching and listening to us? We're not Russians, and we're certainly not terrorists."

"Maybe not, but my guess is that the feds are as confused as we are. If there really is a smallpox outbreak, they're probably looking at anything at all that seems a little unusual to them. And they wouldn't want anyone to know they were doing it in case they stumbled across somebody who was linked to the outbreak. They'd want to follow the trail to its source without letting anyone know they were looking."

"Maybe so, but none of this seems kosher to me. There's more to it. And it's my job to find out what."

"Look Sarah, I'm not sure how I can help here. But one thing is for sure: We need to keep a damn low profile. I'm not happy about how this is playing out. Even if it's an actual terrorist attack, the government isn't playing by the rules. CDC policy really spells it out that clear public communication is a primary part of the response to any outbreak that might be from terrorism. What's happening is just the opposite, even to the extent of removing information from a public website. I thought we were past that."

"So did I. Look, Charles, I'm going to pursue this somehow. How can I get through to you again if I have more questions?"

"Right now, we need to stay away from telephones and e-mail. Maybe in D.C. next week. I have a conference at NIH in Bethesda."

"Do you have your travel information?"

"I think so." Charles pulled out his smartphone and punched a few keys. "Here is it is." He read the information for his flights to and from Reagan National, and Sarah scribbled in her ever-present notebook.

"Give me your cell too. I'll only use it as a backup, and if I need to do that, I'll think of something cryptic."

After writing down the cell number, she paused and asked, "How do we really know where Jake is? We've been making a lot of educated guesses, but couldn't he just as well have flown to Washington to brief people there?"

"I thought the same thing for a while. I almost forgot to tell you. When I used his telephone to call you on Wednesday, I poked my head into his closet. When I last saw him on Tuesday afternoon he was wearing casual clothes and a nylon jacket. Usually, he wears dress clothes when he travels."

"Sure, I taught him that. You get better service that way."

"Well he didn't this time. And more to the point, all three of his suits are still hanging in his closet. He'd never go to Washington without a suit. And here's something else: He keeps his hiking boots in the hall closet. I looked today before you got here. They were gone."

"Then I agree. He didn't go to Washington. He was dressing for the back country. I don't think there's any question. He's gone to New Mexico. I don't know where this is all headed, Charles, but I'm going to keep digging. If I need to talk to you, I'll try to reach you while you're in Washington. Once things settle down, I'll call you for sure."

The conversation had lasted longer than their beer, so they ordered some food with their second round. Once they finished and left the restaurant, Charles paused. "Do you want to stay over? The guest room is clean and the bed is made."

"I should move on. I don't want anyone to know I stopped here. But my duffel and computer are still at your house."

"No problem. You wait right here. I'll go get the car and bring your stuff."

Fifteen minutes later, Evans dropped her at the MARTA station, and Sarah was out of the car almost before it came to a stop. A quick "Thanks" and "Goodbye" had been answered with a "See you next week, maybe." As Charles drove off, Sarah walked into the Avondale station. *They'd have to be pretty quick to identify me if they were following Charles's car.* Nevertheless, she kept her eyes open and tried to believe that she wasn't being followed, right up to the time she boarded the next train to downtown Atlanta.

* * *

Day 25: Tallahassee

Sarah reached the airport at 8:15 that evening and headed directly for the Delta counter, where she tried to put on her most innocent face. "Hi. I really feel dumb. But I stopped for a beer between flights, and then I fell asleep in the waiting area. So I missed my 7:45 flight to Tallahassee. Is there any way I can still get there tonight?"

The agent rolled his eyes and then smiled indulgently. He said there was a flight at 9:22, but she'd have to hurry to make it. He issued a revised boarding pass and pointed her to security. Most of the day's flights had departed, so the line moved quickly. When she reached the gate, she was able to board immediately.

Before the plane reached the runway, Sarah was sound asleep, and she didn't wake until the plane landed. She shook out the cobwebs as they taxied to the terminal. She hadn't made any reservations, so she headed toward the ground transportation area, where there would be hotel information. Professor Granger had suggested the University Inn, and a quick call confirmed that they had an available room.

A little while later, she was checking in at the front desk. "Good thing you didn't try this a couple of weeks ago," said the clerk. "Last-minute bookings just don't happen during football season, at least not here at FSU."

Sarah awoke to the warm feeling of sunlight on her face. It was almost 10:00 a.m., and she felt good. She pulled on a pair of lightweight nylon running pants and a sweatshirt, donned her running shoes, and put some money in her pocket. She ran along Tennessee Street just past the other end of the FSU campus, maintaining an easy pace and enjoying the weather. When she spotted the Waffle House, she decided to stop.

When she finished her breakfast, it was almost 11:30. She didn't want any difficulty finding Granger's building later on, so she walked through campus on the way back to the hotel. She had no difficulty locating Granger's laboratories.

After showering and changing into fresh clothes, Sarah walked over to the chemistry building. Granger showed her around, happily introducing her to several graduate students and postdocs. After talking for more than an hour, Sarah had the information she needed.

Walking back to the hotel, she felt remarkably relaxed and satisfied. The day had gone well, and she had almost forgotten her worries about chickenpox. Or was it really smallpox? The answer to that question would have to wait, at least until she got back to Washington and figured out her next steps. For the moment, she decided she would just focus on her chemistry story.

She got back to the hotel at about 4:00 p.m., booted up her laptop, and spent a couple of hours typing in her notes from the interview. Then she set up a rough outline of her story and sent the electronic files to both her work and home e-mail addresses. That way, her work was safe, even if something happened to the laptop on the trip back to Washington.

With the assistance of the hotel staff, Sarah got a last-minute reservation for one at a nice restaurant. She had a delightful dinner of blue-corn fried catfish and jalapeno-seasoned collard greens, a distinctively southern meal.

After dinner, she checked her e-mail, found nothing that needed her immediate attention, and decided to go to bed early. Her flight departed at 7:20 the next morning, so she requested a wakeup call for 5:30 and crawled under the covers.

* * *

Day 26: Arlington, Virginia

Just past noon on Sunday, Sarah's plane was making its final approach into National Airport, banking hard as it followed the contours of the Potomac River. When Georgetown University appeared on the left, she looked out the window on the right of the plane, to see her apartment building came into view on the Virginia side of the river. She was never quite sure where she wanted to sit when she was on a flight that approached the airport from the North. It was always exciting to see the buildings in where she lived, and she always tried to pick out the balcony of her apartment, but it meant giving up the views of the nation's capital that could be seen from the left side of the plane. Whichever side of the plane she was on, it was always a thrill.

The landing was uneventful, and in just a few more minutes, she was on the escalator to the Metro platform, where a Blue Line train would take her the few miles north to the station by her apartment. By one o'clock, she had unpacked her duffel and thrown her dirty clothes into the hamper. There wasn't a lot of food in the house, but a quick taste test showed that the milk in the refrigerator was still okay, and she had a bowl of cereal for lunch.

Sarah booted up her desktop computer and logged onto her e-mail account. Always worried about making sure her files were backed up and safely stored, she downloaded the e-mail attachments she had sent from Florida to the computer's hard drive. Then, to be doubly safe, she decided to put them on her external hard drive as well. She turned on the power strip for the external drive and reached for the cable to insert it into the USB port of the computer. It was already plugged in! *How the hell did that happen? I unplugged it before I left!* Her memory was clear. She had removed the USB cable when she did her final sweep of the apartment before leaving on Friday.

Sarah was so stunned, she couldn't move. She could barely breathe. She put a hand on her desk to steady herself. *Someone has been in my apartment, and they've been looking at my files.* She opened the computer's "event viewer" to see if there was any information on how the computer had been used. Most of the entries didn't seem significant to her, but one of them caught her eye. It was an entry for her virus protection program. The event was logged for the prior day at 3:47 p.m. *Holy shit! There's no question about it.*

Someone used my computer yesterday afternoon while I was in Florida.

Sarah's first thought was the phone call with Sue Parkinson before she left for Atlanta on Friday. Was the FBI after her because of the FDA stuff? The FDA file was encrypted, but she checked the drawer in her desk, anyway. Her checkbook and calculator were still where she had left them, but the little book of postage stamps that had fallen off to the side the previous week was now sitting neatly on top again. *Shit! They searched everything. And they tried to cover it up.*

Her panic increasing, Sarah began to imagine other possibilities and other problems: Would the FBI start following her? Would they monitor her phone calls? And would all this stop her from following up on the chickenpox–smallpox story? From what Charles had told her, it seemed that they might already be doing some sort of monitoring of calls to the CDC. And if someone had broken into the apartment to check her computer, how did they know she was away in the first place? *Damn! Sue told the FBI agent I was gone for the weekend. That's got to be it.*

The more Sarah thought about it, the more she moved toward a conclusion. She had to find a way to become less visible as she moved forward on both of her stories. It didn't matter which one was the reason people were checking on her. She had to find ways to communicate without being monitored, and find a way to move around without people knowing her every step.

She reached for her cell phone to call her father. He'd spent his entire career selling electronic equipment, so he knew what it could and couldn't do and how people might be able to misuse it. Sarah dialed the Florida number, and Richard Lockford answered on the third ring with a happy "Hi Sarah!"

"Hey Dad! It's been weeks since we've talked. How are you? How's Mom?"

"I'm just fine, sweetheart. We're both fine. Mostly, I've been playing golf and relaxing. Your mom even played nine holes with me yesterday, even though she claims to hate the game. This partial retirement thing is a pretty good deal, and I don't have any business meetings for at least another week. "I tried calling you yesterday, but I didn't get any answer at the apartment. Were you out having fun, or were you off on business?"

"On business, Dad. I just got back. My schedule was tight, and Tallahassee isn't very close to you." Sarah's parents had bought the house in South Florida about 10 years earlier. Now they were spending nearly half the year there.

"Anyway, I'm sorry I didn't get to see you and Mom for Thanksgiving. I hope you'll be coming up here again soon, even if it means that you'll be working." She paused briefly and started again hesitantly. "Dad, how can you make phone calls so that nobody can eavesdrop or trace them back to you?"

Immediately, the tone of Rich Lockford's voice changed to one that was halfway between that of concerned parent and all business. "Are you okay, Sarah-Boo?"

"Huh? Of course I am!" The answer had come out a little too quickly. His use of the nickname had surprised her. He hadn't used it since she was a kid.

She continued her fiction. "I'm working on a couple of stories for the paper, and one of them is about government corruption. So I'm thinking that I need to be extra careful that my activities stay private."

"Look, Sarah, there are a number of things you can do to be safe. So listen up." He was all business now, and he knew that she would be writing notes furiously in one of her notebooks. "First of all, it's hard to be invisible these days. Ever since September 11, the U.S. government has been more like Big Brother than ever before. Part of it is from advances in technology, and I suppose I've been partly responsible for helping that trend, but a big part is also a lack of trust. The last several administrations in Washington sometimes have just acted as though anyone who isn't one of their paid political supporters should be treated as a suspected terrorist. Even in downtown D.C., they've been putting surveillance cameras all over the place. And your cell phone probably has GPS capability, so it might be possible to track you wherever you go, every step you take."

"Then I'll just turn off my cell phone when I'm not using it."

"No, that isn't enough. The only way to shut down that capability on some of the newest phones is to actually remove the SIM card. That's the *subscriber identity module*. It's a kind of smart card, maybe an inch square and as thick as a credit card."

"I know what a SIM card is, dad."

"Yeah, I suppose so. Anyway, it's not hard to take out. Usually, you just have to take off the back cover of the phone. When the tracking stuff was designed, the manufacturers introduced it as a way to locate someone who's been injured, or lost, or maybe abducted. But sometimes it can make it a little tough to maintain your privacy."

Catching himself before he went off on a political rant, he returned to the thread of the conversation. "If you want to be less visible, first off, don't drive your car. Everything from satellite photos to planted tracking devices can be used to follow every move you make. Second, don't use your own telephone, either land line or cell phone. What you really need is a prepaid cell phone. You can get one online or in a cell-phone store, but usually that means providing ID of some sort. Sometimes they don't care as much at one of the kiosks at an airport or train station, so you could try that approach. And third, remember that every time you pay with a credit card or an ATM card, there's a record of what you bought. And a record of where you bought it, and when. Some of these things are getting pretty close to the real-time tracing that they like to show in movies and TV shows."

His tone changed once again, but Sarah couldn't quite figure out the implications. He was calm but wary. "One other thing, Sarah. Just in case you need to do a lot of traveling, keep your passport handy. It's a really good form of ID. My advice is that when you get home from your trip, you should get your passport out of the file cabinet and keep it with you."

"Dad, what are you …?"

Sarah only got out part the question before father interrupted. "Oops, sorry Kiddo, I gotta go! I told some of the guys over at the club that I'd meet them for a game of cards before dinner. Talk to you soon. Or I'll shoot you an e-mail." And with a click, he was gone.

Once again, things had become more confusing instead of less so. Most of Rich Lockford's advice had been reasonable, even if Sarah wasn't yet sure how she would go about following it. But his last couple of statements didn't make sense, and the way he ended the phone call was uncharacteristic. Did he think she hadn't yet returned home from Florida? No, that wasn't it. He knew she'd been traveling, and she specifically told him she was home again. He even recognized her number when he answered the phone.

Even more confusing, he had told her to get her passport out of the file cabinet when she got home. But she kept her passport in a dresser drawer. She didn't even have a file cabinet. Her father knew that.

Then it hit her. He was talking in a sort of code. He was already worried that someone might be listening to their call. And the "file cabinet" wasn't even a regular file cabinet. Ever since she was a little kid, he'd had that big safe that he referred to as his "file cabinet." It was fireproof, and it had a combination lock. Her father had given her the combination and taught her how to open it years earlier. After her parents sold the house in McLean, Virginia, they'd built a log home on a big plot of land out in West Virginia. The more she thought about it, the more certain she was. For some reason, her father was telling her to get out to the house in West Virginia and get something out of the safe.

* * *

8

Intelligence

In the exercise of assigned responsibilities, the USD(I) shall ... (4.1) Serve as the senior DoD intelligence, counterintelligence, and security official below the Secretary and Deputy Secretary of Defense.

—Directive Number 5143.01, Donald H. Rumsfeld, 2005[*]

Day 22: Staking the Claim

Robinson Edwards sat at his desk in the Pentagon, drumming his fingers on the legal pad in front of him. There were some things that even the USD(I), the Under Secretary of Defense for Intelligence, didn't want to enter on his computer. He believed it was the most secure computer network anywhere in the world. It was backed up frequently to prevent any loss of information, whether important or mundane. Consequently, Edwards decided this had to be a completely black operation. It could be disclosed only after he brought it to the successful conclusion that would save thousands, if not millions, of American lives. *Tomorrow is Thanksgiving. We will be thankful.*

A printout of a memorandum was sitting on Edwards' desk, next to a legal pad with his notes. The notes would soon go through his

---

[*] Department of Defense, Directive, No. 5143.01, Subject: Under Secretary of Defense for Intelligence (USD(I)), Nov. 23, 2005 (signed by Donald H. Rumsfeld, Secretary of Defense).

shredder, but the memo would remain in his files. It was a copy of Directive No. 5143.01, which spelled out the responsibilities of his office. It was signed by Donald Rumsfeld, who had been Secretary of Defense in 2005. There was no question in Edwards' mind that he had all the necessary authority to do what had to be done. Nor did he have any doubt that the Defense Secretary Walker would fully support the plan, at least those parts of the plan that Edwards would tell him about. Edwards didn't earn his three stars by being indiscreet. He knew how to take charge. And how to take action.

He glanced down at the memo, reviewing the potential trouble spots. He found what he needed.

> *4.19. Coordinate with the USD(P) regarding intelligence and intelligence-related matters that affect antiterrorism, counterterrorism, and terrorism consequence management policies as well as special operations intelligence elements and special operations-related activities funded through the MIP.*

Edwards put a mark next to item 4.19. Given the urgency of the matter, and knowing where the Secretary would throw his support, he decided that coordination could wait a while. Of greater importance were two specific terms in the item: "special operations" and "terrorism consequence management." Those words encompassed what needed to be done—and gave him the authority to do it. Nevertheless, he was unable to completely dispel a sense of unease about this whole thing, wondering if others in the chain of command might fail to recognize his immense authority.

He moved his eyes down the text of the Directive.

> *4.11.2. Develop, coordinate, and oversee the implementation of DoD policy, programs, and guidance for personnel, physical, industrial, information, operations, chemical/biological, and DoD Special Access Program (SAP) security as well as research and technology protection.*

That would be hard to argue with. The phrases were clear. "Develop ... oversee the implementation ... operations ..." No subordinate would dare to challenge him on those official responsibilities. Another checkmark in the margin of the document.

4.16. Develop, coordinate, and oversee policy and policy implementation for all other sensitive intelligence, counterintelligence, security, and special technology programs and activities within the Department of Defense.

More solid support for his plans. "Develop, coordinate, and oversee ... counterintelligence ... programs ..." These were the exact words for what he was planning, and his plans fit perfectly with the definition of counterintelligence in the Directive's appendix.

E2.1.2. Defense Counterintelligence. Information gathered and activities conducted to detect, identify, exploit, and neutralize the intelligence capabilities and activities of terrorists, foreign powers, and other entities directed against U.S. national security.

It couldn't be more clear-cut. Item 4.16 gave him the authority to undertake programs in the area of counterintelligence. Anything that included "activities conducted to ... identify ... and neutralize the... activities of terrorists." Another check.

The last checkmark went next to the phrase that Edwards thought would trump any possible objection or concern that might remain. The one thing he knew for certain was that the Secretary would have his back, even if he didn't ask explicit permission beforehand.

4.20. Perform such other duties as the Secretary may prescribe.

Edwards punched a button on his phone, and his assistant responded. "Yes sir?"

"Please have Colonel Zaborsky from DJ report to me ASAP. I spoke with him earlier, and he expects your call."

* * *

Day 22: Questions

"Come in, Bob, and shut the door, please." Edwards motioned to the table in his office.

Colonel Robert Zaborsky served in the Defense Intelligence Agency, where Edwards had recently appointed him as his primary military liaison. The position ordinarily would have been filled by a higher ranking officer, but Edwards wanted Zaborsky, even at the rank of Colonel. If he did his job, the stars would come soon enough.

The two men met when both served in DIA in the South Pacific in 1999. Zaborsky had been a junior officer reporting to Edwards, a Colonel at the time. After September 11, 2001, they worked jointly with Philippine military forces in a series of special operations to hunt down members of a terrorist group. Their efforts led to a promotion for Zaborsky and earned Edwards his first star. Zaborsky continued to work in covert operations in DIA until Edwards got him to run the coordinating center for intelligence operations.

"We've got a situation. A terrorist attack. Farmington, New Mexico. Smallpox. I think it may be a trial run for a massive biological attack on the U.S."

Zaborsky was stunned. "Smallpox? I thought that didn't exist anymore. It was wiped out. Except for research. The Russians?"

"No idea. None at all. We don't know who, and we can only guess why." Edwards went on to tell him the sketchy details he did have. What he had first heard from Bradshaw and what he, Colonel Bradshaw, and Secretary Walker had discussed in their conference call that morning.

"Bob, this operation will run out of your shop. You will bypass Counterintelligence completely. You'll get whatever help you need from the Directorate for Human Intelligence. I want to go right to the operational level. Nobody, repeat, nobody outside DJ is to know anything about this. As far as anybody else is concerned, it's just a training exercise. It's fully authorized by the Secretary. Your ass is completely covered. Just try not to piss off too many people unnecessarily, especially the ones that outrank you. Any questions, just tell them to call me. If they're stupid enough to go right to the Secretary, they'll get the same answer, and Walker will tear them a new one while he's at it."

Edwards retrieved his yellow pad from his desk and began making a list as he spoke.

Who?

"You've got to check out the Russians. And the former Soviet states. All those countries that end in *–stan.* You need to check our existing databases. There may be entries that are significant today, even though they weren't yesterday. We need to reach any agents we have in place. And sources in the expatriate community. The expats always have good information from the old country."

"What about CIA and the other agencies, General?" Even though Edwards was now a civilian, Zaborsky still called him "General," when they were alone.

"No other agencies. This has to stay completely under wraps, or we'll have mass panic in the streets. The Secretary agrees. Until we find out what's going on, any inquiry you make has to be disguised by treating this whole thing as a planning exercise. A secret planning exercise. The situation may change, but right now you just make sure that even the people working for you don't know what's really going on."

"Yes sir. I'll check out the Russian side and the former Soviet states, as well. Anything else?"

"Yes. We also need to look into the possibility of state sponsors of terrorism. Some of the countries on that list have a long history of dealing with the Russians. Iran is one of them, and they could very well turn out to be our number one candidate. I'll bet the Vice President is thinking along those lines. He hates those bastards."

"Got it, sir. Russia, former Soviets, and state sponsors. Especially places like Iran that have Russian ties."

"Another thing, Bob. As crazy as it sounds, we can't rule out domestic terrorism. Don't forget McVeigh. He was willing to kill a lot of people. Everything related to smallpox in the United States is supposed to be held at CDC in Atlanta, so start there. Then check on the other level-4 laboratories. Remember that nutcase with anthrax. The FBI said he used samples that he cooked up at Fort Detrick."

Edwards now had three bullet points under his main entry.

Who?— • *russia* • *rogue states* • *domestic*

"What about the other two questions, General? *Why?* and *How?*"

"We can wait on those. Whoever it was, they wanted to hurt us. Once we find out who they are, we'll know why. Whether it a radical Muslim group trying to kill the Great Satan or some local nut job that's unhappy about income taxes. And as for how it was done, we'll have to leave that to people on the ground out in New Mexico.

But to be on the safe side, send a few of your guys out there to make sure that Bradshaw keeps pushing on that part of the investigation."

"I'll take care of it."

"CDC is sending out a medical and scientific team, but those people may not be much help to us unless we push them. Otherwise they'll just focus on treating the locals—the Indians. The smallpox is mostly on the Navajo Reservation. If they can give us an idea of how the attack was launched, we'll be able to wrap up some of the details, and maybe even find the guys who did it. I say guys, but I suppose there could be women, too. Those assholes over in the Middle East have been letting women blow themselves up for a few years already. No reason why they wouldn't use them for smallpox."

The list now had two more entries:

> *Who?*— • *russia*   • *rogue states*   • *domestic*
>
> *Why?*— *later*
>
> *How?*— *wait on new mexico*

Edwards turned the legal pad toward his subordinate but didn't give it to him. His hand rested across the top of the pad, unambiguously conveying the message that the paper itself was not going anywhere. "All right, Colonel, here are your orders. We need these answers yesterday. So use people you can trust, just like back in the Philippines, and get to work. I want to be briefed by you and you alone. At least twice a day. This counts as one, but I'll expect an update by the end of the day."

As Zaborsky stood up to leave the office, Edwards spoke softly. "Bob, you'll probably want to set up a cot in your office. I don't expect you'll have time to go home and sleep anytime soon. Same thing for your staff. Tomorrow may be a holiday, but you'll have to explain that we're trying to simulate reality. When this is all over? If they do it right, that's when they'll be able to give thanks. We all will."

* * *

Day 22: New Teams

At nine o'clock on Wednesday evening, Edwards looked up from his desk in response to the light knock on the door. "Come in Bob. What've you got for me?"

Zaborsky was beat. "Preliminary stuff, nothing definitive. I've got all my teams in place. First off, I was able to reach Colonel Bradshaw in Farmington. His troops can provide security. And he's okay with having our people run the intelligence interface."

"That's good. Bradshaw is first rate."

"I've got a team heading out West. They'll hit the ground running first thing in the morning, assuming that they know how to sleep on a plane. There are six of them, and I briefed them personally. So far, they think this is an exercise. They'll find out about the smallpox when they get there, but then they'll get zero information from anyone but me. Four of them, two men and two women, have backgrounds in surveillance. The other two are tech guys who will take control of communications out there. Basically, that means they'll shut things down. No telephone, no cell phone, no Internet. They'll set up secure lines of communication for official purposes, and all of that will go through us."

"What about roads?"

"Bradshaw will handle all the physical controls. He's shutting down the local airport and closing the roads. That's air and land, and there's no sea. There's a couple of small rivers that go through Farmington, but I don't guess we'll need to bother with that."

"What other personnel have you assigned?"

"We've got four other teams headed out to check up on the level-4 laboratories around the country. The labs have got a history of poor security, and that's worrisome. In addition to CDC, itself, we're checking out five others. That includes the Army lab at Fort Detrick and the lab at Georgia State University. Some of these places *could* work with smallpox. We just need to verify that they never actually did."

"So you're going to send a team of investigators to each site?"

"No, sir. At least, not all at once. The first four teams will do the initial screening, which should be relatively easy. We're pretty sure most of the labs never actually had access to smallpox. The Fort Detrick team will be larger because they'll have to deal with a long history that includes the old biological weapons program. But it's an

Army lab, so they'll cooperate. I've got someone preparing a memo for your signature."

"Make sure the memo makes it clear that we're not asking. We're telling."

"Absolutely. And we're sending the largest team—five investigators—down to Atlanta. They'll check out Georgia State University and then dig in hard at CDC. I've been back in touch with that guy Rasmussen at CDC who first called Colonel Bradshaw, and he understands that he has to work with us. I guess you made it clear to him from the beginning about the need for complete secrecy. In addition to checking anyone who might ever have had access to the smallpox virus, we'll set up surveillance and controls on all members of the CDC team that was deployed to New Mexico. It would be an easy place for an accidental leak, so we've really got to put a lid on things."

"Sounds like you're making progress, Colonel. What are you proposing if there's any sort of leak and we need to do damage control?"

"I talked with Dr. Rasmussen about that. If anything happens, or if anybody gets too nosy, we say that there's an outbreak of chickenpox. But I think we'll be able to control this completely. Bradshaw will have Farmington sealed off by the end of the day, and the people there already think it's chickenpox. The symptoms are similar, and you can even die of chickenpox, so people out there should believe what we tell them. And remember—this isn't a big city with a lot of doctors and lawyers. It's only a damn Indian reservation."

"What about questions from people at the biological laboratories? Won't they get suspicious?"

"We have that covered too. We'll tell them we're running a surprise inspection as part of an anti-terrorism planning exercise. All classified. Nobody is going to object to questions about whether they've ever had smallpox virus in their lab. If they've never had samples of the virus, it's over and done with. And if they have studied the virus, they'll understand how important it is to cooperate with us."

"They'll remember the anthrax."

"Exactly. Nobody wants another snafu like the one at Fort Detrick. But you know what, General? I don't think we're going to find anything wrong at any of these labs. This is America. Sure, maybe some crackpot like McVeigh had a beef with the government.

That kind of bozo might attack a federal building. But biological weapons against innocent civilians? That's got to be from the fucking Arabs. We'll find out and we'll nail the bastards."

"The nailing will be up to others, Bob. You just need to find out who attacked us. What have you got on that front? I mean with regard to Russia and the other countries we discussed?"

"Nothing yet, but we've started making inquiries. The hardest part was finding a cover story for why we're asking questions. We can't just walk up to the head of the FSB—I still have trouble calling those guys anything but KGB—and ask politely if they just carried out a smallpox attack on the U.S. They know damn well what our policy is for responding to a WMD attack. If they thought we suspected them, there's a good chance that they'd launch their missiles before we ever heard an answer to our question. So we're saying that this is all an anti-terrorism planning activity. We're trying to get updated information on anybody that might ever have had access to the Soviet smallpox samples. And we explain the urgency by saying that our exercise is being done just like military war games. That we have a red team and a blue team competing against each other. Each side wants to win the game."

"I like that, Bob. Especially the chickenpox as a backup cover. Just make sure your own people understand that everything is top secret. They can't even talk about chickenpox to anyone who isn't fully briefed into the mission, not even their own families."

"Will do, General. And it's not just Russia. We've also got sources for other countries that are potential sources of an attack. That includes Syria, Pakistan, and Iran. For Iran, we also have the Mujahedeen-e-Khalq. That's the MEK. They've been working against the regime for decades, and they gave us the information that helped us show that Iran was lying about its nuclear programs back in 2007. It may take a few days, but we'll get some good information back."

"We don't have too many days to work with, Bob. No matter how well you control the information coming out of Farmington, we have to worry about one other person besides us. And by us, I mean our entire team. You, me, your team, the CDC in Atlanta, and all of Bradshaw's people out in New Mexico. There's one other person who knows about the smallpox attack."

"I don't understand ..."

"Think about it Colonel. The person who carried out this damn attack. He's out there somewhere—monitoring what we're doing. He probably got out of Farmington at least a week ago—it takes more than a week for smallpox symptoms to even begin developing. So he's sitting out there somewhere waiting to see what we do. Just the fact that there's no news coming out of Farmington may tell him he was successful.

"If you don't get the answer soon, he's going to conclude that the first part of his attack worked. And then we'll be facing the second wave. Armageddon. You can't let that happen, Bob. We need to know who did it. What country did it. And then they'll pay. They'll pay before they ever get a chance to start the second wave. They'll never have the chance to launch another attack. Never."

* * *

Day 23: Looking for Leaks

Zaborsky sat at his desk in his office in the B ring of the Pentagon on Thanksgiving morning, finishing his fifth cup of coffee. He had managed to sleep for a couple of hours after he found a folding cot, which now sat in his office, fully made up and ready for inspection. He'd risen at 6:30 a.m., showered, and shaved. The Pentagon had all the facilities. One of the things he'd learned from all his years in the Army, was to be ready to travel at the drop of a hat, and he kept a change of clothes in his office. Crisis or not, he took great pride in maintaining control of both his appearance and his actions.

Edwards was pacing in the hallway in front of his office when Zaborsky rounded the corner of the hallway at 11:00 a.m. "Morning, Bob. I'm just stretching my legs a little. It's been a long night. Were you able to get any sleep?"

"A little. You?"

"The same. It's just like our operations down in the Philippines. The adrenaline kicks in, and sleep doesn't matter quite so much anymore. Let's go inside where we can talk. I assume you have a few things to show me?"

"Yes sir. I think you'll be pleased. Maybe not pleased—that's the wrong word for this situation. But I think you'll agree that we've been able to make some progress. We've heard back from all four of our field teams. As of now, there's no indication that any of them, except for CDC and Fort Detrick, have ever had actual smallpox samples on site. Ever since the anthrax thing, their security and record keeping has been pretty good. Everything is pointing to this being a foreign operation."

"I agree that it all fits. It probably wasn't somebody from one of the American laboratories. But don't come to your conclusions too quickly. You'll probably be able to refocus your assets on more probable targets, but have some of your people keep looking. Have them look deeper—for anything that could be any sort of irregularity. I keep coming back to the anthrax attacks, when the FBI jumped the gun and named the wrong person as their suspect. As a result, the guy that they later identified as the culprit went around free as a bird for seven years. We sure as hell don't want another fuck-up like that."

"No sir. No question about that. I'll make sure that my teams continue putting pressure on all the labs. We'll tell them it's just for record-keeping, to be sure we haven't missed something important. Unless you object, I'm going to keep the original Fort Detrick team in place and merge the other two field teams into the one at CDC. First, we need to keep searching at both locations for any possibility that a smallpox sample might have been moved off site. The second reason may be more important: we want to put an emphasis on Atlanta, so our people keep an eye on communications in and out of CDC. We don't want any leaks about the Farmington task force."

"How many people did CDC send out there?"

"So far, it looks like about a dozen—all M.D.s or scientists. Colonel Bradshaw is providing support staff, so CDC only needs technical and medical people. Bradshaw said we could slip in a couple of people from DIA. The CDC guys won't know the difference, and we'll be able to keep an eye on them more easily."

"Good thinking. Go back to Atlanta for a minute. What will your team be doing there?"

"Reorganizing the original four teams will give us nine people at CDC. Two of them will be assigned to CDC's Coordinating Office for Terrorism Preparedness and Emergency Response. That's COTPER—the office that sent the medical team out to New Mexico. They'll monitor any visitors or incoming telephone calls. They'll switch off working 12-hour days. During CDC working hours, they'll act as receptionists and screen all incoming telephone contacts."

"What about the people who didn't go to New Mexico?"

"Everybody in COTPER who stayed in Atlanta was told that a highly classified training exercise is under way, and it is not to be discussed with anybody. We'll also assign someone to keep an eye on Rasmussen and Torlander. They're the only two CDC people who have been fully briefed—on the smallpox, I mean—not on our operation. Officially, we'll be providing liaisons for support, but our guys understand that they might need to intervene in a hurry if either Rasmussen or Torlander starts to go off the reservation."

He cleared his throat and continued, "Okay. All this will still leave us with three people who can keep pushing on the historical records. Those three can also provide relief to the others to cover meals and stuff."

Edwards took on a serious tone. "You're doing a good job on the logistics, Bob. But the fact is, it's all just beating around the bush.

The real question has to do with actual intelligence. We agree that the smallpox almost certainly didn't originate inside the U.S. That means we're looking for a foreign source. And officially, that would mean it has to be Russia. It doesn't mean the Russians launched this attack, just that the virus somehow originated with them."

"That's true sir. Our intelligence files indicate that there were at least two biological facilities outside Russia, in Kazakhstan and Uzbekistan. But we can't be sure yet about smallpox virus at those places. We need to wait for confirming information from some of our agents and other sources."

"What about Iran?"

"Right. We've got the reports you mentioned about Soviet materials winding up in Iran. Back in 2001, Putin made a big deal of saying that all smallpox stores, first in the Soviet Union and then in Russia, were safe. And he specifically said that Russia had not provided any assistance to Iran for the development of WMD. But we also know from that business with Project Sapphire that Iran tried to get access to enriched uranium back in 1993. So if they were trying to get Russian uranium from Kazakhstan, it's hard to believe they didn't try to get other stuff, too. They would have been trying to get smallpox samples from the old Soviet biological weapons facility in Kazakhstan at the same time. It seems to me that it everything points to Iran."

"I concur, Colonel. But keep digging. I'll be a lot happier when you provide me with some hard evidence from our own investigation to verify our suspicions. That will make our case against Iran a whole lot stronger when it gets debated at the National Security Council."

* * *

9

Sarah

*We have argued that the Fourth Amendment would
not apply to military operations the President
ordered within the United States to deter and
prevent acts of terrorism.*

—*Department of Defense Directive, 2005*[*]

Day 26: Airport

Shortly before two o'clock, Sarah left her apartment and crossed the hallway to the elevators. Instead of going to the lobby, Sarah pushed P2, which took her to the lower level of the parking garage beneath her apartment building. There she exited and turned toward the far wall, away from the cars. Lining the wall were a series of storage lockers, cages, actually, made from chain link fencing. She came to the one she was looking for. She took her keys out of her pocket, opened locker, and pulled out her Cannondale bicycle. It was the "Bad Boy" model, one that she'd picked out because it was highly rated, lightweight, and tough. Plus, she admitted to herself, the name had sold her.

She checked the tires, put on her helmet and gloves, and took a pair of tinted protective goggles from her handlebar bag. She walked

---

[*] U.S. Department of Justice, Oct. 23, 2001, Memorandum for Alberto R. Gonzales, Counsel to the President and William J. Haynes, II, General Counsel, Department of Defense; authored by John C. Yoo, Deputy Assistant Attorney General and Robert L. Delahunty, Special Counsel, "Re: Authority for Use of Military Force to Combat Terrorist Activities within the United States," p. 34.

the bike up the ramp to the exit door and put the small entry card that was attached to her key ring next to the sensor. As the door went up, she realized that the entry card was yet one more opportunity for someone to track her. She rode several short blocks toward Key Bridge. If anyone were watching, they would assume she was headed across Key Bridge into Georgetown. But as soon as she had crossed Lee Highway, she made a hard right turn onto a bicycle path on the Virginia side of the Potomac River.

Almost immediately, the trail crossed a small pedestrian bridge over the George Washington Parkway and connected to the Mount Vernon trail. Sarah loved the trail, which ran alongside the Potomac for almost 20 miles, all the way to George Washington's historic home. But today, she was only going to ride about three miles. Her destination was Reagan National Airport, and she reached the north end of the runway in 15 minutes.

It was a place that nearly every biker and runner paused to watch the planes take off or land. The runway always operated in just a single direction that depended on wind conditions, and both takeoffs and landings were a thrill to watch as the planes passed directly overhead. Sometimes they seemed almost close enough to reach up and touch. Today, however, Sarah dispensed with the tradition and kept on riding.

In less than a half mile, she neared the terminal buildings. The bike path continued over a small bridge across the airport exit, but Sarah veered off into a small parking lot. At the end of the main terminal, she locked her bike to a lamppost.

Striding around the end of the building, Sarah was immediately surrounded by travelers, suitcases in tow, surging toward the waiting line for taxicabs. Walking against the tide, she entered the baggage claim area and took an escalator up to the departure level. Scanning the concourse, she saw what she was looking for—a kiosk with a large advertisement for cell phones. *Perfect.*

She waited by the arrivals board until another customer finished browsing, and she approached the kiosk looking as frustrated and upset as she could.

The clerk noticed her. "Hi, can I help you?"

"Somebody stole my bag just before my flight left Chicago, and I lost everything. My wallet, my ID, my credit cards—everything! All I have left is some cash, so I'm hoping I could buy some kind of phone to call the people I'm staying with."

Sarah saw the look on the clerk's face, and she knew she had succeeded in getting his sympathy. "Man, that really sucks. We're not supposed to sell any of these phones without proper identification, but I guess this is sort of an exception. If you'll just give me all your information, I'll write down that you showed me your driver's license."

"Thanks. That's really nice of you. Do you have something that's not too expensive?"

The clerk suggested a model that had 30 prepaid minutes and cost $25.

"That sounds perfect." At least for that one response, Sarah couldn't have been more honest if she'd tried.

She gave the clerk she was "Jennifer James," a combination of the names of two kids she'd gone to elementary school with, and she made up a street address in Chicago. When he asked her for a contact phone number, she made up a number with the 312 area code.

Five minutes later, she was walking away feeling like the cat that had swallowed the canary. The clerk in the kiosk seemed pleased as well. Apparently he took her improved mood as evidence that he'd been a Good Samaritan.

She walked back to her bike, she rode slowly back out of the airport onto the bike path. This time, when she reached the area at the north end of the runway, she pulled over to the side of the path and looked up just as a plane was taking off. The power was awesome—all those tons of metal vaulting up into the sky with a mighty roar. After a few moments, she resumed pedaling back toward Arlington. The entire way home, she focused on her next step. Another bit of deception.

* * *

Day 26: Just Good Friends

"Hey Sarah, come on in." Eric Murphy was surprised. He walked over to the coffee table and picked up the remote in order to mute the football game he had been watching. "Half-time," he explained. "Can I get you a beer or something?" Eric had lived in the building even longer than Sarah, and they were casual friends.

"No thanks Eric. I actually need to ask a favor. I have to make a run down to Richmond this evening, and there's this guy I'm trying to avoid."

"Somebody threatening you?"

"No, nothing like that. More like a puppy dog who hasn't quite figured out that the interest doesn't go both ways. But I thought I saw him down the street when I came back from the store, and I just don't want to 'accidentally' run into him. Anyway, I was wondering if I could borrow your car. So if that creep really is looking for me, he won't see me drive out in my car. I'll leave you my keys, and you can use my car if you need to go anywhere."

"No problem with lending you my car, but I'm worried about this guy. It sounds like he's stalking you." Eric hesitated as he fished his keys out of his pocket and removed the Chevy key from his key ring.

"I hear you, but I don't think he's dangerous. I'll keep an eye out for him for a few days, and if he's still hanging around I'll ask the cops to pay him a visit."

"Okay, I'll trust your judgment on this one." He handed her the key. "Anyway, I just filled the tank last week. It's been running pretty good, so a trip to Richmond shouldn't be a problem."

Sarah put her car key on the coffee table. "Thanks Eric. I really appreciate this. It's good to have a friend you can trust." With yet another lie, she felt a pang of conscience.

"Are you really going to do this as a round trip this evening? That's a lot of driving."

"If I'm tired, I can stay over. Do you need the car back before tomorrow afternoon?"

Murphy laughed. "The only place I'll need to go is to work, and that's only a block from Metro. Just promise you'll be careful. And I mean careful for yourself, not the car."

"I will. Thanks Eric, you're a good friend."

Sarah got up and walked toward the door. "If you're not around when I get back, I'll ask the security guard to put them in your mailbox. I have an extra key, so I'll still be able to use my car, even if I don't see you for a couple of days."

"Okay, have a safe trip." Eric turned back to the TV. The second half of the football game had started.

* * *

Day 26: Off the Grid

Sarah put on a canvas field coat that Jake had left in the closet the last time he'd visited. It was too big for her but fit her purposes completely. She added a baseball cap, tucked her hair under it, and looked at herself in the mirror. In the fading light of late afternoon, the clothing might allow her to pass for a man. And it wouldn't be her car, in any case.

She exited the garage and started driving west. An hour later, she crossed the Blue Ridge, soon finding herself on smaller highways that took her into the countryside of West Virginia.

The roads became narrower and more winding, eventually giving way to a dirt road that signaled she was only a mile from her destination. It was well past sunset now, and Sarah was relieved that she'd made the trip previously. Finally, she reached her parents' place, Situated on a steep hill above the South Branch of the Potomac River. She couldn't see much in the darkness. The house was isolated and, even though it was less than 100 miles from Washington. The combination of rivers and mountains made the location difficult to reach.

Sarah pulled the car up to the log house, went around to the side of the building, and retrieved the key from its hiding place. She turned on the gas fireplace to get some heat and found a container of chili in the freezer for her dinner.

She climbed the stairs to her dad's office area. He called the loft his "crow's nest." She sat in her father's desk chair, swiveling it toward the file-cabinet safe. The combination lock worked just as she had remembered. Opening the upper drawer, she looked through the labels on the various files. Most seemed to be business records.

In the lower drawer, she saw a file labeled "Sarah." Inside were several 9 x 12 manila envelopes. She started with the top envelope, which said "college," and examined the contents of the envelope. It was mostly some old correspondence from William & Mary about the tuition bills that her parents had paid.

The second envelope was labeled "sarah-boo." She smiled, thinking about the childhood nickname her father had used. She opened the flap and tilted the envelope. She was stunned when a passport slid out. *Why in hell did he take my passport?*

She picked up the passport and opened it. Sure enough, it was hers. There she was in the standard passport photo, and right next to her picture was her name, Sarah. But it wasn't Sarah Lockford, it was Sarah Wallingford.

"Son of a bitch!" she said aloud. "What in hell is going on?"

Thinking back to the phone conversation with her father, Sarah realized that he had been trying very carefully to tell her about this other passport without actually saying the words, and without saying aloud that it was out in West Virginia. Someone overhearing their conversation would have thought he was simply referring to her own apartment and the same passport she'd had for five years. She looked again at the Wallingford passport. The date of birth was January 12, 1980. Almost the same as hers, but not quite. Sarah had been born on October 12, 1980. This passport merely interchanged the digits specifying the month—from one-zero for October, to zero-one for January.

Sarah reached for the telephone to call her father, but she stopped and put the phone back into the cradle. What he didn't say in their last conversation may have been more important than what he actually said.

His secrecy on the phone meant that she couldn't possibly call him to ask. She couldn't even call him at all. That whole conversation had been his way of saying, "You're on your own Sarah. I've done what I could."

Sarah thought back to her childhood, and the jumbled, random thoughts flying around inside her head began to undergo a weird sort of self-assembly. The house in McLean was just down the road from the headquarters of the Central Intelligence Agency. Her dad worked up the road, a couple of miles in the other direction, in Tyson's Corner. But did he really? Was that the only office he ever went to? She never actually saw him go to work. She only saw him when he left in the morning and came home at night. He'd always said that his office was too boring for a kid.

He'd frequently been on trips to Eastern Europe and developing countries. Were they really sales trips for electronics? Or had all of it been a cover story? How on earth did he learn how to get hold of a fake passport?

As this revelation crystallized among Sarah's swirling emotions, she thought of another explanation for the fake passport. Several years earlier, she'd gone with him on a trip to Europe. That's when she'd first obtained her own passport, the one that was in her dresser in Arlington. The fake passport was issued at about the same time, or at least that's what the date said. And she was sure the photograph was the same as the one in her real passport. He must have used a copy of that photo to make the fake passport.

She remembered that after the main part of their trip through Germany, they had traveled briefly into Georgia and the Ukraine. *Maybe he was worried that something could go wrong there. It was back when Russian troops went into Georgia.* Whatever the explanation, Sarah realized that her dad's expertise was more than just selling electronics. He'd used it to help her obtain a new identity, so she just needed to take it and run with it.

Why didn't he tell me he's a CIA agent? Doesn't he trust me? I wonder if Mom knows about this.

Sarah turned her attention back to the desk, looking at the other envelopes that had been in the folder labeled "Sarah." The next one was marked "high school," and it was exactly what it purported to be. There was some correspondence, a few report cards, and a clipping from the school paper about the time her cross-country team had placed second in the state finals.

The fourth envelope was labeled "resources," and it was stuffed with what felt like a sheaf of printed pages. But what Sarah pulled from the envelope was a very different kind of paper. She was holding a clear plastic sleeve, similar to those she had used in college to protect her lab reports. But this wasn't a report. The sleeve was filled with money!

There were six bundles of bills, each about a half-inch thick. She pulled out one of the two packets closest to the opening of the sleeve and riffled through it. They were all $10 bills. She did the same with each of the other packets, removing them one at a time and examining them. Three of the packets consisted of $20 bills, and the last two were made up of were 50s and 100s.

Sarah slid the bills out of the band that was holding the stack of $10 bills and began to count. The first time through she lost track of the count at 58. She tried it again and got to 89. Realizing that her nerves were getting to her, she counted out piles of 10 that she could easily verify. There were 10 piles. *My God, that's a thousand dollars, in just this first bundle.* Then she thought she must have done that multiplication incorrectly, that there couldn't be that much money in such a small package. So she counted through one of the 10 separate stacks: *10, 20, 30 ...* and realized each of them did indeed contain $100, which made a total of $1,000 in the original bundle.

And that's just the $10 bills. She reached for a pencil and added up the values of the individual stacks. *Twenty-two thousand dollars—in cash!* Sarah took a few deep breaths in an effort to calm herself. She also noticed that the bills didn't seem to be new. They didn't stick together, and they just seemed slightly used. She slid several of the $100 bills out of their packet and looked at the serial numbers. They were random. Her father had made plans for going off the grid long before Sarah even thought of it.

Sarah went back to the envelope that had held the sleeve with all the bills. She turned it upside down and gave it a gentle shake to be sure there was nothing else inside. Something fell on the desk. *A credit card.* It was a Visa card, but she noticed that it looked different from her own credit card. At the top, it said "all-access."

The credit card made Sarah think of something else. She took the legal pad and signed her name. But not her real name, not "Sarah Lockford." What she wrote was "Sarah Wallingford." Then she reached for the passport with the same name and opened it. The signature that she hadn't even noticed before was virtually identical to the one she had just written on a legal pad.

Sarah figured that her father had used a sample of her writing. There would have been enough of a patter to generate the "Wallingford" in exactly the same style that Sarah normally used. As long as she remembered to use the right last name, whatever she signed would look just like the signature on her passport.

Once again, she turned to the file folder. There were only two envelopes left, and the first had just a few more documents from her graduate school days. The last envelope was labeled "drivers." At first it seemed to be empty. But when Sarah shook it, a little, another piece of plastic fell onto the desk. *A Virginia driver's license.*

Once again, her picture was on the front. It was the same photo as her passport, but it was cropped differently, and her hair color looked a little different. Sarah put the two next to each other and thought that someone had intentionally made the photos look different, just enough that nobody would compare them and ask why the same photo had been used for both. The signature was the same. Except it wasn't. At first she thought they were identical, some sort of photocopy. But when she placed them next to each other, she saw that there were small differences. Then she put the piece of paper she had signed in between the two documents and shook her head in amazement. *I wouldn't be able to tell them apart.*

Looking at the driver's license and passport side by side, Sarah noticed for the first time they didn't show her current address. The documents listed her residence as 6138 Stoneham Lane in McLean, Virginia, only a block away from the family home where she grew up. Her friend Jennifer had lived at 6100, the last house on a dead end street.

Sarah spent a few more minutes poking around the file cabinet, but she couldn't find anything. She couldn't eat, so she found a couple of blankets and a pillow that she carried out to the couch. Just before turning out the lights, she looked up at the photograph of her parents on the bookcase. *Thanks Dad. I'm glad you're looking out for me. But you could have told me.*

* * *

10

Antiques

As you approach her the sandstone figure seems to have two heads but when you pass her only the fine features of a beautiful woman remain. ... More exploring reveals more weird rock creatures. When you tire of hunting fantasy figures you drive back onto the main road and head toward Navajo Dam.

—*New Mexico magazine, 1965*[*]

Day 17: Interlude

Gregory Anniston was depressed. Here it was the weekend before Thanksgiving, but instead of having a weekend to relax with his wife and kids and maybe even watch some football with his buddies, he was in Albuquerque. *I'm stuck out here in the middle of the freakin' desert.*

His hotel room had a magnificent view of the Sandia Mountains. He didn't want to play golf, or go sightseeing, or even take in a movie by himself. He would be away from home for the entire week.

The adult movies on TV didn't help matters. *And here I am, almost 2,000 miles from home.*

So he went to the hotel bar and ordered a bourbon. He sipped the drink slowly. It figured to be a shitty Friday night.

Greg had been a defensive back on the football team. Not a star, but he had become a starter by the second half of his senior year. Football practice cut into his moderate scholarly efforts, resulting in

---

[*] *New Mexico Magazine*, 1965, Santa Fe, New Mexico (ISSN 0028-6249).

a grade point average that was just barely above the lower limits for passing. But he managed to graduate.

He was bigger than average, standing a little over 6 feet, and weighing just more than 200 pounds. That was 20 pounds heavier than when he played college football 15 years earlier, but he thought he carried it well.

The bartender came over to ask if Greg was ready for another drink, but he said, "No thanks." He had at least another five minutes left on his first round. He was happy to run up a tab, but he wanted to do it slowly enough that he could still walk back to his room at the end of the evening.

As the bartender turned away, a young woman with long dark hair took a seat at the bar and ordered a Margarita. The next time the bartender came by to ask if he wanted another drink, Greg said yes. Noticing that the woman had looked up, he said, "Could I buy you a refill? No point in being unfriendly."

She laughed. "Thanks. That'd be nice." Again, they returned to their drinks.

They laughed awkwardly when both reached for the bowl of cocktail snacks on the bar between them. Then the woman motioned to the empty seat between them, a nonverbal request to see if it would be okay for her to move over. The nod and smile from Greg provided a clear answer. "Danielle Brandis," she said, extending a hand.

"Gregory Anniston. Friends call me Greg. It's nice to meet you Danielle."

Over the next 45 minutes, the two travelers chatted about their backgrounds and why they were in Albuquerque. Danielle turned out to be an antiques dealer, what she called "antiques and artifacts."

"I specialize in Native American arts and crafts, with a particular focus on the Southwest. Every year, I take a two-week trip out here to hunt for items that I can bring back to sell at my shop."

"I'm going to guess Delaware. Your accent definitely isn't New York or New Jersey, but it's not southern either."

She laughed. "Pretty close. Maryland, actually. Just north of Baltimore, not too far from where I grew up. I have a place there now."

"In the city?"

"About 20 miles northwest. Out in the countryside. It's a low-key life style, but I love it. I studied art history in college, and then I found out I could travel around the country finding things related to

American history. And I could make some money in the process. For a couple of years, I had some dead-end jobs that supported my antiques as more of a weekend hobby. Then I took my savings, along with some help from my parents, and bought the property in Maryland. It's not much, just a small house, but there was a barn next to it that I use as my shop."

"So you just sell stuff from the Southwest?"

"I wish. No, I still deal in all sorts of antiques. A girl has to make a living."

"Sounds interesting. Any really old pieces?" Greg's mood was improving.

"If they're really old, they're really expensive, and I can't afford them. Like Navajo blankets and rugs. Pieces from the early 1800s might go for a half million dollars. And the truth is, I have a hard time when I find a real steal. I mean, how can I buy something worth thousands of dollars and pay only a few bucks to someone who has no money? I'm not rich, but I can't cheat poor people. Usually, if I find something that I think is worth a lot, I'll give the person what I can afford. Then if I can sell it for a lot more, I'll send them half of what I make."

"You're a real saint."

Danielle stopped smiling.

"That came out wrong. I didn't mean it as an insult. It's just that it doesn't sound like very good business."

She recovered. "No offense taken. But you're wrong about the business end. The couple of times I've done it? Those people have stayed in touch with me, and they've found me more bargains. They know I'll be fair with them, and they'd rather sell to me than get cheated by somebody else. That's why I come back and make the same circuit every year. This is five years in a row now."

They talked more about little things, and Greg told her about his job. "A lot classified defense programs, so I can't say too much. The company does software design and instrument development for high-tech manufacturing. Mostly laser-based. Mostly, I manage projects, especially with subcontractors. I make site visits to check on progress. That's why I'm here. It's my job to make sure that we don't get any big surprises."

"It sounds exciting. It's important for the country, and you get to travel."

"I suppose so, but it gets tiresome after a while. And lonely at times." The words caught in his throat, and he felt himself blushing.

He looked away from Danielle and stared down at his drink. *What the fuck am I doing?*

He tried to recast his comment in a more innocent light. "You'll see what I mean after you've done this for a few more years."

"Oh, listen to Mr. Old Guy. What're you, maybe five years ahead of me?"

Anniston laughed. "Okay, I'm being dumb. But traveling does get old."

"Yeah, and I do understand about it getting lonely at times. For me, too."

"Hey, look." Greg hesitated, almost stumbling on his words. "Like this has been really fun talking here, but if we keep doing this we're both going to be drunk off our asses. What do you say we go get some dinner?"

Danielle smiled. "I'd like that. Any ideas where?"

"There's a restaurant on the other side of the hotel. It's convenient, and someone told me it's pretty good."

"Let's give it a try."

Greg paid the tab, advising that he was on a business trip and an expense account. "Part of my job is making new contacts, so it's an investment. Just like when you find an expensive antique."

Danielle accepted graciously, and they stood up to leave. Greg hadn't noticed before, but she was tall and willowy. *All woman.* As they walked across the hotel, they passed a sign for the rest rooms. "I need to stop in the ladies' first, okay?"

"Sure. I'll wait here for you."

Noticing that he was by the gift shop, Greg wandered inside. Looking around, his eyes locked on something not on his normal shopping list. A package of condoms His heart skipped a beat as he reached for it. Then he picked up a second package. *What the hell am I doing?*

Self-consciously, Greg paid for his purchase and the sales clerk discreetly put the items into a small paper bag. Danielle was waiting for him outside. When he walked up to her, she leaned close and said, "I saw what you bought."

Greg turned a shade of red that he was certain must have been brighter than the crimson ribbons on some of the early holiday decorations in the hotel lobby. "I didn't ... I mean ... Oh shit! Look, Danielle ... I've never done this before."

"Of course you have, silly. You told me you have two kids. I'm okay with that."

"That's not what I mean. I'm trying to say that I don't go around doing this kind of stuff. I didn't go out looking for women tonight. I mean, I'm really glad we met and everything, but I wasn't trying to pick you up."

"I know that Greg. I was thinking the same thing." She couldn't meet his eye for a moment; then she looked up and smiled.

She leaned even closer to him, her voice husky. "Dinner can wait. Let's go to your room."

When the elevator doors closed, they were alone. Greg pushed the button for the 18th floor and turned to face Danielle. She reached up, and their kiss was electric. She put her leg between his and pushed her hips into him. He reached down, slid his hand under her skirt, and gasped. "You're not wearing any underwear!"

"I told you we were thinking the same thing. When I was in the ladies' room, I took them off."

The elevator chimed, and they stepped out onto the 18th floor. Fumbling for the key card and again to unlock the door, it took Greg two tries before he finally opened it. They didn't wait for the door to finish closing before their hands were all over each other.

After a few seconds she pushed him away. "Don't tease me anymore, Greg. I want you. Now. Take off your damn clothes." She dropped her skirt to the floor and took off her sweater and bra. While Greg finished undressing, she took one of the packets out of the paper bag from the gift shop. Danielle led him to the bed and sat down in front of him, pulling him toward her. Gently, she unrolled the condom onto him and then lay back. "Please Greg. Hurry up. I want you inside me!"

The first time, it was too fast and too rough. But that was only the first time. The second time was slow and gentle, and it lasted much longer. "Oh, Jesus, Greg. That was wonderful."

"It was. It really was. You're fantastic. I wish I could do it again, but a guy needs a little recovery time."

"Fair enough. Let's get dressed and go have that dinner. That should give you enough time." As they stood up, Danielle pressed her breasts against him and kissed him again as she ran her hand down his back. Then she looked down and giggled. "I'm not sure you'll need to wait that long, mister."

* * *

11

Sarah

*The oversize white envelope bore the blue logo of
the Department of Homeland Security. Inside, I
found 20 photocopies of the government's records
on my international travels. Every overseas trip I've
taken since 2001 was noted. ... My biggest surprise
was that the Internet Protocol (I.P.) address of the
computer used to buy my tickets via a Web agency
was noted.*

—*Budget Travel Magazine, 2008*[*]

Day 27: Romney, West Virginia

Sarah was awake at first light. She made coffee, toasted a
bagel from the freezer, and ate it quickly. Then she poured
another cup of coffee, put on her jacket, and walked out
onto the deck. Looking out over the back railing, she marveled at the
view. The hardwoods had lost their leaves, but there were enough
conifers to provide some color on top of the otherwise gray
landscape. In the distance, she could see larger mountains, and she
could hear the flowing water of the river 300 feet below. It was
peaceful. She wasn't.

She looked at her list: "Four Corners." It had to be her next
destination. But first, she needed access to a computer. *Time to head*

---

[*] "A rare peek at Homeland Security's files on travelers," Sean O'Neill,
Budget Travel Magazine, Newsweek Budget Travel, Inc., Dec. 22, 2008.

to Romney. The population of the county seat was only about 2,000, but it had a nice little library.

After a last look around, Sarah picked up a small plastic bag with the trash from her visit, got into Eric's old Chevy, and began the 45-minute drive to Romney. Just past the old courthouse she found a parking place almost directly in front of the Hampshire County Public Library. Inside, she saw several computer workstations that were clearly intended for public use. She smiled politely at the librarian and glanced at the library policies that were posted nearby. Internet access was available and encouraged, as long as "inappropriate subject matter" was not accessed. *I wonder if the librarian would consider what I'm about to do inappropriate.*

Task number one was to find out more about the new Visa card in her wallet along with the driver's license for Sarah Wallingford. Anything that could identify her as Sarah Lockford was now in a small packet in her backpack, stuffed under the back seat of the car.

Sarah chose one of the computers and checked to see how visible her work would be to someone walking by. She hung her jacket over the back of the chair and stood back several feet to assess the view. She concluded that she could probably use her body to shield specific information on a small part of the screen, but if the librarian wanted to stroll by and see what sort of sites Sarah was looking at, there would be no way to prevent it. *I'll need to be careful.*

A quick Google search for "all-access Visa" told her most of what she wanted to know. Her Visa card was a prepaid debit card that was just about the same as a credit card—except that most car rental agencies wouldn't take it. *Not surprising I guess. This one doesn't even have my name on it.*

The home page for all-access Visa had a menu for obtaining a new card, so Sarah tried an experiment. *It might be a good idea to find out how you go about getting one of these things.*

She entered the name "John Smith," and the next menu asked for a social security number. *Oh, shit! The Post-it!*

On one of the envelopes in the file cabinet Sarah had found a Post-it note. She remembered that it said "Sarah-Boo," And there were some numbers—almost certainly the nine-digit number that her father had used for a social security number. She grabbed her notebook and opened it to the last page she had used. There was no Post-it note. *Damn it! I know I pasted it there. Maybe it's still be on Dad's desk. Unless it blew out the window on the way to Romney or something. Crap! It could be anywhere.*

The experiment was a dead end, so she went back to the home page for the Visa site, where she found a list of "frequently asked questions." There was a link for "How do I check my balance?" *Okay, that's progress.*

The link took her to an account login screen. Now she needed both a username and a password, and she didn't know either one. *Shit! Those were on the Post-it, too.*

The password had to be "Sarah-boo." Her father had used it on the phone, and she was sure it was on the Post-it, as well. And it was also written on one of the envelopes. *That's the password. I'm sure of it.*

By the time she was 10 years old and could read her own stories, Rich Lockford still sat with his daughter at night before she turned out the light. She remembered the time that she was starting to feel much too grown up for such a silly sounding nickname, and she had told her father that he really ought to stop calling her Sarah-boo.

He had understood the conflict between being daddy's little girl and growing up. "It's okay sweetheart, I won't use it when anybody else is around. But it will still help you go to sleep at night. And it will always be our own little secret." It worked just as he had said it would. The comforting phrase always helped her to go to sleep, and it was still their secret. *Amazing. I was just a little kid, and already he was teaching me how to be a spy.*

Sarah tried to remember the other word on the Post-it. When she closed her eyes and concentrated, she thought she could remember that it had part of her new name. "walling" or maybe "swalling."

Then she remembered that her father had used an e-mail name like those for government agencies: part of the last name and first initial. Maybe it was "wallings" for her new identity. Unless it was in the other order, where the initial came first, "swalling." *I can almost see it in my mind. But I can't remember which it was. Wait! There was an "x" in it. It was sxwalling or wallingsx. I'm sure of it!*

She thought about driving back to Levels, but that could be another dead end. She was sure she had pasted the Post-it into her notebook. But it was gone! *I have to figure this out now. I'll try wallingsx first.*

Carefully, Sarah began to type. This was no time for a clumsy keyboard mistake. Then she moved the cursor down to the password box and entered the letters for *Sarah-boo* and clicked on the box that said "log in." For a few seconds nothing happened, and then the icon in the task bar began to show the growing dotted line that indicated progress in exchanging information with the server. The screen went blank, and as Sarah held her breath, a new page loaded. "Oh crap," she muttered to herself quietly, mindful of the library's policies on inappropriate behavior. There at the top of the page, in a bright red font, was the following message:

Log in Error: The Username and Password combination that you have entered is not valid.

She double-checked to make sure the Caps Lock wasn't on and then tried the other Username, *sxwalling*. Again, the screen went blank—and then the same bright red error message appeared. *This isn't an auspicious start to my career as a spy.*

It could have been any of a million different possibilities, but Sarah was absolutely convinced that she was on the right track. But there were some other possibilities. *It has to be the hyphen. A lot of sites don't let you use anything other than the standard letters and numbers. I bet he would have left it out.*

For her third attempt, Sarah returned to the first username, *wallingsx*, but now the tried *Sarahboo* without a hyphen for the password. The result was the same: "Log in Error." If they're tracking by this computer's IP address, I may already have used up my three tries before they shut me out. I hope it's only by username. Trying to be meticulous—this was no time to screw up by entering the same incorrect combination twice—Sarah wrote down the combinations she had tried in her notebook. Next would be *sxwalling* and *Sarahboo*. Once again, the error message appeared.

She tried again to visualize the name on the envelope that she had taken from her father's safe the night before. She closed her eyes … and there it was! *The name on the envelope was completely in lowercase.* Typing carefully, she went back to *wallingsx* and then entered *sarah-boo*.

Sarah clenched her teeth and hit the enter key. For a few seconds there was nothing. Then—*Shit!*—the error message. Sarah looked quickly over her shoulder, worrying that she might have sworn aloud, but she saw the librarian nearby with her head still down, focused on her work.

At least I know that they don't just shut you out after the first two tries for the username. But it was a small consolation, because Sarah knew she was running out of chances. She had used "wallingsx" three times, and her next attempt would be the third try with "sxwalling." If she didn't get the password right this time it was almost certain that the system would not let her try a fourth time.

Deliberately, Sarah keyed in *sxwalling* and *sarah-boo*. But then she erased the password and typed it again, using just her two index fingers. *I can't afford any typing mistakes now.*

It seemed to take forever, and Sarah wasn't even aware that she was holding her breath. Once more, the screen went blank, and slowly a new screen began to load. This time the red lettering was missing. Instead she saw a different word at the top of the screen. It said "Welcome." Finally, her breath came out with an audible whoosh, as she read further and saw the options for her account.

She saw the choice she wanted: "check your balance," and the next screen asked her to enter the numbers on her card. She keyed in the 16-digit card number along with the month and day shown below it and hit the enter key. There it was! "Your current balance is $9,500.00."

Immediately moving to put her body in front of that number, Sarah clicked on the "log out" icon. She certainly didn't want anyone else to see that she was carrying around that sort of money. She also did her best to clean up her tracks on the computer, deleting the history of sites that she, and everyone preceding her, had visited and clearing all cookies that might also indicate what she'd been doing. It wouldn't prevent a serious forensic team from tracing her activities, but she knew it would stop a curious librarian dead in her tracks. Now she had the information she needed about the debit card. She was ready for her next task, the final item on her list.

* * *

Day 27: Tickets

Sarah logged on to a travel site and clicked on "find flights." She selected DCA, Washington's Reagan National Airport, as her starting point and then entered Cortez, Colorado as the destination city. She didn't know if there was an airport anywhere in the vicinity. She specified the next day for departure, and a return date for Saturday, hoping that Tuesday through Saturday would be enough. She clicked on the "find flights" button and waited for the next screen. *Not again!* There was a message in red letters:

Sorry, no flights were found.

At first she thought that there might be no airport in the region, but she noticed that a three-letter code had appeared in the field for the destination city. *Weird. If there's an airport, why aren't there any flights?* A Google search, for "Cortez" and "airport" produced the information she was after.

Cortez Municipal Airport, located at 22874 CR F, Cortez, Colorado serves Cortez as well as the entire Montezuma County area. ... Great Lakes Aviation serves the community's commercial aviation needs.[*]

The link to Great Lakes Aviation sent her on another search, this time for "Essential Air Service," Sarah learned about a federal program that provided a minimum level of commercial air service to small, often remote, communities. There was a link to a list of cities that included Cortez, and it said that there was service to Denver. *All right!* She felt like yelling out a cheer. *This looks like I can do it after all.* Sarah went back to the travel site and this time entered Denver as the point of origin. She hit the enter button and watched the screen go blank before reloading the results.

When the hand fell on her shoulder Sarah almost jumped through the ceiling. She wasn't sure if her heart had actually stopped beating for a few seconds or if it had just started beating so hard that the difference made it seem that way. She turned in her chair to see the face of the librarian. "I'm sorry to disturb you ma'am, I just wanted to let you know that usually we have a 30-minute limit on these

---

[*] This description of the airport appears on the website for the city of Cortez: http://www.cityofcortez.com/government/airport.

terminals, and you've been here longer than that. But I guess since nobody's waiting, you can go ahead for a little while longer."

Sarah choked out a "thank you," and tabbed to another browser window in the hope of hiding the information on her screen from the librarian. She wondered how long the woman had been standing behind her before saying something. *Not much I can do about that. Except to hurry up and get the hell out of here.*

She went back to the other window, and the screen had refreshed to show several alternatives for her request. She selected the one that she knew would enable her to make Denver connections from Washington. To give herself ample time, she decided that an overnight in Denver would be the best way to travel on her return trip. Then she added in the Washington flights.

Tue, Dec 3 Frontier Airlines, depart Washington 9:00am, arrive Denver 11:10am

Tue, Dec 3 Great Lakes Aviation, depart Denver 2:43pm, arrive Cortez 4:03pm

Sat, Dec 7 Great Lakes Aviation, depart Cortez 4:17pm, arrive Denver 5:30pm

Sun, Dec 8 Frontier Airlines, depart Denver 7:30am, arrive Washington 12:45pm

Sarah realized that she hadn't been paying any attention to costs, but if she survived this whole adventure and got the story she expected, the *Post* would pay for everything. In the meantime, the prepaid Visa card did the job, and the computer informed her that her e-tickets were ready to go. She could check in at an automated kiosk at the airport.

One more thought occurred to Sarah. The last thing her dad had said in their phone conversation was that he'd send her an e-mail. Since everything in that entire conversation seemed to have been designed to tell her things in a way that nobody else would understand, she realized that this was one more clue in her puzzle. She had checked her regular e-mail accounts, and was no message from her dad. Suddenly, it was obvious. *He's set up a new account for me, and I'll bet anything that he used the same username and password.* There was only one question. "What service provider?"

She was confident that that it was a free e-mail service, probably Gmail or Yahoo. She decided to try Yahoo first. But when she entered the username and password, she saw the red lettering:

Invalid ID or password.

She hoped one wrong guess didn't mean much. It had taken six tries for the debit card. Still convinced that she already knew the correct username and password, she went to the Google site and selected Gmail. She entered the username and password and hit the enter button. This time, she saw the phrase, "loading sxwalling@gmail.com ..." *There it is!*

There was one message, and clearly it was from her dad, even though it wasn't from his regular account. He'd used the same style as Sarah to set up his username, *rxwalling,* and this meant that another line of safe communication might be available if she really got into trouble.

The subject line of the message was a nine-digit number with hyphens in all the right places. *It's the social security number.* She quickly copied that down in her notebook as she clicked on the message to open it.

The message was short: "You're doing great, and I'm proud of you. When you get that new phone, try 447-245-4477. love." There was no signature, but the word "love" spoke volumes to Sarah. She wrote down the phone number, closed out the Gmail screen, and signed out from the Gmail site.

Worried that the librarian would interrupt her again, Sarah did another quick cleanup of the temporary Internet files and browser history. Then she logged off the computer, made certain she had her notebook and wallet, and walked toward the door, nodding politely to the librarian as she left.

Sarah made one stop on the way home from West Virginia. At the top of the long hill on the outskirts of Romney, she pulled into a shopping center, where there was a retail outlet for a cell phone company. Having another prepaid cell phone might be an absolute necessity as she moved forward with her plans. And now that she had identification as Sarah Wallingford, she could buy another phone without having to make up stories about having lost her wallet and ID.

* * *

12

Redhouse

The first monster the Twins destroyed was Yeetso ('Big Monster'), who roamed the sacred mountain Tsoodzil (Mount Taylor) in New Mexico. One of the best ways to overcome or weaken a monster is to name it. The Navajo name for uranium is Leetso, meaning 'yellow brown' or 'yellow dirt,' after the color of the uranium-bearing ore. Tsoodzil is where the world's largest underground uranium mine would be built. Leetso, the yellow monster, was let loose in Dinè'tah, in Navajoland.

— 'Leetso,' the Yellow Monster: Uranium Mining on the Colorado Plateau[*]

Day 1: Woodrow Sorrelhorse

"I'm back, Dad. Thanks for … for watching Jackson. It's really a big help when you do things like that, when Jack isn't here."

"I'm always glad to help, Evelyn. Whatever I'm able to do."

Evelyn put the groceries away and brought the laundry into the living room so she could watch television while she was folding. The house was small. There was the kitchen and the living room, then a small hallway that led to the bathroom and two bedrooms.

---

[*] "'Leetso,' the Yellow Monster: Uranium Mining on the Colorado Plateau," MaryLynn Quartaroli, http://cpluhna.nau.edu/Change/uranium.htm.

Evelyn's father could no longer live on his own. His lungs were in bad shape. He shared a room with his grandson, Jackson.

Her father had stayed there another time, years earlier, before his illness was so severe. It was back in 2004, when Jack's reserve unit was called up to go to Iraq. Back then, long before the baby was born, the father was taking care of the daughter.

Her dad was still a big help at times. Little Jackson adored his grandfather, and if Evelyn needed to run a quick errand, he could keep an eye on Jackson for a few minutes.

A lot of the older Navajo men suffered lung disease from working in the uranium mines. Woodrow Sorrelhorse had been a vigorous man in his youth, and handsome too. Evie had photographs. But his health had gone downhill the past several years. He needed extra oxygen to breathe, and even with that he was at high risk of getting lung cancer. He had taken care of her when she was a child. Now it was her turn.

Evelyn smiled, and for a moment, she was lost in her own thoughts. "Dad, do you remember when Jack and I first met?"

"Course, I do. Your cousin Annie introduced you. And you were both so worried that he was older than you and I wouldn't approve. That man was scared half to death when he came over to our house to talk to me. To get my permission to ask you out on a date."

"Well, he was a lot older, and he'd even served in the Marines—in the first Gulf War."

"That just made him a little smarter than some of the kids your own age. Jack is a good man, Evelyn. Always has been. I knew that from the beginning."

Evelyn leaned over and gave her father a hug.

"Are you ever sorry that you didn't get to follow your dream, Evie? To go to college and everything? Your high school teacher convinced your mother and me that you could do that."

Her eyes misted slightly. "No way, Dad. How could I ever regret what I have now with my family? You, Jack, and now Jackson? There's nothing to be sorry about. And I'll still go to college. I'm just not getting there as quick as I first planned."

He nodded sadly. "I guess you're right. Jack is a good husband and a good Marine. I was worried when he first came back from Iraq, though. He was pretty messed up then."

"I remember. He was so moody and withdrawn. It was bad. But you helped him, Dad."

"Wasn't really me. He helped himself. But it sure took him a while to get ready for it."

"Yeah, almost a year, I think. He didn't trust anybody. To tell them what he was feeling."

Evelyn remembered trying to get him to go to the VA center in Farmington. "I knew they had a counselor over at the VA, but he wouldn't go. Said he couldn't talk about his problems with the other men he'd served with. That it wasn't the way a Marine handled himself. It was only after you talked to him, Dad. When you took him to the medicine man."

Woodrow Sorrelhorse reached out and took his daughter's hand. "Has he ever told you about that, Evie? About what I said to him? And what the medicine man told him?"

"No, Dad. He's always kept it to himself."

"Maybe it's time for you to know. Not the details. That would be for him to tell you. But I told him that I understood better than he thought. Jack didn't know that I'd been in Vietnam. That when I came back home, I was a lot like him. I told Jack how old Charley Goodluck had brought me to visit an old friend, a Diné medicine man, and he was able to help me. I said, 'Jack, I think it's time I did that for you.'"

"What did he say to you? The medicine man?"

"He spoke in a way that meant something to me as a Navajo. I think I still remember the exact words. 'When we leave the land and ways we know to take up a rifle and kill, we are cursed. We use tradition to remove that curse.' He said those were the words of another medicine man he knew."

"And that's what he said to Jack, too?"

"Can't say for sure what he told Jack, but I bet it was about the same. That was when Jack started learning how to talk with his fellow veterans."

"And to me, too. It was when everything started to get better. Sometimes I think we forget how important it is to rely on our traditions. I'm so glad you were there to help Jack back then. To help both of us. If I never said it before, thank you for that."

Her father simply squeezed her hand tightly. But there was a look of contentedness on his face as his eyes closed.

"You're tired, Dad. Why don't you sleep for a few minutes?"

Evelyn listened to the rhythmic sounds from the oxygen machine. She found it comforting. *Click click click ... sigh. Click*

click click ... sigh. It reminded her of the sound of the aerator in the fish tank that they had at school.

Her father said the sound made him sad. Like a roller coaster that never made it to the top of the first hill. Always a sigh of defeat.

Evelyn worked full time as a teacher's aide, and the teacher she worked with was wonderful. Jillian Sommerset. Jillian came to Farmington as part of a program called Teach for America. She was a mentor to Evelyn, and she had been encouraging when Evelyn confided that she wanted to continue her education.

Jack was supportive, too. More than once, he told Evelyn that she was a born teacher. As soon as he could make enough money, she could stop working and go to college. Now he was the foreman on the construction worksite, and his paycheck had grown. And they had the house, just across the river from Farmington, just inside the reservation. It wasn't large, but it was theirs.

Evelyn looked over at the computer on the small table, near her father's chair. It had been a surprise gift from Jack on her last birthday. She thought back to her high school biology lab, where she learned to use a microscope. She remembered the magic of looking at what she had called "the little bugs that you couldn't see at all just with your eyes." As soon as she could save up enough money, she was going to buy a microscope. She had been looking on eBay, and she knew she would be able to find a real bargain if she just kept trying.

She already had things to look at. Several months earlier, she found a posting for "microscope slides" on eBay. A collection prepared by physician way back in the 1940s. She was excited when she told Jillian about it the next day. "I put in a bid, and I got it. For only two dollars. And free shipping."

Click click click ... sigh. Click click click ... sigh. Evelyn looked up from the laundry and glanced at her father, who had awakened from his nap. She smiled at him, and he nodded back, still sleepy. Her father was one of Dr. Parker's patients now. Evelyn wasn't the only member of the family who was indebted to the physician. "Do you remember when I worked for Dr. Parker, Daddy? He was really good to me that summer. He'll help me when it comes time to go on to college."

A few minutes later, as Woodrow Sorrelhorse looked at TV, Evelyn watched Jackson climb up onto his lap.

She smiled at the scene, but then her smile turned to a frown. "Jackson, what is that in your mouth? Dad, please get that away from him. Hurry, before he cuts himself." Evelyn ran over and took the microscope slide that Jackson had put in his mouth. She was relieved to find that he hadn't cut himself. She even opened his mouth and looked inside to be sure. Then she turned to the box from her eBay purchase. She must have moved it down to the coffee table by mistake, when she was getting something off the bookshelf.

She spoke to her father, but the words were really directed toward herself. "This really isn't safe here. I'm taking this in to school tomorrow. I'm sure Jillian will let me keep it in the science storeroom for a while."

As Evelyn turned to walk back to her pile of laundry, her exasperation grew. "Dad, Please! I've said a million times that you shouldn't let Jackson put your oxygen tube in his mouth. If either one of you has any germs, the other is going to get sick too. And besides, it's just gross."

* * *

Day 16: Complications

For two days after Jackson was seen by Dr. Parker, Evelyn and Jack thought their son was getting better. But then on Thursday, Jackson's symptoms were more severe. When Jack came home from work at the end of the day, he saw it immediately. Before that, they hadn't worried. After all, Dr. Parker had said that Jackson might have a rough couple of days before he got better. But this was different. It wasn't just a rash anymore. The lesions had become really bad. There were more of them, they looked really horrible, and they were filled with pus.

"Evie, he's burning up. We've got to do something."

I know he feels bad, Jack. But remember that Dr. Parker said it would be bad for a few days before it got better. If he doesn't improve by tomorrow, I'll take him to Dr. Parker again. Remember, Jack, I've been with him all day, and my dad watched him when I needed a nap. Dad's sleeping now himself. He's been a little under the weather. When I give Jackson a bath, he feels better. And the antihistamine that he prescribed helps the poor little guy sleep. He'll get better soon. He's got to."

"I hope so Evie." Jack pulled Evelyn to him and hugged her. He held her tighter, his eyes brimming with tears. Then he turned and walked away. He would never let Evelyn see that part of him.

They took turns that night. Between lukewarm baths and the acetaminophen, they were able to keep his temperature below 103. But they knew how hard it was on Jackson. He wasn't screaming anymore, just whimpering. Jack called in sick the next morning.

It was on Friday morning, just before noon, when Jack suggested that Evelyn should wake Jackson from his latest nap. "Let's check him again now. If his fever is still up there, we have to take him back to Dr. Parker."

Evelyn stood up from her chair by the crib and leaned over. "He feels cooler, Jack. Maybe that's good." There was a pause—and then a scream of pure agony. "Jack! Jack, come quick! He's not breathing."

* * *

Day 21: Dr. Akebe

Jimmy Shepherd looked again at Ethan. He didn't like what he saw. The toddler was hot as blazes. His forehead felt like it was on fire when Jimmy touched him with the back of his hand. We've got to get him to the hospital, Stacey, and we have to do it right away. Something's really wrong. We're leaving now. I've got Emily's coat. You can put it on her in the car.

The closest hospital was just across the river, the San Juan Regional Medical Center. When they arrived at the emergency department, the first thing they encountered was red tape. It reminded Jimmy of when he was in the Army. *Hurry up and stand in line.* But this wasn't the same thing, and he had a hard time keeping his temper under control while they made copies of his driver's license and the insurance card. When the receptionist told him to have a seat, that someone would be with him shortly, he almost lost it. He could see that it was a slow afternoon, and there was nobody else in the waiting room.

He was able to avoid yelling, but only barely. "Please ma'am. My son is real sick. We thought he had chickenpox, but something's wrong now. Something real bad." Before the nurse could once again respond in the condescending voice that was making Jimmy angry, a man in a white coat walked up to the desk.

"My name is Dr. Akebe. Please tell me what your problem is." Then he saw Ethan.

Jimmy started to explain the progression of Ethan's illness over the previous several days, but Dr. Akebe interrupted him. "Please follow me. Bring your little girl, also."

"Dr. Akebe, where are you going? Exam room two is available. Dr. Akebe!"

"We are going to the Pediatric Ward. The rooms at the end of the hallway are all empty. We will be in the last room. Please ask the Director to call me on the telephone in that room. In the meantime, I want nobody to go to that group of rooms. No nurses, no laboratory technicians, no other doctors. Not unless they are at least 33 years of age. Do you understand me?"

"Dr. Akebe, what are you …?"

"Nurse, I asked you a question. Do you understand the instructions I just gave?"

"Yes Doctor, but …"

"There shall be no 'buts.' You shall do as I have instructed. Do you understand?"

"Yes, Dr. Akebe."

"Very good."

He turned to the Shepherd family. "Now if you will just follow me, please."

As instructed, Jimmy and Stacey picked up their children and followed Dr. Akebe at a brisk pace along the hospital corridors. They didn't know just what was happening, but they knew it was serious. And Jimmy recognized someone who understood the concept of command and control. When they reached the entry to the pediatric ward, the three women at the nurses' station were visibly irritated. Clearly, they had been warned by telephone of Dr. Akebe's intentions.

"I'm Carrie Castillo. I'm the head nurse in pediatrics. I was born in 1967. And I am 46 years old. And I've been here a lot longer than you have, Dr. Akebe." She pronounced it Uh Kee Bee, each syllable with attitude, hands on hips, spoiling for a fight.

Dr. Akebe didn't notice her challenge, or at least he chose not to show that he noticed. "Thank you Nurse Castillo. Would you please take this family to the last room on the corridor? Please try to make the child comfortable. He is most certainly not comfortable right now." Akebe looked at Jimmy. "The child has a high fever?"

"Yes, doctor. The last time we checked, it was up to 105. We're really scared. Please help him, doctor."

"We shall do what we can." Akebe turned to the other nurses. "Until I give you further instructions nobody other than the parents, the child, Nurse Castillo, and I are to be in that corridor." He paused to look at the nearest rooms. "An exception, please. If there are patients in any of the rooms in that corridor, you will move them immediately to rooms on the other hallway."

"But Dr. Akebe, you have no ..."

He spoke quietly, firmly, and slowly. "You will do as I said. You have no choice in this matter. And you will do it quickly, please."

The nurses were stunned. Jimmy and Stacey were even more confused about the interaction, but already their attention was elsewhere. They had to follow Dr. Akebe down the hallway."

As Jimmy and Stacey stood to one side of the bed, the nurse tried to make Ethan more comfortable. She prepared some cold compresses and gave one to each of the parents, asking them to gently put them on Ethan's body. "It will help ease the fever."

Carrie Castillo turned to Dr. Akebe. "Is there anything I can do to assist in the diagnosis, doctor?"

"Shortly, perhaps. There are other things I must do first."

The phone rang, and Dr. Akebe walked over to it. He moved the base and handset away from the bed to the corner of the room. When he answered, he turned his back on the others and spoke quietly. Stacey couldn't hear most of the conversation, picking up only a few words here and there. "… child … variola … yes, I know … I am sorry, but it is true …" Then, more clearly, he said, "Please would you get for me the main contact number, the reporting number for the CDC. They must learn of this." Then he hung up.

"Dr. Akebe," Stacey began.

Akebe held up his hand. It was less imperious than the orders to the nurses who had objected, and it wasn't an unkind gesture. But it was enough that Stacey knew she should be quiet for a while. The phone rang again, and Akebe said virtually nothing. He wrote something on a pad of paper, uttered a simple "Thank you," and hung up. Then he turned to the others and said, "I'll be in the next room. Please remain here and try to be comfortable."

Once again, Stacey tried her best to overhear. But even though Dr. Akebe was talking more loudly now, it was more difficult to hear anything from the next room. She could again make out the word "variola." It sounded familiar, and she wished she could remember what it was. Whatever was going on, she didn't like it.

At one point, Dr. Akebe raised his voice, clearly frustrated and angry. "I understand that it is not possible. What I am telling you, however, is that it has happened nevertheless. I was a child in Botswana during the outbreak in 1973, and I was in Somalia as a medical student with the WHO for the last known case in 1977. I have treated cases before. I know what it looks like. There can be no question. You must send a team at once."

When he returned to the room with the Shepherd family, Stacey decided that she would brook no further delays. "Dr. Akebe, you've got to …"

Once again, the hand went up, but this time it was conciliatory, almost deferential. "I am sorry to have been so rude to you, but there were things that were necessary. We have a serious problem. I also am very sorry to tell you that your son has smallpox."

* * *

13

Artifacts

Nearly west from us a gap opened in the high table-
lands which limit the view in that direction; that
through which the San Juan flows to its junction
with the Colorado.

—*Report of the Exploring Expedition, J. S.*
*Newberry, 1876**

Day 19: San Juan River

I‍t was late Sunday afternoon, and Greg Anniston, dressed in a
terrycloth robe, looked out at the San Juan River. *What an*
incredible weekend.

When he and Danielle had discovered that each of them needed
to be in Arizona by Monday evening, they decided to spend the
weekend together and drive to Arizona on Monday morning.
Danielle told him about a fishing lodge she had seen on a previous
trip. It was about three hours north of Albuquerque on the San Juan
River, near a place called Navajo Dam.

It was less than an hour from Farmington, where Danielle
needed to scout out possible purchases, but they would have plenty
of time for themselves. On Monday morning, they would drive west
into Arizona. Danielle said she would drop Greg off in Flagstaff

---

* J. S. Newberry, "Report of the Exploring Expedition, From Santa Fe, New
Mexico, to the Junction of the Grand and Green Rivers of the Great
Colorado of the West, in 1859," Government Printing Office, Washington,
D.C., 1876.

before continuing to Phoenix. "This will take us through some beautiful country, Greg, right through the heart of the Navajo Reservation. It's the largest Indian reservation in the United States."

They were able to reserve a cabin for two nights. It wasn't luxurious. In fact, it was a bit Spartan, but the privacy and the views made up for it. And the meals prepared by the chef at the lodge were superb. But in contrast to most of the guests who traveled great distances for the wonderful fly fishing, Greg and Danielle had other things in mind. The first thing they did on arrival was to push the two twin beds together, creating a home-made king-size bed, and they put it to good use.

Along with their extended periods in bed, they went on afternoon antiques expeditions. Danielle had been thrilled with some of the items she'd found, and Greg was in turn delighted to find that this seemed to enhance her physical appetites.

Greg turned when he heard the bathroom door open. Danielle had finished her shower, and she was toweling off. He stared at her, transfixed. She was smart, and he was enchanted by her sense of humor, but her physical nature and ease with her body astonished him. As she finished drying off, she stood there, naked, with no sign of self-consciousness. Instead, she just smiled, facing him with complete self-assurance. Her dark hair fell to her shoulders, highlighting her tall frame. Greg's gaze moved to her breasts. *Damn, they're nice.*

His eyes traveled slowly down her body. That was a long time ago now, but he thought he liked the change. Now, as he admired the exquisite female form standing in front of him, he amazed himself once again. He had thought that he was completely spent—tired, exhausted, depleted. But as he took in this visual feast, he felt himself stirring once again.

Danielle put the towel in front of her naked body again. "Why don't you hop in the shower, Greg? Get yourself all nice and clean."

* * *

Day 20: Cabin Fever

Monday morning was sunny and beautiful. Danielle drove the rented Jeep through the outskirts of Farmington. The Jeep had space for the antiques she acquired, and she felt a lot safer with a four-wheel drive vehicle. It had been in the low thirties at 8:00 a.m., and it was ready to break into the forties an hour later. The morning sun was at their backs as they traveled due west on U.S. 64, the highway following the general path of the San Juan River. Danielle had predicted that they wouldn't make any stops until they were well into Arizona, and the state line was another half hour away.

"Watch it, Danielle. That guy is driving like a lunatic." Greg had been watching the pickup truck as they gained on it, but he wasn't sure that Danielle had noticed the erratic behavior.

"Yeah, I see it. You think he's drunk or something?"

Danielle slowed almost to a stop as they came up behind the truck. It was an old, beat up Chevy, with a paint job that looked like it had been done a few square inches at a time in different shades of gray. The exhaust was acrid, and abruptly it turned to black smoke. Just as suddenly, the driver made a hard right turn from the highway onto a side road. The truck fishtailed as the driver struggled to maintain control and came to a stop by some trees on the shoulder. Danielle made the same turn, although a bit more cautiously, and pulled up behind the pickup.

"What the hell are you doing?"

"We can't just keep on going, Greg. Whatever the problem, he needs help. It doesn't matter whether it's his truck or he's drunk. It's too cold to just leave him stuck out here."

They got out of the Jeep and walked slowly up to the pickup, noticing that the driver was half slumped over the wheel. Danielle spoke first. "Can we give you some help?"

Jack Redhouse looked at Danielle but spoke to Greg. "Uh yeah, man. Yeah, thanks. Little problem here. Just bought some groceries and my truck broke down."

"Looks like we were going the same direction. Can we give you a ride home?" Greg asked.

The man's eyes were glassy, and his speech was slow. Almost like he was drunk, but not quite. "That would be a real help. My cabin is about five klicks from here." He recognized the confusion on their faces. "About three miles."

Greg looked as Danielle for guidance, and she gave an imperceptible nod. "That's not too far. We'll be glad to drive you. Army?"

"U.S. Marine Corps, sir. First Gulf War and again in Iraq. Sometimes I forget that civilians use miles."

"Either way, we can get you there. You just need to show us the way. What about your truck? You can't just leave it here."

"It won't drive anywhere by itself. Or with anyone else right now. I'll just leave the keys in it. One of my buddies will take care of it later."

"Okay, then. Let's get into the Jeep. Hand me whatever you want to bring. You said there were groceries? Danielle is driving. You want to sit up front to give directions?"

"Back seat is better. I'm real tired. Rough couple of days. Need to get some sleep. Name's Jack—Jack Redhouse. I live in Farmington, on the outskirts, but staying at my cabin just north of here. Just inside the reservation. My father built it. Good place to get away from stuff, clear your head. Know what I mean?"

Greg nodded. "Good to meet you Jack. I'm Greg. Greg Anniston." He still wasn't quite sure whether Jack was drunk, or maybe sick, or just very tired. But Danielle was right. It wasn't important. All that mattered was that they could help get Jack to his cabin safely.

Greg walked around to the passenger side of the truck and picked up the backpack that Jack had pointed to. It was beat up, old green canvas, army style. At second glance, he noticed the letters USMC. Jack saw him looking at it. "Yeah, I've been carrying that Alice pack around ever since I got out. About seven years now. Seems like a thousand years ago. It holds all kinds of stuff, and it never wears out."

He noticed the quizzical look on Greg's face. "A.L.I.C.E. Not a person. Stands for 'all-purpose something-or-other carrying equipment.' The military has abbreviations for everything."

Greg put the Alice pack in the back seat next to Jack, and they all climbed into the Jeep. Danielle asked, "Keep on going west on Route 64?"

"Yeah. Two or three miles. There's a big ridge on the right, and you turn north onto 38. That's Indian Road 38. I'm full-blooded Navajo. Sorry if I'm rambling some. I'm real tired. Feel like hell. Tough week at home. It's why I need to get away. Just a couple of days."

Forty minutes later, as Danielle slowed for a hard curve in the road, Jack pointed to left. "Over there—on the left. Head up into that dry stream bed. Cabin's a couple hundred yards back. Can't see it from here."

Following Jack's instructions, Danielle turned off the road. She drove slowly, but this was what a Jeep was designed for. After a few hundred feet she spotted the cabin, part way up a hillside. She pulled to a stop, and everyone got out. As Jack stood, his knees buckled slightly. "Whoa! A little shaky here."

Greg had grabbed the Alice pack, and he was coming around the back of the SUV when he saw Jack lean on the door to steady himself. "Looks like you could use some help, friend. Let us give you a hand." He and Danielle took positions next to Jack, draping his arms over their shoulders. Initially, it was only to steady him, but halfway up the hill, they needed to support him. The last few feet, they were virtually dragging him.

The cabin was ice cold. They got Jack into an old armchair next to the wood stove. "It's probably still burning. I just banked the fire before I went to get food. There's firewood over in the corner. A lot more stacked up out back."

Danielle wrapped Jack in a blanket, while Greg stoked the fire. Soon, it was warm and comfortable, at least near the stove where Jack was sitting. "Are you sure you're going to be okay here by yourself? You aren't looking all that well right now." Danielle sensed that she couldn't push too hard. There was something about Jack, a stubborn streak, maybe, or perhaps just a cultural difference that wouldn't allow him to accept too much help from a woman.

During the drive to the cabin, Danielle had told Jack a little about her interest in Navajo arts and crafts. She misunderstood his grunt as a sign of approval and smiled when he finally said something. "You come see me next time you're in New Mexico."

In view of Jack's condition, Danielle didn't ask him for a phone number or address. Instead, she handed him one of her business cards. "Send me a note, or give me a call. Let me know how to contact you, and I'll stop by on my next visit. But right now, you should get some rest. Can we do anything else? Maybe fix you some food?"

"No, it's okay. Really. Thank you very much. I appreciate your help. Been a real mess if I'd tried walking all the way out here. Be okay now. Probably sleep for a while. Then I'll feel a whole lot better. Couple of my buddies are meeting me up here this afternoon.

To do some hunting. There's some pretty good game out here. My rifle is over in the corner. Probably not supposed to have it. It's military style—some folks call it an assault rifle. Another souvenir from Iraq. But nobody cares anymore. It doesn't matter."

Greg and Danielle walked back down the path to the Jeep. "Do you think he'll be okay, Greg? He doesn't look so good. And he doesn't sound so good either. Part of the time he seemed to be rambling a little. And when we helped him up to the cabin, we almost had to carry him. I though he felt warm, like he was running a fever."

"Yeah. I thought so, too. Probably the flu. And some kind of a rash. I sure hope we don't get it. But he really seemed like he wanted to be alone now. And his friends are coming this afternoon. When I put more wood on the fire, I set the vents so it would burn slowly. It should last most of the day, so even if he falls asleep for a while, he'll be warm enough. If he needs to get to a doctor or something, his friends will take care of him. I'm glad they're on the way."

* * *

Day 20: Parting Ways

An hour after they left Jack at his cabin, Greg and Danielle approached the Arizona state line. As they traversed the Navajo Reservation, the scenery of the high desert was different from anything that Greg had ever seen, and ahead, in the distance, they could see the Carrizo Mountains. Off to the south, Danielle pointed to the remarkable formation jutting up from the flat plane of the desert. "Look over there. That's Shiprock."

"I thought we just passed through Shiprock."

"Yeah, the town. But this is what the town is named for. Apparently people in the last century thought it looked like a big sailing ship."

"It looks big. Maybe a couple of hundred feet high."

"More like a couple of thousand. We're too far away to get the perspective, but it's really huge. You'll just have to come out here again sometime."

He noticed she didn't say, "we." A relief, but it stung a little.

Greg recovered quickly. "It looks steep. Must be a real favorite of the rock climbers."

"It used to be. Shiprock is a sacred place. So you're not allowed to climb it anymore."

"You're a good person, Danielle. I like how you stopped to help that man before. A lot of people would have just kept on driving. I probably would have, too. Maybe it's different out here. Back home, you couldn't stop and pick up someone on the side of the road. All you hear about are robberies, knifings, shootings. Maybe it's just better out here."

"In some ways, I think it is. Maybe that's why I've gravitated to the Southwest. And why the Native American arts are so attractive to me."

"This whole weekend has been incredible for me. Going back home again is going to be a real change. I don't even know if I ..."

"Don't go there, Greg. We met by accident on Friday. We were attracted to each other. You're a good-looking guy, and we were both lonely. So we had a fantastic weekend together. And it's over. So now we're both going back to our original paths. Separate paths."

She looked over at him to be sure he was listening. "It's like Vegas, Greg. You know, that old line about what happens there stays there? I'll always remember this weekend, but when we get to

Flagstaff in a couple of hours, we'll say goodbye. I'll drive on to Phoenix, and it'll be over. It will all have been good, but it will be over."

Greg started to object. But he knew she was right.

* * *

14

Intelligence

*The 2011 plot to assassinate the Saudi Ambassador
to the United States shows that some Iranian
Officials—probably including Supreme Leader Ali
Khamenei—have changed their calculus and are
now more willing to conduct an attack in the United
States...*

—*Director of National Intelligence, 2012*[*]

Day 25: Looking for Links

"The Vice President will see you now, sir."
With authorization granted, Under Secretary Robinson Edwards stood up from the chair in the small waiting area where he had been cooling his heels for 15 minutes. *How in hell does he expect me to get my job done, if I'm sitting on my ass watching his receptionist play solitaire on her computer?* Clenching his jaw, he forced a smile and entered the inner office.

"Sit down, Edwards. What do you have for me?"

"First off, we're making progress on the origin of this outbreak. We've got good data now on all the different possibilities for domestic terrorism. We know for sure it wasn't the CDC labs in

---

[*] James R. Clapper, Director of National Intelligence, "Unclassified Statement for the Record on the Worldwide Threat Assessment of the US Intelligence Community for the Senate Select Committee on Intelligence," Jan. 31, 2012, p. 5.

Atlanta. Every sample of smallpox virus under their control is accounted for. We've got a team down there, and we've checked out every time a smallpox sample was accessed during the past 20 years. They're clean. Just to be safe, we're doing additional background checks on the half-dozen scientists who had access to those samples. But it's not going anywhere."

"What about other labs? There were other places that had access after 2001."

"There are four other highly secure labs at different locations around the country. They all have safety ratings that would let them work with smallpox, but that doesn't mean they've ever had samples of the stuff. They're all checking out clean. We're doing extra investigation at Fort Detrick, even though we're sure they're clean too. We can't look like we weren't careful, especially after the anthrax snafu there."

"So you're confirming, or as good as confirming, that we can rule out domestic terrorism for this New Mexico thing?"

"Yes, Mr. Vice President. It wasn't domestic."

"What about the Russians? If this were 25 years ago, we'd be at DEFCON-1. They're the only ones with known stores of smallpox virus."

"We remain confident that this has nothing to do with the Russians. Not with their current government. We've made inquiries on four fronts. First, we went directly to some of their top military officers. General Radisson flew over to Brussels yesterday for the NATO meeting. We knew that some of the Russian brass were going to be there, and he knows one of them pretty well, Vladimir Koznetzkii. He arranged a private conversation with Koznetzkii this morning, that was about eight hours ago. He asked if there had been any rumblings about restarting their biological weapons programs. Radisson reported back that Koznetzkii was shocked, that he was adamant that there was no such development. Radisson said he thinks this was accurate."

"I still am reluctant to trust them."

"We have other sources within the Russian military, and we put inquiries to two of them. One of them, a reliable source inside their Defense Ministry, has responded already. We asked if there was any indication that the old bioweapons programs might be reactivated. His answer was an absolute negative. He's heard nothing. Same response by our senior military attaché over in Moscow."

"You said four fronts. You've only described three."

"The fourth is the expatriate community, the guys who bailed out when it was still the Soviet Union. Most of them still have a lot of enemies back there, so there's no love lost and no reason to think they'd support an attack against the U.S. We think the expats are the best sources we have. If there were any signs that the Russians were up to something, the expats would know about it. But they confirmed everything we heard from the other three sources. There's no question, sir. The Russians are clean. At least on this one."

"So we're talking about a Middle-Eastern terrorist group. Goddamn it, Edwards! They've attacked our shores once again? And the President hasn't done a fucking thing about it. Our country can't afford another September 11. That attack almost crushed the Bush Administration. I'm not going to let a bunch of fucking ragheads take us down. This time, they're going to pay for what they've done."

The Vice President leaned in toward Edwards. His voice was quiet. "Was it Al Qaeda?"

"We don't believe so. We think this was a different group, maybe an offshoot. Directly linked to the Iranians."

Edwards noticed Richards' sharp intake of breath. The Vice President slowly exhaled through clenched teeth. "Those motherfuckers will be sorry this time. I want everything you have."

"We don't have much yet in the way of specifics. We're waiting to hear from our sources, including one agent in place. He's in Tehran. There's been a whole lot of chatter about efforts to mount a major biological weapons capability. Way too much noise in my opinion. We've got another source—we call him 'Energizer,' because he never stops giving us good stuff, just keeps going and going. He's absolutely insistent that Tehran has been working with the smallpox virus since late 2011. He even pointed to the location of the bioweapons lab. He says it's hidden inside the Research Center of their Reference Laboratories."

Edwards was convincing himself as well as the Vice President. "It's a perfect cover. They've even publicly listed bioterrorism as one of their areas of expertise. Here's an article on brucellosis written by one of their scientists. It's been weaponized before, so if they're working with brucellosis, they sure as shit could be working with smallpox."

"It's pretty goddamn clever. If anybody gets suspicious, they just say they're working on ways to prevent epidemics. They're sneaky bastards, all right. What else?"

"Here's another one. Iran partnered with a European company to bring in botulinum toxin. They say it's for cosmetic use, like Botox, but they're doing some kind of clinical trials inside Iran. They're hiding behind Botox to look legitimate, while hiding the biological warfare aspects. See what I'm getting at?"

"Keep going, Edwards."

"There are public claims that Iran has an offensive biological weapons program. Let me read you an exact quote. It's from the State Department."

> *The United States judges, based on available evidence, that Iran has an offensive biological weapons program in violation of the BWC. Iran is technically capable of producing at least rudimentary biological warheads for a variety of delivery systems, including missiles.*[†]

"We've gone soft, Edwards. Why the hell didn't we take action on Iran a long time ago? People ask for a smoking gun, and I'm seeing a whole fucking arsenal with smoke pouring out. You have any more?"

"We got a report that Iran brought in scientists from the former Soviet Union several years ago to work on things like smallpox and the plague. We were never able to confirm the earlier reports that Iran actually had smallpox, but this attack in New Mexico might be the proof."

"I don't need anything that *might* be the proof Edwards. I want *real* proof. I want information that will convince those assholes on the National Security Council when we meet again on Monday. I don't want the President to have any excuse for just sitting there with his thumb up his ass. Don't let me down."

* * *

[†] "2005 Adherence to and Compliance with Arms Control, Nonproliferation, and Disarmament Agreements and Commitments," U.S. Department of State, http://www.state.gov/t/avc/rls/rpt/51977.htm..

Day 26: Where's Sarah?

"What you have learned, Parsons?" Zaborsky was meeting with Donald Parsons, his senior field agent. Parsons was a civilian, but before signing on at DIA three years earlier, he had put in 10 years in the Army. By that time, it was clear that there would be no further promotions, and he was mustered out at the rank of Staff Sergeant.

"Nothing conclusive, Colonel. We're following up on a lead from the team in Atlanta. We've got a record of all the incoming telephone calls to the scientists who were sent out to New Mexico. There are a couple that caught our attention. One was a call taken by Andrea Mason. She's acting as receptionist down in CDC's bioterrorism offices. A call came in for a Dr. Overman, Jake Overman, who's leading the scientific team in Farmington. Andrea got suspicious when the caller wouldn't leave her name or phone number. We had the number from caller ID. When we checked it out, that's when we found out it came from the *Washington Post.*"

"It was a reporter? Shit! Who was it?"

"We weren't sure at first. The *Post* uses a switching system that assigns outgoing calls to whatever line is open. So all calls show the main number. But it put us on alert. The caller told Mason she would call Overman on his cell, but the CDC team was instructed not to bring cell phones to New Mexico. That gave us an opening. With your previous authorization, we went to the Overman's cell phone provider and asked for his phone records for the last week. It's amazing how cooperative they are when you bring up national security. Overman only had a half-dozen incoming calls that day, and we just looked for any that had come from the D.C. region. It turns out there was only one. The name is Sarah Lockford. We confirmed that she works for the *Post.* She's a reporter, all right."

"Does she know what's happening? Has she gotten past our security to reach Overman?"

"Absolutely not, sir. All the e-mail traffic to the CDC Farmington team has been rerouted to a secure server here at DOD, and I'm the only one with access to it. For the most part, it's harmless, but we're sitting on it in any case. I've released a few messages from their coworkers in Atlanta. Otherwise, we're just letting them stay blocked. One of those messages was one from the Lockford woman. It didn't say anything, just that she wanted to talk to him. That was when we decided to take a closer look at her."

"What did you find out? I don't like this, Parsons."

"Well, she's definitely nosy. She's written a couple of articles on government misconduct in the medical field. So it makes sense that she'd be talking to a scientist from CDC. But she may know too much already. Just knowing that Overman works in terrorism response might make her too curious about why he's gone. So we did some more checking. On Friday, I went over to the newspaper, and I talked with her boss."

"That was stupid! Now they know that we're interested."

"No sir, Colonel Zaborsky. I sort of hinted that I was from the FBI. You know people never look real close at our federal badges. And her boss didn't even ask for my photo ID, so it was even easier. Even if she asked, I would have shown her the fake ID I have for the Federal Investigative Services. People hear that, they just think FBI. So if they ever go looking for Special Agent Joseph Silver, they won't find him. Not here, and not at the FBI."

"All right ... did you learn anything?"

"Not from the boss, except that Lockford was out of town for the weekend. So we put a couple of guys out to watch her apartment. And we also managed to get the cooperation of the phone company. They're giving us daily updates on the phone numbers she's called or that have called her. Next thing we found was that she'd called a guy at Emory University. That's in Atlanta, right near CDC. Guy's name is Evans, and it turns out he's another scientist who studies infectious diseases. That's maybe just a coincidence."

"No such thing as a coincidence, Parsons. Have you questioned this guy, Evans? Or listened to his phone?"

"Not yet. So far, it's just suspicions, so we'd never get a warrant for an actual tap. But we do know Lockford went to Florida. Flew through Atlanta, but only to change planes. So she didn't meet Evans. We had a team watching his house for a while. Here's something, though. He shares the house with Overman."

"With Overman? They're a couple??"

"No sir. Overman just rents out his guest room. The other guy just moved to Atlanta and needed a place to live. We're pretty sure that Lockford is Overman's girlfriend, or at least she used to be. But we did check it out his preferences, just to be sure."

"And ...?"

"Seems like he's been screwing one of the secretaries at CDC on and off for the last year. So he isn't a queer. The secretary started blabbing to Andrea, told her that Overman was a real pussy hound.

Anyway, the head of security at Emory used to work here in DIA, and he told Evans to stop talking with the reporter. Made up some story to keep Evans from getting suspicious."

"Then where do we stand? Is this taken care of? The reporter, I mean?"

"Not yet, Colonel. We confirmed that she'd gone to Florida. The Transportation Security Administration people were real cooperative when we said we needed to check the passenger lists. Then we made a quick visit to her apartment."

"You broke in?"

"Not exactly, sir. Let's just say that she wasn't there to invite us in. But we got to look around, and we checked her computer pretty good. We made a copy of her hard drive. Same thing with an external hard drive. Some of it was encrypted, but we were able to break through that fairly easily. So far, it doesn't look like there's anything there that we'd be interested in. Some stuff about the FDA, but nothing we'd care about. Here's something interesting, though. We could tell that she was looking at a website called HealthMap. It lets you check outbreaks of diseases all around the world. She was looking at chickenpox."

Zaborsky interrupted. "That's what our people told the locals out in Farmington. They still don't know that they're dealing with smallpox. It sounds like this reporter was talking to someone in New Mexico."

"Maybe then, but not anymore. Not since we shut down the communications on Thursday. We also took action on that website. We told them the data on chickenpox was all fictitious, that it was part of our 'training exercise.' So they took it off the website. All we did was suggest that cooperation could be real important for their next grant applications."

"So the reporter is under control?"

"Yes sir. We're still keeping an eye on her. Just a couple of men, but we'll notice if she tries anything funny. If necessary, one of our people could always stop by and have a nice chat with her."

* * *

15

Sarah

F.B.I. officials said the incident came to light as part of the continuing review by the Justice Department inspector general's office into the bureau's improper collection of telephone records through 'emergency' records demands issued to phone providers. The records were apparently sought as part of a terrorism investigation, but the F.B.I. did not explain what was being investigated or why the reporters' phone records were considered relevant.

—New York Times, 2008[*]

Day 27: Preparations

Driving back toward D.C., Sarah began planning her trip to Four Corners. Once she reached Cortez, Colorado, she'd need help from Jillian's friends, but first she wanted to talk to her father. Remembering what he'd said about tracing cell phones, she decided not to create a link to West Virginia. Even with an anonymous cell phone, it would be better to wait until she was closer to home.

An hour later, she exited the interstate just outside the Washington Beltway and pulled into a strip mall. She parked the car near an electronics store that her father had shown her years ago.

---

[*] "F.B.I. Says It Obtained Reporters' Phone Records," *New York Times*, Aug. 9, 2008, p. A15.

After looking in her notebook, she turned on the cell phone she had just purchased and dialed the number her father had sent by e-mail.

He answered on the third ring. "Hi Sarah," he said in a voice that seemed tired or maybe just worried. "Are you okay?"

"Yeah, I'm fine Dad. But things sure have gotten a little crazy around here. As far as I can tell, it's all about this story that I'm working on."

"Don't tell me any more about it. The less I know, the safer you'll be. Look, I really meant it when I said I was proud of you. You figured out the key steps after our last conversation. But now, you're pretty much on your own."

"I think I know what to do, Dad, but I'm a little nervous about it. How did you know that I was going to need all these things in the first place?"

"I didn't know. Mostly it was left over from ..." He paused before finishing, "... from when I was traveling a lot. Just in case of emergency."

"I think I understand. Maybe sometime soon you can fill me in on the last 30 years."

"Yeah, I guess it's time. Sorry if it took you by surprise. I suspect you've already figured out a lot of it. Look Sarah, I really can't say much right now. Are you using a phone that can't be traced?"

"Absolutely, I just got it at ..."

"Don't give any details. You may want to completely avoid using your own phone for a while. Remember, your phone records will show all the people you've talked with, so that would link them with each other. Even more important, whenever you use it, the records will show where you were at the time. I'll keep this phone, so you can reach me in a real emergency. But remember, I'm not as young as I used to be, and it's only little kids whose dads are superheroes. The rest of us are just regular mortals. Stay safe Sarah, I love you."

"Love you too, Dad." The line went dead.

Following her father's advice, Sarah took out her old cell phone, the one that was listed in her real name, and removed a panel on the back. She found the SIM card and removed it. After fitting the rear panel back onto the phone, she put both the phone and the SIM card into her backpack. Then she got out of the car and walked toward the electronics store.

"May I help you?"

Sarah explained what she was looking for, and several minutes later, she departed with a hand-held shortwave radio. The debit card was now worth about $500 less than it had been, but the salesman had given her a huge discount because it was returned merchandise. The salesman had given her a thorough demonstration and had thrown in some spare batteries.

She put the radio in one of the side pockets of the backpack and removed about a thousand dollars in cash from the packet of bills, a mix of denominations. There was one more stop to make. She wanted to go to a store that sold outdoor gear. At the outfitters, Sarah selected a few pairs of hiking socks and a lightweight water-resistant jacket and pants. Walking through the camping and hiking section, she saw something else that might be valuable. It was time to add GPS to her bag of tricks.

By the time Sarah had cleared the checkout counter, she had spent most the thousand dollars. The salesclerk seemed surprised that that someone would pay in cash, but Sarah just explained that she'd been putting aside a little bit every payday for the last year to get ready for a holiday hiking trip. Everyone who worked in the store seemed to approve heartily of hiking trips, so nobody gave her explanation a second thought.

* * *

Day 27: Heading West

Sarah made one final stop to fill Eric's gas tank. Then she started thinking about surveillance. There was no concrete evidence that she was being watched, but there was also no question that someone had searched her apartment while she was in Florida. As she approached her neighborhood, she once again donned her baseball cap, put on her sunglasses, and pulled up the collar on her jacket.

The overhead door at the garage entrance had closed again by the time the car reached the bottom of the ramp. As expected, Eric's space was empty, and Sarah tossed the plastic bag of trash from West Virginia into a nearby trash bin. Then she removed the backpack from beneath the seat, picked up the shopping bag with her latest purchases, and headed to the elevator.

As the elevator door opened to the 12th floor, Eric Murphy was just leaving his apartment. "Hey Eric. Here's your key. Thank you so much for lending me the car. I never saw that jerk once, so maybe he's decided to find someone else to chase after."

"No problem, Sarah. Always glad to help. Let me go get the key for your Accord."

"I've got my spare key, and you look like you're on your way out. You can give it to me later."

"You going camping?"

"Huh?" Sarah looked down at the label on her shopping bag. "Oh yeah, but not camping. I was going to do a little biking. Take a few days off after working all weekend. The weather has been so nice, I thought I might get on the trails and just ride out into the Virginia countryside. Maybe stay at a bed and breakfast." Once again, she was surprised at how easily lies flowed off her tongue.

"Sounds like fun. Enjoy yourself, and I'll probably see you later in the week. Be careful!"

"I will, Eric. Thanks again."

Sarah went into her apartment and started packing. Her large backpack was perfect for the trip. Everything she might need would fit in it. For carry-on luggage, a smaller backpack would hold all her electronic gear. She packed her laptop, GPS, cell phones, and handheld radio, along with her wallet and extra cash.

By late afternoon, Sarah was ready to go. She wanted to be really careful now about leaving tracks, or not leaving them, depending on her goal. Two of her three cell phones were in her large backpack, the one she had purchased at National Airport as well as her original cell phone. She didn't want to use the original phone at all, not unless it became necessary to resurface under her true identity, and the one that had been purchased by "Jennifer James" had to be saved for a real emergency. The third cell phone, Sarah Wallingford's, had only been used to call her father so far, and she would be careful if she had to use it. It was important to minimize the possibility that anyone could make a connection between the two identities—Sarah Wallingford, who would be flying west in the morning, and Sarah Lockford, who was going off on a bike trip.

Sarah booted up her desktop computer logged onto her e-mail account at the *Post*. There were a half-dozen messages, but nothing of real significance. She composed a message to Sue Parkinson saying that she was tired from working all weekend and was taking a few days off to go biking.

She needed to make contact with Jillian, and radio seemed to be the only option. But they had made no arrangements for a follow-up conversation. Maybe Elmer would still be monitoring the same frequency. It was really the only hope. Sarah wasn't sure her new radio had enough range, so she turned on the old Emerson set and set the transmitter to 9,030 kHz. She was glad it wasn't digital. Even if someone had noticed the transceiver, she had turned the dial, so there was no record of the frequency she had last used. To reduce the risk of identification, she violated the rules by not using her call sign. "This is Sarah calling Jillian. This is Sarah calling Jillian." There was no response. She waited five minutes and tried again, "This is Sarah calling Jillian. This is Sarah calling Jillian." Still nothing.

Sarah waited another 15 minutes, growing more nervous with each second. Then she tried again. "This is Sarah calling Jillian. This is Sarah calling Jillian."

She jumped when the set spoke back to her. "Sarah this is Elmer." It was the same voice as the last time.

"Elmer, we need to make this quick. Please tell Jillian I'm going to visit Mr. Cortez tomorrow. Tell him I'll call at 4:30. Do you copy?"

"I copy. Tomorrow. 4:30."

"Thank you. Over and out." Sarah heard nothing more, and she turned off her transmitter. The whole exchange had taken less than 30 seconds, and she hoped that was too short a time for anyone to pick up the transmissions. She also hoped that Elmer and Jillian would understand what she meant. It wasn't "Mr. Cortez" she was visiting but Cortez, Colorado, where she hoped she would find Raymond Morgan. She had a telephone number, and she hoped he'd be ready for the call.

Sarah was exhausted and hungry, but she didn't want to run the risk of leaving the apartment. The same people could break in again. So she used her regular telephone to call a local restaurant that delivered. After a quick dinner, she thought about her early flight in the morning.

* * *

Day 28: D.C. to Colorado

Sarah awoke to her alarm at 5:30. It was still dark. She showered, made a quick cup of coffee, and dressed. A final check reassured her that she had everything. She hefted the large pack onto her back, picked up the small pack, and headed for the parking garage.

She did not go to her car and went instead to the far side of the garage where her bicycle was stored. She unlocked it and attached the lock to the frame. She attached the smaller pack to the rack on the back of the bike, securing it carefully with an extra bungee cord. Then she walked the bike to the exit door and swiped her access card. Mounting the bike, she rode quickly out of the garage, looking carefully for traffic. There didn't seem to be anyone watching. Just like her last ride, she headed for Key Bridge but turned off at the last minute to cross over the George Washington Parkway. She rode hard on the Mount Vernon trail, reaching the airport in about 15 minutes. But this time she kept going. She didn't want any trace of Sarah Lockford at Reagan National.

Rounding one of the curves in the bike path on the side of the airport, Sarah she saw a burly man stopped on the trail ahead, straddling his bicycle. He held up his hand as a signal to stop. She recognized the uniform. Police frequently patrolled the paths on bicycles. *They know! They were watching me!*

She looked around, desperately searching for a possible escape route. But there was no place to turn, no place to go. If she kept riding or tried to run away, the cop would certainly be able to catch her. She had all the extra weight of her backpack. Silently cursing herself for being incautious, Sarah braked and came to a stop as she approached the officer.

"Excuse me, Miss. Do you know how the best way to get to the Washington Monument from here? I think I got myself a little turned around."

He's not a cop! His warm-up jacket was almost the same color as the uniforms that the park police used, but he was just another rider out for a morning of sightseeing.

Sarah pointed back in the direction from which she had come. "Just keep following the path around the airport. In about a mile, you'll come to the 14th Street Bridge. There's a bike path on the last span, just after you pass under the bridge. That'll take you right to the monuments. Have a good one!"

Breathing hard, but not from physical exertion, Sarah got back on her bike and continued riding. *I only lost a couple of minutes. No problem. Damn! I'm really getting paranoid.*

At the south end of the airport, where the bike path crossed Four Mile Run, Sarah veered off onto another path that went underneath the parkway. She followed this trail through a heavy industrial area that looked like a water treatment plant. After another half mile she exited the path and used local streets to ride to the Crystal City Metro station, where she locked her Cannondale to one of the station's bike racks. Using cash to buy a new farecard, she caught the next train to the airport.

As she stepped off the train at Reagan National, Sarah once again put on a baseball cap. Not exactly a disguise, but it would make it more difficult for anyone to recognize her from a distance or from a routine airport surveillance photo. She checked in at one of the electronic kiosks and then handed her large backpack to an airline employee. "Looks like you're going hiking. "I hope you find someplace without too much snow."

"Me too," replied Sarah. "My first stop is Colorado, but California should be a little warmer."

"I hope so. Have a nice flight."

Sarah tried to calm her nerves as she approached the security checkpoint. She had been careful not to bring too much of the cash with her, not wanting to do anything suspicious. Almost half of the money was still in the file cabinet in West Virginia, and she'd also left $3,000 in her apartment. It was on top of the frozen spaghetti sauce in a half-full plastic container in her freezer. When she added up all her funds, she was traveling with about $6,000 in cash. Some of it was in her wallet, and the rest was in one of the zippered pockets of her small carry-on backpack.

Reassuring herself that her identification wasn't fake, just different, Sarah Wallingford presented her boarding pass and Virginia driver's license to the security guard. He smiled, scribbled an approval mark on the boarding pass, and pointed to one of the screening counters. She unlaced her boots and put them into a plastic tray. The laptop went into a separate tray. The screener gave her a momentary scare when he backed up the conveyor belt for a second look, but then the belt resumed its normal forward progress. Sarah was waved through the security scanner, and she began to retrieve her items from the plastic trays.

"Excuse me, Miss. Is that your backpack?"

Sarah nodded, fighting back a wave of nausea. *Stay calm! Maybe it's nothing.*

"Could we take a look at this please?"

She forced herself to answer. "Of course."

"We just need to check it out. There seem to be a few electronic devices in here, and we didn't recognize one of them."

He opened the main compartment, where Sarah had placed the GPS, the cell phone that that was purchased in Romney, and the radio. One at a time, each of them was placed on the counter. The agent picked up the cell phone, turned it over, and put it back into the backpack. Then he picked up the GPS.

"Could you turn this on for me?"

Sarah did as requested, and after a few seconds the screen lit up with its standard message.

"That's fine, ma'am. Thank you. You can turn it off and put it away." He handed it back to her and reached for the radio. "Now just what do we have here?"

"It's just a radio. It's a standard ..."

"Would you turn it on for me, please?" He watched her carefully as she powered up the device. It only took a second or two.

"Do you want me to scan for a signal or something?"

"Please. I need to verify that it really is a radio."

The unit squawked with some local construction traffic, and the screener extended his hand. "Sounds about right. One last thing, though. Would you please turn it off and remove the batteries?"

Sarah did as requested and then handed him the unit. He examined the battery compartment and the frown on his face slowly changed to a smile. "I guess we're okay here, ma'am. We just have to be careful. I hope you understand."

Before Sarah could answer, he spoke again. "I'd suggest you leave these batteries out of the device for now, all right? We don't want anybody thinking that you might try to use the radio during your flight."

"Yes sir. Sorry to cause you any worry."

"Have a good flight, ma'am." The screener turned to go back to his station.

Sarah reached clumsily to gather her other belongings and bent down to put her boots back on. Her legs felt unsteady. *God almighty,*

I hope I don't have to go through that again. I'm sure as hell not going to leave the security area while I'm in Denver.

Sarah relaxed for the first half hour of the flight, and then she pulled out her new GPS and used the laptop to load maps from the CD that came with the unit. By the time the flight crew made the announcement to turn off all electronic devices, she was satisfied that the GPS was ready to go.

In Denver, Sarah had almost three hours before her flight to Cortez. She saw a notice that the airport had free Wi-Fi access, and found a seat in a quiet area. She booted up the laptop, plugging it into an available outlet so that its battery would retain a full charge. Just as she was about to log on to the Wi-Fi system, she realized it would create a link to the location of the laptop. The longer she could wait before risking that sort of exposure, the better off she would be.

Another prepaid cell phone was her next priority. She spotted what she wanted at a small kiosk and asked if it would be possible to get two prepaid phones. "So my mother and I will have the same capability."

"No problem as long as you use your own ID for both phones."

Five minutes later, Sarah—Sarah Wallingford—was now walking back to her gate with another two prepaid cell phones. She was carrying three cell phones, the GPS, and her handheld radio. Two more cell phones were in her checked baggage. *I'd never make it through another security check with all this shit.*

Sarah stopped to get some lunch and then found another part of the concourse that was fairly quiet. She spent the next hour familiarizing herself with the radio. Then she walked to the gate for her next flight.

The flight to Cortez had only eight passengers, and it was only half full. The seats were cramped, but breathtaking views made the 80-minute flight pass quickly.

The plane landed at Cortez Municipal Airport on time just after 4:00 p.m., and after taxiing for several minutes they pulled up at the terminal building. Sarah had noticed the single landing strip and the small terminal building that appeared just large enough to serve the several flights that arrived and departed each day. *Damn! This is one small airport.*

After just a few minutes, the luggage had been removed from the aircraft's hold, and Sarah hefted her large backpack over one shoulder as she surveyed the scene. The sun was low in the sky, and it was clear that it would soon be getting dark. She needed to make contact with Raymond Morgan.

"You need a ride to town, ma'am?" Sarah turned in response to the voice behind her and saw a pleasant looking man, dressed in the neat but casual style that she would come to think of as typical for the region. The airport was several miles south of the city, a very small city with a population of about 7,000, and she hadn't seen any taxicabs. Maybe some of the locals just provided taxi service with their own cars.

She didn't want to be rude, but she wanted to try reaching Raymond Morgan as a first step. "Thank you, but I think a friend is going to meet me. If I can't reach him, I'd really appreciate your help."

He smiled politely and nodded, while touching his right hand to the brim of his hat in a salute. Sarah turned away and walked a few steps to a chair near the side of the terminal. She set down her large pack and removed a cell phone from her small pack. It was the one she bought in West Virginia. The two from the Denver airport were being held in reserve. She opened her notebook and quickly found the phone number that Elmer had given her for Raymond Morgan, not at all sure at this point whether that was his actual name or might even be another name for Elmer. She dialed, and almost immediately a voice said "Hello."

It was only one word, but the voice sounded familiar. "Yes, hello. I'm trying to reach Raymond Morgan."

"Yes ma'am," said the voice. "I told you I could drive you into town."

Sarah nearly dropped the phone, but she turned and looked across the room to see the same man in the cowboy hat smiling broadly at her. Once again, he saluted her by touching the brim of his hat, and he walked over to her in a few long strides. "Sorry if I startled you just then. Our friends told me you were arriving this afternoon, so I just took a chance on meeting the plane. You match the description pretty well, and besides, not too many women come here all by themselves."

Despite her embarrassment—he had, after all, played a joke on her—Sarah was tremendously relieved to have made contact with Morgan. "You are Raymond Morgan?"

"Yes ma'am, and Raymond will do just fine. Why don't we talk more while we're driving." He reached for her large backpack. "Let me help you with that."

Sarah followed Morgan out of the terminal building to a somewhat beat-up pickup truck and lifted her pack into the cargo bed. He motioned her to the passenger side, and they climbed into the cab. Some of Sarah's surprise must have shown in her face, because Morgan said "It's a '75 F150. That was the first year Ford made that model. Out here we don't buy a new truck every year, but we sure do learn how to keep them running. And this one has been humming like a top since I got it in '92, when I got back from the first Gulf War."

Embarrassed once again, Sarah started to answer. "Look, I didn't mean to ... I mean I ..."

"That's okay, ma'am. It's just that most folks from the East don't have a real good understanding of how we live out here. Putting food on the table is a whole lot more important to us than what kind of car we drive."

"Okay," said Sarah firmly. "First off, I'm sorry if I offended you. I sure didn't mean to. And second, if you expect me to call you Raymond, then knock off this ma'am stuff. It's Sarah."

"Well, I reckon you got me there." He chuckled softly as he spoke again. "Fair enough. And I like your style. You seem pretty tough, and that's gonna be real important the next few days."

"Two things before we go any further: Are you going to help me get to my friend Jillian? And what do you know about what's going on?"

"That'll take some time ma'am—I mean Sarah. There's a lot to tell you. Why don't we head back to my house now? My wife is making a nice dinner, and we can talk about everything when we get there. But the answer is yes. We'll help you get to your friend. For tonight, my wife has fixed up a bed for you, so you'll be able to get a good night's sleep. You'll need it before we leave early tomorrow morning."

Morgan's home was on the outskirts of Cortez, and the drive over some rough roads took a half hour. During that time he told Sarah about his background. "I'm a Navajo, but the area around here is mostly associated with the Ute tribe. The Southern Ute and Ute Mountain Reservations make up the northern part of what people call the Four Corners.

"I always thought that it was the Navajo Reservation. It's what my friend Jillian told me about the school where she teaches."

"Most people do think of the Navajo Reservation when they talk about the Four Corners. It's larger than the Ute Reservations, maybe

10 or 15 times larger. And there's an even bigger difference in population. The Navajo Nation—that's what we call it—has a total population of more than 170,000. Almost a hundred times the number of Utes. And that's just the people living in the Tribal areas.

"I had no idea. This is mostly in New Mexico?"

"Actually, no. The biggest part of the Navajo Reservation is in Arizona. But San Juan County, where Farmington is, has a couple thousand square miles inside the reservation boundaries. The population is probably close to 30,000, and Farmington is the only city in the region. So you can see why people think of Navajos when they talk about the Four Corners."

"But Farmington isn't actually inside the reservation, is it?"

"No, it's not. But it's right on the edge. There's always a lot of tension between the communities. People who aren't from around here don't understand that this is our land. We get along pretty well with folks from the outside, but we sure don't like to get pushed around."

A few minutes earlier, they had left the highway and turned east on Road H, a bumpy dirt track that seemed to lead into remote wilderness. Now Morgan slowed and pulled into a cleared area.

In the light of a nearly full moon low in the sky, Sarah saw a small, well-kept ranch-style house. Next to it was a stand of small trees, but otherwise, there was no vegetation, with the dirt, rocks, and sand stretching endlessly to the distant mountains.

Raymond turned off the engine. "This is my home. Please come in."

* * *

16

National Security Council

We'll never use the damn germs, so what good is
biological warfare as a deterrent? If somebody uses
germs on us, we'll nuke 'em.

—*Richard Nixon**

Day 27: Counterintelligence

"Please record that I have called the meeting to order. Is everyone here?"

"Yes, Mr. President."

James Fallon Alexander cleared his throat and looked around the room before he proceeded in a somber voice. "We have a single topic on our agenda today, and it is perhaps the most consequential issue that any of us shall face in our lifetimes. It has now been five days since we first received confirmation of the smallpox outbreak in New Mexico. Following on the initial efforts of the Department of Defense, I have decided that this situation shall remain absolutely secret."

The Vice President glanced at the Secretary of Defense. He might have smiled, but nobody else noticed.

"We cannot risk a national panic. Nor can we allow our adversaries to learn what we have discovered. Everything we discuss

---

* "Iraq's Ton of Germs," William Safire, Essay, *New York Times*, April 13, 1995.

here will remain classified at the highest levels. Not even the senior members of your respective departments and agencies are to be told without explicit authorization from me or Vice President Richards. If anyone inquires about what is happening in New Mexico, we will advise that a biodefense training exercise is being held. That should suffice to keep things quiet for another week or so."

The Secretary of State caught the eye of the Director of National Intelligence. If there was a frown, he was the only one in the room who saw it.

"The primary challenge we now face is to decide what response, if any, we shall undertake against those with whom responsibility for the outbreak lies. If, in fact, the outbreak resulted from an intentional attack against our country ... If it was an act of biological warfare, we are facing the gravest of crises. Our options are extremely broad, as are the responsibilities we bear on behalf of all American citizens. We could no more neglect such an act of war than could our predecessors have failed to respond at the time of Pearl Harbor."

The President's National Security Advisor was watching the Vice President, and he thought he had seen a trace of a smile.

"Within that context, however, we must act responsibly. To facilitate the process, I am asking Vice President Richards to lead our discussions. I shall retain the ultimate responsibility, but I do not want my role limited to that of an impartial moderator of the debate. I shall expect those of you at the table, and those of you who are here to assist the principals, to provide all the necessary evidence. I shall not be rushed to judgment. Nor shall I be deterred from the proper exercise of my responsibilities to protect the people of our great nation."

"Mr. President?"

"Just a moment, Parker. As of now, I'm turning the meeting over to the Vice President." He nodded at Richards, who in turn signaled his recognition of T. Parker Cunningham.

The President's National Security Advisor looked nervously at the individuals seated around the table. He understood full well what was about to happen, and he would not allow his boss to be rushed into a bad decision that could affect, or even end, the lives of millions of people. "Mr. President, Mr. Vice President—I want to emphasize that as of now, we have no evidence to indicate that the outbreak resulted from hostile action. The fact is, we really don't know what happened—nor do we know how it happened. So I urge all of us here to move cautiously before we call this an attack. The simple truth is that we just don't know yet."

The Vice President realized for the first time that he had been outflanked by the President. Richards was in charge of the discussions, but he had been marginalized in the process. He was no longer free to railroad the actions he desperately wanted the NSC to approve. Richards hadn't seen it coming, and now the opening salvo—a call for moderation—had been fired by the other side.

Richards stared wordlessly at Cunningham, the expression on his face unchanged. Only the National Security Advisor recognized the look of hatred. The Vice President glanced casually at others whom he viewed as the opposition—threats to the strength and power of the United States of America. *A bunch of fucking pansies.* He was looking at the Secretary of State, the Director of National Intelligence, and the President's Chief of Staff.

The opening shots had been fired. It was time to launch the counterattack. Richards looked at the several hands that had been raised politely and motioned to the Secretary of Defense. The Vice President knew that Quentin Walker could be trusted to support the positions they had previously discussed. He only hoped that Walker would be able to present them with adequate logic and passion. He had his doubts.

"Mr. President, Mr. Vice President—may I remind our esteemed group of colleagues of a longstanding policy of our country? I'm looking here at a document put out by the Centers for Disease Control. I mention that so that everyone is clear that we're not talking about a DoD policy. It's called the Smallpox Response Plan and Guidelines. Here in the executive summary, it says the following:

A single case of smallpox is likely to represent a bioterrorism release and will require an immediate and coordinated public health, medical, and law enforcement response to control the outbreak and to protect the public from any additional release.[†]

"So I don't think that there can be any question. The established policy of our country is that the disease has been eradicated. It can

[†] "Executive Summary, Smallpox Response Plan and Guidelines,"(Version 3.0), http://www.bt.cdc.gov/agent/smallpox/response-plan/files/exec-sections-i-vi.pdf.

no longer occur as the result of natural causes. If someone is infected by smallpox, it is America's policy that we view it as resulting from an act of terrorism—by definition. We shouldn't be looking for excuses to avoid our duty as leaders of this country. We've got to accept as fact that we've been attacked by terrorists, and we have to formulate our plans to respond accordingly. I do agree with the National Security Advisor that there are certain things that we don't know yet. But we've got to proceed on the basis that we were attacked by terrorists. What we don't know yet for sure is who attacked us. And we're working on that as we speak here."

"Thank you Secretary Walker." The Vice President was relieved by Walker's brief presentation. It wasn't eloquent, but he used established policy instead of personal opinions and emotions. Established policy could not be easily dismissed.

The Secretary of State had signaled that she wished to speak in response. Richards had no desire to hear what she had to say, but he knew that he couldn't ignore her. There had to be an appearance of fairness if his plans were to move forward.

"Mr. President, I respectfully suggest that we act cautiously and judiciously here. The real issue is what response the United States is going to take. We must use the utmost restraint to ensure that we don't take retaliatory measures against another country without clear and unambiguous evidence that the government in question was responsible for the outbreak in New Mexico."

Gotcha, bitch! Only with considerable difficulty was the Vice President was able to hide the smirk that attempted to cross his face. He had no love for Caroline Calebresi. In fact, he disliked her intensely. The Secretary of State had fallen into his trap, just as he had hoped she would. He knew that she was a traditional dove, that her first priority would be to avoid military conflict. And precisely because she was so focused on that goal, she had accidentally undermined the position taken by her ally Parker Cunningham.

The President's National Security Advisor had argued that there was no proof that the smallpox outbreak was actually the result of a hostile action. Secretary Calebresi had focused too closely on the possibility of a military response—so closely that she had tacitly accepted the origin of the smallpox outbreak as a terrorist attack.

"Mr. Morrison—you have a comment?" The Vice President invited the President's Intelligence Advisor, the Director of National Intelligence, to speak, hoping fervently that Morrison would continue along the pathway initiated by Calebresi.

"Yes, thank you Mr. Vice President. Mr. President, as you noted so powerfully at the start of this meeting, we are in the midst of a grave crisis. I feel compelled to reiterate Secretary Calebresi's recommendation for caution. We must be extraordinarily careful to avoid a premature response. The world will be watching us very closely when we act, and we cannot make mistakes."

Beautiful. Richards forced himself to stifle a sneer. *How did these dumb fucks ever get to positions at such a high level? Not only did Morrison support the position that we'll need to undertake military action, he implied that all we need to do is clearly identify the target.*

The DNI continued, "To avoid international embarrassment—or, more accurately, international condemnation—we must first have good intelligence. It needs to be rock-solid, not just a good guess. We cannot afford to go forward on the basis of another 'slam dunk' here."

"Just what have you been able to learn from our intelligence agencies, Mr. Morrison?" The Vice President knew the answer, but he intended to establish just where the real expertise resided among those seated at the table.

"So far, we really don't have that much Mr. Vice President. Since it was agreed that this entire situation would remain under wraps, we haven't been able to go out with specific queries on smallpox. Under the guise of background work on the next Review Conference for the Biological Weapons Convention, we've been asking about any weapons programs or other violations. So far, we've heard nothing, so whoever it is that's been working on smallpox is pretty good at keeping secrets. We've also been looking very carefully at intercepted electronic communications, particularly e-mail."

Nodding to Quentin Walker to acknowledge the role of the Defense Department, Morrison continued. "We have a team at the National Security Agency that we've cleared for this operation. They're looking for anything about smallpox. Anything, anywhere. And as you know, on Friday the President authorized the NSA and our other national security agencies to extend their normal activities to domestic surveillance as well. Unfortunately, our team has reported no hits yet."

"Does this absence of any information suggest that this attack might have been carried out by a non-state actor?" National Security issues weren't in the normal realm of Treasury Secretary E. J.

Salcines, but heads around the table nodded at his perceptive question.

"You raise a good point," Morrison said. "Al Qaeda and its spin-offs, for example, have shown remarkable discipline in their ability to minimize communications traffic before a terrorist attack. But we don't think that this is likely here. Strictly speaking, any smallpox sample must have originated in what once was the Soviet Union, so that means Russia and the various former Soviet Republics. And, of course, we have to include second-generation countries that might have inherited biological materials after the collapse of the Soviet Union."

"You're saying it wasn't a terrorist group?"

"Even the most radical of the regimes in question would never be so foolish as to provide smallpox to terrorists. Those groups have a well-established pattern of changing their minds about just who they think the enemy is. Everything we've learned from across the entire intelligence and diplomatic landscape …" Morrison glanced over to see a reassuring signal from the Secretary of State. "Everything points to a rogue state. Someone with a terrorist background may have assisted, but there can be no doubt that the attack was planned and executed by a national government."

"Then this is getting simpler if not easier." The Vice President was trying to steer the conversation. "It's becoming clear from remarks all around the table that we need to identify the perpetrator of this cowardly attack on our citizens. Secretary Walker, the DoD has been working closely with the CDC. Do you have any updates?" The question was part of a set piece, and Richards knew exactly how the Secretary of Defense would respond. They had practiced the exchange beforehand.

"Yes, I do, Mr. Vice President. Mr. President, with your indulgence, I'd like the Under Secretary for Intelligence to report to this group. It's my understanding that he has some information that he has not even been able to brief me on as of yet."

Robinson Edwards stood up from his chair at the side of the room and walked toward the table where Secretary Walker pointed to an empty seat. He described all the small pieces of evidence that he and his team had collected, not mentioning that they'd had much of it for several days. He, Walker, and Richards had agreed beforehand that they would present this entire package as if it were newly acquired information. There was no need for the Director of

National Intelligence to learn that the DIA had been withholding virtually all its information from him.

When Edwards finished, he turned to Walker. Once again, the conversation had been rehearsed. Walker looked over to Richards at the end of the table. "Mr. Vice President. We still expect to obtain additional information. But this is what Under Secretary Edwards was able to describe to me on the short car trip over here. Everything we have—absolutely everything—points to Iran."

There was a long silence. Finally, Cunningham spoke. He addressed Edwards, but he kept his eyes focused directly on Walker. "You've presented a compelling set of arguments, but I return to my earlier point. We must act cautiously. Cautiously and prudently. Everything we've heard here today has been powerful. I agree that it may point to Iran, but the evidence is entirely circumstantial. We must have something more solid before we can recommend any action to the President."

This time the Vice President actually smiled, albeit only briefly. *It's so much better when you can get someone else to make your points for you.* The President's National Security Advisor had begun the meeting by expressing his doubt that the smallpox outbreak had been the result of a hostile action. Now he was merely advising that they should move cautiously before they responded against Iran. *It's just a matter of time.*

"Thank you Mr. Cunningham." The Vice President's sarcasm was muted. "We appreciate your wise counsel, and unquestionably, this group cannot recommend any action until we obtain confirmation of our preliminary information. And certainly, that confirmation must be strong. It must be unambiguous. But I have no doubt that our very capable intelligence services will be able to obtain the necessary evidence. I can only encourage them to do so with all possible speed."

"Mr. Vice President?" It was Secretary of State Calebresi, again.

Richards didn't like this. *She's no better than a two-bit whore, and she can be just as much trouble.*

He used his most diplomatic voice to respond. "Yes, Secretary Calebresi."

"There is a question that we haven't discussed yet. If we are to respond to this outbreak ..." She paused, straining to control her anger.

"... this apparent biological attack in New Mexico—we must address the type of response that we should undertake. If we anticipate initiating a major diplomatic initiative, I will need to get my people moving. It would involve far more than just the Near East Section. Presumably, we would want to involve all of our allies, in NATO and elsewhere around the world."

"I'm sorry, Madam Secretary, but it appears that you are forgetting. The United States of America already has a policy in place with regard to how we would respond to an attack such as this one. It is an attack with a weapon of mass destruction."

Calebresi glared at the Vice President with a mixture of anger and loathing.

The Vice President continued. "Let me remind you of National Security Presidential Directive 17—also known as Homeland Security Presidential Directive 4. It was signed by President Bush on September 14, 2002. The complete text remains classified, but as you are certainly aware, it has never been rescinded, and it remains in effect. The document clearly enunciates the American response to an attack with chemical or biological weapons. Permit me to read you the relevant quote:

> *The United States will continue to make clear that it reserves the right to respond with overwhelming force—including potentially nuclear weapons—to the use of [weapons of mass destruction] against the United States, our forces abroad, and friends and allies.* [‡]

The room went completely silent. Not a single person dared to look at the Vice President.

* * *

[‡] Federation of Atomic Scientists, National Security Presidential Directives, http://www.fas.org/irp/offdocs/nspd/nspd-17.html; Arms Control Association, "U.S. 'Negative Security Assurances' At a Glance," http://www.armscontrol.org/factsheets/negsec.

Day 27: Contingency Planning

The four officials were gathered in the office of Juan Allesandro, the President's Chief of Staff. The others were Parker Cunningham, the National Security Advisor; Bertram Morrison, the Intelligence Advisor and DNI; and Caroline Calebresi, the Secretary of State. The mood was somber, depressing even.

Calebresi spoke first. "What just happened in there? I feel like I've been run over by a train."

"Worse than that, it's like we're in another rush to war." Those words from Bert Morrison.

"We were blindsided," Cunningham observed. "They had that entire thing orchestrated ahead of time. The Vice President, the Secretary of Defense, and the Chairman of the Joint Chiefs. Plus that weasel, Edwards. This has created an extremely delicate situation. We find ourselves participating in plans to initiate a war—a nuclear war—without any adequate justification. We've have to counteract this push. We have to protect the President."

"The President can protect himself." Allesandro knew President Alexander better than any of the others. "But he needs the rational input that will allow him to do that. So, he does need our help. We have to make sure he is working from facts, not guesses. So far, I don't think he's been given reliable information."

"Are you going to tell him that?" Cunningham, again.

Allesandro answered without hesitation. "I believe the President already understands the problem. If we get hard data that point in a different direction, I can assure you he will learn about it. But we can't act like a bunch of kids tattling on the school bully. If there are hard facts to be presented, and perhaps disputed, the President will want it to be done in an open meeting of the NSC. That's how he makes his decisions. Watching us debate with each other is as much a part of his process as looking at the actual facts."

"Then there are two areas where we need to get better data. First is on the intelligence front ..."

All eyes turned momentarily to the Director of National Intelligence, whose face flushed with a mixture of anger and embarrassment as Cunningham continued his assessment. "The other is in the policy arena. They caught us off guard today, and we can't let that happen again. I should make it clear that I'm not one of those 'peace at any cost' types. If there's proof that Iran or some other government initiated a biological warfare attack on the United States, I'll be one of the first to vote for a military response. But it would have to be the right response, and I can't imagine how nuclear war would be appropriate."

"How did we ever get a policy that even suggests a nuclear response for something like this? And how come I never even heard of it before today?" Allesandro, whose background was in the private sector, was genuinely puzzled.

Morrison leaned forward in his chair. "The answer is amazingly simple. It's a little bit like the Suez–Hungary thing in 1956. In the middle of the Suez crisis, the Soviets sent troops into Hungary. Most people remember only one of the stories—as though the other never happened. Somehow, it's exactly what happened here. Bush signed the policy in 2002, but it was secret. *The Washington Times* obtained the classified wording about nuclear response and published it several months later."

"But why wasn't it a big deal? That should have been front page for every newspaper in the country."

Morrison frowned. "That's my whole point. The story was published on January 31. Early the next morning—February 1, 2003—the Space Shuttle *Columbia* disintegrated on reentry into the Earth's atmosphere. Every TV station, every newspaper, just about every reporter in the country turned their attention to that tragedy. The nuclear policy was completely forgotten. I can only remember one news story. It only said that the White House declined to comment on the original *Washington Times* report. The whole thing just died. It shouldn't have, but it did."

"So it's still in effect?" The Secretary of State was clearly surprised. She had expected to learn that the Vice President was misrepresenting the facts.

"It was never rescinded. At least not completely. It just seems to have fallen off everybody's radar screen. Even mine, and that embarrasses me. The next administration did take it off the table for response to an attack from a non-nuclear state, but Iran and North Korea were explicitly excluded. So the answer is, yes. The policy is still in place."

"Please get each of us some specifics on this, Burt. I need to clarify this for the President before the Security Council meets again on Thursday. If we're not prepared to debate these issues competently, the nuclear option could get pushed through."

Morrison nodded to Allesandro. "I'll take care of it. I'll also get you a copy of the Doctrine for Joint Nuclear Operations, which dates back to 2005. We need to be ready for something that's pretty well buried inside, but it's there. It's the notion that an effective strategy of deterrence means that the U.S. is willing and able 'to preempt or retaliate.' That word 'preempt' is really important, because it could be used by our friends in the NSC to justify an attack against Iran, even in the absence of clear evidence that they actually attacked us with smallpox."

"Bert, may I bring up a somewhat awkward question?"

"Of course Madam Secretary." Calebresi was the only one in this group of power players holding cabinet rank, and the others showed the appropriate courtesy when addressing her.

"If I read the tea leaves correctly, it appears to me that our colleagues from the Defense side were not entirely forthcoming in reporting their intelligence findings to you. Would you concur?"

Cunningham and Allesandro both nodded in agreement with the Secretary of State's observation, while the DNI screwed up his face as he thought for a moment. "I can see why you might conclude that, but I can't say for certain that it was intentional. We're working on an extraordinarily short timeline here, so it's possible that the Under Secretary of Defense didn't get his information in time to share it with me before the meeting."

Calebresi smiled wryly at the DNI. "I thought diplomacy was supposed to be my bailiwick. You're showing remarkable restraint."

"In the absence of more compelling information, I really have no choice but to accept what we heard today at face value. That said, we need to pursue the intelligence side of this crisis really hard. I want each of you to exploit whatever avenues you have available. In particular, I plan to speak with my senior staff to make certain that moving forward, everything from Defense will get routed through my office."

"If I may speak for the others, we'll take your suggestion as our marching orders," Calebresi said. "I'm not quite sure what we can put together over at State, but I'll call ahead and have the Assistant Secretary of State for Intelligence and Research waiting in my office when I get back. Should we agree to use the same dodge that was employed by our DoD colleagues? That we're looking into preparations for the next Review Conference for the Biological Weapons Convention?"

"Yeah, that's a good idea, but make sure they know it's urgent. And you've got to emphasize the highly classified nature of what we're looking into."

"Good point," said Cunningham. "My staff and I are close to key people in the other agencies—people whose loyalties lie with our country and not with any individual. But we all have to be very careful with these inquiries, or we'll cause a civil war with the Defense Department."

"As his Chief of Staff, I'll be meeting with the President this afternoon, and there are a couple of things I can do. I'll discreetly let him know that there are some serious differences of opinion within the National Security Council. That won't surprise him, and it won't appear that I'm speaking out of school. He'll be glad to know that his advisors are taking their jobs so seriously. I'll also make sure that nobody—and that includes the Vice President—nobody meets with President Alexander unless I'm present."

The informal meeting ended, and Caroline Calebresi stood up first. "Gentlemen, thank you for your cooperation. We've been put in a very difficult position, but you are serving your country well. Let me remind you that patriotism reflects people's love and support for their country, even at great personal risk. In contrast to what others have suggested, it's far more important than a pin on your lapel."

* * *

17

Sarah

*Section 4001 of Title 18 states: No citizen shall be
imprisoned or otherwise detained by the United
States except pursuant to an Act of Congress. ... As
we explain below, the President's authority to detain
enemy combatants, including U.S. citizens, is based
on his constitutional authority as Commander in
Chief. We conclude that section 4001(a) does not,
and constitutionally could not, interfere with that
authority.*

*—Justice Department memo, June 2002, on the
legality of military detention of United States
citizens**

Day 28: Cortez, Colorado

Raymond took Sarah's large backpack out of the bed of
the truck and motioned her to follow him into the house.
They were greeted by the gentle smile of a woman who
didn't seem that much older than Sarah.

"This is my wife, Annie. She'll show you to your room, and then
we'll be able to sit down for dinner."

---

* U.S. Department of Justice, June 27, 2002, Memorandum for Daniel J.
Bryant, Assistant Attorney General; authored by John C. Yoo, Deputy
Assistant Attorney General, Office of Legislative Affairs, "Re:
Applicability of 18 U.S.C.§ 4001(a) to Military Detention of United States
Citizens," p. 1.

Raymond stayed behind as Annie led Sarah to a small room at the far end of the house. "I hope you'll be comfortable here, Sarah. The bathroom is right across the hall there. You can wash up and then come and join us for dinner."

Sarah felt greatly comforted. Strangers had taken her into their home and were treating her as one of the family. *I hope I'll be this generous if I ever have the chance.*

A few minutes later, she found Raymond and Annie sitting at a table in the corner of the living area nearest the kitchen. The table was set for three, and they motioned her to sit at the remaining place. Annie pushed a mug of hot coffee toward her and then spoke somewhat hesitantly. "I hope you like coffee. It's a customary drink for us."

"I do." Sarah inhaled the delightful aroma as she took a sip. It tasted wonderful. "It's really good. Thank you so much."

Annie smiled and got up from the table. Raymond put down his mug. "While Annie gets dinner finished, let me tell you more about what's going on in Farmington." He explained that Annie's cousin was Evelyn Redhouse, the woman whose child was the first to die in what people had been calling the chickenpox outbreak. "And it was her husband Jack that introduced me to Annie. We served together in the first Gulf War, back in '90. We're both Marines."

"You're still in the Marine Corps?" Sarah was surprised.

"No, we both finished up by '94, except Jack's reserve unit got called up after we went into Iraq in 2003. But once you're a Marine, you're always a Marine. No such thing as an ex-Marine. Anyway, one time a few years back, Jack invited me over to their place, and Annie was there. Best day of my life. We got married six months later. Jack and Evie have been good friends to us, even though we don't see them so often, what with them living down in Farmington and us here in Cortez. It's less than 50 miles as the crow flies, but it's twice that by car, and it takes at least two hours in good weather.

"Anyway, Jack and Evie have had some tough times, especially after Jack had to go back in—when they sent him to Iraq in 2004. For a long time he wouldn't get help at the Veterans Center. But things got better after a couple of years, and they were really happy when little Jackson was born. And now this sickness … they really loved that kid. Evie called us before they shut down the phones and told us that they lost him. And then Jack disappeared."

"Disappeared?" Sarah asked.

"I think he just couldn't handle it. I remember when he lost a couple of buddies in Desert Storm. He was real broke up about that too. But this time I think he's just gone off into the hills to be by himself while he heals. It's not doing Evie any good, that's for sure. And she still has to take care of her dad. He lives with them, and his health isn't so good anymore."

"Did they tell you anything about what happened to Jackson?"

"All Evie said was that it was chickenpox. But we hear there have been other people dying down there too, and I sure never heard of any chickenpox being that bad. Then the government comes in and seals off the whole area."

"Because of chickenpox?"

"No, something else is going on. I just don't trust them. Jack and I grew up on the reservation. So did Evie, but she's a lot younger. We've learned an awful lot about why Navajos shouldn't trust the federal government. Our dads all worked in the uranium mines, and the government said that was okay too. Eventually, it killed all of them. All except for Evie's dad. He's not dead yet, but it'll get him, too."

"What do you mean, it killed them?"

"The radioactive dust. You keep breathing that long enough, it'll get you. And they wouldn't give them the medical care they promised. Just kept saying it must have been because they smoked or because they didn't eat proper. The government men just sat back and stalled while the Indians died. Sometimes I wonder why we still love this country. Enough to fight for it. And enough to die for it."

Before Sarah could ask any questions, Annie started bringing food to the table. Her soft voice was accompanied by a generous smile. "I hope you'll like this, Sarah. It's traditional Navajo food to help you feel more welcome with us. We know you've come to help, and we appreciate that."

The dinner was simple but tasty. Navajo fry bread, pinto beans, and mutton stew. To Sarah, the fry bread tasted like a large homemade doughnut, but without the sugar on top. There was little conversation while they ate.

"That was delicious, Annie. I'm grateful and I'm honored that you've brought me into your home this way."

Sarah reached for her plate as Annie got up to clear the table, but Annie gently put a hand on her wrist. "That's all right, I'll clean up. I think you and Raymond have some more serious talking to do."

155

Annie refilled the coffee cups, removed the rest of the dishes, and continued working in the kitchen.

Raymond picked up his earlier narrative. "Even though they've tried to shut down all the lines of communication, the government folks really don't understand us. Maybe the roads are closed, but there's a lot of old trails we use to go back and forth. We've been able to keep up on the news. As I understand it, they think it's smallpox, but they don't want anyone on the outside to know."

Raymond gave Sarah an intense look to be certain she understood. "The only way to get out of this mess is for you to get this information to your newspaper. We don't know why they're doing this, but we've suffered too much in the past. I'm talking about all the Indian tribes, not just the Navajos. We need your help, and we're willing to do whatever's needed to help you get this into the news."

"I'll do what I can." Sarah felt overwhelmed by the responsibility. These people were counting on her, but she didn't know what to do. She paused for a moment to make sure she could speak without her voice breaking. "I don't know why they're trying to cover things up, but I do know that hiding the truth never works. My job as a reporter is just to tell the truth, so I have to find out what's really happening."

"Seems to me, we need to go talk to the people in who live there. Maybe your friend Jillian, Annie's cousin, maybe some other people as well."

"One of the doctors who came out from the CDC in Atlanta is someone I know. At least I think he's out here. If I can find him, he may have the answers. I can trust him not to turn me in when he sees me."

"He'd have to be a pretty good friend."

"He is."

"We may need to keep separate if you get to see him. Not much point in both of us going to jail."

"Everything is so crazy now. But you're right. We have to be really careful, and we can't put you at risk. Do you really think you can get me past the roadblocks or whatever they're using to isolate Farmington?"

"I'm sure of it. Like I said, there's a lot of old trails, and they can't watch them all. It's not like a full military occupation. They've just tried to seal the place off by closing the airports and main highways. The real question is whether you're up to it. The terrain is pretty rugged, and you aren't used to the elevation."

"I'm in pretty good shape. I do a lot of running and biking, including some pretty good hills. So if you're trying to say that you don't think a woman can ..."

"No offense, Sarah. It's rugged country, and you're not used to the altitude. Some of this trip may have to be on foot. I make my living guiding people on hiking and camping trips. I need to know what your abilities are."

"Fair enough. Sorry. So, I understand it could be pretty difficult. But if you don't expect me to go too fast, I think I can handle some fairly rough terrain. I went backpacking at elevations above 10,000 feet last year. It was hard, but I did it."

"All right, we'll try to do as much as we can with vehicles, avoiding the major roads. The best way to get to Farmington is through Durango, and they'll be watching those roads, especially near the airport. But they'll never even think about the back trails."

He pushed a map across the table. "A straight line, from here to Farmington would go southeast, right through Mesa Verde National Park, then down through the Ute Mountain Reservation, and across the state line into New Mexico. But those lines on the map indicate deep canyons, so most of the roads don't go through."

"Yeah, I can see why it's a long trip."

Raymond paused. "Something has been bothering me. How could those people have caught smallpox? In the Marines, they told us it had been wiped out except for the possibility of germ warfare by the Russians. So how did we get it out here?"

Sarah shook her head slowly. "I don't know. I guess that's why they're trying to keep it a secret, and we need to find out why. If somebody attacked our country, then people need to know that."

"And if it wasn't an attack?"

"I suppose it could have been an accident, but I can't imagine how it could have happened. And if that isn't the reason ... it would almost seem that our government was responsible. And people sure as hell would need to know about that. None of this makes sense, Raymond."

Raymond took a deep breath and exhaled slowly. "Even if it was just an accident somehow, like the nerve gas thing when all the sheep died up near Dugway in the 1960s, people here in the West don't have a lot of trust in the government. If people found out that the government was doing experiments with smallpox and killing

Indians ... man, that would be war. Our schools teach how white people purposely infected Indians with smallpox during colonial times. There could be a lot more than just hard feelings."

"But nobody would ..."

"I know it doesn't make sense, Sarah. But maybe this is a whole lot bigger than just little Jackson and the people who've already gotten sick and died."

Raymond looked over at Annie and then turned back to Sarah. "I think the best thing right now is for you to get some sleep. We'll have a long trip starting tomorrow morning, and you're going to need as much rest as you can get. You should be pretty tired by now. You go on in and get some sleep."

Sarah said goodnight and went into the guest room. In less than 10 minutes, while she wondered what preparations Raymond was making, Sarah fell sound asleep.

* * *

Day 29: Canyons

It seemed that only a few minutes had passed, when Sarah heard a knock on her door. She was momentarily confused, looking over at her alarm clock, only to find that it wasn't there. She realized that she wasn't at home, when the door opened and Annie entered with a hot mug of coffee. She set the mug on the bedside table and spoke softly. "Raymond says you should get up now."

"Thank you," Sarah said as she reached for the mug. "You've been so nice ... I don't really know how to thank you."

"If you can help, it will be an important thing for our family—and for our people. For all of us."

Sarah didn't know what to say, so she just nodded. Annie went out, and Sarah dressed quickly. She secured both of her backpacks, carried them across the living room, and set them by the front door.

Annie had prepared breakfast and motioned Sarah to the table. Raymond came into the house and went to the kitchen sink to wash his hands. They sat at the table, and Raymond advised Sarah to eat well. "You won't get another good meal for a few days." Sarah wasn't sure if this meant that they might be living on bread and water or just that Raymond liked Annie's cooking. After trying the fry bread with eggs, beans, and chili, she decided it was the latter.

When they finished, Raymond pushed his chair back from the table. "We need to be going." Sarah's watch said it was 6:00 a.m., and a touch of grey in the sky hinted at dawn. Raymond picked up Sarah's packs and took them outside.

Sarah turned to Annie. "Thank you so much for having me in your home."

"We have been honored to have you Sarah. I just hope you will be coming back."

"Oh, I'd be delighted to ..." Sarah began with a smile, before she realized what Annie had meant. "We'll be careful, and we'll be back. I promise." She wished she could be as certain as the words she had spoken.

As Sarah turned toward the truck, she saw the all-terrain vehicles. It looked like Raymond wasn't going to make her hike all the way to Farmington.

"Have you ever ridden an ATV?"

"Yeah. My mom and dad have them at their place in West Virginia. I'm not an expert, but I know not get caught going sideways on a hill."

"Mostly we'll be on trails, so you won't have that kind of problem. If we do go off road, I'll lead so you can avoid getting caught in a bad situation. It's good that you've ridden before. You'll be okay."

Raymond told Sarah that he had built and welded the ATV carrier himself. "Lets me carry two ATVs and still have room for other gear. I have to drive slow, but it's a lot better than hauling a trailer."

Sarah climbed into the cab of the truck and buckled her seat belt as Raymond started the engine. Soon, they were driving steadily on a paved roadway, and Sarah could see the lighter gray of the sky off to the left as they headed south toward New Mexico. She recognized the road they had driven the previous evening as they passed the Cortez airport on the right. A few miles later, they turned east onto a much smaller road. "Now we're on BIA-204. That's a route designation set by the Bureau of Indian Affairs. It's also known as Indian Road 204. After a few miles, it becomes Mancos Canyon Road."

Raymond said they would stay on Mancos Canyon Road—not a highway, but a decent road—for about 15 miles and then take Grass Canyon Road. By the time they reached that turn, daylight had arrived. Raymond handed Sarah a map. "Take a look at this. It'll help you understand where we were and where we're going."

It was a topographical map of the area, and Sarah found the Four Corners with no difficulty.

"Trace your finger in a loop around the Four Corners. There's a belt of highways that make a rough circle about 50 miles in diameter. To most people, that defines the geographic area known as the Four Corners."

As Sarah traced their route from Cortez down to Mancos Canyon Road and then Grass Canyon Road, Raymond explained that their entire trip would be about 80 miles and would take them four or five hours driving time. "We'll follow Grass Canyon Road for about 15 miles in Colorado, and then another 20 miles through New Mexico. It's not a very direct route, but you can see from that map why the mountains and canyons make it impossible to do anything else. After we cross the Ute Mountain Indian Reservation, we'll get to Farmington on a couple of unmarked roads."

At about 10:00 a.m., Raymond pulled the truck over into a clearing on the side of the road. The views were spectacular, with mountains in the distance and rocky ground that looked more like a moonscape than anything she'd ever seen before.

Ahead of them was a rocky outcropping that seemed to be only a few miles away. "That's where we're headed. But you can't get there from here," Raymond added with a wry smile.

"Those dark areas are canyons, some of them four or five hundred feet deep, with walls that are almost vertical. It's pretty much impossible to get across, so we have to go around until we can cut back over there." He pointed to a location somewhere in the distance with no distinguishing landmarks, at least none that Sarah could see.

He reached for a brown paper bag from behind the driver's seat and removed a couple of smaller packages, handing one to Sarah. "Go ahead, open it up." She removed the paper wrapper from what she discovered were two blue-corn patties. After an encouraging nod from Raymond, she tried one.

"Pretty good. I like it."

Raymond took two battered metal cups from the bag, handed one to her, and poured water into them from a canteen. "At this altitude, you need to make sure you drink plenty of water."

The next treat from the paper sack turned out to be sandwiches made with white bread. "Not everything we eat is traditional, and Annie made these from stuff that came right from the grocery store. She makes a mean bologna sandwich."

They ate quickly, again without any conversation. Raymond opened the door of the cab and started to get out. "I'll use this side of the truck, and you can have your privacy over there. Not too many trees or bushes to hide behind, but I can't help that."

"I'll manage."

It was a bright sunny day, but chilly, probably no more than 40 degrees. So the windows stayed closed. Sarah followed the map with difficulty as the truck bounced along the back roads. Then she remembered the GPS unit in her pack, and she reached down and got it out. She turned it on and was bringing up their location on the small screen, when Raymond looked over.

"You have a GPS. That could be a big help. Especially for you, if we run into problems. We're going to hide the truck up in the hills above Farmington and use the ATVs for the last few miles. I'll leave the keys under the seat, so you could always go back to the truck. Just be sure to write down the coordinates for where we leave it."

By mid-day they were well into New Mexico, skirting the small town of Cottonwood on a dirt road. Raymond slowed the pickup to almost a complete stop, turned hard to the left, and pulled into a small cleft beneath a rocky outcropping. The opening was partially obscured by a small stand of scraggly trees.

"Make sure you've got these coordinates. I'm going to unload the truck and make sure it's not visible, even from above."

Once the ATVs were off the truck, Raymond unloaded additional gear from the truck. He put a 5-gallon can in the carrying rack on one of the ATVs. "Extra gasoline. No gas stations out here, but we should have more than enough fuel." When they were done, the ATVs were loaded with extra food and water, two sleeping bags, and a rifle.

Then Raymond removed a sheet of camouflage netting from behind the driver's seat and threw it over the truck. He tied down the corners, and Sarah watched as the truck virtually disappeared. Unless you were within a few feet of the vehicle, it blended completely with the natural vegetation and rocks of the high desert. She understood why Raymond had placed such emphasis on the GPS coordinates.

"Our next stop is a friend's house on the edge of Farmington. He knows we're coming. Let's get started." They had moved the ATVs a few yards onto the rocky path, when Raymond dismounted and walked back toward the truck. He broke off a small branch from one of the trees and used it as a broom to sweep across the slight tire tracks that the truck had left, continuing the process as he walked back to the ATVs.

"Old Navajo trick," he said solemnly, and then he broke into a broad grin. "Actually, we learned how to do that in Marine basic training. It turned out to be pretty important for some of our operations in Desert Storm. I just want to be sure here that anyone happening by this location won't spot the truck—or see the tire tracks leading to it."

"Won't the ATV tracks be visible?"

"We'll drive off the trail for a little bit, and part of the time we'll use that old stream bed. Any tracks that survive a day of normal winds will just look like someone was out doing some recreational riding. We have about 10 miles on these trails before we reach my friend's house. We'll be north of town, and by the time we get to a more populated section, we'll just look like a couple of people out for a ride. Nobody will think twice about it."

An hour later, Sarah saw houses, and Raymond pointed to one of them, a modest one-story cement-block building. They pulled the ATVs behind the house and walked around to the front. Before Raymond could knock, the door opened and an unsmiling face beckoned them inside.

Raymond motioned Sarah go in. "This is Anthony Chee." She stepped through the doorway, as Raymond continued the introduction.

"Anthony, this is Sarah, the reporter I told you about."

As Sarah extended her hand, Anthony turned away. Sarah glanced uncomfortably at Raymond.

Anthony pointed at a small table as he walked toward the kitchen with his back toward his visitors. "I have some food for you. You can wash up if you want. The bathroom is over there." He turned and walked away.

* * *

Day 29: Finding Jake

Sarah joined the two men at the table, where Chee offered some slightly stale fry bread, beans, and coffee. "Raymond says you're okay, so I'll take his word for it. We don't know what's happening here exactly, but it's not good. You think you're going to be able to help us?"

"I don't know. I can only say that I'll try to find out what's going on and get the story in the *Washington Post*. I need to get information from for someone I think is here."

"Anthony has lived in Farmington most of his life, and people will help him."

Sarah had a lot of questions. "Do you have any idea where the medical people are located?"

"Yeah, they're over at SJC. That's San Juan College, a couple of miles east of here. Almost all of the government people have moved in there. They stopped classes, and they took over a lot of the buildings. I used to work there, electrical and plumbing and stuff, so I know a lot of the employees."

"Is that the military headquarters, too?"

"No. Their main operations are down by the airport. That's where the troops are based. Maybe a thousand."

He turned to Raymond. "I just heard that two local men have been detained by the military. One was Jimmy Ayze. He was trying to drive to his mom's place east of the city, and they stopped him on the main highway. Then they came to his house and took away his brother Jeremiah. The people next door overheard something about Jack Redhouse, like they were accusing Jimmy and Jeremiah of helping Jack get out of town."

Raymond interrupted angrily. "They need to let Jack alone. The man has suffered enough. Why would they be after him anyway?"

"I don't know, Raymond. Doesn't make any sense at all to me, but we haven't been able to find out anything more. The unit commander wouldn't even let the lawyer from the Tribal Council see them. Wouldn't even admit that they were in custody."

Chee turned to Sarah. "You asked about the college. They're using classrooms as hospital rooms. They're also using the science labs, and they've brought in a whole lot of equipment."

"That's where we need to look. The friend I'm looking for is a scientist, so he'd need a laboratory. You know that it's probably smallpox?"

"Yeah, word got out pretty quick after Dr. Akebe saw Jimmy Shepherd's kid. That was after Jackson died. I heard that the people in Washington told Akebe he was nuts, but I guess they changed their minds. What are the chances that we'll all get smallpox if we start nosing around those people at the college?"

Sarah knew the question was directed to her. "To be completely honest, Anthony, I really don't know. It depends on whether you were vaccinated when you were a child and how long that vaccination remains effective. I was vaccinated about 15 years ago for a trip to Africa, but most people stopped getting vaccinated a lot earlier."

"Raymond and I were both in the first Gulf War and got vaccinated then. Is it still good?"

"I think we should all be okay, from what I've read. No vaccine is 100 percent, but we have to take the risk."

Raymond and Anthony both nodded. It meant they would all work together.

"We need to find Jake Overman, the friend I told you about. Is there somewhere where we could watch the main entrance to the college?"

Anthony frowned as he considered the question. "I have an idea. Let's go for a ride."

They climbed into Anthony's pickup truck. To Sarah, it looked even older than Raymond's, and it drove accordingly. But it wouldn't attract attention.

Anthony explained as he drove: "We're on Pinon Hills Boulevard. You can see the college up ahead on the right. It's about a hundred acres, maybe two hundred. After we go past, we'll head down toward Main Street. There's a little cantina that my cousin runs. We can see if he knows anything."

A short distance after they passed the campus, Anthony pulled into a parking area to the side of a small but well-kept storefront with a sign identifying it as "Chiquita's Cantina." Five minutes later, Sarah and Raymond were sipping coffee, and Anthony was across the dining room chatting with his cousin.

Anthony joined them at the table with a mug of coffee. "Most of the government people are staying at the Travelodge a mile down the street. A few of them have come here for a snack, but it's a little too *native* for most of them. The typical customers here are local working folks, so maybe the Easterners don't think they fit in. They're mostly eating their meals at Chili's or one of the fast-food places. But my cousin says that a lot of them have been shopping right across the street at San Juan Plaza."

Sarah's frustration was growing. "How are we going to find out if Jake is really here? There have got to be a lot of security people here, and they'll notice if we ask too many questions."

"We just have to ask the right people. Nobody would think twice about me talking to my friends here. You and Raymond have to be a little more careful, though, because there's definitely a lot of security. They walk like military, but they're wearing civvies."

"Can we hang out here without raising any suspicion?"

"Sure. My cousin knows to keep this quiet. The folks working in stores and restaurants are on our side, and they're unhappy because closing off the roads has killed the tourist business. They can't even call their friends and relatives, now that the phones and Internet are down."

"If we do find Jake, I'll need someplace to talk to him." Sarah looked around the room, which had a few small tables and a couple of booths. "Could we talk here?"

"I think it would work real good, don't you Raymond? Let me go talk with my cousin. His name is Joseph, by the way, Joseph Begay." Anthony got up and crossed the room to the counter where Joseph was standing by the cash register. After several minutes the two of them came over to the table.

Anthony made formal introductions, and Joseph spoke directly to Sarah. "Thank you for helping us."

"I think we're all trying to help each other, Joseph. Thanks for letting us use the cantina."

"No problem. If you need to talk with someone, I'll make sure you get that quiet booth over there in the corner."

"That would work fine. And one other thing—do you have something with the name and address of the cantina?"

"That's easy." Joseph reached into a pocket and handed her a business card. "We just had these printed."

"Perfect." Sarah copied the information into her notebook and put the card in a pocket. She had been watching the cars driving down Main Street, and something caught her eye. "Those men getting out of the green car over there in the shopping center? One of them is Jake. I'm sure of it! At least, I think I am."

"We can walk toward the stores and nobody will think twice," Anthony said as they headed for the door. "There's a blue Chevy over there, just this side of the green car that Sarah pointed out. The Chevy belongs to a guy I know who manages one of the stores, so even if he comes out to his car, we could stand next to it and keep talking. For those men to get back to their car, they would have to walk toward us. They wouldn't get too close, but we could get a clear look at them."

As they waited in the parking lot, Sarah took a pen from her pocket and wrote on the back of the business card. Then she focused her attention on the doorway to the pharmacy through which Jake, or at least the person she thought was Jake, had entered. Raymond said he was going in the store to look around. Anthony and Sarah waited by the Chevy trying hard not to look nervous.

Several minutes later, Raymond emerged and strode over to Sarah and Anthony. "They bought some shampoo and stuff, and they're just paying for it now. They should be coming out in just a minute."

The two men emerged from the pharmacy and began walking in their direction. There was no question about it. The man on the left was Jake. "Wait here for me." Sarah walked toward the men, keeping her head down. As she approached them, she kept her gaze directed toward the ground, but she headed almost directly into Jake's path.

He looked up, initially surprised that the person walking toward him wasn't moving out of the way, and then he stopped dead in his tracks as he recognized Sarah. At first it didn't compute, and he didn't say anything. It was exactly what Sarah had hoped for. At the last moment, she turned slightly to the side and walked past Jake, brushing his arm as she did so.

Then she stopped and reached down, as if to pick up something from the ground. Standing up, she turned back toward the man she had bumped against. "Excuse me, but you dropped this."

Still dumbfounded, Jake took the business card. "Uh, thanks," he responded as Sarah began to walk into the store. He turned the card over, saw the simple notation, "6:00 p.m." He put the card in his pocket.

"She sure was clumsy. Maybe drunk," his companion said.

"Yeah, I guess so. Whatever. Let's get back to the lab and finish up for the day. I'm tired." The two men got into the green Toyota and drove out of the parking lot.

Sarah, meanwhile, had continued into the store. After the Toyota pulled away, she rejoined Raymond and Anthony. As they walked back toward Chiquita's, she offered them the package of mints that she had bought in the drugstore. They declined.

"That was really smooth. Who taught you that?"

"I'm not sure, Raymond. Maybe I saw it in a movie. I really don't know." She was shaking.

"He recognized me, Raymond."

"Yeah, I could see.

"It worked, Sarah. You did well."

"Thanks. I was really lucky."

"How well do you know this man? Can you be sure that he won't just go back and tell the security people?"

"I trust him, Anthony. He wouldn't do that. Anyway, I wrote on the card that he should meet us at the cantina at 6:00. I saw him read it."

"I'll ask Joseph if he can use some extra help in the cantina this evening, so if anything goes wrong I'll be close by. You say this Jake is your friend, but he's also working for the government. They haven't been too friendly the last few days. Raymond, maybe you can take point. Stay outside, maybe act like you're taking a nap in the truck until it looks safe. When you come in, I'll put you at the next table. Even if this man Jake is as standup as you think he is, Sarah, he won't notice an Indian at the next table. We tend to be pretty much invisible to most white people."

Raymond shrugged. "I guess I could do that. Okay with you, Sarah?"

"Yeah. We just have to hope that Jake will help us."

* * *

18

Sarah and Jake

*We conclude that the President has both
constitutional and statutory authority to use the
armed forces in military operations, against
terrorists, within the United States. We believe that
these operations generally would not be subject to
the constraints of the Fourth Amendment, so long as
the armed forces are undertaking a military
function. Even if the Fourth Amendment were to
apply, however, we believe that most military
operations would satisfy the Constitution's
reasonableness requirement and continue to be
lawful.*

—*Justice Department memo, October 2001, on the
legality of using military force inside the United
States*[*]

Day 29: Chiquita's

B y 5:45 Sarah was sitting in a booth at Chiquita's,
pretending to read a brochure on local attractions.
Raymond was outside in the truck, and Anthony was

---

[*] U.S. Department of Justice, Oct. 23, 2001, Memorandum for Alberto R.
Gonzales, Counsel to the President and William J. Haynes, II, General
Counsel, Department of Defense; authored by John C. Yoo, Deputy
Assistant Attorney General and Robert L. Delahunty, Special Counsel, "Re:
Authority for Use of Military Force to Combat Terrorist Activities within
the United States," p. 37.

helping Joseph. At 6:00 the door to the cantina opened, and Jake stepped tentatively into the dining area. Sarah caught his eye and motioned to him to join her.

"Can I get you two anything?" Anthony asked.

"A couple of Diet Cokes," Sarah answered.

"I'd like a beer, please."

"Not beer, Jake. We have too many important things to talk about."

Jake turned his head toward Anthony. "A beer." Then he looked hard at Sarah. They were silent.

"I'll have your drinks in a minute."

Jake waited until Anthony was out of earshot. "Jesus, Sarah! What on Earth are you doing here? I mean, it shouldn't even have been possible for you to get here. And why? Why are you out here? You're supposed to be back in D.C."

"Wait a minute, until after he brings our drinks. How are you, Jake? I've missed you."

"Goddamn it! I'm not okay, Sarah. And I'm sure as hell not glad to see you. You shouldn't be here. It's too dangerous."

Anthony brought Sarah her Coke and set a cold mug of beer in front of Jake. Then he returned to the front of the Cantina.

Looking over the edge of her glass, Sarah spoke quietly. "Jake, I know about the smallpox."

His initial response was one of confusion. "Why shouldn't you? That's what I mean about it being too dangerous."

"I should be safe, Jake. I was vaccinated 15 years ago, before I went to Africa with my dad."

"Maybe you're okay. Why did you come here, Sarah? Why didn't you just ask CDC for information? They're not letting reporters in here for a reason. You should know that."

"I'm the only reporter who knows about it, Jake. There's no information available anywhere. The government is hiding the fact that it's smallpox. This place is under quarantine, and there's a complete news blackout."

"Of course there's a quarantine. That's the first step in any smallpox response plan. It's CDC policy. I told you about it when I helped draft the policy."

"That's right, Jake, but the response plan only mandates isolation of people who are infected. Not an entire geographic region."

"Normally, sure. But the military advisors argued that a complete quarantine would be more effective. Because this area is remote, we thought we could stop any further spread of the disease. Previous scenarios were designed for heavily populated areas."

"You just aren't getting it, Jake. It goes directly against your own damn policy. And it sure as hell doesn't explain cutting all communications."

"But there's no *news blackout*. That doesn't even make sense. We lost our telephone service this weekend when a rock slide west of here that damaged the main trunk lines. It also took out fiber-optic lines that carry signals from cell-phone towers, but it was supposed to be all fixed by today."

"That's bullshit! I was told last Friday that the phone lines were about to be shut down. Before it happened! It was done intentionally."

"My e-mail is working fine."

"If your e-mail is working, why didn't you answer my messages?"

"What messages? I haven't seen anything from you in the last two weeks, Sarah."

"That's the point Jake. You haven't seen them. But I sent them, goddamn it! And what the hell is the military doing out here? National Guard, okay. But regular military units are prohibited from active deployment on U.S. soil unless martial law has been declared. And that certainly hasn't happened."

"It's some kind of new response force. There was an Army unit trained in bioterrorism response that could deploy rapidly."

"But that's not how it's supposed to be, Jake! And I don't know why you're trying to cover it up, either. We both know that the official response plan for a smallpox outbreak is to provide open and accurate communication to the public. That's official CDC policy, and you told me about it yourself last year."

"It's not a cover-up, Sarah. CDC headquarters must have just delayed the announcement until we could get things under control here. To avoid a panic. The announcements were supposed to be made over the weekend. I helped draft them, and I signed off on them as head of the medical team from CDC. The entire country should be well aware of this by now."

"Have you seen coverage on TV? Have you seen any news reports on the outbreak?"

"I've been too busy to watch television. In addition to treating patients, we're trying to pin down the origins of the outbreak. But

I've walked past the TV in the motel lobby, and they were discussing the outbreak on the local newscast."

"That's bullshit, Jake. They weren't even admitting to the locals that it was smallpox."

"That was before. At first, we thought it would prevent panic if we told the local population it was chickenpox. But it didn't help, so we started providing accurate information. That was two days ago."

"Well let me tell you, there's no news about this anywhere else in the country. Not a damn thing! They've shut it down Jake, and they did it without you even knowing. If there's news coverage, it's strictly local. There's a fucking cover-up going on. It's time to wake up!"

Sarah told Jake about the initial reports of chickenpox she had found on HealthMap and how the results suddenly disappeared from the website. "I'm not making this up, Jake. It's real."

Jake started to argue but then just lowered his head and stared at the table. "I don't understand what's going on. And you're right about the military involvement. Christ, I've been a fucking idiot. The orders came from Washington, and somebody said it was the White House. We just went along with it."

"What's really going on, Jake? How did this all start?"

"We don't know how it started. We're hoping it's under control, but we really can't be certain. There have only been a few cases so far. There could be another wave, people infected by contact with the first victims. Actually, it would be a third wave. We think that it started with a single case—a child—as the primary and that he infected several other kids and adults. Those are the secondary cases. Tertiary cases could involve many more people, hundreds even."

"But you think it's under control?"

"I didn't say that, Sarah. I said we're hoping—that we got here in time and we isolated the secondary victims before they infected others. We are damned lucky that this area is so isolated. We believe everyone who was in contact with the primary victim is still here. But the truth is, we don't know for an absolute certainty. The outbreak could still get much, much worse. We just got a shipment of vaccine, and we've started vaccinating the local population, but we don't really know how well it's going to work. We're also testing a new antiviral agent for those who are infected, but it's never been used before. We don't even know about the side effects."

"How did it happen, Jake? Where did the virus come from?"

"We don't know. There's no research laboratory in the area, so it couldn't have been an accidental release. Bioterrorism doesn't make any sense either, at least not to me. Why would anyone initiate a terrorist attack in the middle of nowhere? Part of the problem is the CDC smallpox response plan. An outbreak is automatically presumed to be the result of a terrorist attack."

"But why the secrecy?"

"I don't know that either. Keeping the public informed is supposed to be the best way to keep them safe. I guess I really don't know what's going on. But I'm sure as hell going to find out."

"Something's wrong here, Jake. You have to be careful. Someone is directing a major cover-up. God knows what they'd do if they thought you were trying to undermine their efforts."

"Sarah, I'm not sure ..."

"The secrecy won't last. I found out several days ago. Communications haven't been shut down completely and neither has access to Farmington. Otherwise, I wouldn't be here. This is going to get out, and my job as a reporter is to make sure that it gets out accurately."

"We're making progress in the lab. We're close to finding out what happened. You know about our operations here at San Juan College?"

"Yeah, I've driven by. But I didn't try going onto the campus."

"Well, don't. They definitely watch everyone going in and out of that place, and they've got remote cameras in place. Even in the labs. It's really heavy handed. It's been tough for the locals, especially the Navajo and the Hispanic population."

"That's right, Jake. They're being treated like shit. They can't travel, and they haven't been able to make phone calls. Some of them can't even get to their own families."

"How did you manage to get here?"

"I have some friends, Jake. Better if you don't know all the details. Let's just say there are a lot of back roads. With a good guide, it's not as hard as you might think. The security forces have made the stupid mistake of thinking that everyone travels on paved roads."

"Oh."

"That brings up another question. You said the security people watch you all the time at the college. Are you sure they didn't follow you here?"

"I don't think they watch us very carefully once we're away from the laboratory. They have us stuck in this town, so they don't need to keep close tabs on us. Remember, there's something like 40,000 people here, and probably there's over a hundred of us on the medical and scientific team. So keeping the roads blocked seems to be their main approach to controlling things. A couple of times I've seen someone—once it was a guy, the other time a woman—who seemed to be just hanging out in the motel lobby, but I haven't seen any indication that anyone has actually been following us.

"Anyway, some of my colleagues were going out for dinner. About halfway to the restaurant, I told them I changed my mind about a big meal and turned back toward the motel. It was already dark, so I ducked into the shadows. Then I walked here on back streets. I have a map, so I knew how to get here. There's no way I was followed."

"If things get tight, they may decide to watch everyone a lot more closely."

"What about you? Do people back in Washington know you're here? The security people could be looking for you."

"I don't think so, Jake. It's a long story, but people back home think I'm on the bike trails in Virginia."

"Maybe we'll be safe for a while."

"What are you doing in the lab, Jake? It shouldn't have taken too long to identify the pathogen, to find out whether or not it was smallpox."

"That was the easy part. Right off the bat, an electron microscope, convinced us it was smallpox. We used biochemistry to really nail it down. We've been using the ViroChip for a couple of years now at CDC, and that gave us a genetic conformation of variola. I guess it was last Friday when we knew with absolute certainty."

"That's when they started shutting down the whole area."

"Yeah, I guess so."

"Do you have your equipment out here?"

"Yeah, some of it. And we're making progress. By tomorrow, we should know where the virus came from. We're comparing gene sequences between smallpox strains. We already had sequence data for the other strains that are locked up in Atlanta. They only have minor differences in their genetic sequences, but it's enough to tell them apart."

"Is this what they're calling microbial forensics? I've read that the FBI used it to trace the samples back to Fort Detrick after the anthrax attacks in 2001."

"That's it. We finished the first round of preliminary work yesterday. Listen to this, Sarah. The sequence for the virus causing this outbreak didn't fully match any of the known strains. That worries us, so we're doing a more complete analysis. We think we can get a time frame for when the strain was developed. Then maybe we can start to understand what's going on."

"So far you have no leads?"

"All we know is that the first case was little kid they thought had chickenpox. He was in contact with a four or five other small children, and several of them are now showing symptoms. But we're giving good supportive care, and the virus responsible for this outbreak doesn't seem to be particularly virulent. So we're hoping that we can get through this without any more fatalities. We've put all of their families into protective medical care. We've isolated the dead child's mother and the grandfather, but the father has gone missing. That's our biggest concern from a public-health standpoint, and the security guys are pretty freaked out too. Some of them think he may be the person responsible for the attack."

Several minutes earlier, Raymond had taken a seat in the next booth. Jake had noticed, but when Anthony came and spoke in Navajo, it quickly eliminated Jake's concern that someone from security might be eavesdropping. He and Sarah resumed their discussion. Now, Sarah saw Raymond turn his head to better hear the conversation.

"I need to get going anyway. Can we meet again tomorrow afternoon?"

"Three o'clock?"

"I'll be here."

As they stood, Sarah reached across the table and squeezed Jake's hand. He reached for his wallet, but Sarah shook her head. "I'll take care of it."

After watching Jake walk down the street in the direction of his motel, Raymond moved over to the other booth with Sarah. "You understand what he said about their suspect?"

"They think it's your friend, Jack, don't they?"

"It sounds that way." Raymond turned to Anthony, who had joined them. "They think Jack Redhouse is responsible for all this. That's crazy. I've known Jack for 20 years, since we first joined the

Marines. I fought next to him, and he risked his life for me. He's a patriotic American, and would never do anything to cause something like this. Sure as hell nothing that would hurt his son. He loved Jackson as much as any man has ever loved his child. It's too late tonight to go calling, but first thing tomorrow, I'm going to see Evie and find out what's going on."

"Hold on, Raymond. It may not be safe to go to see her. Jake said they had Evelyn and Jackson's grandfather in isolation, so there may be security guards. You can't just go over there without checking into it first. And when you do go, I'm going with you. I can't help you if you leave me out. You know that. We need each other."

Raymond gave her a look, a hard look that quickly softened. He nodded. "Okay, tomorrow morning, we'll start checking it out. Maybe we can start by trying to find Jack. In the meantime, we've had a long day. Let's go back to Anthony's house. If I'm right in my thinking, tomorrow may be a really rough day."

* * *

Day 30: Where's Jack?

Sarah was confused by the soft knock on her door. She had been in a deep sleep and didn't know where she was. It was still dark. Then she remembered. She was in Anthony's house. Raymond and Anthony had slept in the living room, giving her the only bedroom. She had fallen soundly asleep almost as soon as she had put her head on the pillow, and now her watch said it was 6:30. She pulled on her clothes and poked her head out of the bedroom door. She could smell fresh coffee and fry bread.

As Sarah drank her coffee, Raymond spoke. "Anthony and I were talking, and we thought it would be best if he stayed here while you and I go off looking for Jack. Nobody's even aware that you and I are in town, so they won't be concerned that we're not here."

"Okay, what's the plan?"

"We know Jack's not at his house, but I have a pretty good idea where he's gone. My guess is he's at an old hunting cabin just west of here."

"You think he went hunting?"

"No. Jack is someone who needs to be by himself when he's troubled. Sometimes, during the rough times for him and Evie, he just bailed out. She would get really upset, but he told me it was the only way he knew to deal with trouble. Just get completely away from it until he could clear his head. His son died less than two weeks ago. Doesn't surprise me at all that he went off by himself. He wouldn't want anyone asking him a lot of questions about Jackson, and even if it upset Evie, he'd just want to be alone. And Evie would never tell anybody where he'd gone."

"Even if they said he might be implicated in the attack?"

"Especially not then. Question Jack's loyalty and nobody would say a word."

"When do we go?"

"As soon as you finish up your breakfast, Sarah. If we take the ATVs and use trails on the outskirts of town, we'll be at Jack's cabin by late morning. But bring all your gear. If something goes wrong, we might not be able to come back here."

By 7:00 they were ready to leave. As they mounted their machines, Raymond cautioned Sarah to ride carefully. "Some of the trails are pretty rough. You don't want to hit a pothole and lose control."

"I'll be careful."

It was a cold morning, but the sun felt good on their backs as they rode west. Sarah loved the wind in her face. The rocky, mostly barren landscape was beautiful.

The San Juan Mountains were visible as low hills in the distance to the north, and more hills were ahead of them. That was where they hoped to find Jack. *In other circumstances, this would be a great place to be a tourist. Maybe someday, Jake and I could ...*

"Watch where you're riding here," Raymond called. "We're making a detour around the San Juan Power Plant down there. No reason to run into people if we can avoid it. We should be there in another hour.

They continued in silence, Sarah thinking of the challenges that lay ahead and wondering how Raymond would react to whatever they might learn from Jack Redhouse. At a curve in the road, Raymond slowed and drove into an arroyo. Within a short distance, they could no longer see the road. Then Sarah caught a glimpse of the cabin, up the slope from the dry stream bed.

It wasn't what she had expected. It was more shack than cabin, but it had a roof.

As they rode up to the tiny structure, Raymond called Jack's name. There was no answer, but he turned to Sarah and pointed to the footprints leading to the doorway. "He's been here, all right. Last week or so. Otherwise those footprints would be completely wiped out by the wind. But I don't see his truck."

Sarah and Raymond walked up to the cabin. Raymond went to the door and called again, and still there was no answer. He opened the door slightly and took a half step forward, peering into the dim light of the interior. He froze. He turned his head partially toward Sarah and said, "He's here."

"What do you mean? Then why didn't he answer?" And then she saw the expression on Raymond's face. *Oh, God!* "Wait a minute Raymond, don't go in. Can you see what it is?"

"Not clearly. But he's dead, Sarah. It looks like he was trying to stay warm, wrapped in a blanket. There's sores all over his face, and he was with Jackson for the whole time that poor child was sick. Do you have any doubt what it is?"

"No. But we need to be sure. Let me go in. I've been vaccinated more recently than you, and I've seen medical photos. So I think I should be able to tell for certain."

"He's dead, and by our Diné customs, the body should be removed by two men. Nobody else should be going in there now."

Raymond saw the look on Sarah's face, and he decided not to argue. "I guess this isn't the time to insist on traditions. You go ahead."

As she stepped around Raymond, Sarah paused and gently put a hand on his shoulder before continuing into the cabin. Inside, she went directly to the figure lying on the floor by the small wood stove. There was no question. She could see the scab lesions on his face and on his hands. There was no way for her to tell how long he'd been dead. The body had not begun to decompose significantly, because the temperatures had been down in the thirties, even in the daytime during the previous week.

She didn't touch anything, partly to avoid contaminating the scene and partly from a residual fear that her own smallpox vaccination might not protect her. Turning to leave the cabin, a speck of white caught her eye. It was a business card lying on the floor near Jack's body. *That's strange. Why would he have a business card when he was trying to get away from everything?*

"Raymond—do we have a small plastic bag? Maybe from a sandwich?"

"I'll go check." He returned to the doorway in less than a minute. "Will this work?"

"Yeah, thanks." She turned the bag inside out, and with her hand inside she picked up the small card. Then she inverted the bag, squeezed it flat, and zipped it with the card inside. Whatever pathogens might be on the card were now safely inside the sealed plastic bag. Walking to the door, she looked at the card and saw that it was for an antiques collector from Maryland. That didn't make much sense to her, so after showing it to Raymond with a shrug of her shoulders, she put it in her pocket. She'd deal with it later on.

"We need to report this to the authorities, Raymond. It should prove to everyone that Jack was no terrorist. He was a victim, just like his son."

"How do we do that without causing problems for ourselves? They'll just lock us up, even if they use a word like quarantine. If the phones weren't out, it would be easy. Maybe Anthony can find someone to report it without giving us away, but it's asking a lot. It's hard to say what they'd do to someone in order to get our identities."

"Maybe there's an easier way." Sarah rummaged through her pack and pulled out the handheld radio. "I almost forgot about this."

Taking it from Sarah, Raymond gave her an approving smile. "You keep on surprising me. This is even better than a radio, because it's a scanner too. That means we can listen to what happens in response to our call. And if they come looking for us, it will help us avoid them."

"Before you start with the radio, I have to do something." Sarah retrieved her cell phone from her pack, the one registered to her real name, and she reinstalled the SIM card. *It won't hurt to do this for a minute. Nobody would be monitoring cell phones when all the service has been shut down.*

She powered the phone on as she went back inside the cabin and used its camera feature to take two pictures of Jack's body. A patch of sunlight had moved across his face and it showed the ravages of the disease in gruesome detail. As soon as she'd finished, she shut down the phone and removed the SIM card again.

Raymond began to pace slowly around the clearing where they had parked their ATVs, as Sarah turned on the radio and began to automatically scan for radio transmissions. The first few hits were static, but the next channel came in clearly. Raymond walked over to her, and they listened carefully. After a minute he said, "Sounds like work crews from the coal mines at BHP Billiton. Probably 20 miles south of here, so that means we can get reception at least to Farmington. Let's keep scanning."

They both perked up when they heard a conversation between the Arizona Highway Patrol and a Colonel Bradshaw. They were discussing logistics along the Interstate-64 corridor—moving personnel while halting other traffic. As Sarah and Raymond listened, they realized it was a main command channel.

"This is exactly what we need, Sarah. Find a way to mark that channel so we can use it again quickly. We'll tell them where they can find Jack, but we'll be far enough away that they won't find us. They'll need the exact location of this cabin, or they'll never find it. Can you pull the coordinates off your GPS?"

"What if they respond really quickly, maybe send out a helicopter? Won't they see us leaving?"

"We'll put some distance between us and this location before we make the contact. Afterwards, we'll listen for a while and make sure they're not hunting us. Not too many trees for cover, but we've got camo netting. They wouldn't see us unless they got within about 50 feet."

Sarah copied the GPS coordinates into her notebook. Then they tied pieces of dry mesquite to the backs of their ATVs and then drove over their original path along the arroyo to the road. The ATVs didn't leave much in the way of tracks on the rocky surface, and the brush that they dragged behind them completely obliterated any remaining trace of their passage. "Is that something else you learned in the Persian Gulf?"

He laughed as he answered. "Nope, this one's an old Navajo trick."

* * *

19

Tehran also can be expected to strike at America, Europe, and elsewhere. And Tehran likely will unleash terrorists worldwide, possibly with chemical and biological weapons ...

—The Daily Beast, February, 2012[*]

Day 30: Letter of Intent

Edwards went home Wednesday night. He was sick of sleeping in his office, and he needed clean clothes. *Better to be fresh and rested than just to sit around waiting.* When he returned to his office just before 7:00 the next morning, Zaborsky was waiting for him.

"What's up, Bob?"

"A couple of things, sir. We finally got access to some of the CIA's files on biological weapons programs. There must have been some real head-butting at yesterday's National Security Council meeting. We received a bunch of electronic files late yesterday. It was almost nine o'clock. They probably figured we wouldn't look at them until today. I guess I shouldn't be that surprised, since we're stonewalling them, too. We're putting a date-time stamp for the next day on everything we put into the system, and that's only after we've reviewed it pretty thoroughly. Anything we have to give the other intelligence agencies won't leave here until we've spent at least a day going through it."

---

[*] "Israel and Netanyahu, Pipe Down the Threats of War on Iran," Leslie H. Gelb (president emeritus of the Council on Foreign Relations), *The Daily Beast*, Feb. 6, 2012, http://www.thedailybeast.com/articles/2012/02/06/leslie-h-gelb-israel-and-netanyahu-pipe-down-the-threats-of-war-on-iran.html.

"That's good, Bob. It's exactly what we want. Just be careful you don't fuck up. There can't be anything in the record showing that we haven't cooperated. The DNI was pretty damned angry when he suspected we'd been holding out on him." *At least if we do get caught, everything will have Zaborsky's fingerprints, not mine.*

"So here's the first of the stuff we got from CIA. It looks like a Soviet smallpox expert went to both Iran and Iraq. I think she gave them a sample of the smallpox virus. We learned about this in 2002, but CIA wouldn't let us interview their source. It was during the run-up to the Iraq war."

"So they've had this information for a while."

"No question. They were just keeping it to themselves. Mostly, it was just history. But it describes how Iran has been trying to get weapons of mass destruction since the 1980s. First they looked to the Soviet Union, and then, after the Soviet collapse, to the former republics. Remember, we already have that information about Kazakhstan that was related to Project Sapphire."

"Anything further from the MEK? That's the dissident group, right?"

"Right, the Mujahedeen-e-Khalq. Nothing of real value lately, but don't forget that they're the ones who first told us Iran was working with smallpox. We liked them because they wanted regime change in Iran, but they were also aligned with Saddam in Iraq. Since then, the State Department listed MEK as a terrorist group, so we've had to keep our contacts low key."

"We really need something that proves the transfer of smallpox virus to Iran. Something unambiguous."

"With all due respect, General Edwards, we both know that the intelligence business isn't an exact science. But we've got the attack in New Mexico, and we can't ignore that."

"We've got to keep looking, Bob. Those peaceniks in the Security Council want to hand over our country to the fucking terrorists. They don't understand that we need to take the fight to the terrorists, or else we'll be fighting in our own streets."

"There is something else, sir. I said I had two things this morning. The first one was important, but the second one may be even bigger. We think we know who actually carried out the attack in Farmington."

"You've arrested someone? You're interrogating him?"

"No, sir. That's actually the point. The Indian kid that died out there? Well his father has disappeared. We think he's the one."

"Why would a man kill his own kid? Only the ragheads do shit like that."

"There's no sign of the guy, so he has to be on the run. And here's something else. It turns out he's a veteran."

"Why would you suspect a veteran?"

"A couple of things, sir. First, he's not a regular American. He's an Indian. Second, he served in the first Gulf War, and his unit was called up again after we invaded Iraq. So he's been over there more than once."

"That's just circumstantial."

"There's a third part. There was something in his file. Something big."

"Tell me."

"Here's the report. The guy's name is Redhouse, Jack Redhouse, and he was Marine Corps. His unit was stationed in a village east of Baghdad. They were talking to the locals, not in an active defensive posture. This guy Redhouse, Sergeant Redhouse, had his men sitting around with their weapons on the ground when an Army unit came through. The Captain in charge of that unit stopped to talk. This Captain Ferguson, he saw some stuff that he didn't like. He didn't like it at all, and he wrote it up. This is his report."

The photocopy was blurred in a few places, but it was fully legible.

Nov. 14, 2005—Our unit was headed up to Baqubah from Baghdad. We were trying to deal with the increased attacks from the insurgents. I was taking my troops around to the east, so that we could enter Baqubah from the north. This took us much closer to the Iranian border—probably within 20 miles. Instead of the 50 miles to go directly from Baghdad to Baqubah, our travel distance was approximately twice that, and we were under constant exposure to attack by the insurgents. My men were under considerable stress.

At about 12:30 local time, while passing through a small village, we encountered a U.S. Marine patrol. The patrol was led by the above-referenced Sgt. Redhouse. I decided that the extra cover provided by the Marines would allow my men to take a rest break with less concern about sniper fire, so I told them they had 30 minutes to relax. Most of my men stayed together as a group, but a couple of them walked around for a look-see after the Marines assured them it was safe. The Marines claimed that they had good relationships with the locals.

At approximately 13:00 one of my men—Lt. Manzoni (see above)—reported to me what he thought was suspicious activity. He had observed Redhouse go off by himself to sit down with two of the locals. It was just the three of them. As Manzoni walked nearby, he could hear them talking, but not in English. Moreover, Manzoni reported that they were not speaking Arabic. He had studied languages in college, and he said he had heard enough of that to know that it wasn't Arabic. He also said it was not Farsi, the language used by the Iranians.

I attempted to confirm this, but the discussion had ended before I returned to the site. I confronted Sergeant Redhouse, but he claimed he was just being nice to the local teenagers—that this was an approved activity for the Marines in that area—part of a program to win the hearts and minds. I found his explanation unsatisfactory and suspicious. I asked Redhouse if he spoke Arabic, and he claimed he did not—other than the few words that all of our troops pick up while stationed here. He also said he did not speak Farsi. I tried to make this part of a general conversation, and I did not tell him why I was asking.

When we returned to our base, I discussed this with our intelligence officer. He confirmed my suspicions. In view of our proximity to the border with Iran, this could be a serious security risk. We were unable to confirm the language that was used, but we could rule out the three most logical possibilities— English, Arabic, and Farsi. There are two other languages used in the proximate area of Iran—Laki and Luri. I searched the web and found that these two languages are used by a total of nearly 7 million Iranians.

*There is reason to be concerned about the activities
of Sergeant Redhouse. He appears to be fraternizing
with civilians in an inappropriate manner. His
interactions with the civilians seemed to utilize a
foreign language that most likely was an Iranian
language. Altogether this actions add up to a
possible major security breach involving the
Iranians—a country that the United States has
labeled as a state sponsor of terrorism. In view of
the preceding facts and assessments, I recommend a
full security investigation be undertaken.*

"Son of a bitch!" Edwards realized that he had been holding his breath. "Was there an investigation?"

"There's nothing in the Redhouse file, sir. We've concluded that Captain Ferguson's report must have gotten lost for a while. Things were getting really fubar over in the Baghdad area back then. Probably by the time they located the report, Redhouse had returned stateside and received his discharge papers. There would have been nothing left to investigate, so they must have just put the report in his file and forgotten all about it."

"Is Colonel Bradshaw looking for this guy? Out in Farmington?"

"You'd better believe it, sir. Trouble is, the damn Indians aren't being real cooperative. Claim they don't know where he is. We sure as hell can't say we think he's a terrorist without blowing our security. It might tip off any accomplices he might have. For now it's essential that the natives stay ignorant."

"Tell Bradshaw to push. He needs to push really hard."

"I'll do that sir. But you've got what you wanted. This is your smoking gun. You wanted a clear link between Iran and Farmington? Well now you've got it."

"You're right, Colonel. You've done a good job. I won't forget it."

Edwards stood up and squared his shoulders. "I've got to get this to the Vice President."

* * *

20

Sarah and Jake

*... a successful response to a future major incident—
either a terrorist attack or natural disaster—
requires a coordinated, interoperable response by
the Nation's public safety, public health, and
emergency management community, both public and
private, at the Federal, State, tribal, territorial,
regional, and local levels.*

—National Emergency Communications Plan, July
2008[*]

Day 30: Finding Jack

After leaving Jack's cabin, Sarah and Raymond traveled northeast on BIA 38 until the road curved to the southeast toward Farmington. At Raymond's signal, they pulled over by a tall rock outcropping and drove a few hundred feet into a small canyon. Raymond draped the camo netting over the ATVs, picked up a small pack from the ATV, and told Sarah to take her electronic gear. They scrambled up the hill to gain a better vantage point. Raymond estimated that they were about three miles from Jack's cabin, and using field glasses, they'd be able to observe the response to their actions.

Raymond picked up the radio. "I'm going to call this in like I'm still at Jack's cabin. I won't be on the air long enough for them to

---

[*] National Emergency Communications Plan, July 2008, Department of Homeland Security.

triangulate our position, and I'll give them a name based on people I know in the tribal police. They won't figure it out for a while."

The radio was still tuned to the same military command center, and Raymond pressed the send button for the first time. He used the same jargon they had been hearing, and he spoke in a firm and steady voice. "Command Central, come in please. Command Central, come in please."

A moment later, the radio crackled with a response. "Command Central, this is Lieutenant Walters. Who is calling?"

"Command Central, this is Officer Matthew Darby, Navajo Nation Police, Shiprock District. We've located the individual you're looking for. Man by the name of Redhouse. Repeat, Jack Redhouse."

"Roger, Officer Darby. Please state your location. We'll send someone ASAP."

"I'm at a small cabin in the hills east of Shiprock. On the reservation, near the eastern edge."

"Can you provide an exact location, officer? We need to know how to reach it."

"Yes sir, Lieutenant. It's about five klicks north of highway 64 on BIA-38. It's a hundred yards up an arroyo, so it's not visible from the road. Here are the coordinates: 36 degrees 47 minutes 51.71 seconds north, 108 degrees 32 minutes 01.08 seconds west. Please verify."

"Roger, officer. 36-47-51.71 north, 108-32-01.08 west. We've got people on the way. Please stay there to guide them in."

"Copy, Lieutenant, but I've got an emergency call west of here. I'll meet up with your people back down on Highway 64. Somewhere near the Hogback Canal. Over and out."

"Officer Darby, you must remain on site. Do you copy?"

Raymond listened to this command but didn't respond, even when it was repeated twice more. "They have no reason to doubt anything I said. It will take a long time before they even think to look for someone traveling east. Meanwhile, let's get some of that camo netting over us, just in case. And stay still. Anyone who's ever gone hunting will tell you that it's motion that gives you away, even if you've blended completely into the surroundings."

Listening to the scanner, Raymond and Sarah quickly learned that the Command Central was scrambling. A group designated as an "S-team," was being sent out with both Army and CDC members. Sarah wondered if the "S" stood for smallpox.

Within 10 minutes, they heard the distinctive "whup whup whup" of a helicopter. "It's a Black Hawk—a UH60," said Raymond. "They could have a dozen men aboard."

Only seconds after they heard the first sounds, the helicopter screamed past their position, close enough that Sarah could see the crew at the front of the aircraft. Raymond whispered that their speed was probably 150 miles per hour. "Can't outrun one of them."

Raymond handed Sarah a pair of binoculars. "I learned to carry two pairs when I'm working as a guide. My clients always want to look, but if I give them the only pair, then I can't be a very good guide. These both have non-reflective surfaces, so they won't give away our position." The helicopter circled once over the cabin and set down in the road at the mouth of the arroyo. Several people jumped out and took up defensive positions, while others moved slowly toward the cabin.

It was difficult to see much detail from that distance, even with the binoculars, but when the figures neared the cabin, Sarah and Raymond suddenly heard the radio traffic.

"S-Team A to Base. This is Captain Jenkins. We have reached the cabin, and there is no sign of anyone in the vicinity. I don't know where that police officer went, but he sure as hell isn't here."

"Captain Jenkins, this is Colonel Bradshaw. Secure your perimeter, and enter the building cautiously. One person only. Then report back."

After about a minute of silence, the radio again came to life. "Base, this is Jenkins. There is no sign of life in the cabin. There is a body on the floor. The medics are going in now."

Again, there was silence. Sarah's heart was pounding, and she felt like she was in a horror movie, hiding in a closet, while the deranged killer was searching for her. When the next transmission came, she nearly screamed. "Base, this is Jenkins. The medics confirm that the individual is deceased. We're going to bag the body. The CDC medics say they'll do all follow-up work back at the hospital facility at SJC."

"Roger that, Captain. Assign four of your men to remain at the site. We're sending a forensics team by road. They should arrive within an hour. Keep your eyes open for that Indian Police Officer. I don't know why the hell he left in the first place. Tell the men you leave behind to disturb nothing. Allow nobody inside the cabin until the forensic team arrives."

Minutes later, Sarah and Raymond watched the Black Hawk lift off and gain altitude. Within two minutes the aircraft had passed them to the south, maybe a mile away this time. It was completely out of sight in another two minutes. "Let's pack up Sarah. It's time we were getting back to Anthony's house. We need to talk about this, and you need to get ready to meet Jake."

* * *

Day 30: Back at Chiquita's

"Did you know Jack and his family?" Sarah and Anthony were talking while Raymond took his turn in the shower.

"Not as well as Raymond, but I knew Jack pretty well, I guess. I only met the others a couple of times. Some of us tried to go over and visit Jack and Evelyn after little Jackson died, but they wouldn't let us into that part of the reservation. I guess that's where all the smallpox cases have been. Jack and I used to work construction jobs together sometimes. He really loved his kid. It must have almost killed him when little Jackson died. I guess it actually did."

"I just hope Jake can figure out where the disease came from."

When Raymond joined them, he immediately began to describe his plans. "I think we need to go over and talk to Evie. It would be good if your friend Jake could come with us."

"How can we get there if the house is quarantined?"

"It may be okay now, at least the general area. We just need to be real cautious. While you were in the shower, Anthony said there haven't been any new cases of smallpox, so they're starting to lift some of the restrictions. Evie and her father have been staying at her cousin's house. She couldn't go back into her own house, not after Jackson died there. Our customs wouldn't allow that. Her cousin's place is right down the street, and there was enough room for two more people. The neighbors brought groceries and left them at the doorstep, so Evelyn, her father, and her cousin just stayed inside."

"Talking with her sounds like a good idea, if you can get us there. I'll ask Jake to come."

"Then we should go meet him now. We'll take Anthony's truck again. When we go to see Evie later, we'll come back here and get the ATVs."

Sarah nodded and reached for her pack. She had been thinking about how helpful Anthony had been, providing shelter, food, transportation, and gasoline. She pulled a $50 bill from one of the zippered pockets of her small pack and extended it toward Anthony. "This may help cover some of your expenses for all this, Anthony."

Chee's eyes flared with anger as he pushed her hand back, almost slapping it. "We're doing this to help our people. Not for you and not because someone's paying us! We may be poor, but we don't need any handouts. Save your damn money to pay the people who won't do the right thing unless they get paid for it."

Sarah was stunned by Anthony's reaction. "I ... I didn't mean ... I mean I'm sorry ..."

Raymond's look told Anthony that the argument was over.

He spoke gently. "Sarah, you put your money away. Someday you'll understand why Anthony and the rest of us are quick to take offense, but we don't have time for that now. Let us help you by giving what we have. If we need to buy something we can't afford, we'll talk then about how to do it. Right now, we've got more important things to worry about. We're all on the same side here."

Sarah was nearly in tears, more from embarrassment than anger, and Anthony still looked angry, but they both nodded deferentially to Raymond. Then all three got up from the table, Sarah quietly said "Sorry" to Anthony, and he silently nodded.

Driving over to the cantina, Anthony skirted the college by driving further to the north than he had the previous day. "There was a bunch of activity just before you got back this afternoon. They really ramped up the military checkpoints and also the security perimeter around the college. They're convinced this was a terrorist attack, and they're worried about a second wave. Except for the college, the extra effort is on the outskirts of the city. Nobody seems to mind if we drive around in town."

By 3:00, Sarah and Raymond were back at Chiquita's, occupying the same booths they had used the previous day. They were mostly silent as they waited. After 30 minutes, there was still no sign of Jake. Raymond went outside briefly. "I asked Anthony to drive around the area and look for anything unusual. How long do you think we should wait for him, Sarah?"

"I'm really not sure. Maybe he just got caught up in all the fuss about finding Jack's body. If he's not here by four o'clock, maybe we should leave. But then what? We didn't make any fallback plans for a later meeting in case something went wrong. Damn it! We just need to wait, Raymond. However long it takes."

"Maybe Anthony will learn something. In the meantime, just try to relax. It won't help anything for you to get yourself all worked up. I'm going to wait over by the front windows."

It was almost 4:00 when Raymond ducked outside again. Anthony had returned, and she could see them talking outside. Raymond returned and gave a reassuring nod. "He saw Jake walking in this direction. Should be here in five minutes."

When Jake entered the cantina, the others were ready. As Jake slid into the booth, Anthony began walking toward them. Jake smiled at him. "Just a Diet Coke, please." Sarah nodded and held up two fingers to signal the same for herself.

"Sorry I'm so late. Things got really crazy. We had to do a crash analysis for a new victim. They found the father of the first kid that died, and it looks like he died of smallpox, too. He was out in some cabin in a remote part of the reservation."

"Yeah, I know."

"What do you mean you know? How could you possibly know? We only learned about it a couple of hours ago. For God's sake, Sarah, what's going on? You seem to know more about some of this than I do."

"I probably do, Jake. And think about it. It shouldn't be that way, should it? But there's also a lot of things that you know about that I don't. We need to start working together, or we'll never make any progress."

"I want to hear how you know about them finding the latest victim."

"We'll come back to that. Please, Jake, what did you learn today? Any lab results?"

"It's all hard to believe, Sarah. And it's not good. There are nine confirmed cases of smallpox. No, I guess that's 10 now. The first was the child I mentioned, the one whose father was found today. Somehow the mother didn't get infected. It's strange how that works sometimes. We think the child's grandfather may have had a very mild case, but his symptoms weren't severe enough to be certain. We're waiting on the results of some antibody work now to nail that down. He'd be number 11."

"Go on."

"After that first kid, his name was Jackson ... You know that already, don't you?"

Sarah nodded.

"His family doc missed the diagnosis. Thought it was chicken-pox. The symptoms aren't very different in the early stages, and smallpox has been off the list of possibilities for 30 years. There were no more cases until about 10 days later. After they had the chickenpox party, some of the other kids got infected. In a way, we got lucky then. An emergency room doc at the local hospital, a Dr. Akebe, worked in Africa during the last smallpox outbreaks in the 1970s. He recognized the symptoms right away, and set up an unofficial quarantine of the other kids. He also called us. He knew to call the CDC. So the exposure was limited. The families were all from the same neighborhood, and that helped, too."

"There haven't been any other cases? Just the 10?"

"We identified four families in the neighborhood with infected children. Three siblings in one family, two in a second, and two more with one child each. The last two families didn't go to the party but came by the next day. Only five of the children have become symptomatic. So there were six children total, Jackson and then five more in the second wave. There were also three adults infected. Two were mothers of the other kids, and the third was a schoolteacher who came to visit the mom."

Sarah couldn't breathe. *Oh my God, it's Jillian!* The words came only with great effort. "What was her name?"

Jake frowned and said, "I'm not sure. Maybe it was Yazzie—or something close to that. Rena Yazzie, I think that may have been it. Why?" He paused. "Oh, shit! You're worried that it's that friend of your from college, aren't you? She's out here somewhere in that teaching program. Is that her?"

"No, thank God. But she is out here. That's how I first learned there was a problem. I haven't seen her yet. I don't want to do anything that would put her at risk. I didn't come out here for a social visit. Jake, I told you that we each know a lot that the other doesn't. We'll get this all cleared up, but right now, go on with your story."

"The schoolteacher was the only one living in a different neighborhood, but we found her before she became symptomatic. If you remember your old virology studies, transmission doesn't take place until the infected person shows the skin lesions. That usually not for a week or two after exposure. As soon as we got our team out here, we started all the standard parts of the public health response to the outbreak. We tried to secure the area, and we started a mass vaccination of people who were in possible contact with the known cases. Also, we hospitalized or quarantined people as appropriate, and we've tried to identify every person who came in contact with the infected people. We think we've been pretty successful with that. That last group isn't under quarantine, but they're being monitored."

"So they're not in jail. It's just more like a concentration camp, is that it, Jake?"

"Come on, Sarah. Stuff has gone wrong out here. I won't argue with that. But you know that we're doing the right thing with these public health steps."

"Maybe. But this situation isn't good, Jake."

"Let's focus on what you and I can do. I'm worried about the man whose body was found today. We have no record of where he was or who he might have had contact with. I'm hoping hope that he simply went to that cabin and that he had no contact with anyone. But we don't know."

Sarah decided to let Jake finish his story before telling him what she knew. "What did you get from the lab results?"

"That's the really exciting news. But it's also the most frustrating, maybe the scariest. I wanted to tell you the other stuff first, but this is really going to blow your mind. Remember, I said we were comparing the genetic sequences of the samples from here with those in our reference stockpile? The samples from old outbreaks? Well, we've gotten our comparisons using the GeneChip technology. Some of the older samples were *Variola major*, and some were *Variola minor*, the milder form of the disease, so we focused on the parts of the genome that are the same for both variants.

"Now, you remember from genetics how as populations evolve, the number of mutations increases? That fits for all the samples in our reference stockpile. The oldest are from outbreaks dating to 1948 in China and the United Kingdom, and they're essentially identical. By the 1950s, a few mutations developed and there was one more in the sample from India in 1953. By 1965, a South African sample showed another three. The largest number was from Somalia in 1977. That's the last known naturally occurring case anywhere in the world, and we counted 13 mutations. There are some additional mutations in some of the top secret samples from our labs and the Russian labs, because they continued to culture the virus for a number of years even after the Biological Weapons Convention took effect in 1975."

"You're losing me, Jake. What does all that have to do with the outbreak here in Farmington?"

"I'm coming to it. Everything was making sense. The virus from the current outbreak, what we're calling the Farmington strain, isn't very different from the earlier strains. The DNA sequence seems to be more than 99 percent identical for all of them. The genome has almost 200,000 nucleotides, and there are just a few places where a single one of them has been substituted. The technical jargon for that is a single nucleotide polymorphism, a SNP. It's pronounced like 'snip.'"

"I've heard of the term."

"So, when the computer finally spit out the analysis today, there were more differences between the Farmington strain and the Somali sample from 1977 than we expected. More than we found between any of the other samples and the Somali sample. We used that as our baseline because it's the most recent naturally occurring sample."

"Jesus, Jake! Then it really did come from a terrorist lab! Someone must have cultured the virus for a long time to get so many mutations. It's state-sponsored terrorism, Jake. It's real biowarfare. God, this is terrible!"

"That's not it, Sarah. What you just concluded is exactly what my boss is saying. And it's wrong! And I'm one hundred percent sure it's wrong."

Jake reached for Sarah's notebook and pen. "If you look at the number of SNPs for the Farmington virus, it's seems really high. But that's just adding up the numbers. You also have to look at the specific mutations."

Jake began to draw a diagram in the notebook. "We expected that the Farmington virus would have all of the unique SNPs from its ancestor plus new ones that might have developed during the intervening years. Do you remember much about phylogenetics from grad school?

Hesitantly. "A little."

"Nowadays, with DNA sequencing, they call it molecular systematics, but it's a way to get an evolutionary tree." The line in Jake's drawing now showed several branches from the starting point of his diagram.

"We haven't completed the cluster analysis yet, but it's clear that Farmington isn't the last virus in the evolutionary chain of all our samples. It's just the opposite. *It's the first!* If it came from one of the other strains, the previous mutations would be there."

"But those mutations are missing?"

"Exactly." Jake continued drawing. "Just look at the 23 differences between the Farmington virus and the 1977 baseline virus. Do you see it, Sarah? Farmington didn't evolve from one of these other virus samples in our database. Farmington came first! All of the others came later."

"So couldn't someone have made the Farmington virus from one of them?"

"Good question. But there's something else. Look at all the other mutations that have developed over the years. Like the 13 that I mentioned for the baseline sample from Somalia when it's compared to the 1948 sample. None of them show up in the Farmington virus. Not a single one!"

"Isn't there another possibility? Maybe the Farmington virus is derived directly from the 1948 ancestor. It would explain the 23 SNPs differences, and it would be different from all the other strains in the database."

"You're close, but it's not correct. It couldn't have been evolving naturally over the last 65 years, because there would have been smallpox outbreaks from it. We would have seen this strain a long time ago. But we didn't. We'll have the complete statistical analysis later today, and that will confirm the genetic relationships. But the preliminary data already show that the Farmington strain isn't new. It's old, really old! The starting point for all the different strains in our database isn't the 1948 virus from China and the U.K. The Farmington virus came first!"

"I don't see how this proves that it's not terrorism, Jake."

"I suppose it doesn't prove it completely. But it shoots down every other hypothesis that people have been making. They're saying an attack would have to come from one of the countries that maintained a smallpox inventory. That means the United States. Russia, or a former Soviet country. I've just given you hard proof that none of the samples held in those labs could possibly have been the source of the Farmington virus. The Farmington virus predates all of them. That's not a hypothesis. That's a goddamn fact."

"How would this virus have survived, Jake? Doesn't it have to be preserved under special laboratory conditions?"

"Not necessarily. Variola is actually very hardy. As long as it's been kept out of the sunlight in conditions that are fairly dry and cool, it could last for a really long time, maybe even a hundred years."

"If it isn't terrorism, then it solves the whole problem, doesn't it? All you need to do is make sure that you follow up with all the necessary medical procedures to contain the outbreak and treat people who were infected."

"You don't understand, Sarah. When I started my story, I said it was scary. But it's not the smallpox that scares me now. It's what they're going to do about it. I tried to explain all this to the military liaison, but he doesn't want to listen. He twisted my words and told his commanding officers that we had proof that it's bioterrorism. Even worse—and this is the really terrible part—I think they've concluded that either Iran or Syria is responsible."

"Didn't they both sign the Biological Weapons Convention?"

"They're both signatories, but Syria never ratified it. And they've both been on the State Department's list of 'State Sponsors of Terrorism.' I think the military is getting ready to carry out a retaliatory attack."

"That can't happen, Jake! You've got to stop them. Talk to them."

"Talking doesn't work, and there's nothing I can do, anyway. When I tried to send my report to CDC in Atlanta, my e-mail didn't work anymore. The military liaison said it's because security has been increased. They don't trust me and they don't believe me. It's almost like a military coup, and I don't know what to do. They're even saying that the Indian who died—Jack Redhouse—that he was some sort of Syrian or Iranian spy. "

The despair of Jake's statement hit Sarah like a punch in the stomach. She reached out for his hand and squeezed it tightly. "We need help, Jake. It's time to bring in reinforcements."

* * *

21

National Security Council

Unfortunately, senior DoD officials would not allow this intelligence to be placed into proper Intelligence Community channels once it was collected. As a result Intelligence Community officials never became fully aware of the information provided by the Iranians ...

—U.S. Senate, Select Committee on Intelligence, 2008[*]

Day 30: Absence of Evidence

The National Security Council would convene in another hour. The "doves" had assembled beforehand in the office of the National Security Advisor. Although they did not see themselves as pacifists, each of the four was aware of the sobriquet that had been conferred upon them by the Vice President. Instead, they saw themselves as voices of reason. Neither Parker Cunningham nor Bertram Morrison was a stranger to war. Cunningham had served in the first Gulf War and Morrison at the end of the Vietnam conflict. They understood that war was not

---

[*] Senate Report on Intelligence Activities Relating to Iraq Conducted by the Policy Counterterrorism Evaluation Group and the Office of Special Plans within the Office of the Under Secretary of Defense for Policy, June 2008.

something to be entered into lightly. And they knew too well how badly the act of killing could damage a person's soul.

The Secretary of State saw her constitutional obligation as requiring her to strive for a diplomatic solution to whatever crisis she was facing. She understood that war is sometimes necessary, but it would always be the choice of last resort, after all other options had been exhausted both earnestly and honestly.

Finally, Juan Allesandro saw his role entirely from his position as the President's Chief of Staff. He believed his first responsibility was to protect James Fallon Alexander, even if that protection were from other members of the administration, even if it were to shield him from the actions of his own Vice President. He believed that he could best serve by ensuring that the President received advice that was accurate, reliable, and free from the political agendas of others.

The Secretary of State took the lead. "We have two topics to discuss here. The first is the reliability of the intelligence we have so far, and the second concerns the father of the Navajo child who died in New Mexico."

Allesandro responded first. "What about the last Nuclear Posture Review? I've shared it with the President. I don't know if he's read the entire document yet, but I've discussed the implications with him, particularly the idea of preemption and retaliation."

"There's not enough time before the NSC meeting, Juan. Assuming we've each done our homework, we'll be able to address it as necessary."

"What about the withholding of intelligence from the Director of National Intelligence? That directly impacts my ability to act as the President's National Security Advisor."

"Same answer, Parker." Calebresi was getting impatient. "We all know—or, at least, we all suspect—that DoD hasn't been relaying its information in a timely manner. But it will serve no purpose to make a direct accusation in front of the President. We would only look like schoolchildren. Let's proceed. Bert, can you give us an update on the reliability of the intelligence presented at the last NSC meeting?"

"Certainly, Madam Secretary. Let me begin by saying that Under Secretary Edwards has been extremely cordial and cooperative with me since the last meeting. I've been receiving daily intelligence updates that appear to contain everything that the DIA has been able to learn. There's still some delay because they insist on doing the preliminary analysis. I'm actually more concerned about the sources for the DoD intelligence."

"Why is that, Bert?"

"Because so much of it is coming from expats and opposition groups."

"I see. But let me play devil's advocate. At State, our goal is to talk directly with people in a foreign government, but that's been difficult for years in the case of Iran. It's certainly the case with our intelligence agencies. So aren't they forced to talk to the expatriates? Wouldn't the expats be most knowledgeable about Iran? And wouldn't the opposition groups have the best pipelines back into Iran? They might even have operatives in country."

"What you say is correct, Madam Secretary, but only to a point. The opposition groups have their own agendas. So do the expats. Their primary goal is not the well-being of the United States. For many of them, the overriding goal is regime change in Iran, and they would be delighted to have us do that for them—even if the justification were entirely fabricated."

"Are you suggesting that our intelligence has been falsified, Burt?" The question was from Juan Allesandro.

"No, I'm not, Juan. At least not at the present time. On the other hand, there is a long history of ... shall we say somewhat skewed information coming from a few of the leaders in the Iranian expat community. If you recall, back in 2001, a couple of Pentagon operatives bypassed all diplomatic channels and met in Rome with an expat who lied through his teeth. It caused a bit of a flap."

"We shouldn't judge our intelligence colleagues too harshly."

"Perhaps not, but the Pentagon should have known better. The CIA had flagged this man years earlier, saying that his information should not be trusted."

Cunningham jumped in, incredulous. "Edwards is using information from this same guy to get us to endorse an attack on Iran now?"

"I can't be sure. So far, DIA won't identify their sources. Either way, it illustrates my point. They're using expats to get information that may be unreliable. I have examples of groups in the U.S. that may be carrying out a coordinated propaganda program."

Calebresi signaled her agreement to the DNI and turned to the other two. "My intelligence people in State have come up with some similar findings, and I have the documentation here in my briefcase. Have either of you found anything similar? Something that you could use during the NSC meeting if the need arises?"

When both Allesandro and Cunningham nodded in the affirmative, she continued, "Then let's move on to our second topic. I have some curious information on the father of the deceased Navajo child. His name is Jack Redhouse. Have any of you located anything about him?"

* * *

22

Sarah and Jake

Even inside the United States, authorities do not know the number and location of an expanding array of laboratories doing research with potentially dangerous viruses.

—*New York Times editorial, 2008*[*]

Day 30: Reinforcements

When Sarah mentioned "reinforcements," Jake gave her a puzzled look. Then he saw Raymond, who was approaching their table. "Wait a minute. I recognize him. He was sitting next to us yesterday. Sarah, what the hell is going on?"

"Take it easy, Jake. This is Raymond Morgan. You can trust him. We're on the same team." Awkwardly, the two men shook hands. "Raymond has been working with me. Jack Redhouse was his friend, and Raymond's wife is related to Evelyn Redhouse."

"Oh, that's just great." Jake put his head into his hands. "I'm screwed. Even if I walked out of here now, nobody would believe me. I'll never get a decent job again in my life, and I sure as hell won't be able to work for the federal government again. They could even send me to prison for this. You too, Sarah."

Raymond spoke quietly as he sat down next to Sarah. "If we don't do something, thousands of people may die because we weren't strong enough to do what had to be done."

---

[*] "Not Safe Enough," Editorial, *New York Times*, Sept. 14, 2008, p. WK9.

Jake's face was deep red with a mix of embarrassment and anger. He said nothing. Then, slowly, he shook his head. "Sorry, that was really stupid of me. I just wasn't ready for all this."

"Jake, we need to figure out what really happened," Sarah said. "We have to get better evidence and then get that information to someone who can do something about it."

"Oh, brilliant. Why don't I just go back to the military liaison and tell him to put me through to the White House, so I can explain all this to the President? That should save us a lot of effort."

When Jake saw Raymond's look of disdain and the flash of anger on Sarah's face, he stopped. "Give me a minute. I'll get past this. Tell me more. I'll just keep quiet and listen."

Raymond spoke first. "I want you to know that Jack was more than a friend to me. We served together in Kuwait, and he was no traitor. He fought for his country, and he was a hero. He didn't like to talk about it. I'm not even sure his wife knows, but he came back with a Bronze Star. Three men in our unit wouldn't have come home without his heroism."

"Then why do they think he was working with terrorists?"

"I can't say, Jake. It doesn't make any sense." Raymond was shaking his head from side to side, but suddenly, he stopped. His gaze went right through Jake for a moment, focused on something far into the distance. Then he closed his eyes as he took in a deep breath. "I think I know."

Sarah turned to Raymond. "What is it?"

"It was during his Iraq deployment. Something happened when his unit was east of Baghdad, near the border with Iran. I remember Jack said a lot of the other troops were just out looking for someone to shoot at. But the Marines were trying to work with the civilian population. Jack was really proud of this. The Marines were trying to get food and medicine to the locals, and it was working. They didn't need to keep their weapons trained on the civilians all the time. And the children were friendly, especially when Jack's unit had enough candy bars."

"But something happened." Jake couldn't keep himself from interrupting.

"There was one day that Jack was talking with some of the local kids, teenagers, I guess. Another unit came through, and an officer said something really nasty to Jack. Told him he should speak English instead of *Iranian*—I remember Jack saying *Iranian*. Jack said the kids had been teaching him some words in *Arabic*. All the guys in his unit had been encouraged to learn some Arabic as a way to show respect for the locals. Jack was doing it both ways. The kids were teaching him Arabic words, and he was teaching them how to say the same words in Navajo. He was real proud of that. Said they seemed to understand that he was in the minority just like they were. Those kids were on the wrong side of the Sunni-Shiite thing."

"That was all that happened?"

"As far as I know. Jack was really pissed off—excuse me—he was mad that this officer had criticized him for doing something good. Maybe it all got written down somewhere, and Jack didn't just didn't know about it."

Sarah looked over at Jake. "There's still the problem that this outbreak started with his son. So the real question is how did that happen? Did you learn anything?"

"Not much. By the time we got here, Jack was gone. The security people didn't like that, especially since his wife said he took a rifle with him. It was a military assault rifle. His wife was completely distraught. She works as a teacher's aide at one of the local elementary schools, but nobody there was infected. So it's all a dead end. Her father can't get around too much, and Jack seems to be the only one who's traveled outside the Four Corners for years."

Raymond raised a hand slightly. "Maybe I can help. Let's go talk to Evie—that's Evelyn Redhouse. Maybe she'll respond better to me. Her mother and my wife's mother were sisters. She might be able to remember some more details."

"She was one of the first people we vaccinated, because she was exposed to her son when he was contagious. It's been almost three weeks, so she's past the incubation period, and she didn't get sick. But they're still discouraging nonessential contact, and they'd stop us if we tried to see her. Plus, there's only the one bridge over the river, and they're certainly monitoring traffic."

"One of the things I've learned from being a Navajo my whole life is that sometimes we're invisible. I think I can show you a way to get over there for a visit. But there's something you should understand—depending on what we find, you may not be able to come back here again, either to your laboratory or to your motel room. Can you deal with that?"

"If that's what it takes. What was it you said before, Raymond? About being strong enough to do what has to be done? You were right, and we have to do this. There's nothing of great personal value in either my room or at the lab. But I can't leave without some of the data we've collected. I'll need that for proof of what we've found."

Raymond took charge. "Then go back to the lab now. It's past 4:30 now. Can you get it done in an hour?"

"Probably. Almost everyone will have left for dinner by then."

"Here's what I want you to do. Leave the lab at five o'clock. If anyone offers you a ride back to the motel, tell them you want to get some exercise. Leave the campus on College Boulevard, just like you were heading back to the motel. But turn right when you come to 30th street, and in about a hundred yards, you'll come to Harvard Drive. It's a short street, so just go toward the end."

Raymond stood up. "I'm going to introduce you to Anthony now. He's another friend, and he'll go outside and show you his truck. He'll be waiting for you at the end of Harvard just after five o'clock. It'll be getting pretty dark by then, so nobody will take much notice."

Jake stood and began to follow Raymond to the door. He turned halfway and looked at Sarah uncertainly.

Sarah tried to smile and gave a thumbs-up sign.

* * *

Day 30: Across the River

Sarah and Raymond were waiting at Anthony's house when Anthony drove up with Jake just after 5:30. The four of them sat down with fresh coffee that Raymond had made, and they shared some cold tortillas that Anthony had brought from the cantina.

"Raymond wouldn't tell me the plan until you two got here, so maybe now we'll find out what's going to happen this evening."

"Okay," Raymond said, "we're going to the Dayzie house. That's Alfreida Dayzie, Evie's cousin. We have to do this without being seen by any of the security details watching the roads, so we'll go in the back way. The house is on the reservation, just southwest of the airport."

Sarah interrupted. "But Jake said there's only one bridge. How do we get across the river without using the bridge?"

"We'll go in a way that nobody expects. There's an old bridge that goes from the south side of the river out to a small island. The water runs deep under the bridge, but the rest of the river is shallow, and there hasn't been much rainfall. We only have to cross about 50 yards of shallow riverbed, and the ATVs should handle that."

"What if they can't?" Jake asked.

"We'll deal with that later if we have to. Right now, let's get moving. Sarah, you ride with me. Anthony knows this area, and Jake can ride with him. We're only four days past the new moon, so there won't be too much light. That's good and bad at the same time. People are less likely to notice us, but we'll need to be real careful crossing the river. We can't afford to use headlights, but the moon won't set until 9:00 or 9:30. So we should have just enough light."

They finished their coffee, went outside, and got onto the ATVs. They drove down the La Plata Highway for a couple of miles, riding wherever possible on dirt paths that ran parallel to the main road. After crossing West Main Street, they went between some homes and the San Juan River. In less than a mile they reached the crossing point.

Sarah was glad she wasn't driving. They had cut off the taillights, and she could barely see the other ATV in the darkness. The path was nearly invisible at times, especially when they drove through a small stand of trees. At the river's edge, it seemed that she could feel the river, or maybe hear it. But she could sense that it was there.

Raymond spoke to Sarah and Jake. "Keep your feet high. I don't think the water will get up to the engine, but it will likely go above the footrests. No point in getting your feet wet, and the water's cold this time of year."

"Go slow." Sarah realized that her nerves were getting tight. That didn't sound at all like the cautionary warning she had intended, but she was scared. *This is no time for panic.* She gritted her teeth and spoke quietly. "I'm ready."

Raymond signaled for them to follow, and he eased his machine into the shallow water. Somehow, he seemed to know the way, and despite the sounds of rushing water, their route stayed shallow. In less than a minute, they reached the small island and crossed the bridge.

They had entered the reservation, and Raymond guided them slowly for about a mile along the dirt roads. In marked contrast to the city just across the river, they passed only a few houses. Finally, Raymond pulled off into some light brush. "We'll leave the vehicles and walk from here. Let me and Anthony do all the talking for now. We'll speak in Navajo, and in the dark all four of us will just seem like local residents. How did you make out with the water back there, Jake? Stay dry?"

"Yeah, I was lucky. I had my hiking boots in the lab, and they're waterproof."

They walked a few hundred yards into a small residential area. Raymond paused in front of a small house and spoke in a barely audible whisper. "I'll go by myself. I need to find out if Evie's heard about Jack."

He knocked softly, and a woman opened the door. Following a brief exchange that the others could not hear, the woman embraced Raymond. Sarah thought she caught the sound of a sob, but she couldn't be sure. Raymond signaled the others to come inside. As they approached the doorway, he nodded somberly. "She knew."

Raymond introduced the visitors to Evelyn. She remembered Anthony and was polite but reserved toward Sarah and Jake. They all sat down in a small circle. Alfreida had gone to sit with Evelyn's father, who was asleep in the bedroom. They tried to talk quietly. Raymond sat next to Evelyn and spoke gently. The others remained silent. "Evie, we're trying to find out how the smallpox started. It's really important, so I want you to remember everything, even though it's painful. Did anyone come visit you—or Jack—before Jackson got sick?"

"That's what the federal people all wanted to know. 'Who came to see Jack?' That's all they seemed to be interested in. At first, it was some doctors, and they were nice, and they asked other questions, too. But then it was just people in uniform, soldiers, and they acted like all this was Jack's fault. 'Where did he go? Who did he meet with? Why did he leave?' And then it got even worse. 'Why did he take his rifle? Did he say he was going to kill people?' I told them I didn't know. I said that he was probably just going hunting. Maybe I should have told them about the cabin."

She turned toward Jake and Sarah. "It was his father's, and it's where he'd go to hunt or sometimes just to get away when the pressure got real bad. But I was afraid they would hurt him, so I didn't tell."

"Did anybody from outside come to visit your house, Evie? From someplace outside Farmington? Somebody who could have come in contact with Jackson? Maybe even at his school rather than at your house?"

"I don't think so, Raymond. Nobody came to the house, except our friends. The government people said they talked to the teacher from my school who came to visit, but she wasn't any help. She didn't know anything about it. She got sick too, but I heard she's getting better now."

"Mrs. Redhouse," said Sarah softly, "may I ask you a question?"

"You can ask, but if you're really here to help like Raymond says, you can't call me Mrs. Redhouse. That's what the government people called me. If you're really my friend, I would like you to call me Evie."

"Okay, Evie. We think that whatever made your son sick was something old. Was there anything really old at school or at your house? Maybe an old photo album or something from your grandparents?"

"No, we don't have any old family heirlooms. I wish we did, but we don't."

Her voice caught. "I mean I don't. There's nothing like that. I'm sorry."

"That's all right, Mrs. ... Evie. We just need to keep trying to figure this out."

"There was something ..." Evelyn turned toward Raymond. "But it wasn't from our family. The stuff from eBay."

"What stuff was that Evie?" Raymond asked gently.

"I've been reading a little now and then. Hoping that sometime I could take a course up at the college. Maybe get an Associate's degree someday. One of the teachers at my school was helping me. Not the one who got sick, a different one, Jillian. She's been really nice to me. And she said she'd teach me how to use a microscope to learn about water pollution."

She nodded her head at the small desk in the corner of the living room. "I was using the computer that Jack gave me for my birthday, and I saw this really nice collection on eBay. It had everything I wanted. All kinds of different specimens and slides. I put in a bid for just two dollars, and I got them. I was so excited. I didn't even have to pay for the shipping, and that was five dollars. It was even more than the slides. As soon as I could save up enough money, I was going to buy a microscope."

When Sarah spoke again, her voice combined sympathy with urgency. "Where are the slides now, Evie?"

"I haven't seen them for a while. Since before Jackson got sick. About a week before. I forgot all about them. They're over at the school, now. Apache Elementary School, where I work. I took them there after I found Jackson playing with them. He was putting them in his mouth, and I was afraid he would cut himself. So I put them over in the biology room to be safe. That was okay for me to do, wasn't it?"

* * *

Day 30: Apache Elementary

As Sarah and the three men walked through the darkness to the ATVs, she started to say something but was cut off by Raymond. "Not until we get back across the river. We can't risk being stopped now. We need to go someplace where we can talk and figure out just what to do next."

They retraced their path back to the old bridge. Crossing the shallow river was easier this time, perhaps because they knew it was possible. The only problem was a wet shoe for Anthony, who momentarily lost his balance when a tire went into a small underwater pothole. Once they were safely on the river bank, Raymond led them down another dirt track for a half mile and stopped in an industrial area with only a few scattered houses. He signaled for the others to remain in place, while he walked around a corner to one of the houses and knocked on the door. A man answered, and after a brief conversation, he and Raymond walked to the street, where they went in opposite directions.

Raymond returned to the others. "Another old Marine buddy. He was just going out and said we could use his living room for a few minutes."

Inside, Sarah felt ready to explode with the information she had. "I have a good friend out here, Raymond. I've known her for years. She's the teacher at the Apache Elementary School that Evie mentioned, Jillian Sommerset. She called me last week. It's how I found out all this was happening out here."

"I know about that, Sarah. I just didn't know we'd find a connection to the outbreak. Remember the man who contacted you by shortwave radio? 'Elmer?' His real name is Walter Lewis, and he's the Principal at Apache Elementary School. He's Jillian's boss, and he's my friend, too. That's why he told you to contact me."

"Then we need to find him. Jillian, too. One of them will know where the biology room is, where Evie put the microscope slides."

"They'll be here soon." He paused. "And don't look so surprised. I've been in contact with Jillian and Walter for more than a week, so when Evie mentioned Apache Elementary I knew what we had to do. This is Walter's house. He's gone to get Jillian."

Sarah's head was spinning. She looked over at Jake, who was equally stunned. "What will we need to look for, Jake? If we can get into the school."

"We just have to look through the slides. And we'll need to do that carefully, since they may be the source of the virus. It sounds like one of the slides might actually be a variola specimen. If so, we need to find it. Is everyone here vaccinated against smallpox? I'm not worried about Walter and Jillian. As coworkers of Evie, they would have been among the first. How about you, Raymond? ... Anthony?"

"Both vaccinated," answered Raymond. "Back in the first Gulf War. Even then, the U.S. was worried that Saddam Hussein had biological weapons."

"That should be okay." Jake paused, as a puzzled look on his face developed into a frown. "Wait a minute. You told me that you and Jack Redhouse served together in the Marines, Raymond. Then he would have been vaccinated too. How come he got sick and died from smallpox? The protection provided by the vaccine decreases over time, but it shouldn't disappear. Jack shouldn't have been hit so hard. Not hard enough for it to kill him. Sarah showed me the pictures she took with her cell-phone camera, and his was a particularly bad case."

Raymond shook his head slowly. "That's the sad part. Jack always hated needles shots, and he'd do anything to avoid getting a shot. The day our unit was scheduled to be vaccinated, he managed to get assigned to a work detail on the other side of the base. He didn't come back until the medical team had left. There was supposed to be a second round, but we got shipped out before it happened. And somehow, he managed the same kind of trick when he was deployed in the Iraq war. He told me about it after he got back."

A soft knock on the front door preceded the entry of two individuals. As soon as Sarah recognized Jillian, she crossed the room and they embraced. Words seemed inadequate, and Jillian was in tears. "Oh, Sarah, I'm so glad you came. It's been so terrible out here." Introductions were then made all around, but with first names only. Raymond had said that it might give them a little extra time in case one of them should be picked up by the authorities.

Raymond brought Walter and Jillian up to speed and explained Jake's conclusion that the military authorities were no longer searching for the origin of the outbreak. "They just want to blame it on Jack Redhouse. They want to call him a terrorist. They're trying to say he was working for a foreign country. And they're talking about a military response. Our only hope—to clear Jack's name, to clear the honor of the Diné, and maybe to prevent a war is to find the true source of this smallpox outbreak. Jake and Sarah think the answer is in a box of microscope slides that Evie Redhouse took to your school."

"I remember them." Jillian looked at Walter. "I think I know where they are. Can we get into the classroom tonight without getting caught?"

"Probably. At least, if we do it in between police patrols. Even if we're spotted, I probably know all the patrol officers. Most of 'em are just kids who were in my classes when I taught high school. I could just tell them that I needed to get some paperwork."

"Then you'd have to stay near your office. Good thing it's in the middle of the main building. I could go over to the science room with Sarah and Jake. The room has dark shades for when we show videos. And I've got some flashlights that we could use."

"Then let's try it," said Raymond. "Can you drive, Walter? The ATVs are too noisy. Four of us can go to this science room while Walter goes to his office. I'll stand watch, so if someone comes to Walter's office, I'll let the rest of you know to lie low. Anthony, you wait outside. If something goes really wrong, you could create a diversion."

They crowded into Walter's car and drove onto Apache Street, which traversed the length of the airport. They could make out parts of the military encampment on the airport grounds. As they neared the school, Walter stopped for a moment to let Anthony out. Then he pulled into the school's parking lot and stopped in front of the main doors to the school. He got out first, unlooked the doors, and held them open while the others quickly entered the building. Only after they had followed Jillian down the hallway, did he turn on a light and enter his office.

The hallway was dark, but Jillian had walked the same path countless times. She extended her left hand, touching the wall as she walked, counting the number of classroom doors they passed. Then she stopped and lifted her key ring. "Aha!" she said softly, as the lock turned. "Stay here for a minute, while I get the shades." The others listened as Jillian lowered the shades, and then they were shocked by a sudden, bright light. They relaxed, when they realized it was just the flashlight, and Jillian was being careful to keep it pointed down.

She guided them to a table on the far side of the room. "The chairs are a little small, but we won't be here long. I have a pretty good idea where Evie would have put the box. There's a place in the cupboard that she uses over here. Hold on a second ... Damn! Not here ... not on this shelf ...wait a second ... maybe ... This looks like something. An old wooden box, and ... yes! It's filled with microscope slides. Organized in little slots."

She put the box in front of Sarah and Jake, and then started to walk around behind them so that she could shine the light on the box of slides and not in their eyes. "Let me get something else from the closet. Don't touch them yet!" A moment later she handed disposable plastic gloves to Jake and Sarah. "I always try to teach the children the importance of safety."

Jake started removing slides, one at a time, so he and Sarah could examine them. The first dozen were disappointing, having labels such as "pond water," silk fiber," and "mildew." There was nothing that was the least bit medical in these slides. But then Jake removed one out that was labeled in a different handwriting. It said "H. Hamilton, var. pos."

His heart raced. "Look at the next one, Sarah. A medical specimen? Hamilton could be someone's name. Someone who tested positive for variola."

Sarah removed the slide. It was "J. Hamilton, neg" and the one after that was a name followed by "neg" as well. Then came three more, all of which ended with "pos."

"It has to be, Jake. What else could it be? The 'pos.' and 'neg.' have to mean positive and negative test results."

"Oh, shit! Look at this one."

Jake handed Sarah a slide that did not abbreviate the description. It said "R. Webster, variola positive."

"This is it, Jake. It must be. We ..."

They were interrupted by the sound of the classroom door opening. It was Raymond. "It's not our lucky night. A patrol car just stopped out front, and the officer got out. We'll see how smooth an operator Walter is. But we need to get out of sight. Get behind a cabinet, get into a closet, whatever it takes. But get where nobody can see you, and stay quiet. Don't talk. Don't whisper. Don't move. If you can avoid it, don't even breathe. Starting now!"

It was the longest five minutes Sarah had ever experienced. She had never even thought before about how difficult it could be to stay still. When she ran or biked, the difficult part was always to keep moving. This was much harder. Every muscle in her body began to hurt, and she desperately wanted to move her legs into a new position to keep them from cramping. But she followed Raymond's instructions.

She nearly screamed when someone jiggled the doorknob. "Look here, Mr. Lewis. This door's unlocked!" The door swung open with a creak, and a flashlight beam swung back and forth across the room.

Sarah was frozen in place in the darkness, lying on her side behind some cardboard boxes. The beam of light created strange shadows, and her heart pounded. She could see Jake's feet under a small table. But they were illuminated only by a reflection of the flashlight beam off the classroom wall, and she was sure that he was not in the policeman's line of sight. Then the beam stopped moving. Sarah could see one of her boots. It was in the beam. That meant that the police officer could see her boot as well. *It's the motion. Raymond said it's the motion that gives you away.* Using all her will power and every ounce of her physical energy, Sarah kept her body motionless, especially her leg. *Maybe he won't notice.* Suddenly, her foot was again engulfed in darkness.

"I guess it's okay, Mr. Lewis. But you really ought to tell your teachers to be more careful about locking up their classrooms. If someone did break into the school, you wouldn't want them to get into the classrooms so easy." The door creaked shut again, and the four intruders heard a key turn in the lock. None of them could understand the muffled conversation from the hallway.

They could breathe again, but they waited another minute before moving. Then a soft knock on the door. It was followed by the sound of a key in the lock. *Please, don't let it be the police again.*

When the door opened, they heard Walter's voice. "He's gone. But you need to hurry. I told him that I'd be done in five or 10 minutes." He closed the door and went back down the dark hallway toward his office.

They resumed their places at the table, and Jake removed a few more slides. "It looks like whoever made these slides—probably a physician—was tracking patients during an outbreak. A smallpox outbreak."

"But there hasn't been an outbreak for 30 years, Jake. Probably twice that in the U.S. How could these slides explain what's happened here in Farmington?"

"It's possible. Maybe even reasonable. The virus can survive for very long times if it's kept dry at moderate temperatures. The wooden box must have been enough."

"How many should we take, Jake? The whole box?"

"No. We should leave the box here as part of the chain of evidence. We have to make people in Washington and Atlanta believe us. Then they can take over and do things all the right way. Let's just pick three slides that are marked as positives and take them with us."

"Jake look at these two. They're both dated 'Apr. 1947.' These slides are almost 70 years old."

Sarah handed Jake three slides, including one of the two that were dated. One at a time, he removed his disposable gloves, using them to separately wrap two of the slides. He motioned for Sarah to give him one of her gloves for the third slide. Then he folded all three inside a paper towel and put the entire package inside Sarah's other glove. "Not quite standard procedure, but it'll do. Jillian, would you put the box back in the closet? Then we can all get the hell out of here."

* * *

23

National Security Council

*Our intelligence agencies get burned by human
sources sometimes—it is a fact of life in the murky
world of espionage.*

—Commission on the Intelligence Capabilities of the
United States Regarding Weapons of Mass
Destruction. 2005[*]

Day 30: Hatred's Origin

The Vice President sat behind his ornate desk, glowering at the Secretary of Defense, the Chairman of the Joint Chiefs, and Under Secretary Edwards. "Gentlemen, this meeting may be our best chance. It may be our last chance. Every time we present evidence that Iran is behind the smallpox attack, the Secretary of State and her friends dream up new reasons why we should disregard the facts. They're stalling. They're preventing our country from doing what needs to be done. They're just a bunch of pussies, and we've got to take charge. If the President hadn't been such a candy-ass and asked for more documentation, those assholes over in Tehran wouldn't be thumbing their noses at us this morning."

"Exactly right," added Walker.

---

[*] "Report to the President of the United States," The Commission on the Intelligence Capabilities of the United States Regarding Weapons of Mass Destruction, March 31, 2005, unclassified version, p. 87.

Neither Walker nor Richards noticed the growing discomfort of the Chairman of the Joint Chiefs. General Radisson's title made him the highest ranking officer in the U.S. military, yet he had no command authority. He was the principal military advisor to the President, yet his appointment had been made on the recommendation of the Secretary of Defense. These inconsistencies made it extremely difficult for him to publicly, or even privately, disagree with Quentin Walker.

Radisson advised the Secretary in private, but once Walker had made up his mind on an issue, Radisson was expected to support the decision without reservation. It was his job. Those were the rules. If he broke those rules, it would be tantamount to resigning. Now Secretary Walker was supporting Vice President Richards in a vulgar slur against the Commander in Chief. *This is going too far.*

Richards continued with his diatribe. "That bitch Calebresi should be taught a lesson. Maybe after we take care of the fucking ragheads, we can send her over to do some of her diplomacy with their ashes. Come to think of it, I'd like to send her over there now to talk to the Revolutionary Guards. We could see how much she feels like negotiating after one of them shoves a broomstick up her ass. Christ, she'd probably like it. Right now, we need to be sure that she and her pansy friends don't outflank us in today's meeting. Edwards, do you have something that will finally convince those assholes?"

The Under Secretary quickly summarized the report connecting Jack Redhouse to Iran. "It's the link you wanted between the smallpox outbreak and the Iranian biological weapons program. And I have additional intelligence pointing to Iranian efforts to weaponize smallpox."

The Vice President waited until Edwards had finished before he issued instructions. "Let's not have everything come from one person. Edwards, your new material ties the Navajo Marine—the one who's on the lam—to Iran's weapons program. That's going to nail this whole thing down, so it should come last. Quentin, you introduce the new reports on Iran's weapons development as soon as the meeting starts. This will be better, coming right from the Secretary of Defense. And it will make it look like you know what you're doing, too. Edwards, make sure the Secretary knows what to say."

Richards gave his final instructions. Alexander put me in charge of the meeting, so I have to appear neutral. So it's your collective responsibility to make the necessary arguments. Iran has been trying to undermine our country for three decades now. I lost a squad of good soldiers in Afghanistan because of those Iranian bastards. A simple mission with 25 men and 21 of them died, some of them probably tortured first. All because the Iranians set up an ambush near the border."

Richards looked at the others intently. "They've been threatening America for years. They've been trying to get nuclear weapons. They've been threatening to wipe Israel off the map. We should have done something about it a long time ago. We should have gone into Iran—not Iraq—back in 2003. We didn't do it then, but we sure as hell can do it now. We can do it, and we must do it. Don't let me down, Gentlemen. Don't let your country down. Do not ... I repeat, do not ... fuck this up. Do you understand? All of you. Do you understand? No fuck-ups."

* * *

24

Sarah and Jake

As soon as you set up a camp, you set up camouflage
netting over any vehicles; that disguises the shapes
from the air, so if there's any kind of air attack, they
won't know that they can hit a fuel truck or a
Humvee over there.

—Bill Katovsky and Timothy Carlson, Embedded:
The Media at War in Iraq, 2004[*]

Day 30: Getting Out

Walter drove directly to Anthony's house, where Raymond insisted that Jake and Sarah remain. After Sarah and Jillian said a difficult goodbye, Walter drove Jillian home and took Anthony and Raymond to the ATVs. When Raymond and Anthony came back to the house, they brought food from a local takeout restaurant, and everyone ate in silence. Only when the food was gone and Anthony had brought out a fresh pot of coffee did they begin the next stage of planning.

Raymond spoke first. "You and Jake need to get out of here, Sarah. You've got to get someplace where you can talk to reasonable people. They'll be looking for Jake pretty soon, so if you don't go first thing in the morning, you'll never get out."

"And there's another reason," Anthony said. "The forecast is for snow tomorrow afternoon. You need to get to Cortez by then, or the

---

[*] "Embedded: The Media at War in Iraq," Bill Katovsky and Timothy Carlson, Globe Pequot, 2004, p. 213.

roads won't be safe. Even with the ATVs, you'd be leaving tracks. Jake, you're going to need some warmer clothes. You're pretty close to my size, so you can take my heavy parka."

"You can't just give me your clothes," Jake began, but Anthony cut him off.

"I already had that conversation with Sarah. We're all in this together, and we all help however we can. No complaints, no objections."

Hoping to steer the conversation in a new direction, Sarah turned to Raymond. "You want us to take the ATVs all the way to Cortez?"

"No, just to the truck. Then drive the truck to Cortez. Retrace the route we used to get here. You've got the maps and your GPS, so you should do fine. Anthony and I will get the ATVs in a few days and bring them back here."

"Should we go to your house? And tell Annie what's happened?"

"Can't do that, Sarah. It would just increase the risks that you'd be stopped. When you get to Cortez, don't go anywhere near Annie. Besides, she'd only worry about me if you did that. Go to the airport. There's a man who can get you out of the area safely. You can trust him."

Raymond handed Sarah a business card that said "Diné Charter Flights, Cortez, CO" along with the name Alvin Keeswood. On the back of it he had written something that Sarah couldn't decipher. "Just find Alvin and give him this card. He'll help you. It'll cost, but he'll help you."

As Sarah took the card, her face suddenly went pale. "Oh my God! The business card. The card in the cabin, Raymond. I forgot all about it."

"What card?" Jake asked.

"I found a business card on the floor of the cabin, right next to Jack's body. I put it into a baggie, but in the excitement I forgot all about it." She reached into the pocket of her jacket and extracted the baggie.

"Holy shit, Sarah! That's a hell of a thing to forget! What if it was someone Jack met after he was sick?"

Jake studied the card. "Danielle Brandis. It says she's an antiques dealer from Maryland. She could be spreading the virus across the whole damn country."

Jake stood up. "Goddamn it, Sarah! I've got to report this right away."

Raymond blocked Jake from moving. "No. You and Sarah have to get away and tell people what really happened. If you tried to call in something now, they might not do a thing—except arrest you. Get out of here with this information—the business card as well as slides and your DNA data. Get it to somebody you can trust. You can report it tomorrow, when you're safe."

"You can't ask me to just sit on this, Raymond."

"He's right, Jake. Once we get out of Farmington, you can reach people who will follow up. We'll figure out a strategy tomorrow on the drive up to Cortez."

Jake said nothing, but after a few seconds he nodded.

Raymond picked up the coffee pot and put it in the kitchen. "Right now, everyone should get some sleep. Sarah gets the bedroom, and the men bunk in the living room. You two need a good rest before you spend the morning on the ATVs. Have you driven one before, Jake?"

"Only once. But I'll be okay. I'll just follow Sarah's lead."

"Let's turn in. Anthony and I will get things ready in the morning. You should start at first light."

* * *

Day 31: North to Cortez

It was 6:15 a.m. and dark. Anthony and Raymond had been up for an hour, working quietly, preparing the ATVs, packing food and water. Raymond made sure the camouflage netting was in the cargo carrier.

Anthony spoke quietly to Jake. "Time to get up. It's 6:20. When you finish washing up, give a knock on the bedroom door."

The others were sitting at the table when Sarah joined them. "I'm going to miss the fry bread when we leave here."

Raymond nodded. He understood that she had meant more than the food. "Sarah, be sure you have all your gadgets. I brought the map in, and I've marked the trails. If you get yourself caught on the wrong side of a canyon, just backtrack until you can match your GPS to the right trail."

He handed Sarah a folded piece of paper. "When Walter dropped us off last night, he said you should listen to your scanner. He wrote down these frequencies. Said you should monitor them every hour, on the hour, starting at 8:00 a.m. He said he was going to drive over to the school early, so he could spot any unusual activity on the road near the airport. The receiver is in his office at the school.

"Your GPS is synchronized to the correct time, so pay attention to it. If there's no news, he won't broadcast. And he won't switch frequencies until he's used the first one. He also said you shouldn't respond unless there's a crisis. You don't want anyone to trace you. You might also want to monitor the military frequency we found yesterday. It would give you a chance to hide if someone comes looking."

He turned to Jake. "When do you think they'll notice that you're missing?"

"I'm not sure. I've been getting to the lab building by 7:15, so by 8:00 they'll probably call the motel. When there's no answer, they'll think I'm on my way in. That would give us another half hour. When they check the room and find out that I didn't sleep in my bed last night, all hell will probably break loose."

"Then figure that by 8:30, they'll be looking for you. They could have patrols out less than a half hour after that. Maybe even helicopter flights. In any case, there should certainly be some radio traffic by then, so listen to the radio. Especially anything Walter might have to say."

Raymond glanced around. "I think you're all set. It's 7:00, and it's getting light enough to travel."

Jake shook hands with Raymond, thanking him for his help and then turned to Anthony. "I really appreciate the jacket and the other gear. I hope that I'll be able to repay you."

"If you can help end this mess, you will have repaid me. Just be careful. And take care of Sarah. She's a good woman."

Sarah had said her goodbye to Anthony, and she was talking quietly to Raymond. "I don't know how to express what I'm feeling. It's only been three days, but I'll always think of you as a close friend. I'll be back again, Raymond. Maybe the next time will be under better circumstances."

"I hope so, Sarah. I know already that you are a good friend. Travel carefully. And trust Alvin. He'll get you to safety, so you can do what's necessary. Until then, you and Jake watch each other's backs."

* * *

25

National Security Council

*Bush turned to Tenet. 'I've been told all this
intelligence about having WMD and this is the best
we've got?' From the end of one of the couches in
the Oval Office, Tenet rose up, threw his arms in the
air. 'It's a slam dunk case!' the DCI said.*

—Bob Woodward, Plan of Attack, 2004[*]

Day 30: Absence of Malice

The Secretary of State looked earnestly at her colleagues. "We must have a plan, Gentlemen. The Vice President sure as hell will. Has anyone learned more about Jack Redhouse?"

All eyes turned to the Director of National Intelligence. According to policy, he should have received all relevant information from the Defense Intelligence Agency, but nobody in the room actually expected that to happen.

"Nothing new for me," Morrison said. "But that shouldn't be a surprise. DIA gave us only what Under Secretary Edwards presented at the last NSC meeting."

The President's Chief of Staff spoke next. "I'm too isolated over here in the White House. Anything I tried would have undermined our effort to be discreet. Maybe Parker has something, though. He

---

[*] "Plan of Attack," Bob Woodward, Simon and Schuster, 2004, p. 249.

has a little more leeway than I do." Allesandro turned toward Parker Cunningham.

"I have the same problem in my role as National Security Advisor, Juan. But there was something really useful in the information that DIA provided about Jack Redhouse. I recognized the name of someone I served with in the first Gulf War. He stayed in as a career Marine officer, and he was stationed in the same area as Redhouse. It turns out that he remembered him."

"Did your contact have anything of value?"

"Yes ma'am. He sent me this report. But it could undermine our arguments. It accuses Redhouse of being disloyal. It isn't something that I'd ever want to believe of a U.S. Marine, but this is what we've got."

"Tell us, Parker." The Secretary of State was grim.

Deliberately, the National Security Advisor read the brief report that had been written years before by Captain Arthur Ferguson, U.S. Army, detailing the incident that he had witnessed in the small village east of Baghdad. When Cunningham finished, the mood in the room had become even more somber.

The DNI was the first to speak. "I see what you mean that about undermining our efforts. But it strikes me as a very weak report. This Captain Ferguson may have jumped to conclusions. Unwarranted conclusions. Presumably, there was a follow-up report. An allegation this serious wouldn't have just gone away."

"Apparently it did. My colleague did a careful search of the records. There was nothing else. Redhouse returned stateside just after this event, and the brass didn't see it as a priority. The insurgency in Iraq was at its peak, so a complaint related to Iran might not have been viewed as a big deal."

Morrison suddenly sat up straighter. "Jesus, do you know what this means? If you found this Ferguson report so easily, the DIA must have it, too. The Secretary of Defense and the Vice President presumably know about it as well."

"Then why didn't they share it with you?"

"Think about it, Juan. If they gave it to us in advance, we'd be prepared for it. You wait and see. When we meet in an hour—in a half hour, now—they'll drop it on us. Edwards will say he just learned about it this morning. They're going to use it in an effort to force the President's hand."

"But now we know about it. They can't."

Cunningham interrupted. "Juan, just because we know about it doesn't mean they can't use it. The report may be weak, but it's damning. We may be really f... We may have been outfoxed here."

Secretary Calebresi had been silent during these exchanges. Her head was bowed, cradled in her hands. She looked dejected, utterly defeated.

Morrison noticed her posture. "Madam Secretary, are you all right."

Calebresi lifted her head, shaking it slowly from side to side. "I've been trying to understand something—it didn't make any sense at all before. Our Bureau of Intelligence and Research came up with an old internal report on Redhouse. It didn't seem to make any sense at all. But it does! It does now! It answers everything. Let me read some of this to you. Just the key parts."

> *... interviewed Lieutenant Johnstone, who was Sergeant Redhouse's commanding officer. I also interviewed Major Thomas Slayton, who was in charge of all the Marine Corps operations in the area.*
>
> *... both officers claimed to know Redhouse fairly well. Both spoke highly of him. Lt. Johnstone said he was courageous under fire and also worked well with the locals. Moreover, Lt. Johnstone emphasized that trying to work closely with the locals was part of the USMC operational plan at that time. They were trying to show that U.S. troops were there to help, not to occupy.*
>
> *... Major Slayton said he had assigned Redhouse to work directly with him on several occasions. Apparently they had some success working with the local teenagers, a really tough group to work with. They were usually very hostile to our troops in the area. Redhouse was able to establish a rapport with these teenagers. A lot of these locals were Sunni, and they were a minority, just like the Indians in the U.S.*
>
> *... that one of the techniques Redhouse used to build relationships with the locals was to teach them a few words of the Navajo language. Apparently, they*

loved it. It was a secret language that nobody else understood, even if they only knew a few words. Redhouse is said to have learned some Arabic as well, but he wasn't fluent.

"There are some other things, but those seem to give the essence of the report. Somewhere in there, it says that the Lieutenant was going to write up a citation for Redhouse—for a Bronze Star—but he was killed by an IED before he had the chance to finish writing it."

"I don't understand, Madam Secretary. What was the point of this report? To whom was the report given? And why?"

"It was handled entirely within the State Department, Burt. I asked our people, the Bureau of Intelligence and Research, to find anything we had on Redhouse, and this is what they gave me. When I first looked at it, there didn't seem to be anything relevant. We didn't know about the Ferguson complaint, and it's never mentioned here. But this report almost certainly was done in response, as part of an investigation. The Army and Marines didn't care. They were fighting an insurgency over there. But we cared ..."

"We?" Morrison interrupted again.

"The people at State. When they heard about this guy who might have been working an Iranian group near Baghdad, they had to follow up. It might have been something could compromise our diplomatic efforts. But that's the whole point. There was nothing! Redhouse wasn't a spy. He wasn't speaking in some minor Iranian language. He was just a Marine doing his job. And apparently, he was doing it really well. Well enough that he got the attention of ..."

She ran her finger down the page as she scanned the text. "Here it is. He got the attention of a Major Slayton, who encouraged his efforts."

Morrison banged a fist on the table. "Now we know the truth. If Edwards and the others try to use that Ferguson report, we'll nail the bastards."

The Secretary of State smiled slightly before she continued. "Let's play this close to the vest. If they don't know about the original Ferguson accusations, we won't bring it up. But if they try to spring it on us, if they try to claim that Redhouse was tied to the Iranians, I'll bring out this State Department report. We'll cut them off at the damn knees. Let's go."

* * *

Day 30: Selective Recall

The mood in the meeting room was grave. The members of the National Security Council were seated around the conference table. Staff assistants took positions in a ring of chairs that lined the walls. There was none of the usual buzz. No conversations about skiing during the holidays, no mention of who would make it into the NFL playoffs.

Most had arrived several minutes early. When all the principals were seated, the President entered, taking his position at the head of the table. He nodded to Trevor Richards. "Mr. Vice President, you may begin."

"The meeting will come to order. You all know our agenda, and I won't waste your time on a recap. The situation is becoming increasingly urgent. We cannot keep a lid on the smallpox situation much longer. Consequently, our decision regarding a military response must be made promptly, if we wish to avoid jeopardizing the brave men and women of our armed forces. If there are no other reports of new information, I'll proceed directly to the Secretary of Defense." Richards scanned the room, but no hand was lifted. Most participants avoided eye contact, and not even an eyebrow had been raised. The Vice President motioned to Quentin Walker.

Walker cleared his throat. He was nervous. Richards had charged him with laying the groundwork. It was his job to get all the other players on board. "Ladies and Gen–"He started over. "Mr. President, Mr. Vice President, Ladies and Gentlemen—we have a decision of major consequence before us. Our country has been attacked, and we must fight back. We cannot shrink from the responsibility that we share to protect our homeland. Our decision may result in the deaths of many hundreds, or even many thousands, of individuals in a faraway land."

He glanced nervously at the Vice President before continuing. "That may sound as though we are preparing to strike in a callous way, and also in an asymmetric way, because far more will die than have been killed so far in the biological attack that was launched against America. But that view would be shortsighted. It would be shortsighted, and it would be wrong. Moreover, it would be dangerous. If we fail to respond now, this first attack—and make no mistake, this can only be the first attack in an effort to destroy our country. If we fail to respond now, this first attack will embolden the enemy and encourage him to take the lives of hundreds of thousands, even millions, of American citizens. We cannot allow that to happen."

The Secretary of Defense saw several heads nod in agreement with his argument. That was good. But he also noticed that most continued to stare down at their briefing books. No eye contact meant no support. This would be a tough sell.

"I want to summarize some additional intelligence reports that we have assembled on this matter. Some are from the Defense Intelligence, and others were provided by Central Intelligence. Others in the intelligence community have provided corroboration, but they gave us no new findings. Let me read you several excerpts:

> We can say with certainty that the Iranian regime now has the capability of mass production of biological material for weapons use. One of the pathogens being worked on is smallpox.

> Iranian Revolutionary Guard Corps Imam Hussein University. Located in Tehran, the university complex houses extensive, but highly secret research departments led by scientists, members of the Iranian Revolutionary Guard Corps (IRGC). ... this establishment focuses on weaponisation of several biological agents, including anthrax, smallpox, typhoid, plague and cholera bacteria.

> Experiments have been taken place at the IRGC Imam University, testing of microbial bombs using anthrax, smallpox, typhoid fever, as well as high dosage aflatoxin.

"There are others, but the intelligence is clear. Iran has been developing smallpox as a weapon. They built facilities for that purpose. They hired scientists to do the work. They have obtained smallpox. They have weaponized it. And they have tested a delivery system. They want to take over the world. They call us the 'Great Satan,' and they want to destroy our country. It is our responsibility to prevent that from happening."

The Secretary of Defense was pleased to see that the number of heads nodding agreement had increased. He thought perhaps he had won a few converts. "Are there any questions to this point?"

He knew he had made a mistake as soon as he asked the question. He should have forced all questions to the end, after Edwards had made his presentation. Now his opponents could snipe at his arguments one at a time, before he and Edwards had finished making their case.

"Mr. Secretary—" It was Bert Morrison, the DNI. "You didn't provide any attribution to your intelligence citations."

"That is quite correct, Mr. Director. We discussed this at some length, and we concluded that even with this august group, it would be unwise to reveal the actual identities of specific agents."

It was apparent to all in the room that the Director of National Intelligence was not pleased by the response. In fact, his anger was barely concealed. "I happen to have the same reports from which you've just quoted, and I believe the identities of the sources are highly relevant."

The Vice President interrupted. "I'm afraid that I need to rule you out of order here, Mr. Morrison. The security of the United States must be protected at all costs, and we cannot afford to compromise it by revealing intelligence sources."

Before anyone could say another word—and it was clear that a heated argument was ready to erupt—the President spoke. "Mr. Vice President, please forgive me for interrupting, but these are extraordinary circumstances. We're discussing military options that could affect our country—the entire world—for many years to come. Everyone in this room is cleared at the highest levels, and secrecy might allow the wrong conclusion, one that could lead us to the wrong action. I'd like the DNI to proceed."

The Vice President was enraged. But he could do nothing other than let Morrison continue, recognizing that he had to follow the President's instructions.

"Thank you Mr. President. Mr. Vice President, the first of those quotes can be sourced directly to an Iranian political opposition group. The other two are from a retired Israeli military officer."

Walker wasn't giving up. "That's precisely why I gave you those reports, Mr. Director. Who better than the Iranians themselves, those who recognize the horrible flaws of the regime, to deliver us the truth? They have the contacts, they have the resources, and they have the knowledge. We are fortunate that they share it with us. And a former Israeli military officer? This man is a real expert. We know him and we know we can trust him. I am afraid, sir, that you are attempting to discredit our friends when you should be focused on our enemies."

Morrison raised an eyebrow. "I know that you've used opposition groups for a long time. Opposition groups and expats, too. You are not alone, because we've been doing that across all the intelligence services for many years, for many decades. But doing so carries a very high risk. These people have a vested interest in changing the regime in Iran, but they don't necessarily give a damn about the United States of America. If anybody wants specific examples of the risks, just look at the historical results of using intelligence from expats. That's how Eisenhower got the debacle in Hungary in 1956. It's how Kennedy got the Bay of Pigs in 1961. And it's how Bush got Iraq in 2003. It's exactly what I said it was. It's very high risk. In the absence of reliable information from other sources, we can't use it."

Walker saw his arguments circling down the drain. "What about the Israeli? The Israelis are trusted allies. Surely, you aren't going to impugn his integrity?"

"No, Mr. Secretary, I am not. Your Israeli source has provided a great deal of well-researched and well-documented information. In fact, it's so good that I'd like to read a bit more of it to this entire gathering. I have in front of me the full document from which you pulled your quotations. Here's another from the same document, one that you didn't read to us:

> *Most of the information for this part was supplied by the National Council of Resistance of Iran (NCRI) early 2003. There are conflicting attitudes over the reliability of the NCRI reports, mainly due to the U.S. State Department statement on August 15 naming the NCRI as affiliate to the Mujahidin-e-Khalq (MEK) terrorist organization ...*[*]

"As you can see, I don't need to attack the credibility of your Israeli source. He was quite rigorous, and he explicitly discredited the intelligence himself. Mr. Vice President, I believe we should all recognize that we are attempting to make a decision, a

---

[*] "Iran's National Deterrent: Weapons of Mass Destruction Program," Defense Update – News Analysis by David Eshel, April 4, 2004, http://www.defense-update.com/2004/04/irans-national-deterrent-weapons-of.html

recommendation to the President, on the basis of extremely unreliable and incomplete information." The DNI was careful to avoid any hint of smugness in either his voice or his expression, but he knew that he had fully discredited the intelligence reports presented by the Secretary of Defense. A discreet look around the room confirmed his conclusion. Those nodding in implicit agreement, if not outright approval, represented a clear majority.

Walker was livid and unable to disguise his emotions. Moreover, he understood fully what had just happened. Rather than attempt to rebut the DNI, he decided to press forward in a new direction. Barely keeping his voice, and his chin, from trembling, he motioned to his Under Secretary for Intelligence. "With your permission, Mr. Vice President, I would like to ask Under Secretary Edwards to present some new information. Something very important." After a moment's hesitation, Walker added, "He just got the information this morning. We haven't had an opportunity to share it with the other side ... I mean our colleagues ... I mean, not even with Director Morrison. But the Under Secretary has copies for all of you now."

With studied calm, Vice President Richards directed Edwards to proceed.

After handing a packet of papers to an aide, Edwards cleared his throat. "Mr. President, Mr. Vice President—I recognize the gravity of our situation. And I also recognize that emotions are running high. Whatever the results of these discussions, the implications for the American people are enormous. Consequently, you will understand the importance of the document that is now being distributed."

Edwards made a compelling presentation of the Ferguson report. By the time he was done, he thought that everyone in the room finally understood they were talking about an American traitor. Jack Redhouse somehow had been directed and supported by one of the three rogue states that had been defined as the "axis of evil" a decade earlier. He had launched an attack on America.

"Mr. President, it was a terrorist attack with one of the most dangerous and horrible diseases in all history. The report now sitting before the members of the National Security Council makes it crystal clear that the United States of America has been attacked by a foreign power. We were attacked by Iran, in the most reprehensible and immoral way imaginable. The facts speak for themselves sir. The choice of response is yours."

Edwards was correct that his presentation had swayed the views of many in the room, among them the Secretary of Treasury, the

Legal Counsel to the President, and the Attorney General. He hadn't expected to convince the hard-line doves, so he hadn't been looking at them. As a consequence, he had failed to notice that both the DNI and the National Security Advisor had each been following the text of the report as Edwards discussed it, taking notes. Had he looked carefully, he would have noticed that they indeed were marking on copies of the Ferguson report—but not the copies that Edwards had distributed. Similarly, had he looked, he would have noticed that the Secretary of State was also annotating a document while Edwards reviewed the Ferguson report. But her markings were on another document entirely.

The Vice President was also unaware that his opponents were focused on something other than the presentation Edwards had so carefully rehearsed. He, like Edwards, believed they had won their case. Incautiously, he asked "Are there any questions before we move toward finalizing a recommendation for the President?"

The Attorney General raised her hand to signal a desire to speak, an unusual move for Samantha Chernikov. She tended to remain silent during meetings. Now she directed her question to the Secretary of Defense. "What about genetic information? We've found, or more accurately, the FBI has found microbial forensics to be extremely valuable. In 2008, the technique provided a definitive answer to the 2001 anthrax attacks. Has CDC done a gene sequence? Wouldn't that identify whether the virus originated in Russia, for example? If that were the case, it would prove that the virus didn't originate here in the U.S. After all, if it came from our own country, attacking Iran would be tantamount to mass murder."

Quentin Walker suddenly looked like a deer caught in the headlights. He was not prepared for this. A quick glance over at Edwards resulted only in a slight shake of the head—Edwards had no idea either. The Vice President, still calm, stepped in. "I believe we have somebody here from CDC. Yes, could you identify yourself sir?" He motioned to a man at the back of the room.

"Yes sir. My name is Dr. Steven D. Rasmussen. I'm a physician at the Centers for Disease Control and Prevention in Atlanta. I'm the Director of the Coordinating Office for Terrorism Preparedness and Emergency Response. "

Trevor Richards didn't want the conversation to go too far astray. "Dr. Rasmussen, can you answer the Attorney General's question, using lay terms if you please, about genetic testing?"

"Certainly. Well, in the simplest terms, without going into how it's actually done, we now have scientific instruments that provide a complete genetic sequence of an organism—a virus in this case. Basically, it's like a fingerprint. So we can tell whether two organisms are identical or not. In this case, we were able to get samples of the original Russian—actually, original Soviet—virus cultures and compare them with what we found in Farmington. So far, we only have preliminary data, but we do know that the Farmington virus is different from all of the Russian samples."

Once again, the room went silent. The Attorney General followed up her original question. "Then what you're telling us doctor, is that this virus must have originated in the United States?"

"That may not be the case at all. The situation is much more complicated. It turns out that all viruses mutate. They evolve with time. Most of the mutations don't have any effect on the pathogenicity, the ability of the virus to cause disease, but they do create differences in the molecular structure. So the only thing we can say for sure right now, is that this outbreak didn't result directly from one of the actual samples that the Russians have had in cold storage for 30 years."

"But you're not entirely ruling out the Russian samples as the source?"

"No, ma'am, we can't do that. But let me clarify: I can say the same thing about the samples that have been retained in the United States. The Farmington virus doesn't match any of them, either. The only thing that we can say right now—and this is based on the information that our team of experts has sent back from New Mexico—is that the Farmington virus does not match any known smallpox sample."

"Then it's definitely a terrorist attack from overseas." The Secretary of Defense had been unable to control his excitement.

"It's possible. We believe that the Farmington virus has undergone normal mutations in the course of being cultured, very likely cultured to create a weaponized form. There are reports that Iran has tried to create genetically modified smallpox virus. The Farmington virus might have resulted from intentional genetic modification, and it might be resistant to our vaccines. If that's what we're facing, the consequences could be truly horrific."

Richards didn't want anyone suggesting that decisions should wait until CDC completed whatever tests they were conducting on the Farmington virus. Action was needed now. "Thank you Dr. Rasmussen. You may take your seat again. Now, I think we are ..."

"Mr. Vice President?" It was the Secretary of State.

"I have something here that I think everyone should know about. It's something that was provided by the State Department's Bureau of Intelligence and Research. I just received it this morning." Calebresi looked over at Edwards and Walker. "We haven't even had the opportunity to make copies yet. I've been reading it during these discussions, trying to make some sense out of it. Now I think I understand it. May I read part of this aloud?"

"This is highly irregular, Madam Secretary." The Vice President suspected he had been outmaneuvered. Calebresi was playing this well enough to win an Oscar, while Morrison and Cunningham looked as innocent as newborn babes. A discreet glance toward the President told Richards that this was no time to force the issue. He had to let the scene play out. "Very irregular—but we're all seeking the truth here. Please proceed."

Caroline Calebresi was in top form—sincere, forceful, and eloquent. When she was done, everyone in the room knew that Jack Redhouse was no traitor. Even Richards.

As he saw his window of opportunity closing rapidly, the Vice President made one last lunge before it slammed shut. "Mr. President, I thank the Secretary of State for helping us to avoid making a terrible mistake. We were ready to take an American hero and tar him with the brush of disloyalty, to brand him a traitor. Fortunately, the Secretary has corrected that error, and now we can focus more clearly on the task before us. I have been listening carefully to everything that has been said here, and I think we know what must be done. The exoneration of Jack Redhouse confirms that the smallpox outbreak in New Mexico was not an example of domestic terrorism. There can no longer be any question of that.

He turned toward his foe and smiled at her. It was not a friendly smile. "But what the information provided by Secretary Calebresi does do for us—what it makes absolutely clear—is that the attack can be attributed to Iran and to Iran alone. We must act accordingly. Mr. President, on behalf of the National Security Council, I recommend that you commence immediately with final instructions for a tactical nuclear strike on Iran."

In contrast to the dead silence that followed several of the previous speakers, the room was suddenly filled with sounds. There were whispered conversations on the sidelines, and several of the principals at the table tried to speak at the same time. "Mr. Vice President, I object—"

"Mr. President, you cannot—"

"This is an outrage!"

Before things could spin completely out of control, James Fallon Alexander rose from his chair. His deep voice was soft but powerful, and his imposing frame dominated the room, even from the end of the conference table. He brought almost instantaneous quiet to the room. "I shall not tolerate mob behavior in this meeting. Everyone please sit down."

The President remained standing after everyone else was seated. "Mr. Vice President, I thank you for your acute analysis. You have done everything I asked in chairing these last few meetings of the Security Council, and I am deeply grateful. We have now reached the point at which I must make my own decision, and I am reassuming chairmanship of the Security Council."

The other participants, the principals as well as those seated on the periphery, realized that something had just happened, but they weren't quite sure what it was. They knew only that a major power play was occurring, or perhaps had just ended. Now they could only wait to see how things would develop further.

"There are two specific questions that I must address when I make my decision. The first is whether to undertake retaliatory action against Iran. That is a very serious question, and it has lasting import. The second, and that is assuming the answer to the first question were to be affirmative, is whether nuclear weapons should be employed. The significance of that decision is far greater. I am aware of the nuances in what may or may not be the official U.S. policy on responding to WMD attacks and whether the attack in New Mexico would mandate such a response. But that analysis can come only after a decision has been made on the first question. I must first reach a decision on whether we should retaliate against Iran."

The Secretary of State was the first to signal a desire to speak, waiting only until Alexander finished. "Mr. President, I believe there are still unanswered questions with regard to the causes of the outbreak in New Mexico. It is my constitutional duty to strive for diplomacy rather than resorting to war. I urge you to proceed slowly, to allow me and my colleagues in the Foreign Service to serve the American people in peace."

The Secretary of Defense didn't wait for the President to recognize him. "May I point out Madam Secretary, that it was your office, the Department of State, that listed Iran as a state sponsor of terrorism? Your efforts at peaceful solutions have failed. This outbreak of smallpox in New Mexico is real. It is no theory. I concur with the Vice President that a rapid military response is necessary. When the Japanese bombed Pearl Harbor, we didn't debate the topic for weeks on end. Our leaders then understood what needed to be done. We must stop this before it goes any further. We must act now."

Before Walker could go on, a stern look from the President caused him to stop speaking and lean back in his chair. The President then nodded in response to a signal from the Chairman of the Joint Chiefs of Staff, another member of the NSC who rarely spoke up in front of the full assemblage.

"Mr. President, I am deeply disturbed by what we have heard here today." He looked around at the others in the room, most of whom were steeling themselves for a further onslaught against Iran.

"What we have heard here today from representatives of the Department of Defense should have every person in this room paralyzed in fear. You may have concluded this was a minor attack with only a few deaths. Or you may believe it was the first wave of a massive biological onslaught. Those issues do not matter to me. Not today. Today, I must respond in my official capacity as the principal military advisor to the President and as the statutory military advisor to this Council."

Radisson paused to take a deep breath. "We are witnessing the use of predetermined political goals in an attempt to drive a military decision. I understand that I am breaking ranks with the Secretary of Defense, and it is he, not I, who delivers orders to the troops from the Commander in Chief. Consequently, I am aware that some of you may take these remarks as my resignation speech. If that is the case, so be it. But I cannot endorse the proposed attack by our military. We must not commit our brave men and women, and we must not undermine our nation's morality by attacking a sovereign government so lightly. That would require unambiguous proof that the New Mexico outbreak resulted from a planned attack by Iran. Mr. President, we have no such proof."

Once again, the mood in the room changed dramatically. Some were shocked. Others were frightened by the significance of George Radisson's short speech. But most had begun to better understand what had happened. Secretary of Defense Walker and Vice President Richards glanced at each other. They were visibly angry, though it was impossible to tell just who or what was the target of their wrath. The Secretary of State and the DNI exchanged a brief look, one of immense relief engendered by General Radisson's remarks.

For a second time, James Fallon Alexander stood. "It is apparent that feelings run high on these topics, and there is nothing more to be gained by additional discussion today. General Radisson has offered the caution and wisdom that I expect from a military leader, someone who can prevent a war as well as win one."

The President slowly surveyed the room. "We cannot act without unequivocal evidence. Go back to your offices and work with your colleagues. We need evidence, real evidence. Not evidence that selectively supports a particular outcome but evidence that will bring us to the truth. We will reconvene on Monday, and I shall make a decision then. If we find that Iran is indeed to blame, then God help them."

* * *

26

Sarah and Jake

A person who has a communicable disease "in the communicable period" shall not travel from one State or possession to another without a permit from the health officer of the State if such a permit is required under the law of the destination State.

—U.S. Code of Federal Regulations (42 C.F.R. § 70.3)[*]

Day 31: Apache Pursuit

Sarah and Jake followed Troy King Road for several miles on the outskirts of Farmington until they were well north of populated areas. Anyone who saw or heard the ATVs would assume that a couple of locals were out hunting for the day. They only had to cover about six miles as the crow flies, but their actual route would be at least twice that distance. Several times they paused to check their GPS coordinates, and they also stopped at 8:00 a.m. to listen for any communication from Walter. His voice came through clearly.

"Slide One, this is Elmer. Slide One, this is Elmer."

"Roger, Elmer. I copy."

"Cease transmitting please. Nothing yet to report. Over and out."

---

[*] U.S. Code of Federal Regulations, Title 42: Public Health, Part 70.3: All Communicable Diseases (42 C.F.R. § 70.3).

"I guess we don't have to worry about them tracing his transmissions if he's going to finish that quickly," Sarah said. "We'll listen again at 9:00."

"Let's keep moving. But drink something first." Jake handed Sarah one of the water bottles.

Sarah drank quickly and handed the bottle back. "I think we'll be able to get to the truck before nine o'clock when we need to start listening to radio traffic again."

At about 8:45 Sarah recognized the rock outcropping where Raymond had left the pickup. Remembering what Raymond had said a few days earlier, she rode most of the last several hundred yards in the arroyo. Their tire tracks would be less noticeable, if they could be seen at all. Then they stopped the ATVs next to the truck.

"Jake reached out to touch the camouflage netting. "That's amazing. I was looking right at this spot when we turned off the path, but I didn't see anything. Not until we were right here."

"I hope it works as well if anybody comes looking for us. We've only got about five or 10 minutes, so let's get everything ready." She took more netting from the cargo carrier on her machine and gave it to Jake. "Put this over the ATVs, while I go sweep our tracks. And put one flap over toward the truck so there's room for us to crawl underneath." Sarah retrieved the branch that Raymond had broken off and walked quickly back toward Jake, sweeping the branch back and forth to erase any tracks leading off the road.

"I'm impressed. It looks like Raymond taught you a lot over the last couple of days."

Sarah smiled. "Where's my pack with the radio?"

Jake pointed to an opening in the camo netting, and they crawled through it. "Here's some food and water. Looks like they made us a couple of sandwiches. And here's your radio."

Sarah turned on the radio and began scanning. According to her watch, which was synchronized with the GPS, they had at least five minutes before they could expect a signal from Walter. There was nothing on the military command channel, but a conversation came in on another frequency. "… his pickup truck. Road 6900, just off Highway 64. Looks like he might have had engine trouble … keys are still in it."

A burst of static preceded the response. "Stay with it. But don't touch anything. Remember what happened to him. We'll let the medical people know about it, and they can decide what to do next."

"It's Jack's truck. They've found it."

"Where's Road 6900 on your map, Sarah?"

"Let me see ... Here it is. Looks like it must be about three miles from his house. About halfway to the cabin, which is up ... here."

"Shit. You know what that means? If he was getting sick, that would have been too far for him to walk."

"So what? People here knew him. Someone would have given him a ride. Oh, crap. I see what you're getting at."

"If it had been someone local, we would have heard about it. Or, at least, Anthony would have heard. And people around here knew about Jackson."

"Then it had to be a tourist ... Oh Jesus, Jake! The card. The antiques dealer."

"Yeah. Before it was possible. Now it's a probability. I have to call Frank Wirth at CDC. His section tracks infectious diseases, and he knows the issues with smallpox. He also knows how to work with local authorities. But I don't know how to contact him. If I use a cell phone, they'll be able to trace our location. We'd never get the chance to present our evidence."

"I think there's a way. I've got a cell phone that ... Wait a minute, that's Walter transmitting now. I'll tell you later."

"Slide One, this is Elmer. Slide One, this is Elmer."

This time, Sarah didn't respond. She just listened.

"Slide One. We have activity. Patrols heading both directions on Highway 64."

Sarah realized that he could see the "activity" from his office windows. The school was only a few hundred yards from the edge of the airport, where the military units were based. Raymond had told her that Walter's shortwave radio was in his office. It was part of the emergency equipment that he was given in his capacity as school principal.

"Helicopters heading north. Everything is locked down tighter than it was. Over and out."

"Damn! Can you get any of the military communications, Sarah? Maybe we can figure out what's happening."

Most of the military communications didn't seem relevant, but one message caught their attention. "This is Rover 3. We are turning west for our northern sweep."

Only when Sarah heard the "whup whup whup" did she realize a helicopter was approaching them. Fast.

"Don't move, Jake!" Moments later, as the sound began to fade, she peered cautiously through an opening in the netting. It was the same kind of helicopter that she and Raymond had seen the day before. "That must have gone almost directly overhead."

"Yeah, but they didn't find us, Sarah, so they may make a second pass later. The sooner we put some distance between us and Farmington, the safer we'll be."

"If they come back too soon, we'll be sitting ducks. Help me get the camo off the truck and transfer the gear from the ATVs."

In a couple of minutes, they were driving as fast as they could on the dirt road, retracing the route that Raymond and Sarah had followed two days earlier. Sarah was driving. "Two days! It was only two fucking days ago that I got here, Jake!"

They monitored the radio as they drove, and 20 minutes later, they heard a communication that sent chills down their spines. "Base to Rover 3. Make another sweep in the north and west sectors. Expand your radius from three miles to six miles."

Jake was looking at the map. "If that's the same helicopter that came over before, it means they'll be coming right over us again. They're flying a larger radius, and we've driven north by about that much."

Sarah slowed down until she saw a relatively flat place to the side of the road. There were a few small trees. She braked hard, and they jumped out to get the netting. Jake pulled it out of the bed of the pickup and tossed it over the top of the cab. It was only partially secured, when they heard the "whup whup" again.

"Get under the truck," Sarah screamed, and they both dove between the wheels, holding the ends of the netting. "Do you think they might have seen us?"

"I don't know, but we'll find out pretty damn quick. Christ, those things travel fast. We're lucky we were on the far side of the truck. I think we were already out of their sight line when we scrambled underneath. Listen—it seems to be getting farther away."

"Wait until we can't hear it anymore before we move, Jake. Oh, shit! It's getting louder again."

"They're coming back. They must have seen us when we pulled off the road. Goddamn it! We're totally fucked." The sound of the rotor blades continued to get louder, until the aircraft seemed only a few feet away.

Once again, the noise level changed. "They're moving away, Jake. They're leaving!" The din of the helicopter decreased rapidly as the craft sped away from them a second time. This time the sound continued to fade until it was inaudible.

The radio squawked a message, "Rover 3 to base. We thought we saw something, but it was a negative. Repeat, it was a negative. We are continuing west and then back southwest toward Shiprock as planned."

* * *

Day 31: Cortez, Take Two

As Sarah continued driving toward Cortez, they monitored the radio continuously. There was some chatter on the military channel, but nothing of significance. Otherwise, it was surprisingly quiet. Shortly before 10:00, Sarah pulled over into a small copse of trees on the right side of Grass Canyon Road. They put the camo netting over the truck, and quietly shared some water and a candy bar.

Their solitude was interrupted by the radio. "Elmer to Slide One. Elmer to Slide One. Things are quieting down. Snow is starting. Aircraft grounded. Over and out."

"The sky is clear to the north, but look over to the southwest. It's pretty gray. If there's snow moving our way, we should get as far as we can before it hits. Are you okay to keep on driving, or do you want me to take over for a while?"

"Thanks, I think I'm okay. But it sure isn't comfortable. I swear, I can feel every damn pebble we run over."

"Next time, we'll ask for a free upgrade," Jake said. They laughed, surprised that they still could.

Radio traffic was minimal for the next hour, as they had expected from Walter's last transmission. As the time approached for his 11:00 call, they just kept driving. This time, after identifying himself, he simply stated, "Nothing to report. I'm signing off. Good luck." And then there was silence.

"We're on our own now, Jake. I think we'll make it by 12:30 or 1:00, based on the trip down with Raymond. I remember him saying it was a five- or six-hour trip in total. How close are we to the Mancos Canyon turnoff?"

"Not far. It looks like only a mile or so according to the map. Oh, shit! Do you see that?"

Sarah's heart nearly stopped. For a moment, she thought he'd seen another helicopter. But that wasn't it. It was a snowflake.

Within minutes, the occasional flake progressed to a steady snowfall. "Maybe we'll be all right, Jake. Most of it's blowing off the road. How much farther do you think it is to the main road?'

"If I'm right about where we are on the map, it looks like another seven miles, maybe a little more if you count the curves in the road. How fast are you going now?"

"I'm still doing about 15, but it's getting slippery. If it doesn't get too much worse, we'll be okay."

After another 10 minutes, they were doing under 10 miles per hour. The road now had a light but complete covering of snow, and at times it was difficult to see exactly where the road was. They entered a stretch where the road snaked along the bottom of a channel through the rocky outcroppings that went up some four hundred feet above them on both sides. One of the front wheels hit a small pothole as they entered a curve, and the truck began to slide sideways. Sarah spoke through clenched teeth. "Shit!"

Jake tightened his grip on the front of the seat as he looked over at the ditch to the side of the road. It was only a few feet down, but they wouldn't be able to get the truck back out again if they went into it. Sarah regained control, and drove forward white-knuckled. They were down to five miles per hour.

After what felt like longest half hour either of them had ever experienced, Jake looked up from the map. "I think the intersection with the main road is only about a mile away."

"Can't come soon enough for me. This has been a real bitch to drive in. Will our tracks give us away?"

"As long as it keeps snowing for a few more minutes, our tracks should be covered. And they can't use any aircraft until it stops."

"There's the highway! Hot damn, Jake! We did it. Now what?"

"We try to find the guy Raymond told us about. Alvin. The airport is just a few miles to the north, and this road is almost clear. A plow must have gone through."

They were able to drive north at a good pace for the next ten miles. "There's the entrance to the airport up ahead, Sarah. Turn in over there."

Sarah was the first to see the small sign. "Jake. Look! Diné Charter Flights." She eased the truck into a semi-industrial area across the street from the airport entrance. Driving cautiously through the two inches of snow that had built up in the parking area, they spotted another sign for Diné Charter Flights, this one a sign on the door of a small building. Sarah pulled off to the side, keeping the truck out of sight, and they climbed stiffly out of the cab.

"We're starting to get lucky, Sarah. The snow has stopped, so maybe we'll be able to fly out of here. Let's get inside and find Alvin Keeswood."

They stepped through the door into the tiny one-room building and saw a single desk littered with dusty papers that had turned yellow with age. To the side was a wood stove, a coffee pot, a rocking chair, and two small wooden chairs. A fire was burning brightly inside the wood stove. The aroma from the coffee pot suggested it had been brewed quite recently. The rocking chair was occupied by a smallish man who looked to be in his sixties. His brown skin was wrinkled and leathery. He nodded slightly but otherwise didn't move as he asked, "What can I do for you folks?"

"Mr. Keeswood? Alvin Keeswood?" Sarah took the slight tilt of his head for a yes and continued. "Raymond Morgan sent us. He said you could help, and we really need help." She fished the card from her pocket and handed it to him. "He said I should give you this."

There was a noncommittal "um hmmm" but no movement other than to extend a hand to accept the card. The man looked at it and frowned slightly, as if unsure what to make of it. When he turned it over and saw the writing on the back, his posture changed. He sat up straighter, and moved the card into the light from the standing lamp to his side. The puzzled look changed to one of recognition, and he nodded his head. Not the slight movement that he had made when Sarah and Jake first entered, but a full nod. Not one but several, without saying a word. Then he repeated himself. "What can I do for you folks?"

"We need to get to the East Coast, probably to Washington, D.C.," Sarah answered cautiously.

"I could fly you to Denver real easy. Lotta flights back east from there."

"We need to find a way without using commercial airlines. There may be some people who ..."

"You're in trouble with the police."

"No, we're not. Well, not exactly. Look, do you know about the outbreak down in Farmington?"

"I heard."

"Do you know what it is? The disease?"

"I know it's not what they're saying."

"So you know that they're trying to cover it up?"

"Yep."

"We have information about what's really happened. And we need to reach someone in Washington who can help prevent something much worse."

"Don't imagine I need to know about that."

"Can you help us? Raymond said we should trust you."

"I reckon I can help you. But not to Washington. If people are looking for you, we can't fly right into the biggest government city in the country. Maybe somewhere a little west. Maybe Ohio or Pennsylvania. A small airport. Wouldn't attract so much attention."

"That could work, Sarah. I have an uncle who lives in Moorefield, West Virginia," Jake said. "Mr. Keeswood, do you have a list of airports for that area?"

Alvin slowly lifted himself out of his rocking chair and walked over to his desk. From the pile of clutter, he pulled a loose-leaf notebook and flipped through the pages until a small bob of his head indicated that he had found what he wanted. "See if you recognize any of these towns. General aviation airports. A small plane coming in wouldn't be unusual."

Jake scanned the list and stopped when he saw the listing for Petersburg, WV. "Grant County Airport. I'm pretty sure Petersburg is close to Moorefield. Do you have a map?"

The dusty pile of materials on the desk yielded a U.S. Road Atlas. Jake turned to the page for West Virginia and found Moorefield and then Petersburg. "Only about 10 miles."

"Okay," Sarah said. "Do you think you could get us to the Grant County Airport?"

"I could. Not sure you'd want to do it, though. It would be expensive."

"Raymond told us to trust you. We'll pay what you say is a fair price. We don't have any choice."

Alvin turned to another page in his loose-leaf binder and pored over a table of data, writing down several numbers with his pencil. He had the curious habit of licking the end of his pencil, just like a character in an old movie. Then he furrowed his brow and began his explanation. "It's about sixteen hundred miles. Normally, I'd charge between two-fifty and three dollars per mile. This one is more difficult, since I have to come back by myself. And also, we'd need to make stops."

"Stops?" asked Sarah.

"We're not flying an airliner here. My plane is a Cessna 172, a Skyhawk. It's one of the best aircraft out there, and mine is only 30 years old." Seeing the sudden look of concern on the faces of his visitors, he went on, "It's in good shape. Best aircraft ever made. More 172s were made than any other plane in history. So it's safe. And it's reliable. It'll go above 13,000 feet. That's enough to clear all the mountains."

"How far can it go without stopping?"

"It can cruise at about 140 miles an hour, depending on our tailwinds flying east. That's 12 hours of flying time for the trip. Even if I could stay awake that long, it only carries enough fuel to go about 700 miles per leg. Maybe a little less with the extra weight. Can't do it without two stops. One stop is too risky."

He paused and tapped his pencil on the desk. "Like I said, this is an expensive trip. Call it five thousand, and we're all set."

"That would be fine, Mr. Keeswood." She hesitated. "Would it be all right if we paid you in cash? This isn't a good time for us to leave a paper trail."

A pause. "Cash would be fine. What do I call you? I'm Alvin, not mister."

This time it was Sarah who nodded. "Sarah." She tilted her head to the right. "And Jake."

"All right, Sarah and Jake. If people are looking for you, we should get out of here. They've cleared the runway, so we can leave this afternoon. You stay here while I get the plane ready. You have any gear?"

"It's outside. Raymond let us use his pickup. He said we should leave it with you."

"Show me what you need to take on the plane. I'll put Raymond's truck someplace safe. Coffee's fresh. Cups are over on the table."

* * *

Day 31: Phone Home

As soon as Alvin had left, Jake turned to Sarah. "I need to call in the information on the antiques dealer. You started to say something before about a cell phone."

Sarah reached into her small backpack that she'd been carrying with her, "Try this. I bought it with a fake name, so there's no way anyone will trace it to us. You're going to call the guy you work with in Atlanta?"

"Yeah, Frank Wirth. I don't know who else I can turn to right now." Jake removed a business card from his wallet. "At least I have his cell number."

He keyed in the number and held the phone to his ear. "Frank? I'm glad I got through to you. This is Jake Overman. Can you talk for a minute? It's important."

"Christ, Jake, where the hell are you? People around here are going nuts. They're saying that you're ill. That you've gone off the deep end. Your boss is furious that you've stopped providing updates. Just your message yesterday that the training exercise was going fine."

"Frank, it's not a training exercise. It's smallpox. There's been an honest-to-God outbreak of smallpox in New Mexico."

"That's what they've been saying, Jake. About you, I mean. That you've lost it. You were supposed to use the smallpox protocol to test our medical and emergency response. But Jake, it's just chickenpox."

"Something strange is happening, Frank. I don't know why, but it is. The military has taken over in Farmington. The area has been completely sealed for a week now. No communications except through the military. I was sending e-mail messages to Margaret Andrews every day with all the details, but I haven't received a response."

"That's not what Margaret told me. Jake, I repeat, she said that she hasn't heard from you."

"Something is really wrong, Frank. There's something you have to do, and it doesn't matter if you think I'm crazy. Take down this name … call it an anonymous report if you have to. Okay … ready? Danielle Brandis. She's an antiques dealer from Catonsville, Maryland. It's just a few miles from Baltimore. She was exposed to *Variola major* about 10 days ago."

For a few seconds, Jake held the phone away from his ear, unwilling to listen to what Frank was saying. "It doesn't matter whether I'm wacko, Frank. You have to follow up on this and follow up right away. An outbreak in a city like Baltimore with an international airport could cost a million lives before it's over. Even if you think I'm lying, you have to do this. Even if it kills our friendship forever. Do it Frank. I'm begging you."

"I'll have to see, Jake. This is really outside of channels."

Jake used every ounce of his energy to keep from screaming at his colleague. Very softly, he said, "Frank, are you willing to risk people dying—people like your wife and children—because you think I might be wrong? I'll be in touch."

Jake had begun to put down the phone, but he stopped. "Oh, and one last thing, Frank. If you can find this Danielle Brandis, and you realize that I'm right? Get somebody in my lab to do a complete gene sequence. Don't fuck around with it. Just get it done as fast as it can possibly be done." And with that, Jake broke the connection.

Shaking, Jake handed the phone back to Sarah, but she declined. "No, you keep that one. I've got more. Right now, I think I need to do the same thing you just did and call my editor. I'm missing in action, too."

Sarah took out the other two cell phones that were in the name of Sarah Wallingford. In response to Jake's astonished look, she said, "That's all of them—except for the one that's in my real name, and I can't use that unless we want them to find us before we get back to Washington. Oh, yeah—and there's also another one in a different fake name that I used to call my dad. It wouldn't be good to use that one either." After some thought, she changed her mind and put both phones back into her pack.

"Maybe it would be a good idea to save this other one, Jake. It's never been used. You keep it, and I'll call my boss with the same phone you just used."

The phone rang twice at the other end before Sue Parkinson answered. "Sue, it's Sarah."

"It's about time you called. We were beginning to get worried about you. I hope you've enjoyed your biking, but there's work to be done here. Newspapers don't run by themselves."

"Sue, just let me talk for a bit. This will be hard for you to believe, but what I'm going to tell you is the absolute truth. I haven't been biking. I've been working on a story—a big one. There's been an outbreak of smallpox in Farmington, New Mexico. The entire thing has been covered up, and all communications in and out of the area are blocked. It's being treated as a terrorist attack, but I have evidence that it isn't. I need to get you that evidence, but I can't do it yet."

"Sarah, have you been drinking? Where are you?"

"This is real, Sue. It isn't a joke, and I haven't lost my mind. I'm going to need your help."

"Sarah, we can't do something like this over the phone. Just come into the office, and we'll sit down and discuss everything. If you really have the makings of a story, we'll go from there."

"This is the real deal, and I will tell you everything. But I can't come in now, not yet. I know it sounds paranoid, but there are people trying to stop me. I'm scared. And I'm running. But it's too important to let it go. Give me another day. Maybe two. If I'm right, this will do for us what Watergate did 40 years ago. I'm going to need your support on this, Sue. We'll get pressure from the government, probably from the Defense Department. Or maybe one of the security agencies. And we'll probably need legal help. But I'm right on this. I've got to go. I'll be in touch."

Without waiting for a response, Sarah ended the call and turned off the phone. Even though the wood stove had kept the temperature inside Alvin's office comfortably warm, she shuddered when she realized just how much she and Jake were out in the cold.

* * *

27

Intelligence

*Offensive CI operations ... are clandestine CI
activities run in support of DOD military national
security objectives and programs against individuals
known or suspected to be foreign intelligence
officers with connections to foreign intelligence or
international terrorist activities.*

—*response to a question at a DIA press conference
about counterintelligence activities*[*]

Day 31: Tightening the Net

"Grab a chair, Parsons. I'd like an update on anything you've learned on the domestic front. Have there been any more attempts to breach security at CDC?"

"No, sir. Just a few incoming phone calls to people who were sent to New Mexico. We checked them all out, and there's nothing there. One was from an old boyfriend. When he couldn't get through, he didn't even ask where she was. Guess he just figured he'd look elsewhere if he wanted to get laid that night. There was also a call from another guy's former girlfriend—actually, maybe not so much

---

[*] Defense Intelligence Agency, comment by Under Secretary of Defense for Intelligence Toby Sullivan, "Transcript: Media Roundtable about the Establishment of the Defense Counterintelligence and Human Intelligence Center," August 5, 2008, Transcript by Federal News Service, Washington, D.C.

former as current. The trouble is the guy's married. We had to follow up, and I think the wife figured out what's going on. Apparently, she was really pissed. Poor guy's gonna be in trouble when he gets back to Atlanta. He'll probably wish he'd managed to catch smallpox out in Farmington. At least that would've bought him some sympathy."

"What about the girl? The reporter." Zaborsky really wasn't interested in the gossip.

"Nothing at all. We haven't seen her since Monday. The lookout we posted outside her apartment building saw someone fitting her description leave the parking garage on Sunday afternoon. But it wasn't her car. He got the license plate, and it belongs to her next door neighbor."

"Did you talk to him?"

"Not right away. We didn't want to spook her. When there was still no sign of her by yesterday afternoon, we paid the neighbor a visit when he got home from work. We used the same trick with our badges. He actually asked why the FBI was interested before we got to plant the suggestion."

"And ..."

"Well, first off, I think she must have noticed our guy. She told the neighbor she was trying to avoid an old boyfriend. Said she'd noticed him outside the apartment building and asked if she could borrow the neighbor's car to dodge the boyfriend. Said she needed to go to Richmond for the night."

"She's friends with this neighbor? But she lied to him. If she spotted your man, she knew it wasn't an old boyfriend. She's up to something."

"Maybe, but we don't know what. She was back the next day. We saw lights in her apartment Monday night. The neighbor confirmed it. Said he ran into her in the hallway."

"And you haven't seen her since? That was three days ago."

"No, she seems to be gone. But it fits. Early Tuesday morning, the lookout thought he saw her ride out of the garage on a bicycle. She got onto the bike path that heads toward National Airport, so he phoned his partner. The partner drove down the GW Parkway toward the airport, and he saw someone fitting the description—woman on a bike, carrying a backpack, same blue jacket. She rode right on past the airport."

"You didn't try to stop her?"

"We couldn't get to her. The bike path is on the other side of the parkway. But our man saw her stop and talk to a guy on a bike. We thought maybe she was meeting a contact. So our man made a U-turn and talked to this other biker."

"And ...?"

"Nada. Guy was just a tourist out for a morning ride, and he stopped the woman to ask directions. We checked him out, and we don't think he was bullshitting us. He never got to do any sightseeing, though. Not after all the time he spent talking with us. But he won't complain. He thinks he was helping the FBI work a bank robbery case."

"What about the woman?"

"Like I said, our man couldn't follow her any farther. He had to focus on the guy she talked with. She was headed down toward Alexandria, and that path goes all the way to Mount Vernon."

"What does Mount Vernon have to do with it?"

"Nothing direct. But the neighbor said when he saw her on Monday, she had new camping gear she just bought. He asked her, and she said she was going to go on a bike trip for a couple of days, somewhere out in the country. It fits. The weather was good, and the person riding the bike was heading out of town with a big pack. If she'd been trying to go somewhere in a hurry, she would have taken a plane. But she just cruised right on past the airport. We think she's on a little vacation."

"I don't like it, Parsons. We know she's up to something. She's a fucking reporter, for Christ's sake. This is the only security breach we have, and it could be a real problem for us if she finds a way to contact this guy Overman in New Mexico."

"I don't think she'll be able to do that, sir. I followed up with Colonel Bradshaw in Farmington like you asked. He said they'll keep tabs on Overman. If she tries to contact him, we'll know about it. Bradshaw is monitoring the secure phone lines out there, and we're getting all the e-mail traffic here."

"It's time to ramp this up another level. I want everything on this reporter tracked—cell phone, land line, e-mail—all of it. We're talking national security and terrorism here, so get the telecom companies to do full monitoring. And not just lists of phone numbers. I want full transcripts of anything she sends or receives. If anybody gives you trouble, I'll get you whatever signature authority you need. I'll sign it, or I'll go to Under Secretary Edwards or the Secretary of Defense. We'll go right to the fucking Vice President if we need to, so make sure they know that."

Parsons stood up to leave.

"One more thing, Parsons. We need to talk to this reporter. Next time you find out where she is? Don't fuck around. Take her."

* * *

Day 31: Local Service

"What is it Parsons? I'm pretty busy right now."

"Sorry, Colonel, but I thought you'd want to know. We've got active wiretaps on both of the woman's phones, her home phone and her cell. No traffic yet, but as soon as she uses her phone, we'll be listening. I've got two people on it at all times. Since you bumped this up to an official antiterrorism action, we've been able to get a lot more resources on it. Nobody but me knows why, though. They all think we're following up on some kind of Al Qaeda thing. Just like you told me."

"What about her office phone? Edwards signed off on all of this, but we only have seven days. The Foreign Intelligence Surveillance Act requires us to get concurrence by the DNI and the Attorney General after that. Edwards says we're lucky we've got a whole week. Before they amended FISA in 2008, those numbnuts in Congress used to think we only needed three days before we had to follow all the legal procedures."

"We've got her office phone covered, too. Your buddy Atkinson over at the National Security Administration is handling that. NSA has computers that scan everything. So we just picked out some keywords, like her name, Farmington, smallpox. You get the idea. If they get any hits, they'll have someone listen to the conversation. If there's something of interest, they'll send us a transcript."

"Make sure you stay in touch with Atkinson. Just you. If this operation goes south, I don't want anybody else to know what we've been doing. Are all of your people okay with doing the things you've asked of them?"

"Yes sir, Colonel. These guys are solid. They're all contractors, just like me. All ex-military, so they know how to take orders without asking questions. Every last one would like to crack a few heads, but they understand that they probably won't get the chance."

"Okay, Parsons. I want to be notified of any developments. Anything at all."

Parsons left Zaborsky's office and returned to his office by the cluster of cubicles his group occupied. Overall, he thought this was turning into a pretty good gig. Not as boring as usual. And if he caught up with this woman, it might get a whole lot more interesting. He'd seen her picture, and he thought she wasn't too bad. *Not exactly hot, but definitely fuckable. Talking to her—getting some information out of her—that could be kind of fun.*

Parsons signaled his team leaders to join him. "Give me an update. Anything on the Lockford phones?" He'd already checked his desk, and there was nothing from NSA about any calls at the *Post*.

Jimmy Tarkington and Pete Harkness pulled their chairs up close to Parsons' desk in the cramped office. After they reported that there had been no telephone activity, Parsons gave them their instructions. "Look guys, it's Friday afternoon, and I don't think we're likely to hear much more today. So wait until 1800 hours, and then send your people home for the night. I want them fresh in the morning, and they should all be happy that they'll be getting lots of overtime this weekend. Both of you need to stay on alert in case I have to call you. And make absolutely sure that you each have an unmarked car ready to go. If anything goes down, we need to move quick. Zaborsky is getting nervous."

In just a few minutes, all the cubicles were empty. One of them, occupied all day by the newest and lowest ranking member of the group, still had the Post-it note affixed to the bottom corner of the computer monitor.

To: D. Parsons

From: A. Cummings

Re: MSA—pls call H. Atkinson about your leak

Cummings had received his discharge papers only a few weeks before, and he was excited with this new job as a contractor for DIA. Growing up in Las Vegas, he had driven past MSA Engineering on countless occasions. They did electrical and plumbing, and the incoming message had triggered that memory. It never occurred to him that he was thinking of a business located more than a thousand miles away. In addition, he had heard the first letter incorrectly—it was NSA, not MSA.

The message came in after five o'clock on Friday, so Cummings figured it could wait until Monday. Unless it was something important. In that case, the plumber would surely call Parsons at home.

* * *

28

Sarah and Jake

First there were just 20 sick people—all in Oklahoma. Two weeks later, there were thousands, spread across many states. Three months after that, 1 million people in 25 states were dead. Those were the results of 'Dark Winter,' a government-sponsored exercise conducted last summer, in which researchers simulated a smallpox attack on Oklahoma City.

—*New York Times, 2001*[*]

Day 31: Skyhawk

"Let's move out. I want to be airborne before sunset." Alvin waved Sarah and Jake to the door, turned off the light, and followed them outside.

"I was wondering, Alvin. Do we need to go through a security check? Because Jake sort of lost his wallet, and ..."

"Don't have to do that here. They've been pushing for new rules, but my plane is way under the limit. It only weighs 2,300 pounds, even with the fuel tanks full." With that explanation, he pointed at a dilapidated panel truck that was idling at the side of the building. "Jimmy will give us a ride over to the plane."

No further introductions nor explanations were offered, and Jimmy drove them to a single-engine aircraft on the tarmac near the runway. Alvin directed his passengers into the small plane's cramped seating. "If you two aren't friends yet, you will be by the time we get to where we're going. The cabin's only 42 inches wide." Sarah and Jake watched the truck drive off as Alvin closed the hatch and started the engine.

Alvin turned and offered each of his passengers a set of headphones. "Nothing fancy. They're just to cover your ears and make it quieter. We'll make it to our first stop in Wakeeney, Kansas, by about 9:00 p.m. That's Central time."

Alvin pulled the plane onto the runway after a short radio exchange with somebody. Without further communication, they were airborne. The distant mountains were majestic, and they looked huge. Alvin had said the plane could fly above the mountains, but Sarah hoped he would go around them instead. She looked at Jake and tried to smile, but his response looked more like a grimace. She reached over and held his hand, then put her head on his shoulder. She was asleep before the plane had reached its cruising altitude, and Jake nodded off shortly afterward.

Alvin flew north of the Colorado-New Mexico line, hugging the southern edge of the San Juan Mountains. Staying below the rugged peaks to their north minimized their radar visibility, and Alvin didn't want to fly above 10,000 feet without oxygen supplies. About 100 miles to the east of Farmington, he turned the plane briefly to the southeast and then east again, to skirt the last of the big mountains. An hour and a half later, all the mountains were behind them, and Alvin dropped the plane even lower as they began crossing the Great Plains. There was no unexpected radio traffic and no weather to worry them. It was an easy flight.

Sarah and Jake awoke as the plane was making its approach into the Trego-Wakeeney Airport. They could see the runway lights, and they watched as the ground came closer and closer until, finally, the plane touched down gently and settled in after only one light bounce. Alvin taxied to the far end of the runway and opened the plane's single door. He climbed out and motioned for Jake and Sarah to follow.

"See those lights? That's Interstate 70. Walk around the truck stop over there, and head up the road under the interstate. There's a McDonald's on the far side. A couple hundred yards past the entrance ramp. I'll be there in 15 minutes. Order me one of those hamburgers with the special sauce. And some French fries. Super-size."

They watched as Alvin climbed back into the plane and taxied back down the runway toward the airport buildings. "I'm not sure what he's doing, Jake. But Raymond told us to trust him, so let's go."

As they walked through the darkness, Jake said, "I feel like we're fugitives."

"We are."

They were already eating when Alvin walked in. "Friend gave me a ride. You get that burger?"

Jake stood as Alvin sat on the opposite side of the booth. "The kid behind the counter over there said he'd keep it warm for you. Do you want something to drink with it?"

"Coke would be good. Regular, not diet. Don't forget the fries."

Alvin remained silent until Jake returned. He nodded his thanks and began to eat. When he was half finished, he started to talk between occasional bites of food. He reached into his pocket and pushed a motel key across the table to Jake. "Right there across the street. One room for the two of you. Didn't want to give them too much information. I've got the room across the hall."

Pulling a map from his pocket, he unfolded it on the table. "Here's how far we've come. This is a small town with a small airport. Anybody starts asking about this flight after we leave, folks here saw me come in alone. I said I was meeting two passengers here in Wakeeney and taking them back East. Tomorrow morning, I'll file a flight plan for Salem, Illinois. That's here. That leg will be a little over four hours, so make sure you're ready to go at 7 a.m. The motel has free breakfast, and you might want to bring a candy bar or something on the plane in case you get hungry. But don't drink too much, understand? No restroom."

Sarah and Jake both nodded, and Sarah asked, "What about the last leg?"

"That's here. I'll file a flight plan once we're in Salem. No point in saying too much too soon. From Salem, Illinois, to Leesburg, Virginia."

"Wait a second—"

"Hold your horses, Jake. I know what we said. 'Petersburg, West Virginia.' And that's where I'll take you. But if somebody's looking for you as hard as you're hoping they're not … Well, we don't want to give them advance warning. I figure that nobody has made any connection so far between you two and my plane. They will, though. Maybe sometime in the morning, but by the time they find out we've gone to Salem, we should already have left there. So anybody wanting to welcome us would be waiting in Leesburg, just sitting there and thinking about how smart they are. They'll have to wait a long time, though. When we get over West Virginia, I'll call in and ask to divert to Petersburg. Tell them I'm running low on fuel. Nobody argues with that."

Jake smiled. "It seems like you've thought of everything, Alvin. I understand why Raymond told us to trust you."

"And for me to trust you. Trust is good, but pretty soon you'll need to give me that money."

"Oh, God!" Sarah reached for her backpack. "I'm so sorry. I forgot all about it."

"No. Not here. Too many eyes. In the morning. Right now, let's get some sleep."

They walked across the street and past the lobby to their rooms at the Best Western. Most of their gear was still on the plane.

"I don't have any clean clothes, Jake. And I'm too tired to shower now anyway. I just want to go to sleep."

"My watch has an alarm on it, Sarah. I'll set it for six."

* * *

Day 32: Cross Country Run

Alerted by the beeping sound, Sarah realized that the military truck was backing up directly toward her hiding place in the ditch at the side of the runway. She tried to jump to the other side of the ditch, but her foot was wedged between two rocks. She couldn't move. When she screamed for the truck to stop, no sound came from her mouth. Three more feet, and the rear wheels would crush her.

The gentle touch of a hand on her shoulder was followed by a voice from somewhere distant. "Sarah, it's six o'clock. Time to get up." Jake silenced the alarm on his watch.

"Huh? The truck! Oh … Jake, it was … Shit, I guess I was dreaming. Give me a minute. Where are we?"

"We're in Kansas. You need to get up and get dressed now so we can be ready to leave with Alvin in an hour. Do you want to shower first?"

"You go. I need to try to wake up."

They were eating cold cereal in the breakfast room at the hotel at 6:15, and there was no sign of Alvin. "He's probably getting ready for the next leg. Jake, do you have any idea for what to do once we reach West Virginia?"

"Alvin said we'll have two five-hour flights plus refueling, so we won't reach Petersburg until 6:00 p.m. By the time we get to my uncle's place it's likely to be closer to 7:00. No, wait. There's another time-zone change. It might be closer to eight o'clock."

"We need to get to D.C."

"Not today. By the time we got there from West Virginia it would be way too late to do anything. We should stay overnight with my aunt and uncle. And I'm sure we can borrow their pickup truck. They mostly use their car these days."

"Here's another idea. I saw on the map that Petersburg isn't that far from the place my folks bought north of Romney several years ago. They're in Florida, so it's empty. If you can borrow the truck, it wouldn't be much more than an hour. We need privacy to make plans, and we could be ready to start in the morning. That would be Sunday, right? Today's Saturday, I think. At least, I'm pretty sure it was Friday morning when we left Farmington."

"Yeah, today's Saturday. And that's a good idea. We can try to reach someone on Sunday. I just don't know who. We need to think more about that."

"You know your uncle well enough to just drop in on him this way?"

"He's my mom's brother, and we've always been close. He'll help us. I'll call him when we reach Petersburg."

After finishing their breakfast, Jake and Sarah were waiting in their room with the hallway door ajar, when Alvin arrived. "I paid for the rooms. You can just leave your key card on the table. A friend at the airport lent me his truck. We can drive right to the plane."

"But it's still dark," Sarah said.

Alvin shrugged. "Doesn't matter. We're in the western part of the Central zone. Sunrise here won't be until almost eight. But the runway lights are on here from dusk to dawn, so we're good to go."

Sarah and Jake clambered back into the plane, while Alvin spoke with someone to the side of the runway area. Sarah found the cash-filled envelope in her backpack. It contained $5,000, half of the original bundle of $100 bills that her father had left for her. She counted them once more to be sure.

"You're freaking me out, Sarah. Where'd you get all that cash?"

"My dad left it for me. I'll explain tonight when we have time to talk. It's another reason for going to my parent's place in West Virginia. I didn't take all of the cash he left for me."

Alvin climbed in, and Sarah leaned forward to give him the envelope. As he settled into his seat, he looked inside and looked at several of the bills. "Unmarked and not in sequence. Don't know what's going on, but I'm sure glad Raymond said I could trust you. Let's get buckled in. We're ready to go here."

Sarah spent much of the flight reading two newspapers from the motel—*USA Today* and *Western Kansas World*. She caught up on the news around the world and learned more than she wanted to know about current events in Wakeeney, Kansas. Jake didn't relax. He was angry but didn't want to say anything in front of Alvin. The flight seemed to take forever, but it was only about noon, still central time, when they reached Salem, Illinois.

Alvin took them in for a smooth landing and continued in the same direction until he turned into the service area at the north end of the runway. As he switched off the engine, he turned to his passengers and announced, "No secrets here. I put both of you on my documentation. John and Mary Smith. Talk to folks if you want. We'll take off in a half hour." As he climbed out of the cockpit, he indicated a building about across the tarmac.

A man in coveralls greeted them and pointed to the restroom. Several minutes later, he walked over and handed them a paper sack from a fast-food restaurant. "Alvin radioed ahead and asked us to pick up some lunch for you folks. We're always glad to help out." And after a pause, he added, "Uh, I do need you to pay for it, though. They stapled the receipt on the side of the bag."

Sarah had left her small pack in the plane, but Jake quickly removed some cash from his wallet. "Thanks for getting this. We really appreciate the help."

"Glad to be of assistance. That's why we're here. Not too many folks come through this way. To Salem-Leckrone Airport. So it's nice to have someone fly in. Someone to talk to, you know? Where'd you folks fly in from? Been on vacation?"

Before Jake could say anything, Sarah responded, "We've just been off on a long weekend, trying to get away from it all." And then, with a slightly embarrassed tilt of her head, "Somewhere that his wife wouldn't find out about it." As the man started to turn and walk away, Sarah leaned up and kissed Jake. Glancing over his shoulder, the man walked away, no longer interested in chatting.

Jake turned a shade of scarlet, but he didn't say anything until they were walking back to the plane. "Goddamn it Sarah, what was that about? Why did just you do that in front of him? My wife?! And you still haven't said where you got all that money."

"He was asking too many questions, so I figured it was a way to make him feel a little uncomfortable. And it worked. He didn't want any more of that conversation. Try to chill, Jake. I'll tell you everything later."

Alvin was waiting for them by the plane. "Got a couple of bottles of water for us here, and I see you got the food. The burgers may be a little cold, but they'll get us through to our next stop. We can eat them in flight."

"Can you do that?" asked Sarah. "I mean can you drive this thing, steer or whatever, while you're eating?"

"Oh, that's not a problem. I'll just set her on autopilot after we've reached our cruising altitude. This plane can just about fly itself the whole rest of the way. If it looks like I've fallen asleep, just give me a knock on the shoulder."

Alvin's comment didn't make the flight any shorter, but it guaranteed that neither Sarah nor Jake would fall asleep.

* * *

29

Intelligence

*The provisions include the use of "roving wiretaps,"
which allow the government to keep tabs on suspects
who switch cell phones or other means of
communication. This provision makes sense in an
age of disposable communications devices, and it
extends to terror investigations a power used for
years by federal authorities investigating organized
crime.*

—*Tampa Tribune editorial, 2011*[*]

Day 32: Long Distance

Parsons' phone was ringing, and he picked up the receiver. It was Harvey Atkinson from NSA. It was 7:30 on Saturday morning.

"We have something that will be of interest to you, Parsons. I called late yesterday, but I missed you. Whatever you people are up to over there is pretty freakin' wild stuff. I don't want to talk about it over the phone, so bring up your secure e-mail account. I sent a file. It's called 'paranoid,' and it's encrypted."

Moments later, Parsons had brought up the message and entered his encryption key. Text filled his screen:

Caller: Sue, it's Sarah.

---

[*] "Extend the Patriot Act," editorial, *Tampa Tribune*, Feb. 28, 2011.

Recipient: It's about time you called. We were beginning to get worried about you. I hope you've enjoyed your biking, but there's work to be done here. Newspapers don't run by themselves.

Caller: Sue, just let me talk for a bit. This will be hard for you to believe, but what I'm going to tell you is the absolute truth. I haven't been biking. I've been working on a story—a big one. There's been an outbreak of smallpox in Farmington, New Mexico. The entire thing has been covered up, and all communications in and out of the area are blocked. It's being treated as a terrorist attack, but I have evidence that it isn't. I need to get you that evidence, but I can't do it yet.

Recipient: Sarah, have you been drinking? Where are you?

Caller: This is real, Sue. It isn't a joke, and I haven't lost my mind. I'm going to need your help.

Recipient: Sarah, we can't do something like this over the phone. Just come into the office, and we'll sit down and discuss everything. If you really have the makings of a story, we'll go from there.

Caller: This is the real deal, and I will tell you everything. But I can't come in now, not yet. I know it sounds paranoid, but there are people trying to stop me. I'm scared. And I'm running. But it's too important to let it go. Give me another day. Maybe two. If I'm right, this will do for us what Watergate did 40 years ago. I'm going to need your support on this, Sue. We'll get pressure from the government, probably from the Defense Department. Or maybe one of the security agencies. And we'll probably need legal help. But I'm right on this. I've got to go. I'll be in touch.

"Holy shit! I've got to get this over to Zaborsky." Parsons spoke aloud, but there was nobody else in the office to hear him. He clicked the print icon on his computer and waited a few seconds for his laser printer to spit out the message. To be on the safe side, he grabbed his inkpad and stamp, marking the document SECRET. He reached for an opaque envelope and his briefcase, and then he noticed that a second page had printed. He was about to toss it in the scrap bin, thinking it was just useless header information from Atkinson at NSA. Then he noticed the additional text.

Time of call: Friday, Dec. 6, 17:30 EST

Call origination: Cortez, NM
cell phone—tower location 37 18' 43"N 108 37' 27"W

Call recipient: Washington, DC (Washington Post, Susan Parkinson)

Call originator: prepaid cell phone, registered to Sarah Wallingford

Parsons sat back down. He reached for his stamp and marked the second page SECRET as well. He put both pages inside the envelope and placed the envelope into his briefcase. He clicked the latches closed and checked that the combination lock was functioning properly. When he reached Zaborsky's office, the Colonel was already working at his computer. "I've got something important to show you, sir."

"The person who took this call? That's who I interviewed at the *Post*. Sarah Lockford's boss. But the caller isn't Lockford. It's somebody named Wallingford."

"Think back to your training, Parsons. When people make up an alias, they usually just make minor changes to their real names. It's probably her, but we need more. Did you trace the phone number?"

"Not yet sir. I'll get right on it as soon as we're done. I wanted to get this info to you as quickly as possible." The mistakes were piling up. Zaborsky hadn't mentioned the time lag between the intercept and the present discussion, but Parsons knew his superior wouldn't have missed it. Now Parsons knew he'd dropped another ball as well.

"Find out everything you can. I want to know every call that's been made to and from this cell phone. And don't stop there. Find this woman. She's becoming a real threat to our country."

A minute later, Zaborsky was alone, but he spoke aloud. "Goddammit. Goddammit. Goddammit. I need to see Edwards."

* * *

Day 32: Distance Learning

Robinson Edwards finished reading the intercept of Sarah's call to Sue Parkinson. "The shit has really hit the fan, Colonel. We've got to get this under control."

"If we can find her, can we stop her from publishing her story? What about going to the *Post* and asking the editor to put a hold on it? It's a legitimate question of national security."

"I wish it were that easy. Some new information just came in. It's probably on your computer by now. Remember the doctor running the CDC team out in New Mexico? Overman? He's missing."

"You think somebody took him out?"

"No, I think he took himself out."

"Killed himself, sir?"

"No Bob, he's AWOL. According to our team in Farmington, he disappeared for a couple of hours on Wednesday. On Thursday, he did it again, and at the end of the day he just left. Nobody has seen him since."

"Maybe he's just goofing off. What do we have to make us think he's on the run?"

"There's more that you haven't seen yet this morning. Our people in Atlanta sent us information on Overman's background. It turns out he has a girlfriend."

"Yeah?"

"Her name is Sarah Lockford."

"Oh fuck."

"Another thing. The Indian that we think was the terrorist agent? You remember he disappeared too?"

"Yes sir."

"Well he isn't disappeared anymore. They found his body on Wednesday. They didn't notify me until last night, because they wanted to confirm the identity. But it's him, all right. I think we're looking a terrorist cell. The Navajo was in on it. We need to find Overman, and Lockford."

"The phone call! The transcript—the call was made from Colorado."

"Right, it says Cortez. Are you familiar with it?"

"Not yet, but I think we probably should be, sir. Can you bring up a map?"

Edwards launched a classified version of Google Earth and entered the coordinates from the telephone intercept. The two men watched the image of Earth grow larger until the sphere was wider than the screen, and they were zooming into the American southwest. Finally, they were looking at a close view of some roads and buildings."

"Back out a little, sir."

"It's an air strip."

"Back out a little more …"

The city name showed up at the next level. It was Cortez.

"Keep zooming out. We need to see what part of Colorado this is."

Edwards zoomed out a few more clicks. The two men recognized the location at the same time. The map showed state lines, and they both knew that there was only one place in the United States where straight lines for the borders of four states meet at a single point. "They got out, Bob. I don't know how, but they got out."

"You think Overman met the woman in Cortez?"

"I'd bet anything on it. Fuck! Bradshaw said he had the area sealed off, but obviously he didn't. Get on the phone and tell him to get a chopper to Cortez right away. I want to know everything about every goddamn plane that's flown out of that airport for the last three days. If he gives you any shit about outranking you, just remind him that I'm in charge here. You're relaying my explicit orders."

Zaborsky stood up to leave.

"One more thing, Colonel. When you talk to Colonel Bradshaw? Tell him to have his troops break out live ammunition."

* * *

Day 32: Learning Distance

"Colonel Zaborsky? I've got some information." It was three hours after Zaborsky's meeting with Edwards, and Parsons waited hesitantly at the office doorway.

"Come in, Parsons."

"Sorry to bother you, sir, but we've got progress on several fronts. Start with Colonel Bradshaw. You must have scared the shit out of him when you called. I mean I never got above the rank of sergeant, and he was treating me like I was a general or something. We got the passenger manifests for the only commercial flights. There's only a couple a day, but nothing fits. We've identified all the passengers on the flights out of Cortez for the last three days, and we're positive that the fugitives weren't on any of them."

"Shit."

"But we also checked incoming flights earlier in the week. On Tuesday, the flight from Denver had a female passenger by the name of Sarah Wallingford."

Zaborsky made a fist and smacked it into his other hand. "Good work. Have you traced her?"

"Not yet. I mean, not exactly. We got the name and address on her photo ID—but it's a fake. A Virginia address that doesn't exist."

"That confirms our suspicions—she's an agent. What about money? Did she pay with a credit card?"

"Yeah, but there's no paper trail. It was a prepaid card."

"Get a tracer on it. If she uses it again, I want to know about it. If the credit card company doesn't want to cooperate, make damn sure they know this is a national security issue. These aren't just suspicions anymore. We have the full weight of everything in the Patriot Act working for us now. Anybody gives you a hard time, just make sure they understand their choices. They can help us right off, or they can sit in a fucking cell while we convince them."

"Will do, sir." Parsons was starting to like this. He actually missed combat. And this was about as close as he was going to get right now.

"Did Bradshaw check private flights?"

"Yes sir. In the works. Only a few flights out of Cortez would fit. Small aircraft in every case.

We've got results for three so far. Two went to Albuquerque, one to Phoenix. All three check out, even with witnesses."

"But there were other flights?"

"Just one. Some local guy. Another Indian. Calls his business Diné Charter Flights—little accent over the e, sounds like dee-nay. Bradshaw says it's the Indian name for what the Navajos call themselves. Anyway, this pilot, name of Alvin Keeswood, left Cortez late yesterday afternoon. Everything last minute. Nobody saw any passengers, at least none they told our people about. Keeswood filed a flight plan to somewhere in Kansas. The locals in Cortez screwed up the paperwork."

"Or maybe they're just not cooperating. This terrorist ring is starting to look even bigger than we thought. Maybe these Navajos are still fighting the old Indian wars, and they're taking it out on us. Somehow they got the Iranians to work with them, and now they're trying to cut this virus loose on real Americans. Tell Bradshaw to get rough if he needs to. I want to know where that fucking plane went."

Parsons started to get up, but he remembered that he hadn't brought up his second piece of information. "Oh, the other thing. We found the cell company for phone under the name of Sarah Wallingford and asked for all the calls, everything sent or received. Turns out there was only one other call, just before this call to the *Post.* Somebody in Atlanta, name of Frank Wirth."

"Find out who he is."

"We're working on it. And there's one more thing. The cell company asked us if we wanted reports on the other cell phone, too."

"The *other* cell phone?"

"Yeah. Turns out that this Sarah Wallingford, the one we think is Sarah Lockford? She bought two phones in Denver, at the airport. We faxed the airport police in Denver a photograph of Sarah Lockford—the one we got that from her passport when we checked her apartment. The sales clerk made a positive I.D. She's definitely the same person as Sarah Wallingford."

"Has she used the other cell phone?"

"Not yet, Colonel. But the cell company knows to call us immediately with location and receiving number."

"She's smart, this Wallingford. Way too smart for a reporter. Watch your step with her, Parsons. And with Overman."

By late Saturday morning in Cortez, the airport staff found the missing flight plan for Diné Charter Flights. The destination was Wakeeney, Kansas, but people there weren't helpful, either. They confirmed that Keeswood's plane landed at 9:00 p.m. local time on Friday and took off again on Saturday morning, but nobody saw any passengers. They did, however, provide the next destination according to the flight plan that Keeswood filed. It was Salem, Illinois.

Zaborsky's staff discovered that the paperwork filed for arrival and departure from Salem showed two passengers on the plane, John and Mary Smith. Zaborsky was sure that his team was closing in on the fugitives.

When he learned at 2:30 p.m. Eastern Time that the final leg of the flight was to Leesburg, Virginia, Zaborsky called Parsons to his office. "Set up a team at the Leesburg airport, but stay out of sight until they land. Otherwise the tower could alert the pilot. They might try to land somewhere else if that happened, and we could lose them."

* * *

30

Sarah and Jake

*The online behavior of a small but growing number
of computer users in the United States is monitored
by their Internet service providers, who have access
to every click and keystroke that comes down the
line.*

—*Washington Post, 2008*[*]

Day 32: West Virginia

The airplane touched down in Parkersburg at 6:30. When Alvin cut the engine, he announced, "Ladies and Gentlemen, welcome to your final destination. We hope you've enjoyed flying with Diné Charter Flights." He turned to them with a big grin.

"No problem changing our destination when I told them our fuel was low. Everyone always defers to the pilot. You two going to be okay now?"

"We'll know in a few minutes," Jake answered.

"I'll get my plane refueled. I'll check back with you before I take off."

Jake led Sarah toward one of the buildings, stopping at a payphone. He handed her his cell phone, the one that had never been

---

[*] "Every Click You Make: Internet Providers Quietly Test Expanded Tracking of Web Use to Target Advertising," Peter Whoriskey, *Washington Post*, April 4, 2008, p. D1.

used. "Pretend you're calling someone, and talk loud enough that anybody walking by wouldn't notice I'm on the payphone."

As they played their charade in the darkness, Jake quietly placed two calls—the first to directory assistance and the second to his uncle. He said little except that he was at the airport and needed a ride. He hung up quietly and turned toward Sarah.

In response, Sarah finished her own conversation. "Thanks Carol. We'll see you out front in a few minutes." They were already walking away from the building.

Anyone who might have overheard could report only that a woman whose name they didn't know had used a cell phone to call someone called Carol, who was coming to meet the woman and her companion.

Jake and Sarah said their goodbyes to Alvin. "Thank you for helping us, Alvin. And please say thanks to Raymond for sending us to you."

"I'll do that. You two take care of yourselves. I don't know what kind of trouble you're in, but I know it's not because you're criminals. So whatever it is, I hope you can get through it okay."

Jake and Sarah hefted their gear, and after Alvin gave them a salute, they headed toward the airport entrance.

They didn't have to wait long. "That's him, Sarah. The green Honda. It's not much to look at, but he's had it for years and keeps it in great shape. C'mon." They climbed into the car, Jake into the front seat, where he shook hands with his uncle. "Hey, George! Thanks for coming to get us. This is Sarah. She's a good friend."

"Hi, Jake. And hi, Sarah. It's good to meet you. Maybe you can tell me what's going on here, Jake."

"I'm sorry, George. It's something I can't talk about. At least, not now. It's related to my work at CDC. I haven't done anything wrong, at least not by my standards or yours. But there are some people who are looking for us, and we need to keep moving. I just need you to trust me on this."

"Okay, son." He hesitated. "After all, your mom is my little sister."

"Then there's one more favor I need to ask. Could I borrow your truck for a few days? We want to get out of here as quickly as possible."

"Of course you can. Want to come in and have dinner first? When I left for the airport, I told Mary not to put the food away."

"George, we really ..." Jake's anxiety was showing.

"Okay, Jake. I understand. We'll just put you in the truck as soon as we get to the house. You can tell me what this is all about later on. But at least let your Aunt Mary come out and give you a hug before you leave."

"Thanks, George. It's a deal. When I bring back the truck, I should be able to tell you the whole story."

Twenty minutes later, Jake and Sarah were driving toward the house in Levels.

* * *

Day 33: Making Plans

They drove north past Romney, following the river valley of the South Branch of the Potomac, in the direction of Cumberland, Maryland. It was an hour later when Sarah spoke excitedly. "Up here, Jake. At the top of the hill—turn right. You'll see a driveway. There, just past that reflector."

Moments later, the light from their headlights showed in the front windows of the cabin. "We're here Jake. We're safe. Let's get inside."

Sarah found the house key in its hiding place on the side of the cabin and opened the door. It was chilly inside, and Sarah switched on the gas fireplace. "This will get things warm pretty fast, at least in this part of the house. Right now, we can get cleaned up. I feel like I've been in these clothes forever. Do you want to shower first, or should I?"

"You go ahead, Sarah. What can I do here to help out?"

Take a look in the freezer, and see if there's anything for supper. Last time I was here there was some chili, but there may be something better." She walked into the bathroom and turned on the shower. "I'll try not to use up all the hot water."

Sarah thought that she had never felt such wonderfully warm water before in her life. It was absolutely luxurious. She stepped out of the shower and opened the small closet to find several towels, along with a large terrycloth robe. She used one of the towels to dry off and put on the robe, leaving the other towel on the counter for Jake.

"The bathroom's all yours, Jake. You'll love it. I haven't felt this good in ages. Did you find anything in the freezer? Was there any more chili?"

"Something even better. This is beef bourguignon, so if your mom is any kind of cook, it's going to be great."

"If it's beef bourguignon, it was my dad who made it, and he's a good cook. You go ahead and shower. I'll get this on the stove." Sarah put the stew on a low light, and went into the main bedroom, where she found a pair of khakis and a wool shirt in the dresser. She figured that Jake was close enough to her dad's size that they would work for the time being. She opened the bathroom door and put them on a chair next to the doorway. "Here's some clean clothes, Jake. They should fit okay."

Returning to the main room, Sarah bent down next to the cabinet that held the dishes and glasses. And the wine rack. She selected a California cabernet sauvignon, and took two glasses from the cupboard. Then she went into the guest room and took the blanket and pillows from the bed. She spread the blanket out in front of the fireplace and dropped the pillows on top. She was standing there, enjoying the fire, when Jake emerged from the bathroom.

"You're absolutely right, Sarah. I feel a million times better. And thanks for the clothes. They fit okay."

Sarah looked over her shoulder at Jake, who was wearing just a towel. The thoughts she had been suppressing all day suddenly came to the surface. She untied her robe and let it fall open as she turned toward Jake. "Maybe you don't need those clothes quite yet."

They made love, slowly at first, but then with increasing passion and abandon. It wasn't the first time in their relationship, but it felt that way to both of them. Afterward, they held each other closely, maintaining their embrace silently for a long time, and then they kissed gently. "I wish we could just stay like this, Sarah. If we can get through this, I want to always be with you. Someplace peaceful, like this."

"We'll get through it, Jake. We have to believe that. And being together ... it sounds wonderful. A few more days. Then we'll be able to think about the future. Right now, though, I'm hungry as hell. Let's have some of that stew and some wine."

When they finished their meal, Sarah put on a pair of sweatpants and an old sweater. "Let me show you what my dad left for me out here." She sat at the desk, turning the chair toward the adjacent file cabinet and spinning the dial on the combination lock back and forth, until the drawer clicked open. She removed the file folder labeled "Sarah," and pulled the plastic sleeve containing the remaining money from its envelope. She watched Jake's eyes go wide as she slid the cash onto the desk.

"Holy shit! That's a lot of money." He picked up a packet of $50 bills, the packet from which Sarah had previously removed about half the cash, and did a quick count. There's 40 or 50 bills here. That's a couple of thousand dollars. And this stack of hundreds is worth twice as much. There's probably five or 10 thousand dollars here, Sarah. How did you get this?"

"It's more than 10 thousand dollars, something my father left for me. I'm really not sure why, but I found it last week, when I came out here. I think he was some sort of spy before he retired. I don't know for sure, but there are a lot of clues. He also left me a prepaid Visa card that had a balance of another 10 thousand dollars. I was floored when I found it."

"If you didn't know about this stuff, how did you even know to look for it?"

"Last week, before I went out West, things started to get strange. I thought someone was following me, and I know for a fact that someone was in my apartment. So I called my dad for some advice, and he was strange on the phone, kind of guarded. Especially after I asked how I could make sure nobody would be able to track my phone conversations. That was when I first used a fake name to get a cell phone. My Dad said that in case I needed to travel, I should get my passport out of the file cabinet."

"Doesn't sound like a bad idea. I wish I had mine with me, the way things have been going."

"Yeah, but the point is, he said to get it from the 'file cabinet.' I don't even have a file cabinet."

"I don't understand. Then why would he say that?"

"It was a code. He was telling me to come out here. To check the safe out here. But he never called it a safe. He always called it his 'file cabinet.'"

"So it was to get you out here and find the money?"

"Yeah, but that's not all. Check this out." Sarah took reached into the small pack she'd been carrying and slid the passport toward Jake.

He opened it and looked at the photograph of Sarah. "Okay, it's your passport. What about it?"

"Look at the name, Jake."

"*Wallingford*—who in hell is Sarah Wallingford?"

"It's a fake passport, Jake. And look at this, a driver's license, also for Sarah Wallingford, and with the same fake address."

"He created a false identity for you? That's fucking amazing. He was CIA or something? And he never told you?"

"I don't know. He was a real businessman. But there was always a lot of travel to Eastern Bloc and to developing countries. So maybe he was part-time. It all fits. And the smallpox vaccination. Why did he have me get a smallpox vaccination in the late 1990s? I think he was worried about bioterrorism, even then."

"But what about the money? And fake identity?"

"Somehow, he must have always been afraid that I'd have to go on the run, or maybe the whole family would. I don't know why. But it was all in place when I needed help."

"Jesus! I don't even know what to think."

"What to think about is a plan for getting us out of this jam. And not just us. A whole lot of other people, besides."

"I was worrying about that all day on the plane. We have to get to the President. There's no other way."

"Jake, that's ridiculous. What are you going to do, call up and say 'Hello White House, could we please see the President, right away? We've got this really important information. And we're not really nut cases, despite what it sounds like.' They'd lock us both up, Jake. And they'd throw away the key."

"That's exactly the problem. We need to find someone who can get our information to the President. And it needs to be someone really high up. Who do you know in government circles? You've been in Washington for a few years now. You must know some people from working at the *Post*."

"Nobody like that, Jake. Sure I've met some senior people, but that's all it is. I shook a few hands, but I don't know anybody well enough to call them. I certainly don't know anyone in the national security area, and that's who we need. You'd be better positioned to do that with your CDC connections. And you grew up in Maryland near D.C."

"CDC has been compromised. When I called Frank Wirth yesterday to have him check on the potential smallpox victim in Maryland, he acted like I was from another planet. I don't think there's a chance in hell that I could get further up the chain."

"Then we need to find somebody we could trust who's directly tied to the national security enterprise."

"There was a guy who lived across the street from my parents, back when they still lived in Bethesda. He was an FBI agent, but I haven't seen him for years. He was a deputy something, back then. If he's still at the FBI, he'd have to be pretty high up by now. He might talk to me, though. But I'm just some kid who lived in the neighborhood, so it's a long shot."

"How do we find out what he's doing now? Can you call him?"

"I don't even know his number."

"We can't call directory assistance. It would be a link to us. To where we are now. "

"You think they might know about this house?"

"We can't be too careful, Jake."

"What about the computer?"

"The last time I was here, I used the library in Romney to buy plane tickets online. But if we're just looking up some names and addresses, it shouldn't be a problem. And it's pretty clear that they don't have this location under actual surveillance, or they would have arrested us by now. Let's try it."

In just a few minutes, with Jake at the keyboard, they were on the FBI's website looking at a list of senior FBI executives. "There he is! Carter Fitzgerald Jennings, III. He's the Executive Assistant Director of the National Security Branch. He may be high enough up to help. Now we just need to get through to him."

Jake went to an online telephone directory and searched for 'Jennings.' "There it is," said Sarah, leaning over Jake's shoulder. She grabbed her ever-present notebook and wrote down the phone number. "Is it the same address as before?"

"Yes. Westmoreland Hills. It's in Maryland, just a few hundred yards from the D.C. line. What do you think? Should I try to call him tonight?"

"Not the land line. Way too risky. And it could link you to the 'Lockford' name. I was already being watched last week. We need to wait until morning and look for a pay phone. There used to be one across from the fire station on our way out of town. If not, we could try a cell phone on the way back toward D.C. It would be harder for them to find us if we're moving, wouldn't it? But even then, it might help them link our names. It would blow Sarah Wallingford out of the water, and they could trace my flights to Cortez and everything."

"Then tomorrow morning it is. Let's get some sleep now. Is there anything else we need to do first?"

A sly smile came across Sarah's face, and a few minutes later, they were again lying on the blanket by the fireplace. Jake took Sarah in his arms and kissed her softly.

"It's nice and warm here, Jake. Warm enough to take off these sweatpants. They'd just be in the way."

* * *

Day 33: Making Contact

Part way through their breakfast, Sarah put down her coffee cup. "Something I can't figure out. How do we prove that the smallpox outbreak in Farmington came from the slides we found at the elementary school?"

"I've been thinking about that, too. If I could get to my lab, it would only take a couple of hours. We don't need the complete gene sequence, only the key portions."

"You know they're watching your lab. Is there anybody at Fort Detrick who could help? It's only an hour from Washington."

"Not anybody we could trust at this point. But you know who we could ask? Charles Evans. We need to get a sample to him in Atlanta."

"The labs at Emory can't handle something like smallpox. He couldn't help."

"Yes he could. He's got a joint appointment at Georgia State now, and their Viral Immunology Center was added as one of the few level-4 biosafety labs a few years ago."

"And he's been doing gene-sequencing?"

"Yeah, it would just be a question of getting him the sample."

"Maybe I could go down there. Oh shit, Jake! We don't have to do that. Where's my notebook? This might work." Sarah jumped up from the table and went to get her backpack.

"What are you talking about?"

"Charles. I told you I saw him in Atlanta, and he said he had a trip to D.C. this week." She opened her notebook. "Here it is. He's still here, Jake! Until tomorrow."

"How do we contact him? And how do we get him the slides?"

"All I know for sure is that we can't call him from here. It's too risky. After you call the FBI guy, we can try Charles. Then maybe meet him somewhere with the slides. We just have to keep a really low profile until you get the facts to the right people."

They reached the intersection by the fire station in Levels at 7:00 a.m. "We're in luck, Jake. The pay phone is still here."

Jake stopped the truck and took the handful of quarters that Sarah had found at the cabin. Sarah read off the phone number for Carter Jennings, and Jake dialed.

"Mr. Jennings? Carter Jennings?"

"Speaking."

"Sir, this is Jake ... Jake Overman. My parents used to live across the street from ..."

"Yes, Jake. Of course, I remember you. How are you, son? It's good to hear from you. But it's Sunday morning. Is something wrong? Are your parents okay?"

"Yes sir, we're okay. No, wait. Actually, I'm not. I need to talk to you, sir. It's really important."

"Then go ahead and talk, Jake. I'm listening. Are you still working at CDC?"

"Yes I am, but I can't talk about this over the phone. It's a national security issue."

The tone changed. "Jake, you should be calling your superiors at the CDC. Or if it's some sort of emergency, you should go through regular channels at the Bureau. Our families are long-time friends, but that's social, not business."

"Mr. Jennings, this is more serious, and more important, than you could possibly imagine. Please see me sir. I won't take up much of your time. I think you'll understand why we need to talk. Why I need your help."

There was a pause before Jennings spoke again. "All right, Jake. If it's that important, I'll see you. Can you come to my office tomorrow morning?"

"No sir, I can't do that. It might be too late. And besides, I need to see you in a more private location. Your house would be much better."

Another pause. "When can you be here?"

"This morning. We're a couple ... I'm a couple of hours away." He glanced at the note Sarah had scribbled. "I can be there by 10:00. There's something I need to show you, sir. You'll understand when you see it."

"Ten o'clock, then." The line went dead.

"That didn't sound too good. Maybe it'll go better with Charles."

"I hope so. Christ, that conversation started off cold and went downhill. But at least he said he'd see us. Let's call Charles now."

Sarah read off the number for Charles's cell phone, and Jake dialed. After a few moments, Jake shook his head. "No answer." Then he suddenly held up his hand. "Hello, Chuck!" Charles Evans detested the nickname, and Jake hoped it would put him on alert. "Chuck," he continued, "my girlfriend told me you were coming up to D.C. Maybe we could get together."

There was a pause, followed by an initially hesitant reply. "Uh yeah, how are you, buddy? What's up? It's like you've just disappeared lately?"

It was clear that they understood each other. "Sorry, Chuck. I've just been working kind of hard. Look, I know you're heading out this afternoon, but we'd love to see you. And Angie has something she wants to give you before you leave. Something special."

"I'm leaving pretty soon. Where do you want to meet?"

Jake looked at another word Sarah had scribbled in the notebook. "Airport."

"The best bet would be the airport, Chuck." Sarah and Jake had already outlined a possible plan during their short drive from the cabin. "If we don't catch you beforehand, Angie will see you at the departure gate. I've got some conflicts, but she's got a ticket on the same airline. It's Delta, right?"

"Yeah, it's Delta. Okay, my friend. I'll look forward to it. See you at about noon."

"That's good, Chuck. And remember, this is my girlfriend, so be discreet."

"Sure ... No problem. You can count on me. She and I know how to be discreet. See ya."

Jake smiled as they rung off. "We're making progress. Let's go visit the nation's capital."

They got back in the truck and began driving to their meeting with Jennings. "He's our only hope, Sarah."

* * *

31

Sarah and Jake

*Federal law enforcement attempts to use cell phones
as tracking devices were rebuked twice this month
by lower court judges, who say the government
cannot get real time tracking information on citizens
without showing probable cause.*

—*Wired, 2005*[*]

Day 33: Bethesda

It was 9:45 a.m. when Jake and Sarah exited the Beltway, the ring of Interstate highways that encircles Washington, D.C. and its closest suburbs in Maryland and Virginia. They were on the Clara Barton Parkway, driving along the Potomac River. Jake took the Glen Echo exit and turned onto Macarthur Boulevard. "We're almost there."

They cut across to Massachusetts Avenue, and soon turned onto a side street. "That was my house, across the street. This is the Jennings house, and we're exactly on time."

Jennings answered the doorbell quickly and ushered them inside. Jake and Sarah were both struck by his demeanor. He was a large man, physically fit, and impeccably dressed. Jake was glad that he had shaved, but his casual clothing was no match for the suit and tie that Jennings wore. "My wife has left for church."

There was something about his poise and military bearing along with a quiet strength that reminded Sarah of Colin Powell. She had

---

[*] "U.S. Cell-Phone Tracking Clipped," Ryan Singel, *Wired*, Oct. 27, 2005;

always admired Powell, even when she was young, first as a general, then as a diplomat, and later as a statesman.

Jennings guided his visitors into the kitchen, where the table was set with plates, coffee, and breakfast pastries. "Please help yourselves." Jennings poured more coffee into his own half-full mug. "There's cream and sugar, if you'd like it."

"Thank you for seeing us, Mr. Jennings. And by way of introductions, this is Sarah. We'll make our explanation quickly. Everything that we're going to tell you concerns an outbreak of smallpox that began last week in Farmington, New Mexico."

Jennings slowly took a sip of his coffee. "That's not possible, Jake. Don't take me for a fool. You do realize that I'm now running the National Security Branch at the Bureau? If anything like that happened, I'd be one of the first to hear about it. And you, of all people, must be aware that CDC wrote the response policy. An outbreak of smallpox would automatically be interpreted as a terrorist attack. The Bureau would be a central element of any response."

"That's why we're here. I was sent to Farmington to investigate what we first were told was an outbreak of chickenpox. When we got there, we learned that one of the local doctors had made a diagnosis of smallpox. And his diagnosis was correct. We confirmed that fairly quickly. So far, there have been only a few cases, all traced to the original infection of a small child. That first one was fatal, and the child's father also died. The entire area has been sealed off."

"I sincerely doubt your interpretation, Jake. But for the sake of argument, if what you're saying were true, why wasn't I notified? Why wasn't the official policy followed?"

"Mr. Jennings? I think maybe your office, or at least some part of the FBI, did know about this. Last week, my boss was confronted by one of your agents." Sarah opened the notebook she'd removed from her pocket. "Joseph Silver, that's the name he gave her. He wanted to know where I was, but he wouldn't give her any information about why he was asking."

"I don't know an Agent Silver. I'll check that name, but what you just told me doesn't fit with the Bureau's procedures."

"That's the disturbing part of all this," Jake interrupted. "I didn't even know that CDC policy, our official national policy, wasn't being followed. I only found out four days ago, when Sarah came to Farmington."

"What is your role in this, Sarah?"

"I have a friend out there, Mr. Jennings. She works with the woman whose child died, and she called me when she heard that they were about to shut down all telecommunications in the area. She thought I could help because of my job. I work at the *Post*—I'm a reporter."

Jennings raised his hand in a signal to stop. He looked icily at Jake and then turned his glare to Sarah. "I don't know what the two of you are up to, but if you had any thoughts that you could manipulate me, you're going to be very sorry. If you wanted an interview, you should have asked for that in the first place. You may leave now. This discussion is over."

Jake was stunned. "No! No! No sir! Please Mr. Jennings. That's not what we're trying to do."

"We're not here for me or for my newspaper, Mr. Jennings. Something horrible is happening in New Mexico. Something is really wrong out there. We won't do anything that will compromise you. That's a promise. This isn't about us. Our country needs your help, sir. Please. We're begging you."

Jennings sat down again—very slowly, all business. "All right. So we know how you found out. How the hell did you get there, if all traffic and communications were blocked?"

"My friend has a contact in Colorado, about 50 miles north of Farmington. He brought me in the back way, mostly through the Indian reservations. The military personnel weren't watching those roads."

"The military? Are you saying they brought in the National Guard?"

"No sir," said Jake. "I interacted with some of the troops, and they were from a unit that's normally based in Fort Bliss, Texas. I didn't get any serious information, other than learning that their commander was a Colonel Bradshaw. I don't know much about the insignia they wore, but the uniforms were U.S. Army."

"The military isn't supposed to be used for civilian operations, not unless there's some sort of insurrection. You've heard of the Posse Comitatus Act? Even the new domestic security outfits have to abide by that. I don't like this. Go on, Jake."

They had gotten through to him.

"The only thing I can really add is from a conversation I overheard among the military commanders. It sounded like they were discussing a retaliatory strike on Iran. One of them said the Iranians had launched a smallpox attack against us."

"That's not an unreasonable conclusion, Jake. It's official policy. Maybe not Iran, but that it was terrorism. After all, natural occurrence of smallpox is impossible. The disease was eliminated a couple of decades ago."

"That's what we thought. But we analyzed the Farmington virus—that's what we've called it—and we compared it to other strains from the U.S. labs and even from the Russian labs. All the genetic evidence points to a virus that predates any other known sample. In other words, it was something that was probably lying around undiscovered for a very long time."

"You're saying it wasn't terrorism? That you have evidence?"

"Yes sir. And we're pretty sure that we know exactly where it came from—from a family doctor in New York City who treated smallpox victims in the 1940s. He saved his medical specimens, and some of the microscope slides wound up in Farmington."

"If you knew all this, why didn't you tell your people in New Mexico? And how the hell did you get here, anyway? How did you get to Washington, D.C., if Farmington is still sealed off?"

"We came out the same way Sarah went in. With the help of some Navajos from the area. They believe the government has betrayed them. Nothing new about that. And I did try to tell my superiors. They wouldn't listen. I tried to send an e-mail message directly back to Atlanta, and someone blocked it. I know it sounds crazy, but it almost seems like a military coup."

Jennings didn't say a word. He stood up and walked slowly across the kitchen, Jake and Sarah watching his every move. When he reached the sink, he picked up an empty glass and filled it with water from the tap. Then he turned around and stared at his two visitors. He continued staring at them silently, as he raised the glass to his mouth and drank the water, looking at them over the rim of the glass. When he had drained the glass, he set it down carefully and, again walking slowly, returned to the table. He folded his hands and placed them on the table before he spoke again. "I believe you're telling me the truth, or at least what you believe is the truth. But it's not enough. I need real proof if you're going to get any help from me."

"How about this?" Sarah had turned on her cell phone, and she gave it to Jake, who then handed it to Jennings with the picture of Jack Redhouse's dead body showing on the screen.

"This is the father of the little boy who died. I previously confirmed the smallpox diagnosis for the boy, and the authorities reached the father's body shortly after we left Farmington. As far as we know, these are the only two fatalities. At least so far. I haven't heard that the CDC team officially confirmed this case as smallpox, but there's no question from that photograph."

"You're telling me that you took the photograph, but the other people on your team didn't know about the body?"

Sarah answered the question. "Not exactly, Mr. Jennings. I went with a Navajo man who was helping me, and we found the body. The dead man was Jack Redhouse, the man guiding me was one of his relatives. We were trying to find him to see if he could help us learn how the outbreak started."

Jake took over the explanation. "The Navajos aren't being treated very well by the military, which has destroyed any desire to cooperate. Some of the enlisted men seem sympathetic, but up the chain of command the Navajos are being viewed as the enemy. Despite the fact that a lot of them have been in the service. Redhouse, the dead man, fought in the first Gulf War and again in Iraq."

"So tell me again. Why exactly did you leave Farmington?"

"Because we have evidence that it wasn't terrorism. That it was an accidental exposure from an old smallpox sample. But the military command wouldn't listen to me, and they blocked my efforts to communicate with my superiors at CDC."

"You've got more evidence than just this photo?"

"Yes we do. We're waiting for final confirmation. Probably later today."

"In other words, you don't want to tell me."

"Respectfully, sir—we can't. We're trying to trust you, but we really don't know for sure that you won't turn us over to the Army when we try to leave here."

Jennings stared at Jake for several second before answering. "Fair enough. I understand your position. But you need to give me something concrete to work with. I need a copy of that photo." His eyes locked with Sarah's.

"I can send it from my phone, if you'll give me a number to send it to."

Jennings gave her a number and watched as she keyed it in. Then he left the room, motioning that Sarah and Jake should stay put. When he returned moments later, he was holding a ringing cell phone. He pushed several buttons. "I've got it. Let me do some checking with what we have so far. Can you come back here this evening? Let's say 8:00 p.m. My wife will be at her church auxiliary until 10:00, so that will give us adequate time to discuss our business in private."

Without further discussion, Jennings walked them to the door. After he shut the door behind them, he closed his eyes as he leaned back against the door frame and shook his head slowly. *Dear God, don't let this be true.*

* * *

Day 33: DCA

"Christ, that was one hell of a conversation, Jake."

"No shit. Somehow, telling him about the troops from Fort Bliss changed his mind. I'm not sure why, but it did, thank God. Now we have to link up with Charles. What time is his flight?"

"He leaves at just about noon. That means he'll go through security by 11:00, so we've got less than an hour."

"If we go down Massachusetts Avenue and get on Rock Creek Parkway, we can make it in 20 minutes."

Sarah was startled by the ringing. It was her cell phone. "Oh, fuck, fuck, fuck!" She grabbed the phone, looked at the name on the caller ID, and flipped the phone open. It was Susan Parkinson. "Hi Sue."

"Sarah, what's going on? You haven't called in since Friday. My sources at CDC and CIA wouldn't tell me a thing, and that's enough to make me think they're stonewalling. So, this storyline you told me about is dynamite. But you haven't given us anything. We need details. And we need hard proof. I can't even go to the senior editors until you give me more. So I repeat, what the hell is going on?"

"I'll have more by tomorrow. I'm sending you a photograph now, and if this doesn't convince you, I might as well quit. I'll call you tomorrow." Hanging up abruptly, Sarah sent the picture of Jack Redhouse with a simple message. "More to come."

They reached the end of Rock Creek Parkway and were driving along the Potomac, passing the Watergate Complex on the left. "Get into the left lane, Jake. We need to take a detour."

They drove beneath the Arlington Memorial Bridge onto Ohio Drive. "Over there, Jake. By that group of tourists. There's a parking place. Take it."

"What's going on, Sarah?"

"We may not have much time. Just get out and walk with me for a bit. Now!" As she talked, Sarah worked furiously with her phone. "I've gotten rid of the important stuff. Okay … over there. Do you see the people getting into that car? The blue one … with the New Jersey license plates. Go up to the man and ask him if he knows how to get to the Air and Space Museum at the Smithsonian. He's probably been there, so pretend to listen to the directions he gives."

The man's directions weren't very clear, because he was only a casual visitor to Washington. But he did his best, as he pointed and waved his hands. His wife did her best to help.

While Jake provided a distraction, Sarah reached into the front passenger seat of the car. Then she nodded to Jake.

"Okay, I think I've got it. Thank you very much for the help. Are you off to see more sights?"

"Unfortunately, no. Our weekend is about over, and we have a long drive back to New Jersey this afternoon. You folks enjoy your trip to the museum."

Jake and Sarah walked back to the truck. "What was all that about? Ever since you talked to Sue on the phone, you've been acting a little crazy. And why were you even talking with her? I thought you didn't want to use the phone."

"That's why I'm so freaked out. I never turned the damn thing off after I sent the photograph to Jennings. Someone could have been tracking our location ever since we left his house. Even worse, they would know from phone records that we've talked with Jennings."

"Then why did we stop? Turn off the phone, and let's get out of here."

"I've already gone one step better than that. Anybody tracking that phone … Even better, anybody following that phone, is going to wind up in New Jersey."

"You mean that couple …?"

"You got it. I slipped the phone under the front passenger seat. I deleted my contacts list and recent calls before we even stopped. The photo of Jack, too. So that nice couple will just be a little confused when they find the phone—or when some cop finds them."

"We'd better get down to the airport. We lost about 10 minutes here."

"Don't drive to the airport, Jake. If they've been tracking us, they could be waiting for us. We'd be sitting ducks."

"If we don't go, we'll miss Charles. We've got to get him those slides."

"There's a way. Go across the 14th Street Bridge, just past the Jefferson Memorial. That will get us to Crystal City. I'll meet Charles, and you wait for me. If I get caught, you can work with Jennings using what you already have. The photo of Jack's body says a lot, and Jennings certainly will have found out that there's some sort of cover-up going on."

"Stop here, Jake. At the Metro Station."

"You're going to use the Metro to get to the airport? That seems like a sure way to get trapped. The airport Metro station is the first place they'd stake out."

"There's a better way. People don't know about it, but there's a tunnel right behind us that goes underneath the railroad tracks. The airport's only a few hundred yards in that direction, and my bike is right over there in that bicycle rack. I'll get in and out of the airport, and nobody will even see me."

Sarah climbed out of the truck. "Wish me luck, Jake. Keep your cell handy. If I'm not back here by one o'clock, get the hell out. If something goes really wrong, and I can't get back here in time, I'll try to meet you at Jennings' house tonight. And if that doesn't happen, you'll have to do the rest of this yourself."

"Just be careful, Sarah."

Sarah unlocked her bike, put on her helmet, gave Jake a thumbs-up signal, and began riding toward the airport. She went through the underpass and followed the bike path along the side of the airport. A spur off the bike path led to a construction area. *It's Sunday, nobody's going to be around.*

On the far side of the construction area was the entrance to a tunnel beneath the airport entrance road. *Here goes nothing.* Riding quickly through the tunnel, Sarah emerged at the rear side of the airport parking garage. She set the bike down in a grassy area, walked through the garage, and crossed over to the terminal building.

She checked her watch and saw that it was almost 11:15. *I need to get moving.*

She entered near the Delta counter and went directly to one of the self-service kiosks. *Here's hoping that there aren't any alerts out on Sarah Wallingford.* The prepaid credit card seemed to work, and the departures board showed a flight to Cincinnati departing at noon from the gate next to Charles's flight. *Perfect.*

She selected a return exactly two days later. *Just enough to keep them off the track.* Boarding pass in hand, she headed for the security lines.

The first official hardly gave her a second look, only checking to make sure her boarding pass matched her photo I.D. When she reached the carry-on screening lines, she realized she hadn't checked out the contents of her small pack. *Too late now.* But no alarms went off, and she reached for the pack as it emerged from the x-ray detector.

"Excuse me, Miss. We'd like to take a closer look at your carry-on baggage."

Oh, shit. I'm totally screwed. What did I forget?

"You have a lot of electronics here Miss. We just need to take a quick look, if it's okay."

"Of course." She thought her reply sounded more like a wheeze than a normal statement. *Keep calm!*

"I was off on a hiking trip last week, and I'm bringing this gear back to my parents." *Not too much information. It would sound like I'm making excuses. God, it's amazing how quickly—how easily—the lies are coming now.*

As the screener removed the transceiver from the backpack, a small paper-wrapped package fell onto the counter next to it. It was the package containing the slides. "Well look at that."

Oh, fuck! I should run. Sarah looked over her shoulder. By sheer force of will, or maybe just from fear, she stayed where she was.

"That's really a nice radio, Miss. Just be sure you keep it turned off while you're in the air. You should remove the batteries, just to be sure. You want to stay on the good side of the TSA, remember."

"Okay, sure, I'll do that." She choked out the words and tried to smile. As the inspector replaced the radio, Sarah reached over and picked up the packet with the slides. She managed a sickly smile. "Thanks, have a nice day."

She put the pack over her shoulder and walked toward the departure gates. *I'm not sure how much more of this I can take.*

Charles's flight was listed for Gate 15, and it was scheduled to depart on time. Sarah took a seat by the adjacent gate, where she could see the passengers as they lined up to board the aircraft. *Charles isn't here! Damn, I hope he's not already on the plane. No, they haven't started boarding. And he wouldn't do that. He knows I need to see him.*

She wrote a message in her notebook and ripped out the page. "Need sequence on samples. Partial sequence OK. Start with 'R. Hamilton, variola positive.' Send output ASAP to sxwalling@gmail.com—critical by 8 p.m. today." She wrapped the note around the packet that now held two slides. She had removed the third slide, wrapped it in another piece of paper, and put it in her backpack. Her note had all the information that Charles needed.

Making another scan of the waiting area, Sarah spotted Charles as he edged up to a small group of people at Gate 15. She walked in his direction, stopping just behind him, out of his line of sight. Then she turned suddenly and stepped directly into him, nearly knocking him down. "Oh, excuse me!" She grabbed Charles by the arm as though she were trying to keep him from falling, and she pressed the packet into his hand. After looking him directly in the eye to be sure that he recognized her, she walked quickly away, turning to add, "I'm really sorry. I just wasn't paying attention."

Sarah returned to the security area, but she went through the exit lane with other arriving passengers. She began walking directly toward the passageway to the parking garage. *Well done, Sarah! We'll get through this after all.*

She paused and turned her head when she heard someone shouting on the upper level of the terminal. "There she is! Down there, coming out of security for the Delta gates."

* * *

Day 33: Airport Departure

Sarah didn't know who was shouting. She only knew that they'd found her, so she started running. She reached the walkway between the terminal and the parking garage and sprinted as hard as she could.

Somewhere behind her, she heard the voice again. "The passageway—quick! She's headed for the garage."

As soon as she reached the end of the walkway, Sarah ran past the elevators and into the garage. She didn't hear any footsteps yet, so whoever was pursuing her hadn't reached the end of the passageway. They wouldn't know for sure what level she was on. *Thank God I have my running shoes on.*

She quickly reached the end of the garage and continued through the open doorway onto a path toward the rental car building. But she didn't stay on that path, darting instead into a grassy area that appeared to be a small park. It was the remains of the Abingdon plantation, on which National Airport had been built nearly a century earlier. She ducked behind a small hill and ran the last 50 yards at a crouch so nobody inside the garage would be able to see her. Finally, she reached the end of the grassy area and dropped to the ground by her bike. On her hands and knees, her chest heaving, she tried to catch her breath and think about what to do next. She yanked her cell phone from her pocket and keyed the speed dial to call Jake. "Start the engine, Jake. Get ready to move."

Her next decision was made for her, when she heard the voice again. It seemed to be coming from directly above her. "She's either got a car or she's doubling back to the Metro station. Call Kupper and Nichols and tell them to cover the Metro entrance. I'm going down to ground level. Get the car and be ready to move."

Sarah got on her bike and started pedaling as hard as she could. Then there was another cry. "Steele—I see her. She's on a bike. She's headed toward the parkway. There's a bike path. Take the car around the north end of the garage!"

Sarah turned the corner. *He probably can't see me now.* It was less than a hundred yards before the long building behind the parking structure would hide her completely. Then she would be in the tunnel under the airport access road. Just as she slowed to turn into the tunnel entrance, she glanced over her shoulder and saw a man run out from the corner of the parking garage. She made her turn, thinking she was clear. She heard the loud noise behind her. *Not quite an explosion, more of a 'crack.' No! I don't believe it. It can't be ...*

But it didn't matter. She was in the tunnel under the access road, and within moments she'd be back on the bike path. Her pursuer was on foot. *No way can he catch me.*

The screech of brakes and honking of horns made her reconsider. But she was on the bike path heading north. If they were in a car coming from the parking garage, they'd be going south. *They can't get to me from there.*

More honking was followed by the roar of an engine and screeching tires. She looked back and saw a gray sedan cutting across the lanes of southbound traffic and into the grassy strip between the access road and the bike path. *Goddamn it! He's going to get me on the bike path!*

Sarah pushed even harder, cursing herself as she lost speed on the uphill portion of the flyover across the airport entrance from the northbound lanes of the George Washington Parkway. *He can't follow me over this bridge. It's too narrow.*

More honking. More screeching tires. *He's staying down at ground level, cutting across the airport entrance, right through the traffic. Keep pushing! Don't let up now. He's still behind you, Sarah.*

She was on the downhill portion of the flyover, making up the speed she'd lost on the uphill part. *I should be okay now. The bike path is narrow where it goes under the parkway. He won't be able to follow me.*

Fuck! I don't believe it. More honking. *The maniac is driving against traffic. Keep pushing!* She was less than 100 yards from the pedestrian tunnel beneath the railroad, but the car was closing rapidly. She could hear the engine. It was getting louder. She didn't dare look back.

Then she was in the tunnel, and a fraction of a second later she heard the crunching and tearing of metal behind her. She was through the tunnel, and there was no longer a gray car chasing her.

Sarah still didn't dare to ease up. She was only a few hundred feet from the garage where Jake was waiting with the truck. She rode across the side street without stopping, barely avoiding two cars whose drivers honked in anger. She turned the corner and rode into the parking garage. "Jake!" she screamed. "Let's go! Move it! Move it!" She heaved her bike into the bed of the pickup and scrambled into the cab. Instead of sitting on the passenger seat, she crouched in front of it, below the dash. "Get the hell out of here, Jake. Anywhere, but get out."

Less than a minute later, Jake told her they were driving north on Bell Street. "Turn when you get to 15th, Jake. We need to get away from here. Let me know when you've cleared the shopping area, and then I can sit up and help navigate. Take Route 50 heading west. There are a lot of strip malls out this direction. We can stop somewhere so I can tell you what happened. I don't fucking believe it, Jake. Those bastards tried to shoot me!"

* * *

32

Intelligence

The problem, he said, is that court rulings over the last few years have made it 'perfectly acceptable' to use military troops within U.S. borders for 'logistical support' ...

—*CNSNews.com, 2009*[*]

Day 33: Calling It Close

Earlier that day, Parsons was working in his office. He hadn't slept much. He felt terrible, and his mood was worse. *All because of that bitch, Lockford.*

The previous evening, while he was waiting for Lockford and Overman at the Leesburg airport, air traffic control contacted him to say that the pilot of the Cessna had diverted to Petersburg, West Virginia. The controller said it was just a pilot exercising good judgment by putting safety first. Parsons knew otherwise.

Parsons had alerted Zaborsky, who immediately asked the West Virginia State Police to intercept the plane and its passengers. But by the time an officer reached the airport, there was no sign of Sarah and Jake. Even the plane was gone, and once again there was a mix-up with the flight plan. Nobody at the airport seemed to know what its next destination would be.

---

[*] "Army MP's 'Just Showed Up' and 'Didn't Cross the Line,' Alabama Law Enforcement Official Says," Pete Winn, *CNSNews.com,* March 18, 2009; http://cnsnews.com/news/article/army-mp-s-just-showed-and-didn-t-cross-line-alabama-law-enforcement-official-says.

Parsons' Sunday morning funk was interrupted by a shout. "We got something here!"

He rushed to the cubicles where Tarkington and Harkness were looking at computer screens. "This is the real-time feed from NSA on Sarah Lockford's cell phone. She started using it at about 10:20 this morning. She placed a call about 45 minutes ago. We don't have that number yet, but she hasn't turned off the phone. We're tracking her. Look over here ..."

The other screen showed a map of the D.C. area. "Here—she was in Bethesda, just north of D.C., when she made the call. She stayed there until 10:30 and then started moving south. First on Massachusetts Avenue and then on Rock Creek Parkway. She stopped again near the Lincoln Memorial. Now she's headed north again. It looks like she's probably heading toward I-95, maybe toward New York City."

"Keep on it. I want to know who she called."

A technician interrupted. "Got the number here sir. I should have the name in a minute."

Parsons frowned at Tarkington and Harkness. "I don't like this. Everything this woman has done so far shows she's real smart. And now she just leaves her cell phone on for us to follow her? She knew we could track a cell phone from the beginning, or she would never have bought those disposable phones. I think she's trying to fuck with us. She's got someone else in their terrorist cell driving north, but she's going somewhere else."

"Here's the information on the call she made. It was to somebody in D.C. named John Smith. Address is 2900 Constitution Avenue, NW."

"Fucking bitch!" Parsons was red with anger.

"What is it, sir?"

"Are you a complete idiot, Tarkington? Look at the name. 'Smith?' And the address. Don't you know anything about Washington? There is no such place. Constitution Avenue ends by the Old Naval Observatory on 23rd Street. The 2900 block would be middle of the fucking Potomac."

Harkness pointed to the map. "Until she stopped by the Lincoln memorial, she was going toward Reagan National."

"You could be right. You and Tarkington get down to the airport. She'll have to go through security to get on a plane. Take two men with you so you can cover all four of the gate areas. She might be meeting someone, but she'd wait near the security checkpoint. Make sure everyone has two-way radios and photos of both the woman and Overman. I'll be there as soon as I update Colonel Zaborsky. Use your cover names. I'm Silver."

"Roger that. I'm Steele, and Tarkington is Gold. The other two are Kupper and Nichols."

"All right, get moving. And Harkness ... Everyone carries a sidearm."

Parsons returned to his office, where he found an update on the phone call that was made to Frank Wirth. *Son of a bitch. Someone else at CDC. This is getting out of hand.* There wasn't time for him to walk to Zaborsky's office, so he picked up the phone.

After learning that Frank Wirth worked at CDC, Zaborsky said he'd have their people in Atlanta bring him in for questioning. "I'll tell them that they don't need to be polite."

"Colonel, things are happening pretty damn quick all of a sudden. We've got a lead on the Lockford woman." Parsons explained that he was meeting his men at the airport.

"Stay in touch, Parsons. And don't fuck up."

Parsons ran to the parking place where he had left the unmarked car. He drove as fast as he could toward the exit of the Pentagon parking lot, the blue flasher on his dashboard warning others to get out of his way. In less than five minutes he was inside the airport perimeter, approaching the main parking garage entrances. That was when his two-way started squawking. "Nichols, this is Steele. Subject is on bike path heading north out of the airport. Gold is pursuing on foot. Intercept if possible."

The car jumped forward as Parsons hit the gas. He was speeding north in front of the passenger terminal, and he swung left onto the access road that looped back behind the parking garages. As the road turned south, he looked to his right. *There she is!* He saw the woman on the bicycle. It was her, but he had already passed her going in the opposite direction. *There—up ahead!* Parsons saw a turnoff to the right.

The sign said "no access," but that didn't matter. He turned into a construction area and saw a small asphalt strip going through the trees to the west. He gunned the engine and shot between the trees to the bike trail. He turned on His flashing lights again and used his horn to warn anyone on the bike path. He thought he could see the woman a hundred yards ahead.

Parsons was driving nearly 50 miles per hour, when he realized he had to slow down—fast. He saw the bridge ahead. It was a flyover, clearly designed for bicycles. His car wouldn't make it over. At the last minute, he swung the car onto the grass, and bounced across the northbound airport entrance from the GW Parkway. Cars were honking at him—no surprise, since he barely missed two of them—but he made it across.

There she is! Goddamn it! She's even farther ahead. He was back on the bike path, and once more he gunned the engine. The path turned left beneath the parkway, and there was a railing separating the narrow path from the roadway. Again, the path was too narrow for his vehicle.

Parsons was driving against oncoming traffic on the southbound entrance ramp to the airport. Cars were coming at him head on. He leaned on the horn, hoping they would hear him, even if they didn't notice his blue flasher.

Then he was clear. The bike path turned left away from the roadway, and the railing ended. He crossed the shoulder and bounced over the curb. He could see the woman ahead, no more than a hundred feet in front of him. He pushed hard on the gas pedal, and the car accelerated rapidly. For a moment, the woman seemed to disappear as the bike path went through a patch of trees, but Parsons hardly noticed. She wasn't stopping, so he would have to try to knock her down. He hoped it wouldn't kill her. He wanted to talk to her first.

Parsons knew the chase was over when he saw white on both sides of the path. Not on the ground, but something going up from the ground. By the time his brain had interpreted what his eyes had seen, there was no time to stop. "Fuck!" he screamed, jamming on the brakes as he crashed into the tunnel entrance.

When the crunching and scraping sounds stopped—it had seemed to Parsons that they had lasted forever— he sat in the car, looking at the airbag that had deployed. His horn was blaring. Once again, he spoke aloud. "Broke my fucking nose. Shit."

Otherwise, he was physically okay, but he knew that wasn't going to help. Now he'd have to explain to Zaborsky that he'd let the woman get away. And that he'd totaled a government vehicle. Even worse, he'd have to explain to somebody else just what the hell he'd been doing on the bike path in the first place. That particular somebody had just pulled up behind him in a car with red and blue flashing lights and the words "Airport Police" on the side. Already, his nose had swollen shut. He tried to lower his window, but that was jammed, too.

* * *

Day 33: Close Calls

His face hurt like hell. He couldn't breathe through his nose, and the bandages made it hard to keep his eyes focused. "That's it, Colonel Zaborsky. I guess I fucked up pretty bad. I'm real sorry. Especially about Tarkington, about him discharging his weapon. He says it was an accident, that he had it out just in case, and then he tripped. Damn I wish he hadn't missed. That would have solved everything. Sorry, Colonel."

"We'll worry about being sorry when this is all over with, Parsons. Right now we have a job to finish. While you were out playing games at National Airport, we got a lot more data. First thing, both of the Wallingford cell phones, the disposable ones, were used at the same time, right about noon today. That's right when you were chasing the woman. One of them called the other. And we got the locations. One was at the airport, and the other was just across the parkway in Crystal City. That's where the woman was headed when you were chasing her."

"So at least we know they're still working together."

"Right, but there's more. Your hunch about Lockford's cell phone was correct. It was a ploy. Remember how she stopped near the Lincoln Memorial?"

"Yes sir."

"Well, it turns out she was making a deliberate effort to send us off in the wrong direction. About an hour ago, a husband and wife from New Jersey stopped to get coffee while they were driving back home from a trip to D.C., and the wife found a cell phone on the floor of their car. She said that she thought it might belong to the 'nice young couple' that they had met by the Lincoln Memorial, and she called the cell phone company to report it. Of course they notified us immediately, and we've recovered the phone."

"How does that help us? I mean now that Lockford can't use it, what difference?"

"To start with, take a look at this image that was on the phone. Lockford tried to delete it, along with almost everything from the phone, but our tech guys are good."

Parsons glanced at the full color printout, and he looked like he was about to lose his lunch. "Christ, Colonel, what the hell is that? I mean, I've seen guys who've been shot up pretty bad, but even they didn't look like this."

"That's a full-blown case of smallpox. I haven't confirmed yet with Bradshaw, but I think it's probably the Navajo guy in Farmington. We know they've found his body, but now it looks like Wallingford, or Lockford, took a picture first. I don't know why. I thought maybe it was to share with other members of their cell, but now I'm not so sure."

"Why's that, Colonel?"

"When Lockford first turned on the phone, she used it to send that image. It wasn't a voice call. NSA has confirmed this. And now they've confirmed your assumption about Mr. Smith. It's a fake name, all right. NSA followed up with some of their state-of-the-art tracking technology, and they think they pinpointed the location of both the caller and the recipient. They were both in the same place. It's a residential area, and one of the houses is owned a guy named Jennings. He's FBI, the head of their national security division. Why would they be sending the photo to him?"

"Could it have been a threat? They were warning him about what they'll do next?"

"I'm not sure, but I can't think of anything else. I told Under Secretary Edwards, and he just told me to sit tight, that we're not sharing our information directly with FBI or any of the other agencies. He says that it's all going through the Secretary of Defense first. The only thing that I can see here is that we've got to find the woman. And once we find her, she'll talk to us. You can be damn sure of that."

"I'd be happy to run that interrogation, sir."

"One other thing, Parsons. Atlanta called back, and they've been able to talk to this guy Frank Wirth that Lockford called on Friday. Actually, it was Overman that called him. Wirth said that Overman asked him to check out a possible case of smallpox up in Maryland. He admitted that he thought it was crazy. Remember, none of the other people at CDC know anything about this stuff yet. But Wirth agreed to check it out. He said that was SOP when a request like that came in."

"Where in Maryland?"

"He wouldn't give our people any other details. Said we'd need to go to the head of CDC to get that information. I'm waiting to see how hard Edwards wants to push to get that information, but it could be important. They could have launched another attack here on the East Coast, and maybe they told this guy Wirth in CDC just to show them what they're capable of doing. Maybe that's what they told the

FBI guy. I sure as hell don't like it. We need to take these people down."

The phone rang, and Zaborsky picked up the receiver. He listened for several minutes, occasionally saying "uh-huh" or "yeah."

When he hung up, he turned back to Parsons. "We've got a new lead on them. Overman has an uncle in West Virginia. Lives right near the Petersburg airport."

"Have you picked him up?"

"We talked to him. He wasn't very cooperative—used to be a damn professor somewhere—but he finally admitted that he let Overman take his pickup truck. We've got the make, model, and plates. We don't have many field men for this, but I want every one of them out looking for that truck. They were up near Bethesda earlier today. Let's focus on the west side of D.C. from Bethesda down to the Lincoln Memorial. And also on Virginia side of the river going north from the airport. We don't know for sure why they were in Bethesda, if it might be more than the FBI guy Jennings. But we can sure as hell look around there. Tell your people to be careful if they start cruising the area near Jennings' house. If Jennings has a security detail, we don't want them asking us questions."

* * *

33

Sarah and Jake

The Defense Intelligence Agency is seeking an exemption from American law to give officers greater latitude in interviewing potential intelligence sources inside the United States, the agency's top lawyers said Friday.

—*New York Times, 2005*[*]

Day 33: Noodle Soup

Sara and Jake were sipping hot tea in a small Vietnamese restaurant in Falls Church, Virginia, five miles west of the airport. It was in one of the strip malls that Sarah had mentioned. They had chosen it in part because there was parking in the back, where the truck couldn't be seen from the highway, in case someone had seen them when they left the parking garage in Crystal City. The proprietors, an elderly couple, spoke almost no English, and Sarah and Jake were able to order only because there were some English labels on the menu.

Sarah had told Jake most of her harrowing story during the 15 minutes it had taken them to drive to Falls Church. "At least you got the slides to Charles. You completed that mission successfully."

"Mission? Who's sounding like a spy now?" With some difficulty, she managed a smile. "But you're right. We're one step closer to being able to make our case to Jennings."

---

[*] "Agency Seeks Freer Hand to Recruit Spies in U.S.," Douglas Jehl, *New York Times,* Oct. 8, 2005.

As they waited for the bowls of Vietnamese noodle soup, Jake asked, "Does Charles know how tight our deadline is for getting an answer?"

"Absolutely. The note I gave him said we had to have it by 8:00 this evening. I used the word 'critical.' Is it really possible for him to do the analysis that quickly? When I was in grad school, people used to take weeks to do a gene sequence."

"Things are a lot faster now. He'll understand about the kinds of markers we're after, and he'll focus on that kind of information. And don't forget, a lot of this is being done using mass spectrometry these days, rather than the old digestions followed by gel electrophoresis. So if you put that together with the GeneChip technology, a whole lot of data can be obtained in just a few minutes. Did you tell him how he should get us the information once he has it?"

"I gave him an address for a Gmail account that my dad set up to communicate with me when this all started. The only time it's been used was when my dad sent me a message, and I accessed it from the public library in Romney. So I think we can be pretty confident that it's still secure. And it only has to stay secure long enough for us to get the results from Charles."

"That would be fine, except we don't have a computer. And we sure as hell can't go to your apartment to retrieve a message."

"Of course we have a computer. I have a laptop I got from the *Post* just before I went to Atlanta."

"I know. That's exactly my point. Think about it, Sarah. They were waiting for you at the airport. They know who you are. If you use the laptop from the *Post,* they could probably trace it just like the cell phone. So we really don't have a computer."

"Yeah, I suppose you're right. But we do have money. Both cash and the prepaid credit card."

Sarah took out her notebook. "We need to make a list, Jake. Item number one is a new laptop. It has to be ready to go, with software and wireless Internet. We have to go shopping."

"Who do you think they were? The people who tried to stop you at the airport? They can't be regular police. If our names had been on an alert list, Jennings would have known about it."

"Who else could it be? Shit, that's a dumb question. They've got to be military, the Defense Department. And it would explain why Jennings was in the dark."

"It also gives the reason, Sarah. The military in Farmington wanted to keep the smallpox secret. They're building a case against

Iran, and they want to keep a lid on everything until they do. They've tried to cover up any data that could contradict them. Right now they're trying to put a lid on us, to squash us with it."

"They started checking up on me right after I called your office last week. I didn't get your voicemail. A woman answered instead."

"I've never had a receptionist, and before I left the office, I switched my phone so it would roll over directly to voicemail."

"Somebody wanted to monitor your incoming phone calls. That makes it seem like CDC was cooperating with the cover-up right from the start."

"It sounds that way. But it doesn't sound like the people I know. They really screwed us over, and what happened has to be illegal."

"Where did it start, Jake? This Colonel Bradshaw you talked about?"

"No, it had to have come from much higher up. Somebody in Washington. Do you remember those stories when the Quentin Walker, the Secretary of Defense, went through his Senate confirmation hearings? He'd been a congressman for a long time, and some of the senators were concerned that he always supported military requests, no matter what. What if people in the Defense Department were behind this? It could be the same ones who were so convinced that Iran was behind the Shiite insurgents during the Iraq war. The Secretary of Defense might be supporting them. And he has his own intelligence arm, the Defense Intelligence Agency, the DIA. That would explain everything."

"It would say why they've been following me, but not how."

"Start with the phones. Couldn't they have traced your call to my office back to your cell phone?"

"I didn't use my cell phone. In fact, I didn't even use my office phone. I called from one of the conference rooms, so there was no direct link to me."

"But it still would have been a link to the *Post*, wouldn't it?"

"I guess so. The guy who Sue Parkinson thought was from the FBI came looking for me two days later. And there was the call to Charles! If they were checking phone numbers, that was probably it. The first time I called him, it was from my apartment, and I called his home number. The second time, I called his office at Emory, and I remember using the phone at my desk at the *Post*."

"There's the link. They probably don't have your actual conversations, but I'll bet they have the phone records. Remember all that crap back in 2004, when the White House Counsel tried to get the Attorney General to approve warrantless wiretaps when he was sick in the hospital?"

"Only vaguely. But I think you're right about the phone records. When I called Charles again, he basically hung up on me. Then he called me later at home, but he didn't use his own phone. He used your line at the condo. He figured nobody would be watching that, since you were out of town."

"But it would have been in the records, wouldn't it?"

"Sure, but when I met him in Atlanta, I was careful to stay out of sight. We already were worried that someone might be watching the condo. My guess is that whoever these people are, they didn't know about my relationship with you, at least not then. They probably were just freaked out that a reporter was nosing around."

"Wouldn't they have known about your trip to Atlanta?"

"I don't think so. I was on an official reporting trip to Tallahassee, and I just stopped off for a few hours in Atlanta. There shouldn't be any record that I ever left the airport before flying on to Tallahassee. And another thing, Jake. I also sent you an e-mail last week when I couldn't reach you by phone. It was short. It just asked, 'where are you?' But I didn't get an answer."

"I never got that message."

"Then that's one more piece of evidence that someone was monitoring your e-mail."

"Sounds like it. Okay, let's go on the premise that they didn't want you to learn anything about what was happening in Farmington. Were there any other phone calls?"

"I don't think so. I talked to my dad, but I didn't mention anything about the outbreak. And before I came out here, I just sent my boss an e-mail saying that I was going biking for a few days. So there was no reason for anyone to suspect that I went to Farmington."

"What about your cell phones? You called your boss from Cortez before we left."

"Yeah, but that was with one of the phones in the fake name of Sarah Wallingford. How would they be able to make any connection to me?"

"It's the same phone I used to call Frank Wirth at CDC. Suppose they just started looking for coincidences? They could've been using a computer to do that."

"Shit. You're right. If that's the case, then they may have been trying to trace Sarah Wallingford. Even if they don't know it's me, that name now has links to the *Post*, to CDC, and to Cortez. Damn it! If they ever find Alvin Keeswood, he won't be able to keep our trip to West Virginia a secret."

"We have to assume that they'll find out about that, Sarah. If they start tracing stuff, they can show your photograph to the person who sold you the phones and to the airline clerks. They probably have surveillance videotapes from the airports."

"Then we can be pretty sure they'll discover that Sarah Wallingford and Sarah Lockford are the same person. They're both me. They've probably figured it out already."

"That's right. It means we need to operate on the basis that these guys know we're together and that we came back here from Farmington. It means they know that we can blow the lid off what they're trying to cover up. We need to be careful, Sarah. This is really dangerous."

"No shit. I'll bet it was my cell phone that let them track us after we left Jennings."

"The main thing is that you got away."

"Wait a minute ... the photograph! I sent it to Jennings and to my boss using that cell phone."

"You said you deleted it."

"No, that's not the point, Jake. They probably have our location when I made the calls, and they certainly know who I called. They probably know we've talked to Jennings."

"But they can't be sure that Jennings actually met with us."

"Maybe not, but you can bet your ass that these guys will be watching for us when we go back to see Jennings tonight. We can't use the truck."

"There's another way, Sarah. His back yard is right on the edge of Little Falls Park, and there's a bike path. We could go that way, and somebody watching the street would never know we were there. The bike trails go all the way to downtown Washington. All we need to do is ride across one of the bridges from Virginia."

"Okay, that's item two for our list. You need a bike. And shoes, too. You'll want something better than those hiking boots."

"This is really nuts, Sarah. The whole damn world is ready to come apart, and you're making a shopping list. If it weren't so serious, this would be pretty funny."

"Just trying to make sure we don't forget anything. Don't give me shit about it."

"Okay, sorry. At least you have enough cash. It might not be a good idea to use that credit card anymore. They may figure out that you used it to buy a ticket at the airport."

"Well, at least if they discover that, they'll start looking for me in Cincinnati." She paused and shook her head. "That's just bullshit, isn't it? They're not going to be that stupid."

"Probably not. Look, we haven't talked about it, but the biggest risk is that they may take it to the next level. They could name us as terrorists, just like they did with Jack Redhouse. They could have every law enforcement agency in the country looking for us."

"Yeah."

"Let's get going. We have to become completely invisible. After we get the things on your list, we have to ditch the truck and stay out of sight. And we have to hope that they don't get to Jennings before we can give him our evidence."

* * *

Day 33: Presentation

The first stop for Sarah and Jake was a Best Buy. A sales clerk, just a kid, tried to help them by recommending models that could run all the latest high-end video games, but Sarah stopped him.

"Hey, you may not believe it, but I'm not gonna play games with this. I'll be using the word processor and the Web browser, but that's about it. All I really need is a netbook with the software loaded and ready to go."

They spent a few more minutes haggling over which model would be best and convincing the kid that they really didn't need a printer to go with it. Jake looked around at accessories, and he added two USB flash-memory drives to their order. Sarah completed the paperwork, using a name and address that she made up randomly, and she paid with cash. The cash brought a look of surprise, but it didn't seem to pose any problem.

"Okay, I just verified that it's in stock. We should be able to have it ready for you to pick up by about four this afternoon."

Sarah responded in a carefully measured tone, "You didn't understand before. I explained that we needed something that was ready to go. We've got a big project we're working on, and we need to finish it this afternoon. Not tomorrow, not tonight. This afternoon."

"Geez, I'm sorry. But I don't know if I can speed it up too much. It's 1:30 now, and my boss always says that we should give the tech guys at least three hours to get something ready for a customer. The guy working there is a buddy, so maybe I could get him to cut that down to two hours. He'll need at least that much time to charge up the battery for the first time."

"You still don't understand. I need to get working on my project now, not later."

Sarah decided to improvise. "My desktop machine died this morning, and I was lucky enough that I backed up almost all of my work onto a flash drive before that happened. But I'm running out of time, and I'm going to get fired if I don't finish this. So I need your help."

She reached for her wallet. "I'll tell you what. Here's $100. You can keep it for yourself or share it with your friend. It doesn't matter to me. All you need to do is find a battery that's already charged, and give the owner of that battery a brand new one. Whoever it is won't mind. Then you can put the charged-up battery into my computer, hand me my computer, and everybody will be happy. Especially you and me."

The clerk's puzzled look changed to a frown and then to a smile. "Yeah, I guess I could do that. I'll have to split it with Jerry, but 50 bucks apiece is a pretty good deal. Hold on a minute, and I'll be right back."

Sarah gave Jake a look that made it clear he shouldn't say what he was thinking, and they just stood at the counter silently for several minutes watching the exchange between the sales clerk and his friend Jerry. Then the clerk gave them a cautious thumbs-up signal and turned to help his friend unpack a box. In less than five minutes he returned to the sales counter with the laptop.

"You should be good to go. I've got the word processor up and running and I used my password to verify that the Internet browser works on our house Wi-Fi system. You'll have to connect to another Wi-Fi network, but it means that you've got everything you asked for. And Jerry said this battery should last for at least two hours before you need to recharge it. You can see the icon down here that says it's at 98 percent now."

Sarah and Jake let the clerk put everything into a shopping bag, and they walked out of the store. "I guess we made his day, Sarah. Even if he thinks we're a couple of loonies."

At the far end of the strip mall, they pulled behind a dumpster, where Sarah tossed all the boxes and packaging.

She put the laptop and charging unit into her small backpack, which now contained only the items they expected to need for the rest of the day. Everything else was in the large backpack stashed with Jake's bag behind the driver's seat of the truck. "Let's head in the other direction, Jake. We have to get you a bike."

The young woman who helped them only asked for 15 minutes to get the bike ready. Jake found a pair of shoes in the right size, and Sarah had another suggestion. "We also need helmets, two of them. I lost mine at the airport. And it'll be dark soon. Let's get some sort of lights."

Sarah used the prepaid credit card in order to conserve their cash. They had talked more about it, deciding that even if someone could identify the purchase, it wasn't like a computer that could be tracked electronically. She turned and whispered to Jake, "Do you think they might start watching the bike paths?"

By the time they had paid for everything, the sales clerk was waiting by the door with the bicycle. "I hope you enjoy it. It's a perfect day for a ride before winter hits. You've still got a couple of hours of daylight, and you made a good choice with those bike lights. The LED bulbs are great."

Jake put the new bike next to Sarah's in the bed of the pickup. "Our shopping's done. What now?"

"Starbucks. They're all over the place. We can get coffee and something to eat. And they have free Wi-Fi. We can keep the computer plugged in, so the battery will have a full charge."

"Let's wait to check e-mail. I don't like the idea of staying in one place for too long. Definitely not after we've logged on to a server that might give us away."

"You're right, Jake, that wouldn't be a good idea. I'll work offline and write a draft of a story. Whatever happens tonight, it's all going to come to a head by tomorrow, and I want to be prepared.

"What about checking e-mail?"

"Let's wait until just before we head out to meet Jennings, We can drive around and piggyback onto a wireless network that isn't password protected. I'll also send my draft to Sue Parkinson. That way the *Post* will be ready to move when the time comes, and the paper will have the story even if something happens to us. It's kind of insurance."

"Don't talk like that, Sarah."

"I have to, Jake. We have to acknowledge that one or both ..."

"Not now! Just write the damn story."

They found a Starbucks near Seven Corners, about five miles from D.C. They hoped it was outside the area where people would be looking for them. Sarah began typing on the laptop, and Jake bought pastries and coffee.

Jake read a copy of the *New York Times,* while he drank his coffee and listened to Sarah tapping away on her keyboard. After a while, he got them refills. By the time those were finished, he was getting impatient. "It's 4:30, Sarah."

"Okay, I'm almost done. Give me another five minutes."

By 4:45 Jake was driving slowly through a residential neighborhood, while Sarah searched for available Wi-Fi connectivity. "Hold it, Jake. I think this is a live one." As Jake pulled over to the curb, Sarah connected to a wireless network called "BillyBoy." Whoever Billy was, Sarah thought that he shouldn't mind helping his country, even though he'd never know what he'd done. First she checked her Gmail account, but there was nothing yet from Charles. It was still too early.

"Is it safe to check my regular e-mail accounts?"

"It should be. Even if they find a way to trace us, we'll be long gone before they could link us to Billy and send anyone out here."

Sarah checked the other e-mail accounts, but there was nothing. She handed the laptop to Jake, who did a quick check of his e-mail accounts. "No messages. I was kind of hoping that I might find an update from Frank Wirth on the woman from Maryland, but I guess that was a little optimistic. Even if they're not monitoring my account, he'd probably be reluctant to put anything onto an unsecured e-mail server. Okay, what next?"

"Let me have the laptop back. I'll send the file of my draft story to Sue, and then we can get the hell out of here." Less than a minute later, Jake heard an emphatic "Okay," as Sarah made a pronounced motion with her right index finger to hit the enter key. This was followed by five seconds of silence before Sarah spoke again. "It's gone. Let's go, Jake."

Jake put the truck in gear and headed down the street. "Where to?"

"We need to find a compromise. It would be nice to be really close to Jennings' house. But we don't want to be so close that someone might spot us. So I think we should probably keep the truck on this side of the river rather than bringing it into D.C. or up to Maryland. That's probably where they'll be looking hardest for us. Do you know the parking area by Roosevelt Island?"

"I don't think so. It's right across from Georgetown, isn't it?"

"Right. Take Arlington Boulevard, over to the GW Parkway. There's a turnoff into the parking area just past the Roosevelt Bridge. There aren't many parking spaces, but there aren't usually very many cars there. It's one of those National Parks that nobody knows about."

* * *

34

Intelligence

*It is clear from the legislative history of 18 U.S.C.
Sec. 1385 and the above cases, the intent of
Congress in enacting this statute and by using the
clause 'uses any part of the Army or the Air Force
as a posse comitatus or otherwise,' was to prevent
the direct active use of federal troops, one soldier or
many, to execute the laws.*
—*U.S. District Court, U.S. v. Red Feather, 1975**

Day 33: Key Bridge

"I'm not sure what it means, Colonel." Parsons had told Zaborsky about the new activity on Sarah Wallingford's credit card. "It was at Reagan National, 11:15 this morning. Maybe a half hour before we spotted her. She bought a ticket to Cincinnati, leaving at noon and returning Monday."

"But you saw her outside security at noon. She should have been on her plane by then. The ticket was a diversion, Parsons. She was meeting somebody at the airport, and she needed a ticket to get through security. Either that, or she was just trying to throw us off track. We need to find out who she was meeting there."

"Maybe so, but I don't think we'll be able to. It would take weeks to sort through all the passenger lists for flights using that

---

* *United States of America v. Geneva Red Feather et al.,* No. CR73-5176, United States District Court, D. South Dakota, April 7, 1975: United States v. Red Feather, 392 F.Supp. 916, 921-923 (D.S.D.1975).

concourse today. And we still might not even recognize the name of whoever she was meeting."

"Stop making excuses, Parsons. Just get the goddamn passenger lists, and have your people start looking through them."

"Yes sir."

Parsons stood up to leave and then sat down again. "Almost forgot. There was another purchase on the credit card this afternoon. She bought a bicycle."

"Maybe she damaged the one she was using at the airport."

"I don't think so. She also bought two helmets. We found one at the airport, right where she was running away from Tarkington. This looks like she and Overman are both going biking. The cashier at the store confirmed that it was a man and a woman."

"They're not going biking for exercise. They've figured out that we may be looking for their truck, and they're trying to avoid us."

"Shit, that'll make things even tougher."

"Maybe so, Parsons, but alert your people. In addition to the pickup truck, they're looking for two people on bikes. The temperature is dropping, so there won't be as many bikes out there."

"Yes sir. I'll get back to you with any developments."

It was just about five o'clock when Parsons frantically called Zaborsky. "We've spotted their truck. One of our guys saw it driving right past us, right in front of the Pentagon. Can you believe those dumb shits? They got onto the GW Parkway going north. They're trying to get into D.C., and we'll be waiting for them. We have all the bridges covered. Two of our cars are following, but they haven't made visual contact yet."

"Don't forget the bicycles, Parsons."

"Even if they have the bikes in the back of the truck, there's no way to use them. They'd have to park, and there's no place to park along the GW."

"Jesus Christ, Parsons! Of course there are parking places. If you ever got off your lazy ass to exercise, you'd know about them. There's the Lady Bird Johnson Park just north of here. Have your cars swing through that first. Then check by Theodore Roosevelt Island. There's another parking area there. And stay in your office, Parsons. I'm going to double-time over there to make sure you don't screw this up any worse."

By the time Zaborsky reached Parsons' office, two technicians were already there. They had to squeeze together to make room for the Colonel. Parsons and the technicians had been listening to a two-way radio.

"Tarkington found the truck, Colonel. The subjects were already on bikes, and they left just as he got there. They rode across a pedestrian overpass before he could stop them. They were headed toward Key Bridge."

"Have you alerted your man up there?"

"Yes sir. Harkness was in his car near the woman's apartment. He's pursuing them across Key Bridge now. At least we think they've gone across the bridge."

The radio squawked. "Silver, this is Steele. We have visual confirmation. They're ahead of us on the bridge. They're turning west onto Canal Road. Nichols and I are caught in traffic, but we'll fight our way through it." Sounds of angry honking could be heard on the radio.

"Steele, this is Silver. Stay on them. Don't let them out of your sight. Take whatever action is necessary."

* * *

35

Sarah and Jake

*... the lawyers said the change would merely give
the Defense Intelligence Agency an authority
already granted to the Central Intelligence Agency
and law enforcement agencies for their intelligence-
collection missions. They said the D.I.A. had no
intention of spying on Americans, but needed the
new authority to help identify and recruit sources
knowledgeable about terrorist groups ...*

—*New York Times, 2005*[*]

Day 33: Biking

Sarah and Jake parked the truck by Roosevelt Island at 5:00 p.m. Their meeting with Jennings wouldn't be for three hours, but they wanted to get the truck out of sight and maintain a low profile. They were just about to get on their bikes, when they heard a screech of brakes on the parkway only 100 feet behind them. A car had come to almost a complete stop in the roadway, and it was starting to drive over the curb toward them.

"Let's get the fuck out of here, Jake! There's a ramp up there at the end of the parking lot. They can't follow us." Sarah led the way on another sprint.

When the car reached the bottom of the ramp, Sarah and Jake already were halfway up. In seconds, they were out of sight, as the

---

[*] "Agency Seeks Freer Hand to Recruit Spies in U.S.," Douglas Jehl, *New York Times,* Oct. 8, 2005.

ramp made a hairpin turn over the parkway. Sarah turned and shouted. "Stay low, just in case they start shooting."

On the other side of the bridge, trees and bushes hid them from their pursuers, and they paused briefly. "Up here, a couple of hundred yards, Jake. Key Bridge. We can cross into the District."

"They'll follow us. We'll be out in the open."

"They can't get there from the northbound lanes of the parkway."

"They'll just turn around, Sarah."

"No. There's a center barrier until farther up. We've got a couple of minutes. Not much more."

"Then let's get moving."

Sarah led the way as they pedaled full speed along the sidewalk across Key Bridge. Georgetown was getting closer by the second. At the end of the bridge, the road was a dead end. They would have to turn right onto M Street or left onto Canal Road. They both were hoping that nobody was following. But their hopes were dashed, when they heard horns honking and brakes screeching. It was followed by a crunch of metal and more honking.

Their only hope would come from the traffic. Key Bridge was always congested. There had been times that it had taken Sarah a half hour to cross in her car. She called back to Jake. "Get ahead of those cars and turn left at the end of the bridge. The traffic will provide a barrier. It'll give us a couple of minutes before they get past the jam."

They raced down the sidewalk along Canal Road, Sarah in the lead. *Probably only a half mile.*

She yelled over her shoulder. "The turnoff is close, Jake. Push!" Her words were almost drowned out by more honking. She looked back to see a car weaving through traffic at high speed. It was closing on them, and the driver could certainly see them in the overhead street lights. "Here it is!" she screamed, as she turned her bike off the sidewalk.

To Jake, following close behind, it looked as though Sarah had turned into the woods on the side of the road. But then he saw the narrow paved path. After just a few feet, it curved steeply downhill and turned hard to the left. To his surprise, they were riding through a short tunnel—a tunnel that was much too small for a car to follow. Sarah stopped at the other end, and he pulled up next to her. "Where the hell are we?"

"It's a tunnel underneath the Canal. It's how you get to the towpath on the canal from upper Georgetown. It's been here forever, but almost nobody knows about it. I'm hoping that whoever is following us will think we went the other way, through the woods."

"I hope you're right, but just in case, let's keep moving."

They were on the Capital Crescent Trail, on the far side of the C&O Canal. "The towpath is right up there, but this is paved. And most of the way it's not visible from Canal Road, so they won't be able to see us. It takes us up to the tunnel under Macarthur Boulevard."

"I can find Jennings' house from there."

They rode hard for ten minutes, trying to get as far as they could from Georgetown before anyone might figure out where they were. Then Sarah slowed down. "Let's catch our breath for a minute, Jake. That's the trestle over the canal and Canal Road up ahead. This whole trail was built on the old right of way for the Georgetown spur of the B&O railroad. If we turn of our lights and walk the bikes across, we'll be pretty much invisible from the road below. After we get across, we should be home free."

A mile later, they emerged from the tunnel beneath Macarthur Boulevard. "Just up ahead there, Sarah. There should a turnoff to the right."

When they reached the turnoff to the other trail, Jake was excited. "We did it, Sarah! His house is just a couple of hundred yards up the path. But we've got almost two hours before we meet him."

They found a place to sit down by the tunnel entrance with their backs to the wall. After a while, Jake put an arm around Sarah, and they leaned together to keep warm. She pulled his arm tighter around her. She found a couple of candy bars in her pack and handed one to Jake. "Raymond gave me these. It seems like a year ago."

During their wait, they encountered only three people. Each of them asked if the couple needed help, and each was satisfied by their answer. "Thanks a lot, but a friend is meeting us. He's supposed to be here soon."

Finally, the time arrived. "It's 7:50, Sarah. Let's go. We'll leave our bikes in the bushes at the side of the trail and walk up to his house from the back."

Five minutes later, they were climbing a small hill leading from the edge of the park to the Jennings property. They went slowly, not wanting to use their lights. When they reached Jennings' back yard, they stayed in the middle of the lawn to avoid being seen from the street. There was just enough light from an upstairs window to help them find their way.

Jake motioned for Sarah to follow him up to the back door. There was a small concrete pad, with a walkway leading to a raised deck on the side of the house. Just as Jake raised his hand to knock on the door, they were startled to find themselves suddenly bathed in light. Nearly blinded by the floodlight above the door, they heard a voice from behind. "Turn around slowly, and keep your hands in the air."

* * *

Day 33: FBI

Sarah began to tremble as she and Jake turned around. Their eyes hadn't adjusted to the sudden light, and they couldn't see the man who had given the instruction. The only thing they could see was the .45 automatic that was pointing at them at chest level. Before they could do more than recognize the strange taste of fear in their mouths, the voice spoke again.

"Goddamn it! What are you two doing back here? My motion detectors went off, and I didn't know what was going on. There have been three break-ins in our neighborhood the last month, and one was an armed robbery."

"Mr. Jennings! Thank God, it's you. We didn't mean to cause trouble, but we had to come this way. We're being followed. Actually we're being chased. Someone even fired a shot at Sarah."

A pause. Then a deep breath. "Get in the house."

Jennings led them through a laundry room into the kitchen. Without turning on any lights in the kitchen, he said, "Wait here." Sarah and Jake waited silently, while Jennings went to the front of the house and closed the drapes. Returning to the kitchen, he closed the blinds that hung from the kitchen windows before he turned on the overhead light. He spoke calmly. "It would be better if we stayed in this part of the house. Let's sit down. We have a lot to discuss. I've learned a few things today that make me believe you two have been honest with me. But I still need to see some real evidence if we're going to push this to the next level."

Jennings suddenly noticed how disheveled they appeared. "You two look terrible. How did you get here?"

"The bike trail, sir. By bicycle. After we left here this morning, we were followed. Well, actually we think we were tracked with Sarah's cell phone. She accidentally left it turned on after she sent you the photograph. Sarah went to National Airport to meet a friend, and they were there waiting. She barely got away."

"I think they fired a shot at me, Mr. Jennings. I only got away because I cut through the pedestrian tunnel to Crystal City. I'm pretty sure their car crashed when they tried to follow me. It was too narrow for them."

The intense, measured stare was interrupted, as Jennings' eyebrows arched momentarily. "Sarah. I am correct that the full name is Sarah Lockford? I'm afraid we've never been fully introduced." Jennings looked at Jake and then returned his attention to Sarah.

"Y... Yes sir."

"I told you I'd learned a few things today. There aren't that many people named Sarah at the *Post*. And the number gets smaller when you start looking at science reporters who could write a story about irregularities in new drug approvals at the FDA."

Sarah relaxed slightly. "Yeah, I guess it was pretty obvious."

"Maybe you were very lucky today, Sarah. I'm not sure what's going on yet, but you are correct about one thing. That car did crash. The driver wasn't injured severely, broken nose, I think. And he wasn't available for questioning by the local authorities. The car was an unmarked police cruiser, and the airport police—they have jurisdiction—were unable to identify the agency it belonged to. It appears the driver was taken away in another unmarked car before he could be questioned."

"But isn't that ...?"

Jennings put up a hand and continued calmly. "Please. I said the airport police couldn't figure out what agency was responsible. My people have better resources. I didn't know for certain until just now that you two were involved, but I was able to learn that it was DIA, the Defense Intelligence Agency. There are a half-dozen federal bodies with antiterrorism responsibilities, and they're constantly fighting over jurisdiction. The FBI is has responsibility for all the domestic issues, but some of these other outfits have been running cowboy operations. In 2008, the Pentagon announced plans to have 20,000 uniformed troops stationed inside the United States for possible response to terrorism."

"That's why you reacted the way you did, when I told you about the troops in Farmington?"

Again the eyebrows arched briefly. "You don't miss much, do you Jake? Well, I always knew you were a smart kid. That's good. If we're going to work together, I'd rather be working with smart people. There are limits on how much I can tell you. You understand that what we're dealing with is highly classified?"

They nodded.

"I can say that we've had our eyes on the DIA for several years, especially since Robinson Edwards was appointed as Under Secretary for Intelligence at the Defense Department. Edwards is in a powerful position, and I think he's been making an end run around official intelligence channels. The Under Secretary is required by law to be a civilian, but this guy is military through and through. He was on active duty in Air Force Intelligence as a general, two stars, until just before he was nominated."

"So he'd be in a position to control the flow of information? And maybe to run, or at least condone, some kind of rogue operation?"

"I didn't say that, Sarah. But you didn't hear me argue with you either."

She nodded.

"Today, I asked some of my top staff to see what they could learn about a possible smallpox outbreak. I told them to say our office had heard a report about a tourist out West. Most people were cooperative—Homeland Security, CIA, State Department—but they said they hadn't heard anything. And then we have DIA. They weren't cooperative at all. They claimed they didn't know anything about any outbreak, but they were very uptight about it. They said if there was something about bioterrorism in Utah, we needed to give them all the details. They started talking about their biological defense systems at Dugway. My people couldn't tell them much, because I hadn't given them much. What we learned was that the DIA response was all wrong. They were stonewalling us."

Sarah looked over at Jake and then back at Jennings. "Doesn't that convince you we were telling the truth?"

"I know it's the truth. At least the part about a smallpox outbreak. I finally got through to Attorney General Chernikov, and she told me that the National Security Council has been meeting over the last week to develop a response. She said the President decided to keep it secret, even from agencies like mine that would normally have a major role in the response."

Jennings paused to stare intently at Jake. "You've said you have evidence regarding the origin of the outbreak, but what you've told me so far amounts to little more than speculation. What I need now is real evidence. This morning, you said you'd bring it to me."

Jake and Sarah looked at each other hesitantly, and then Jake said, "We're not sure yet. Sarah needs to check her e-mail. The answer should be here by now." *I hope.*

"Do you have Wi-Fi here in the house?" Sarah asked.

"That would be out of the question. How do you think it would look if some neighborhood kid hacked into the wireless network of a senior FBI official? But I can give you something a lot better. He went to a small desk in the corner of the kitchen and pulled out a cable. "The other end of this is linked to a top-of-the-line high-speed connection. It's secure, so I'll have to enter a password for you. But it will get you onto the Internet. You have a portable computer with you?"

Sarah nodded and reached for the backpack that she had placed on the floor next to her chair. She went over to the desk, and powered up the laptop. After a few keystrokes, she backed away. "It wants the password."

Jennings entered the code. "Go ahead."

Sarah went to the Gmail site and entered her username and password. In a few seconds her in-box appeared. There was a single message—the old one from her father. But her initial excitement turned to utter disappointment. "It's not here, Jake. Nothing from Charles."

"It's only 8:15. He wouldn't let us down, Sarah. Try again. Hit the refresh button."

Sarah did as Jake asked. *Nothing. Just the old message.* For about three minutes, each of which seemed to last an hour, Sarah periodically clicked the refresh button on the screen. Each time the result was the same. Jennings had started to pace back and forth across the kitchen, when Sarah nearly screamed. "Here it is! He sent it."

The message was from C_Evans@hotmail.com. "He didn't use his university account. Maybe that's a good sign."

The message was short.

> *Attached file has data. Only enough time for partial analysis. Results are preliminary. Also strange. Tried to focus on same regions of genome as Sulaiman. Results don't seem to match known strains.*

"That's good. He used the same protocol that we've used at CDC, so we can compare his results with we did in Farmington."

"Who is Sulaiman?"

"He's a CDC scientist, sir. He led the pioneering work on this."

Sarah opened the attachment and then opened a second file from the flash drive that Jake handed her. She put the images into adjacent windows on the screen and moved away, so Jake could get a better look at the two images that were displayed.

Jake studied them for a few moments, and then he started moving his index finger back and forth between the two windows. "It's a match! There's your evidence, Mr. Jennings. It's not bioterrorism. What my colleague just sent me is the genetic analysis of the sample from 70 years ago. It's identical to the virus that killed the child in Farmington. And it didn't come from a terrorist."

"You told me this morning it came from a physician's microscope slide. How did it get to Farmington?"

"The slide was part of a collection that a teacher's aide bought on eBay. Her child put the slide in his mouth, and he was infected. It was an accident. You're looking at definitive proof that it wasn't terrorism!"

Sarah and Jake both looked at Jennings, waiting for his reaction. His expression was completely unreadable. "This is bad. Extremely bad."

"No sir. You must have misunderstood. The news is good. It was all accidental, and there's a good chance that the outbreak has been contained. Even better, the strains from the 1940s resulted in low CFR outbreaks."

Jake noticed the puzzled looks on the faces of the other two. "Sorry, that means low Case Fatality Rate, it's a standard term in epidemiology. But it means we can be optimistic that the outbreak will turn out to be relatively minor."

"That isn't what I was referring to, Jake. You already told me that you thought the outbreak had been contained. Pardon me, if this sounds cynical, but I'm not worried about the possibility of a few more deaths from this smallpox outbreak. My concern right now is a few *million* people dying—innocent people in Iran."

Jake and Sarah both went numb. "You heard me correctly. The National Security Council is meeting in emergency session tomorrow to make a final recommendation to the President. There's a proposal on the table. It was put forward early today by the Secretary of Defense. If the President accepts the proposal, tomorrow night the United States will launch nuclear missiles against Tehran."

* * *

Day 33: Gathering Evidence

Sarah and Jake were dumbfounded by Jennings' revelation. Jake, still incredulous, responded first. "With all due respect, sir, they can't possibly recommend an attack. Not now. Not now that we know that it wasn't terrorism."

"No disrespect taken, Jake. But you have to understand the real world of international politics and diplomacy. And how things are done here in Washington. This idea did not suddenly pop up in the minds of senior politicians because of the outbreak. There are people throughout the federal government—in Defense, State, Homeland Security, even inside the White House—who have wanted to attack Iran for a long time."

"You mean because of their efforts to develop their nuclear capabilities?"

"That's part of it. But it goes back much further. Ever since the overthrow of the Shah and the Islamic Revolution in the late 1970s, our relations with Iran have been a disaster. Oil has always been a part of it. Iran has huge oil reserves. And don't forget the hostage crisis. The Islamic student revolutionaries attacked the American embassy and held our diplomats, more than 50 of them, for nearly a year and a half. So you've got lots of reasons for some government officials to harbor a long-term hatred of the Iranian regime."

"But that was a long time ago."

Do the math, Jake. In 1979, people who were at an early career stage in government or the military, or whose parents were in senior positions, would have been in their mid-twenties. That was 35 years ago, so it would put them at around 60 now, just about the age for someone to be in a senior government position, someone still harboring a grudge."

"Can't you just tell them what we've learned? What *you've* learned about the smallpox outbreak. That it wasn't terrorism. And it didn't involve Iran." Jake was pleading.

"The people we're talking about don't care. They only need an excuse. And if the excuse turns out to be wrong, they won't mind. It won't stop them."

"But it can't be a gigantic conspiracy. There are too many honest and ethical people in government service. I know. I work with them."

"I know that Jake. And you're right. It isn't a giant conspiracy. It's only a small one. But it has potentially catastrophic aims. The intelligence has been distorted. And now the distortions—some would say 'lies'—have taken on a life of their own. I need to get this information you've shown me directly to the President, or at least to a senior member of the cabinet. If I try to use regular channels, it will almost certainly get torpedoed by someone in the Defense Department."

"You talked about the Under Secretary for Intelligence ..."

"Right, Robinson Edwards. He's a problem, but I can't be sure if he bears any responsibility. Things are highly compartmentalized in Defense, and he may not even know how his intelligence reports are being used. All I can say with any certainty is that the problem is somewhere between his level and the President's National Security Advisor. I need to circumvent that chain. And it will be difficult."

Jennings walked several steps away from Jake and Sarah. Then he turned back. "This is going to be a long night. I assume I can count on your help?"

Both nodded.

"All right then. As I said a few minutes ago, a lot of this is classified." Jennings had walked over to his desk and removed two pieces of paper.

"I'm glad I had these forms lying around. I was planning to review them for possible revision, but they'll work fine in their present form. He wrote a few words on each of them and then handed one to Sarah and one to Jake. "These are nondisclosure agreements. I can't issue you a security clearance, but by signing these, you are agreeing that you won't talk further about any of the classified information that I convey to you."

"But ..."

"Don't go there, Sarah. We'll talk about your role as a reporter after this is over. Right now, these are legal and national security issues that need to be covered, in large part for me. If I don't establish the legal cover, our efforts could be undermined at the last minute. And all three of us might spend Christmas in a cell."

Reluctantly, Sarah and Jake signed and dated the documents and gave them back to Jennings.

"Oh, shit!"

Sarah turned to Jennings with an embarrassed expression. "Sorry, sir." Then she turned to Jake. "I just remembered, Jake. The antiques dealer. What do we do about her?"

In response to Sarah's query, and even more to an intensely questioning look from Jennings, Jake answered cautiously. "The picture that Sarah took? The photo of the dead smallpox victim? She found a business card near his body. From a woman who deals in antiques and Indian artifacts. We think that she might have been in contact with the deceased during the time he was contagious. I passed the information to a CDC official in Atlanta after I left Farmington. He didn't even know that there had been an outbreak in New Mexico."

"You mean to tell me there may be somebody just walking around spreading the disease across the whole United States? After you told me that the outbreak was contained?"

"I still believe it's been contained. The incubation period is usually about two weeks. Jack Redhouse, he's the man in the photograph, left his house in Farmington almost exactly two weeks ago. He went to a cabin in the nearby hills, where he died sometime later. His vehicle was found abandoned a few miles away, and we think this antiques dealer gave him a ride. If she was exposed two weeks ago, she wouldn't have been contagious until the last couple of days. I called my colleague at CDC on Friday, so there's a high probability he got to the woman in time."

"A 'high probability' isn't enough now, Jake. We need to find out about for certain. Otherwise, it could undermine all our arguments. You have to call your colleague for an update."

"We've been a little reluctant to make any phone calls. We called you from a pay phone in West Virginia, and we've pretty much used up our anonymous phones."

"Anonymous phones?"

Sarah was embarrassed. "Uh, yeah. I bought several prepaid cell phones. For one of them I said I'd been robbed and all my ID had been taken. And I gave a fake name. For the others, I used a fake ID."

Jennings frowned. "I'll just forget you said that. This isn't the time to worry about it. I have a secure line here in the house, but using it could have repercussions. The content of the call would be scrambled, but if someone is monitoring your colleague's calls, they could get the number. And that would lead them right back to the FBI. If we have an advantage now, we'd like to keep it."

"Two things, Mr. Jennings," Sarah said. "The good part is that there's no way anybody could trace this one phone to me. It really should be clean. I just made up a random name, and it's never been used. We've been keeping it for an emergency, and this sure seems like an emergency. Could they trace a call back to this location?"

"Only to the general neighborhood. Even the newer units with GPS don't give exact locations immediately. They might figure out you were in this area, but they wouldn't pinpoint this house. At least, not if they're only working with the technology available to local law enforcement. But if they brought in the NSA, all bets are off. Maybe that's something to consider, since NSA is administered by the Defense Department. What's the other thing?"

Sarah winced. "That one may be a real problem. Remember, we said that they found me at the airport? Because of my phone? Well I called your number to send you the photograph. So they may already have the link right back to the FBI. We're screwed. Uh, excuse me again."

Once again Jennings raised an eyebrow. He almost smiled. "You're not the only one who knows how to obtain an anonymous cell phone. Let's just say you don't have to worry about that telephone call linking you and Jake to me. At least, not directly. If they've got NSA looking at us, there isn't anything we can do about it. Right now, I think it would be a good idea for you to call your colleague, Jake."

Sarah handed Jake her notebook, opened to the page where she had written Frank Wirth's cell number. Wirth answered on the fourth ring. "Frank, it's Jake. I need to find out what you learned about Danielle Brandis."

"I'm not sure I should be talking to you. This is very fucked up, Jake."

"Were you able to find her?"

There was a long pause. "Yeah, we found her."

"And? Goddamn it Frank, tell me what's going on!"

"Our team went to her shop. We were lucky. She was sick as a dog. She couldn't even leave her house. None of the neighbors even knew she had returned from her trip. So she's had no contact with anybody for about four days. When she first came home, she was tired from traveling, jet lag and all. She didn't even start to feel sick until the next day. But she never went back outside."

"What was it Frank? Do you have a diagnosis?"

"Smallpox."

"Were you able to do anything on the genetic sequence?"

"We've started. But the lab guys are confused. The sequence doesn't match any of the known virus strains, from here or Russia.

The data suggest something much earlier in the evolutionary chain. Basically they're saying it's impossible. Except for the fact that they're looking at it."

Another pause.

"One more thing, Jake. There was another person exposed."

"Oh, fuck! Besides the antique dealer? How bad is it? How many contacts?"

"We lucked out, Jake. The guy is ex-military, name is Gregory Anniston, and he was vaccinated just a couple of years back. He was still in the reserves when the Iraq war started."

"So he's okay?"

"Yeah, he's okay. At least as far as smallpox is concerned. We've got him and his family under full medical surveillance in a Type X facility at Fort Detrick. He's happy he doesn't have smallpox, but I think he's having a real problem trying to explain to his wife how he was exposed to it. Anyway, it's a good result from a public health standpoint."

"So you're pretty sure there were no other exposures?"

"Almost positive. Anniston was never infectious, and the woman, Danielle Brandis, was already isolated in her own house by the time she became contagious. And by the way, she's been getting better over the last day or so. This seems to be a fairly mild strain of the virus. And the man who died in Farmington? You know about him? Name of Jack Redhouse?"

"I know about him."

"Well, I learned about him, too. But only after I reported this new case up through the chain of command. That was really fucked up, Jake. I should have been told about him first thing. For Christ's sake, I'm in charge of monitoring and tracking infectious diseases. Especially if there's a bioterrorism question."

"We tried to get the information to your group, Frank. They were blocking our communications."

"I don't know what's going on with all the secrecy, Jake. From the beginning, I was told it was just a training exercise, but that sure as hell wasn't the case. Anyway, Redhouse seems to be the source of the infection, although everything is still hush-hush. Only a few of us have been given any of the details. If you hadn't called me about this Baltimore case, I'd still be totally in the dark."

"Did you get any details on the contact with Jack Redhouse?"

"Yeah, we did. The antiques dealer and her ..." He paused. "... her companion met Redhouse while he was contagious. His truck broke down, and they were the first people he met. They gave him a ride to his cabin and kept on going. So the chain of exposure seems to have stopped there. It looks like the outbreak was contained. Was it terrorism, Jake?"

"Can't say anything now, Frank. We'll talk soon. Thanks for all your help. You've done more than you know. Take care of yourself."

Jake turned to the others. They had only heard half of the conversation, but it was enough to know that the news was good. Jake shook his head in resignation. "The woman has an active case, but she's been in complete isolation since before she became contagious. And the man she was with—he was exposed, too, but he'd been vaccinated. They've isolated him and his family just in case. We dodged a bullet."

Jennings stood up. "Now all we have to do is stop some other bullets from ever being fired."

* * *

36

Sarah and Jake

*While the last smallpox case in Somalia marked the
end of the natural disease, the smallpox threat was
not yet fully vanquished, as was dramatically
demonstrated in England in late August 1978. A
medical photographer, working in the Birmingham
University Medical School, was infected by the
smallpox virus, which had escaped from a nearby
laboratory and circulated through an air vent. The
photographer was immediately placed in hospital
and 200 of her contacts were put into isolation. The
professor in charge of the lab with the variola virus,
upon hearing the news, cut his own throat. The
photographer also died, smallpox's last victim ...*

—*Canadian Journal of Public Health, 2002*[*]

Day 33: Preparations

Sarah and Jake were sitting in the kitchen, waiting for
Jennings, who had excused himself to make a telephone
call. It was 9:30 at night, and they were startled when
someone opened the front door. It was Mary Jennings, returning
home earlier than expected. She recognized Jake immediately. "It's
good to see you Jake."

---

[*] "The Speckled Monster: Canada, Smallpox and its Eradication," Luis
Barreto and Christopher J. Rutty, *Canadian Journal of Public Health*, Vol.
93, July/August 2002, No. 4, p. I-1.

"Mrs. Jennings. This is … this is Sarah Lockford."

"It's nice to meet you, Sarah. I hope Carter has offered you something to eat and drink. You both look a little ragged. You have had dinner, haven't you?"

Sarah answered honestly. "No, we'll get something as soon as we finish up here."

"I'm afraid that isn't possible." Carter Jennings had just returned to the kitchen. "It isn't safe for you to leave this house tonight. But I trust you'll find it comfortable downstairs. And secure."

Jennings pulled a chair back from the kitchen table so his wife could sit down, but he remained standing. "Just before Mary came home, I was on the phone with my deputy. He's arranging a security detail for the house until this is over. There will be two undercover units on the street, and two agents will stay in the house. They will remain on duty through the night, so they won't need sleeping accommodations. I'm sorry for the inconvenience, Mary, but I have to make sure you're all safe."

"It sounds like you aren't going to be here with us, Carter."

"Unfortunately, I need to go to the office tonight. I will return for our guests in the morning. There's an important meeting scheduled for 9:00 a.m., Jake, and I want you and Sarah there with me. Please prepare a brief presentation. You'll have five minutes at the most, maybe only three. It may be the most important presentation of your life."

"I'll be ready."

Jennings handed Jake a flash drive. "You may want this. We'll leave here tomorrow morning at 8:30. Promptly."

"Mr. Jennings, I'm not sure what kind of meeting this will be, but we don't have any clothes other than what we're wearing."

"Clothing will be provided, Jake. For both of you."

Jennings turned to his wife. "Evan Brady will be here shortly. He'll be in charge of the team. If anything comes up, he'll know how to reach me." Jennings kissed his wife and left by the front door, picking up his coat from a chair as he walked past.

"You'll have to forgive my husband. He can be a bit abrupt when he's focused on something about work. And it sounds like this is something important. Why don't I get you two some dinner? Carter roasted a chicken this afternoon, and we only ate a little of it. I can heat it with some mashed potatoes and green beans. Would that be all right, Jake?"

"That would be really nice. Thank you."

"Wonderful would be a better word for it," Sarah added.

A few minutes later, Sarah and Jake were starting to relax. They both jumped at the sound of the doorbell.

"Both of you stay right where you are." In contrast to her previous, almost motherly, tone, Mary Jennings' voice was dead serious. It wasn't a suggestion she'd made but an order. She walked briskly to the front door, and standing slightly to the side, she asked, "Who is it?"

Sarah and Jake couldn't hear the reply, but Mary turned to them and relayed the information in a voice that had undergone a partial return to the motherly. "It's all right. It's Special Agent Brady." Then she opened the door to admit two men. Both younger looking than Jake, both neatly dressed. "This is Special Agent Brady, and..."

"And Agent Tomlinson, Mrs. Jennings. You don't need to make any further introductions. Director Jennings gave us some background, but our job here is just to make sure that you and your guests are safe here this evening. We've secured a perimeter." He looked at Jake. "We don't want anybody else sneaking up from the back of the house."

"Our bikes are down there in the bushes."

"We found them, and they're being brought up to the garage for safekeeping. If you don't mind, we'll do a walk-through to make sure everything is secure now, including the alarm system. We'd appreciate it if you'd keep all the drapes and blinds closed. Please don't open any of the doors or windows or try to look outside. It's the only way we can be sure of your safety."

The agents went about their check of the house, and Mrs. Jennings, after indicating that Sarah and Jake should finish their meal, went into the living room and turned on the television. She left them undisturbed, returning only when she heard them clearing the table.

"Please, I'll take care of cleaning up. From what Carter said before he left, I think you still have some homework to do this evening. Why don't you go on downstairs and make yourselves comfortable. The den and guest rooms are to the left at the bottom of the stairs. There are fresh towels in the bathroom, and I put a couple of robes in the closet down there. I'll wake you at 7:30."

* * *

Day 33: Assembling the Arguments

"Who do you think we'll meet with tomorrow morning, Jake?"

"I'm not sure, but the FBI has a real hierarchy, so Jennings has to convince his superiors. They may trust him, but he'll still need us to show them the evidence."

"The proof has to get to the FBI Director, but Jennings would certainly have to go up the ladder first. And then the Director would have to talk to the Attorney General. He's the one who represents the Justice Department in the National Security Council. Maybe we'll get to see some somebody in the Director's office, if Jennings can convince them we're worth listening to."

"He has to get through a lot of people tonight, but this is Washington. And it's a crisis. People may not be happy about it, but they'll meet with Jennings, no matter how late it is."

"You have to get your presentation ready. I turned on the computer."

A half hour later, Jake was hunched over the laptop, alternately frowning and typing, with an occasional nod of satisfaction.

"Got anything ready to look at yet?"

"The first slide needs to be high impact, Sarah. I really have to get their attention."

"What are you thinking of?"

"Jack Redhouse. The photograph you took of his body. It's on the flash drive that Jennings gave me upstairs. It's not pretty, but it's real."

"You'll get their attention, all right. How will you keep it?"

"The key is to convince them that the Farmington virus traces back to the microscope slides from the 1947 smallpox outbreak. Charles sent us genetic information on the microscope slide that Evelyn Redhouse purchased on eBay, and I've compared that with all the data that I brought from Farmington.

"You can't just give them tables of numbers, Jake."

"No, of course not. I've got some charts, but they need to be polished up. Here, look. This one shows key parts of the sequence for four archival samples. Two are from CDC and the other two are from the Russian lab. It demonstrates that the Russians have remained cooperative, and I think it shows how mutations increase over time. The dates are at the bottom."

"It's a real oversimplification, but you can't do details in three minutes."

"Right. This next one sets up a timeline for the Farmington virus and the other four samples. It illustrates the phylogenetic relationships for all five, and it shows that the Farmington virus is actually the first—that it's much older than the others."

"I like it, but you'd better be careful. Just show the trend and say that it means that Farmington came first, not last. Don't go into technical detail. And don't use terms like 'phylogenetic relationships,' or you'll lose them completely."

"Good point. I'll keep it simple. Even if they don't understand the details, they'll see that the samples are all different. But this last one should wake them up. It compares the gene sequences for the Farmington virus that killed little Jackson with the data that Charles sent us for the eBay slide. Look at it, Sarah. They're identical."

"That's incredible, Jake. And the comparison is completely legit?"

"Absolutely. I used every piece of information Charles sent us, and I pulled all the comparable data from what we did out in New Mexico. They match in every single place. There's no question whatsoever, and even a newcomer will be able to see it!"

"This will convince them. No question about it."

"Too bad we don't have a picture of the microscope slide. With that old-fashioned handwriting, it really would have been a neat way to wrap it all up."

"We can still get one, Jake."

"How? We can't ask Charles to do anything else."

"No, I mean we can take the picture ourselves. The other slide is in my backpack, and the laptop has a camera."

In just a few minutes, the photograph had been incorporated into Jake's presentation.

"The only thing left is to write exactly what I want to say. Let me do a draft, and then you can make suggestions."

It was 2:00 a.m., when Jake yawned and rubbed his eyes. "I'm beat. If we don't get some sleep, I won't be able to tell them my name tomorrow morning, no less make a clear argument. Let's turn in now, and I'll set my alarm for 6:30. I hope Mrs. Jennings makes coffee in the morning."

"It won't matter. There's a coffeemaker and a jar of ground coffee on the table in the corner. And Mrs. Jennings put two new toothbrushes in the medicine cabinet. And toothpaste and a razor. So we'll both be able to look halfway decent in the morning. Although I have to admit, it makes me a little nervous that we might be talking to the actual Director of the FBI."

"I know what you mean. But it shouldn't be that bad. I've lectured in front of senior people before. Even the head of CDC once."

They climbed into the bed in the larger of the two guestrooms and turned out the lights. Sarah put her head on Jakes shoulder and snuggled up to him. "Good night, Jake. I'm proud of what you're doing."

She kissed him on the cheek, but he was already asleep.

* * *

Day 34: Fine Tuning

Jake's alarm began beeping at 6:30. He turned it off, but it took him another 20 seconds to figure out where he was. When it came to him, the adrenaline followed quickly. "Time to get up, Sarah. Today's the day."

Jake turned on the coffee maker. "I'm glad you got this thing ready to go last night. I hope the coffee is strong. I really feel like crap."

The coffee helped. During the 10 minutes it took them to drink their first cup, they sat in bed and stared blankly at each other without speaking. Then they realized they needed to start working. Sarah booted up the laptop, now fully charged, and handed it to Jake. "Try it again. I'm ready to listen."

When Jake finished his presentation, Sarah had only a single suggestion. "I think that's it, Jake. It was already really good when we stopped last night. Change that one label on the graph, and I think you're good to go."

Jake practiced it twice more, and each time he felt greater confidence in the words he was saying and the way he was saying them. "It took you exactly three and a half minutes, Jake, and that's inside the window that Jennings gave you. And there's no way anyone is going to ask you to stop during the last thirty seconds. Not with this presentation."

Jake had just finished storing a copy of the file on a flash drive, when there was a knock on the door. "Time to get up. I'll have breakfast ready in 15 minutes. Your clothes are on a hanger just outside the bathroom door."

When they walked upstairs, Mary Jennings, dressed in jeans and what must have been one of Carter's old shirts, was putting a platter of bacon and eggs on the table. "That smells wonderful, Mrs. Jennings. Thank you so much for taking care of us this way."

"You're welcome, Jake. You have a big day today. And I have a feeling that my husband has his neck on the line, so you make sure your presentation is a good one. Watching you grow up, we always knew you had it in you, even if you did put tire tracks in our yard with your bicycle."

Jake grimaced and looked over at Sarah, who just smiled at him. "Is Mr. Jennings here? Have you heard from him?"

"He's upstairs showering, Jake. He got home a few minutes ago. Didn't get any sleep at all."

"That's not entirely true." Jennings walked through the door, looking a lot better than might be expected. "I was too tired to drive, so one of our people drove me home. I got in a quick nap. We needed a car anyway, to take us all downtown. I'll bring you up to date on the drive. We'll be able to use Rock Creek Parkway, so it should only take us a half hour."

The comment struck Sarah as odd. FBI Headquarters was on the far side of the downtown area. So was the Washington Field Office. Massachusetts Avenue would be the logical route, and Rock Creek seemed to be a detour. But she was too tired to object, and Jennings was in charge. *He must have his reasons.*

They ate their breakfast in near silence. The only interruptions came when Jennings asked Jake if he were ready, and then if he had rehearsed sufficiently. The first question was answered by a nod of the head and something resembling a grunt, which seemed to Jake to be better than the alternative of trying to talk with a mouthful of scrambled eggs. The second question earned a more respectful, "Yes, I have."

The third question was whether Jake had save his presentation on the computer. "Yes, sir. And on this flash drive, too."

When they finished eating, Jennings told Jake and Sarah to finish getting ready. "We leave in 10 minutes exactly."

Jennings stood and left the kitchen. Mary turned to her guests. "He gets a little brusque when he's under a lot of pressure. Sarah, I'm glad we had a chance to meet. I hope we'll see you again, and that next time will be under better circumstances."

Downstairs, Jake and Sarah made a quick attempt to tidy up the guest room. "Packing up isn't hard when don't have anything to pack. The computer is in my backpack, and so is the package with the slides. You've got the flash drive?"

Jake patted his pocket. "All set. And I've got this piece of paper with my notes. I want to keep reviewing it."

"You'll do fine, Jake. And you look pretty good, too."

"All things considered, I don't think I look too bad. I just looked in the mirror, and the suit fits pretty well. So does yours. You'd look good to me no matter what, but it's more than that. You just look really sharp this morning."

"Thanks, but let's just say I look okay. And it doesn't matter. We need to get moving."

"Yeah. And by the way, I'm scared shitless."

"So am I, Jake." She gave his hand a squeeze, and they walked upstairs.

* * *

37

Sarah and Jake

Somehow that was twisted into 'a slam-dunk.' You go to war with the army you have, but the facts you want.

—*Maureen Dowd, New York Times, 2011*[*]

Day 34: Arrival

Jennings was waiting in the kitchen with his coat on, and Mrs. Jennings was nowhere to be seen. "Let's go. Special Agent Brady just confirmed that the area is secure." As the three of them walked to the front door, Brady opened it for them, offering each of the three civilians a sober nod of the head in lieu of a salute as they walked by.

At the curb, Sarah was surprised to see another agent holding open the door of their vehicle. It wasn't just a car—the word Jennings had used. It was a full-sized limousine. *If this thing had flags on the front fenders, we'd look just like the diplomats when their motorcades drive through Washington.*

Then she noticed the other two cars idling nearby. Escort cars. *Damn! This is some shit.*

As they drove down Massachusetts Avenue toward Rock Creek Parkway, Jennings appeared to be lost in his own thoughts. Jake continued studying his notes. And Sarah looked out at the passing scenery almost like a tourist, all the while hoping she wouldn't throw

---

[*] "Simply the Worst," Maureen Dowd, Op-Ed, *New York Times*, Feb. 12, 2011.

up. She admired the white dome of the Naval Observatory, where the Vice President lived. Then they passed the British Embassy, the start of embassy row.

They turned right onto the entrance to Rock Creek Parkway. Their escort vehicles were been joined by two large black SUVs. *Chevy Suburbans. Just like the Secret Service uses.* Several times she'd seen the Vice President's motorcade traveling the same route.

Sarah expected their car to stay on the parkway until they reached Constitution Avenue, a relatively direct route to FBI headquarters. But they turned off even before they reached the Kennedy Center and the Watergate Complex. As they curved around the exit ramp, she looked up at the brick building on her left. It was the Four Seasons Hotel.

We're getting on Pennsylvania Avenue. That's weird. We'll hit all sorts of traffic going across town. She looked over at Jake, who continued to study his notes. He was oblivious to their route.

As they drove down Pennsylvania Avenue past the World Bank complex, Sarah was surprised at how quickly they were moving. *It's almost like the traffic signals were timed for our trip.* Then the car turned and came to a stop.

When she recognized where they had stopped, Sarah poked Jake with her elbow. They were at an entrance to the White House!

The driver rolled down his window, and a voice said, "We need to see your badges, please. I'll need each person to hold his own badge while I inspect it."

Oh my God. Oh my God. Sarah was confused. *This is ridiculous. Why did he have the car stop here? We'll just have to turn around and leave, anyway. Unless Jake and I are going to wait in the car. We sure don't have any badges to show them.*

Jennings reached into his shirt pocket, and removed his badge. Like most Washington bureaucrats, he was never without it.

Sarah was startled yet again when Jennings reached into the pocket of his suit coat, and retrieved two more badges. He handed them to Sarah and Jake. Sarah went wide-eyed, and Jennings smiled slightly. "You're not the only one, Sarah. Other people can also generate ID cards. We pulled your digital photo from the *Post's* website. This ID isn't fake, either."

Her head swimming, Sarah followed the actions of the others and held up her ID card as the uniformed guard peered through the window that Jennings had rolled down. After a moment, the guard looked at Jennings and nodded. Then he stepped back, called "All clear!" to somebody, and saluted the car as it drove past him.

They stopped beneath a covered portico, and another uniformed guard opened the door of the limousine. They climbed out and followed the guard through a maze of corridors to an elevator. Sarah couldn't even tell whether they went up or down. Finally, they were delivered to a small room with several armchairs.

Jennings finally broke the silence. "Please wait here. I'm not sure how my next meeting will go, so just be ready, in case I need you. Keep your computer turned on. If we need it, there won't be time to wait for it to warm up."

* * *

Day 34: Final Arguments

After 15 minutes that seemed like an eternity, their wait was ended by a sharp knock. The door opened to reveal yet a different uniformed guard. "If you folks would please follow me ..."

The guard led them down a corridor and around a corner to a doorway that was flanked by two armed guards—Marines. "Showtime," Sarah whispered to Jake.

One of the Marines inspected the badges that Jake and Sarah had been instructed to clip onto their clothing. As he inspected each badge, he made a notation on a clipboard. "They're clear."

The second Marine opened the door and waved Sarah and Jake into the room.

They were stunned. Instead of the two or three people Jake had been expecting, there were probably two dozen people in the room. Most were sitting on chairs positioned around the periphery of the room. A smaller number were seated at a large conference table. At the far end of the room, seated at the head of the table was a face they recognized instantly. It was James Fallon Alexander—the President of the United States.

Jake and Sarah reached the astonishing conclusion at the same instant. They weren't giving Jennings and his boss arguments that they could take to the National Security Council. They were in the middle of the meeting he had told them about—a meeting of the National Security Council. Sarah looked around the table and recognized some of the other faces as well—Trevor Richards, the Vice President; Quentin Walker, Jr., the Secretary of Defense; Caroline Calebresi, the Secretary of State—it was the whole crew. Presumably the people around the periphery were key members of their staffs.

"Jake, Sarah—please have a seat over here at the table." It was Jennings speaking. "Mr. President, members of the Security Council, these are the two individuals that the Attorney General told you about. They came to me at great personal risk, and they have information that bears directly on the momentous decision you must make today."

As an aside to Jake, Jennings said, "Please give this Marine your flash drive and tell him the name of the file. He'll put your presentation up on that screen over there according to your instructions."

Jennings turned back to the larger group. "Dr. Jake Overman, an M.D. with a Ph.D. in biochemistry, works for the Centers for Disease Control, where he directs one of their crisis intervention teams. As soon as the first report came into CDC in Atlanta that there was a possible case of smallpox in New Mexico, Dr. Overman was tasked to lead the medical and scientific response effort. He had been led to believe it was only a training exercise, but once his team arrived, they discovered it was not.

Jennings looked around the table as he continued speaking, and his gaze locked on the Vice President.

"Part of his team was assigned to finding and treating victims. But Dr. Overman's first responsibility was to identify the actual pathogen and learn if it was indeed Variola. That's smallpox. He confirmed that diagnosis.

"Instead of following the longstanding federal policy for response to a smallpox outbreak, the Defense Department deployed a military unit, one of the Consequence Management Response Forces, from Fort Bliss. They instituted a quarantine. In addition, they improperly—and, I am sorry to say, illegally—restricted communications in and out of Farmington.

"We all know that official U.S. policy in the event of a smallpox outbreak is to assume that the disease resulted from a terrorist act. However, that is an assumption, not a fact. Dr. Overman obtained definitive evidence on the origins of the smallpox strain that caused the current outbreak, but he was prevented from delivering that information to his superiors. He was able to reach us only with the help of the woman seated next to him.

Sarah Lockford is a highly respected journalist. She, in turn, was able to bring Dr. Overman key information only with the assistance of members of the Navajo Nation. Once again, our government caused grave injustice to those whose ancestors were here before ours, and it was only because those courageous people helped Ms. Lockford and Dr. Overman escape—to escape, Ladies and Gentlemen, as if they were common criminals—that they are now able to bring you the evidence they have assembled.

"Today, you are about to make a final decision about whether to wage nuclear war against a country halfway around our globe. What Dr. Overman is about to tell you will answer any questions you may have about how that outbreak began. What you will hear from him will not be thoughts, nor will they be opinions. No, Ladies and

Gentlemen, what he will give you are facts—scientific facts based on scientific evidence—the best science that our country has to offer.

"Dr. Overman." Jennings half turned and extended his arm in Jake's direction.

Sarah had been watching the others at the table during this remarkable speech by Jennings that sounded like a summation to a jury. She remembered that for many years the FBI recruited lawyers when they hired agents.

She was riveted by the emotions she observed. The Vice President glared at Jennings with undisguised contempt the entire time, while the Secretary of Defense scowled at the Vice President. The President, while not looking at anyone other than Jennings, nevertheless seemed just barely to be controlling his anger. Clearly, whatever had preceded Sarah and Jake's arrival had not been a pleasant conversation.

Jake turned to the Marine seated at the computer console. "Would you initiate my presentation, please."

When the image appeared on the screen, there was a collective intake of breath—followed by nothing. Nobody in the room seemed able to exhale.

"Mr. President, this is a photograph of Jack Redhouse. A Navajo man in Farmington, New Mexico. What you're looking at is a full-blown case of smallpox. It's not pretty. This picture was taken when he was found dead."

"Mr. President, Jack Redhouse died of smallpox, but he didn't die because of a terrorist attack. I will show you incontrovertible proof that it was not terrorism, along with equally clear evidence of the actual origin."

Jake looked over at the Marine.

"Next slide please."

* * *

References

Chapter 1

5 *the disease had been eradicated completely:* World Health Organization, Weekly Epidemiological Record, Vol. 55, No. 17, p. 121, April 25, 1980.

6 *smallpox virus for research:* Convention on the Prohibition of the Development, Production and Stockpiling of Bacteriological (Biological) and Toxin Weapons and on Their Destruction. This commonly known as the Biological Weapons Convention. See: http://www.un.org/disarmament/WMD/Bio/.

Chapter 2

10 *vaccinations have really cut down on chickenpox:* Centers for Disease Control and Prevention, Varicella Vaccine Q&A. The CDC website provides a thorough discussion of vaccination risks and benefits: http://www.cdc.gov/vaccines/vpd-vac/varicella/vac-faqs-clinic.htm.

Chapter 6:

39 *smallpox response plan:* "Smallpox Response Plan and Guidelines,"(Version 3.0). The CDC website provides complete descriptions of public health policies and responses that would be implemented in the event of a smallpox outbreak: http://www.bt.cdc.gov/agent/smallpox/response-plan/.

43 *Dark Winter:* Operation "Dark Winter," was a bioterrorism exercise conducted at Andrews Air Force Base, June 22-23, 2001. See "Shining Light on 'Dark Winter,'" Tara O'Toole, Michael Mair, and Thomas V. Inglesby, *Clinical Infections Diseases,* Vol. 34, No. 7, pp. 972-983, 2002.

43 *except for an article in the Post:* "U.S. Called Vulnerable to Biological Attack; Smallpox Simulation Alarms Officials," *Reuters, The Washington Post,* July 24, 2001, p. A05.

45 *The first bioterrorism attack:* "America's First Bioterrorism Attack," Philip Elmer-DeWitt, *Time,* Oct. 8, 2001.

Chapter 7:

56   *accidental exposure from a research laboratory accident:*
     "Smallpox," *Global Alert and Response,* World Health Organization,
     http://www.who.int/csr/disease/smallpox/en/.

Chapter 8:

75   *the Mujahedeen-e-Khalq:* "U.S. protects Iranian opposition group in
     Iraq," Michael Ware, *CNN,* posted: 11:53 a.m. EDT, April 6, 2007,
     http://www.cnn.com/2007/WORLD/meast/04/05/protected.terrorists/
     index.html.

77   *the FBI jumped the gun:* "Amerithrax Investigative summary," The
     United States Department of Justice, Released Pursuant to the
     Freedom of Information Act, Feb. 19, 2010;
     http://www.justice.gov/amerithrax/.

79   *Project Sapphire:* "Project Sapphire," John A. Tirpak, *Air Force
     Magazine Online,* Vol. 78, No. 8, Aug. 1995, http://www.airforce-
     magazine.com/MagazineArchive/Pages/1995/August%201995/0895s
     apphire.aspx.

Chapter 12:

104 *lung disease from working in the uranium mines:* "Lung Cancer in a
     Nonsmoking Underground Uranium Miner," Karen B. Mulloy,
     David S. James, Kim Mohs, and Mario Kornfeld, *Environmental
     Health Perspectives,* Vol. 109, No. 3, March 2001;
     http://www.ncbi.nlm.nih.gov/pmc/articles/PMC1240251/pdf/ehp010
     9-000305.pdf.

105 *We use tradition to remove that curse:* Derek Meurer, "Ancient ways
     go around the world," *The Daily Courier,* Prescott, Arizona, Dec. 17,
     2007;
     http://www.dcourier.com/main.asp?SectionID=1&subsectionID=1&a
     rticleID=50750.

Chapter 14:

122 *the location of the bioweapons lab:* The Reference Laboratories of
     Iran, Research Center: http://www.reflabs.hbi.ir/en-site/en-intro.htm.

122 *brucellosis:* "Isolation of Brucella from blood culture of hospitalized
     brucellosis patients," Massoud Hajia and Mohamad Rahbar, *Iranian
     Journal of Clinical Infectious Diseases,* Vol. 1, No. 2, 2006, p. 63;
     http://journals.sbmu.ac.ir/ijcid/article/viewFile/124/112

123 *smallpox and the plague:* Nuclear Threat Initiative, Iran Profile,
     Biological,
     http://www.nti.org/e_research/profiles/Iran/Biological/index.html.

Chapter 16:

144 *the next Review Conference for the Biological Weapons Convention:* Convention on the Prohibition of the Development, Production and Stockpiling of Bacteriological (Biological) and Toxin Weapons and on Their Destruction. This commonly known as the Biological Weapons Convention. For information on the Review Conferences, see: http://www.opbw.org/.

149 *the classified wording about nuclear response:* "Bush signs paper allowing nuclear response: White House makes option explicit to counter biological, chemical attacks," Nicholas Kralev, *The Washington Times*, Jan. 31, 2003, p. A1, Article ID: 2003031311255020010; "Bush Approves Nuclear Retaliation," NewsMax.com Wires, Feb. 1, 2003, http://archive.newsmax.com/archives/articles/2003/1/31/112516.sht ml.

Chapter 17:

156 *when all the sheep died:* "America's Struggle with Chemical-Biological Warfare," Albert J. Mauroni, p. 29ff, Greenwood Publishing Group, 2000, ISBN 0275967565, 9780275967567; Kindle Edition: http://www.amazon.com/Americas-Struggle-Chemical-Biological-Warfare-ebook/dp/B000PC6CQO/ref=sr_1_1?ie=UTF8&qid=1325961222&sr=8-1.

157 *killing Indians:* "Jeffrey Amherst and Smallpox Blankets: Lord Jeffrey Amherst's letters discussing germ warfare against American Indians," http://www.nativeweb.org/pages/legal/amherst/lord_jeff.html; "Colonial Germ Warfare," Harold B. Gill, Jr., *Colonial Williamsburg Journal*, Spring 2004, http://www.history.org/Foundation/journal/Spring04/warfare.cfm.

Chapter 18:

169 *Of course there's a quarantine:* "Large-Scale Quarantine Following Biological Terrorism in the United States," J. Barbera, A. Macintyre, L. Gostin, T. Inglesby, T. O'Toole, C. DeAtley, K. Tonat, and M. Layton, *Journal of the American Medical Association*, Dec. 5, 2001, Vol. 286, No. 21, p. 2711.

173 *ViroChip:* "A Conversation with Joseph DeRisi," Claudia Dreifus, *New York Times*, Oct. 7, 2008, p. D2.

174 *anthrax attacks in 2001:* "Tracing killer spores: The science behind the anthrax investigation," Christine Piggee, *Analytical Chemistry, Online News*, Sept. 18, 2008;

http://pubs.acs.org/action/showStoryContent?doi=10.1021%2Fon.20
08.010.10.108576.

Chapter 19:

182 *gave them a sample of the smallpox virus:* "Threats and Responses:
   Germ Weapons; C.I.A. Hunts Iraq Tie to Soviet Smallpox," Judith
   Miller, *New York Times*, Dec. 3, 2002.

182 *first told us Iran was working with smallpox:* "Iran Said to Be
   Producing Bioweapons: Opposition Group Names Anthrax as First of
   Six Pathogens in Intensive Effort," Joby Warrick, Washington Post,
   May 15, 2003, p. A22.

Chapter 20:

193 *transmission doesn't take place until the infected person shows the
   skin lesions:* Centers for Disease Control and Prevention, Smallpox
   Fact Sheet, Smallpox Disease Overview,
   http://www.bt.cdc.gov/agent/smallpox/overview/disease-facts.asp.

194 *comparing the genetic sequences:* See Tables 1 and 4 in "GeneChip
   Resequencing of the Smallpox Virus Genome Can Identify Novel
   Strains: a Biodefense Application," I.M. Sulaiman, K. Tang, J.
   Osborne, S. Sammons, and R.M. Wohlhueter, *Journal of Clinical
   Microbiology*, Feb. 2007, Vol. 45, No. 2, p. 358.

194 *GeneChip:* "Meeting of Computers and Biology: The DNA Chip,"
   Nicholas Wade, *New York Times,* April 8, 1997.

196 *even a hundred years:* "Smallpox and its Eradication," F. Fenner,
   D.A. Henderson, I. Arita, Z Ježek, I.D. Ladnyi, *History of Public
   Health*, No. 6, World Health Organization, 1988, Chapter 2. Variola
   Virus and other Orthopoxviruses; *see* discussion pp. 115-116;
   "Century-old smallpox scabs in N.M. envelope," *USA Today,* Dec.
   26, 2003.

197 *State Sponsors of Terrorism:* U.S. Department of State, Country
   Reports on Terrorism 2010,
   http://www.state.gov/g/ct/rls/crt/2010/170260.htm.

Chapter 21:

199 *Nuclear Posture Review:* "Nuclear Posture Review Report,"
   Department of Defense, April 2010,
   http://www.defense.gov/npr/docs/2010%20Nuclear%20Posture%20
   Review%20Report.pdf.

200 *caused a bit of a flap:* Senate Report on Intelligence Activities
   Relating to Iraq Conducted by the Policy Counterterrorism
   Evaluation Group and the Office of Special Plans within the Office

of the Under Secretary of Defense for Policy, June 2008, p. 34; http://intelligence.senate.gov/080605/phase2b.pdf.

200 *his information should not be trusted:* James Risen, "How a Shady Iranian Deal Maker Kept the Pentagon's Ear," *New York Times*, Dec. 7, 2003.

200 *coordinated propaganda program:* "Exiles: How Iran's Expatriates are Gaming the Nuclear Threat," Connie Bruck, *The New Yorker,* March 6, 2006, p. 48.

Chapter 22:

215 *almost 70 years old:* "Smallpox Danger Over; Free Vaccinations End," *New York Times*, May 3, 1947.

Chapter 23:

218 *trying to get nuclear weapons:* "2005 Adherence to and Compliance with Arms Control, Nonproliferation, and Disarmament Agreements and Commitments," U.S. Department of State:
The United States has warned publicly for more than ten years that Iran was engaged in a covert effort to develop nuclear weapons, but it was only in 2002 that much information began to appear in public about the Iranian nuclear program.
See: http://www.state.gov/documents/organization/52113.pdf

218 *wipe Israel off the map:* "Wipe Israel 'off the map' Iranian says," Nazila Fathi, *New York Times*, Oct. 27, 2005.

Chapter 25:

232 *axis of evil:* The President's State of the Union Address, George W. Bush, Jan. 29, 2002:
States like these, and their terrorist allies, constitute an axis of evil, arming to threaten the peace of the world. By seeking weapons of mass destruction, these regimes pose a grave and growing danger. They could provide these arms to terrorists, giving them the means to match their hatred. They could attack our allies or attempt to blackmail the United States. In any of these cases, the price of indifference would be catastrophic.

233 *microbial forensics:* "Microbial Forensics: DNA Fingerprinting of Bacillus anthracis (Anthrax)," Paul Keim, Talima Pearson, and Richard Okinaka, *Analytical Chemistry,* 2008, Vol. 80, No. 13, p. 4791.

234 *genetically modified smallpox virus:* "Iran's Accelerating Military Competition with the U.S. and Arab States: Chemical, Biological, and Nuclear Capabilities," Anthony H. Cordesman, Center for Strategic & International Studies, Oct. 17, 2011,

http://csis.org/publication/irans-accelerating-military-competition-us-and-arab-states-chemical-biological-and-nucle.

237 *state sponsor of terrorism:* "Country Reports on Terrorism 2010, Chapter 3—State Sponsors of Terrorism," U.S. Department of State: *Designated as a State Sponsor of Terrorism in 1984, Iran remained the most active state sponsor of terrorism in 2010. Iran's financial, material, and logistic support for terrorist and militant groups throughout the Middle East and Central Asia had a direct impact on international efforts to promote peace, threatened economic stability in the Gulf, and undermined the growth of democracy.* See: http://www.state.gov/g/ct/rls/crt/2010/170260.htm.

Chapter 27:

256 *Foreign Intelligence Surveillance Act:* Foreign Intelligence Surveillance Act of 1978 Amendments Act of 2008, Public Law 110–261, http://www.gpo.gov/fdsys/pkg/PLAW-110publ261/pdf/PLAW-110publ261.pdf; http://www.gpo.gov/fdsys/pkg/PLAW-110publ261/html/PLAW-110publ261.htm

Chapter 31:

286 *Posse Comitatus Act:* Posse Comitatus Act of U.S. Code, Title 18, § 1385: *Whoever, except in cases and under circumstances expressly authorized by the Constitution or Act of Congress, willfully uses any part of the Army or the Air Force as a posse comitatus or otherwise to execute the laws shall be fined under this title or imprisoned not more than two years, or both.*

Chapter 33:

309 *warrantless wiretaps:* "Gonzales Hospital Episode Detailed. Ailing Ashcroft Pressured on Spy Program, Former Deputy Says," Dan Eggen and Paul Kane, *Washington Post*, May 16, 2007; p. A01.

Chapter 35:

324 *uniformed troops stationed inside the United States:* "Pentagon to Detail Troops to Bolster Domestic Security," Spencer S. Hsu and Ann Scott Tyson, *Washington Post*, Dec. 1, 2008, p. A1.

326 *same protocol that we've used at CDC:* "GeneChip Resequencing of the Smallpox Virus Genome Can Identify Novel Strains: a Biodefense Application," I.M. Sulaiman, K. Tang, J. Osborne, S. Sammons, and R.M. Wohlhueter, *Journal of Clinical Microbiology*, Feb. 2007, Vol. 45, No. 2, p. 358.

Chapter 36:

338 *phylogenetic relationships:* "Genome Sequence Diversity and Clues to the Evolution of Variola (Smallpox) Virus," Sammons, A.M. Frace, J.D. Osborne, M. Olsen-Rasmussen, M. Zhang, D. Govil, I.K. Damon, R. Kline, M. Laker, Y. Li, G.L. Smith, H. Meyer, J.W. LeDuc, R.M. Wohlhueter, *Science*, Vol. 313, Aug. 11, 2006, p. 807.

Chapter 37:

347 *Consequence Management Response Forces:* "Statement before the 110th Congress, Committee on Homeland Security and Governmental Affairs, United States Senate," The Honorable Paul McHale, Assistant Secretary of Defense for Homeland Defense and America's Security Affairs, June 26, 2008, p. 5; http://hsgac.senate.gov/public/_files/062608McHale.pdf.

About the Authors

Doug and Linda Raber are scientists who have spent their careers investigating the interplay of cutting-edge science and U.S. foreign and domestic policy.

After graduating with bachelor's and Ph.D. degrees in chemistry from Dartmouth and the University of Michigan, Doug spent 20 years on the chemistry faculty at the University of South Florida. In 1990, he moved to Washington, D.C., as Director of the Board on Chemical Sciences & Technology at the National Academy of Sciences, where he directed studies on topics ranging from chemistry research and development to forensic analysis of bombings to combatting terrorism. He is a sought-after consultant in science policy arenas.

Linda graduated in chemistry and history at the College of William & Mary and began her career as a legislative aide in the Senate before moving to a chemistry research position at the National Institutes of Health. She worked as a reporter at Chemical & Engineering News for more than 20 years before going solo in 2010.

The Rabers have homes in both the Nation's capital and in West Virginia, near the two ends of the C&O Canal that runs alongside the Potomac River. Both locations serve as backdrops for FACE OF THE EARTH, their first novel.

Forthcoming

ROOF OF THE WORLD—scheduled for release in the fall of 2012

A family of immigrants from Tajikistan becomes caught up in an international web of espionage and terrorism. The CIA learns of a plot to launch a nuclear attack against the United States, but nobody knows the identity of the target or when the attack is scheduled. Will careful investigations be enough? Even with the discovery that the planned attack is aimed at Washington, D.C., will a government team be able to locate the plotters? And even if the conspirators can be found, can they be stopped before the nuclear device is detonated?

EASTERN COLONIES—Early 2013

A team at CDC detects a slight but significant increase in food-borne illness across the United States, but all the experts have to go on is a mathematical algorithm developed by a computer expert. The cases are so sporadic that nobody can find the origin of the illness. Is it only a random set of infections, or is it something more?

Jake Overman returns to work with a team at CDC, and they make the frightening discovery that the illnesses are not accidental. Someone has found a way to infect the food supply. The trail leads across the ocean, first to Germany, and then further east to Russia and finally to Kazakhstan. A genetically engineered strain of deadly *E. coli* bacteria is about to enter the American food supply.

13593884R00210

Made in the USA
Charleston, SC
19 July 2012